INVOLUNTARY TOUR

INVOLUNTARY TOUR

A novel by Robert Flanagan

Book I of The ASA Trilogy

Connemara Press

Yellow Spring, West Virginia

authorHOUSE®

AuthorHouse™
1663 Liberty Drive
Bloomington, IN 47403
www.authorhouse.com
Phone: 1-800-839-8640

First published by AuthorHouse 10/2/2009

ISBN: 978-1-4490-1767-5 (e)
ISBN: 978-1-4490-1765-1 (sc)
ISBN: 978-1-4490-1766-8 (hc)

Library of Congress Control Number: 2009908197

Printed in the United States of America
Bloomington, Indiana

This book is printed on acid-free paper.

Book cover and dust jacket by Liam M. Flanagan

Acknowledgments

Every author must acknowledge the vast body of writers who have gone before from whom he has learned his craft. So, to Hemingway, to Conrad and Melville, to Shakespeare, Joyce, Cervantes, to Hardy and Joseph Heller, Yeats, William Eastlake, James Jones, and Scott Fitzgerald—to the entire roster of artists, craftsmen, and scribe laborers who do our language proud, my tip o' the hat and eternal thanks.

And to the legions of U.S. military who keep us and have kept us free, giving me this opportunity to realize ambitions; and who, during my military service, provided the models—however transformed—from whom the characters of this book are drawn, and those who otherwise inspired creations of (almost) pure fiction.

A special nod of the head to the No-Name Writers of Winchester, Virginia, with whom it has been my special pleasure to caucus for more than five years. This gifted coterie of serious writers—men and women, yearlings and grizzled curmudgeons—have given unstinting support and valuable suggestions in the course of mutual manuscript review. It has been a challenging climb. Thank you all for being there to push or pull me up to the next ledge.

Some segments of this book have appeared in various publications, albeit in altered format: short fiction, articles, and poetic form.

> A portion of Chapter 8 appeared as a short story, "An Ordinary Imperative," in an edition of *phoebe*, literary journal of George Mason University.

> Chapter 14 appeared as a short story, "Token Spook," in an edition of *sou'wester*, literary journal of Southern Illinois University.

> Chapter 18 was published as a short story, "A Game of Some Significance," in *phoebe*.

> "Vicarious Hero," "Sleight of Hand," "Pastorale," "Mayday," "Wire," "Semi-Private Mirages," "Street of Hondas," "Another Kind of Understanding," and "Disquietetude," drawn from the prose in these works, appeared as poems in various publications.

Dedication

This trilogy of novels is dedicated to soldiers of the U. S. Army Security Agency, a defunct organization. This Military Intelligence element, when extant within the U. S. Army, served multiple masters, often to its disfavor. The players contributed their time, efforts, skills, and in some cases, their lives, in the far corners of the world without acknowledgment or recognition by the very American citizens whom they protected That their service occurred within a clandestine environment accounts for much of this so-called "Spook" outfit's public invisibility. In their time and place, these soldiers, within their confines, were anything but invisible. ASA has long deserved the telling of their story. This is, at least, one such telling.

In abiding respect for the barren hours and years in far-flung field stations, border sites, DF sites, logistics support bases, and covert locations on the ground, at sea, and in the air, this book is humbly proffered in the hope that its author has managed to capture a bit of the work, some of the play, the often grim realities, and the mad, zany improbabilities of such service. The established need for secrecy in that world impacted not only the job, but inevitably affected personal lives. Veterans of this service often still live in denial of their bizarre lives and times in the surreal world of ASA.

Despite the surreptitious nature of this vital service, and ignorance on the part of those served, non-fiction (historical and analytical) publications now emerging do recognize the great value these sub-rosa outfits provided our national defense through the Cold and otherwise War years. But fiction offers a powerful enticement beyond fact.

Enough time has passed, and technology advanced beyond operational techniques of those days—the days encompassed in these three books: the 1950s and '60s—to allow some of that story to be told. But I caution, lest the reader forget: *This is a work of fiction!*

Author's Notes

This book has grown as grey and grizzled as its author over the decades taken to write it, to—as Hemingway said— ". . . get the words right." It is not a temporal record, an honor that likely falls to the Bible; but this trio of books—written as a single story, converted to a trilogy only due to manuscript size—has truly been a long time coming.

I began keeping a journal in Viet Nam, spring, 1964, with the intent of perhaps producing a novel. Journal entries continued through that tour, subsequent assignments in California and Germany, then Viet Nam again, until late fall 1969, the conclusion of my second Viet Nam tour. By the time "The End" was written to the full story in the fall of 2007, I had incorporated events and military service of the two protagonists prior to the inherent timeline of these books, providing a far broader canvas on which to paint. And the novel which was the goal of that early journal segued into three linked, contiguous novels—The ASA Trilogy—in early 2009. A mere forty-five years in gestation to arrive at publication.

One risk of writing such a long-lived story, peopled with so many characters, is the complexity of the final product. I never envisioned a "linear" story, a story that begins on day 1 and moves smoothly forward through day $1 + n$. Rather, through the use of flashbacks (back story), the basic linear progress of the story is enhanced by recall of character introductions, events, and sidelight issues which make for a richer reading experience.

Here are tendered no apologies for anything that appears in the following work. If there are errors of fact, remember: *This is fiction!* If there appear to be syntactical blunders, that's likely the author's voice, or the voice of his characters projected through the prism of the author's experiences. Spelling errors, if there be such, are simply goofs, though utilizing the English language's incredible flexibility, I am prone to manufacture a word, now and then. These are not errors, but proclaimed artistic license.

If there is one element for which I feel some explanation is due, it is the heavy use of slang, military jargon, acronyms, and other terminology more familiar to military and military veterans than the general public. Also the use of a variety of foreign language phrases. But these books attempt to portray events and characters within a military world as truly as possible, in dialogue as well as narrative. The trilogy is written primarily for those veterans, and if there are others who find the going tough — despite my belief that most information of a utilitarian and/or necessary nature will be obvious by context — there is relief.

A glossary of slang, jargon, acronyms, old and new phonetic alphabet, and foreign language phrases is available to those who desire it. As a writer, I do not subscribe to the practice of explaining each and every ambiguity, whether in parenthetical enclosures or open text; nor do I recommend the use of a glossary as one reads. The distractions in both cases create rifts in the literary flow–the vision that is the story. If you would avail yourself of this asset, it is available to download on the internet from my Connemara Press website <connemarapress.org> free of charge.

This book and its two subsequent volumes were not written to be "easy on the reader," a thing I might have done to enhance sales. But the primary readership, those whom I truly wish to read these works, have an inherent interest that will enable them forward through author arrogance, structural complexity, and impressions of abstract unbelievability. I trust that other readers, using intelligence, diligence, and perhaps a few leaps of logic enhancing literary probabilities, will persevere on their journey from start to finish.

Robert Flanagan
Yellow Spring, West Virginia

Contents

Sky Queen caresses the engine cowling and squints across the blazing plain of airfield. Straightening from engine check, beading oil with dust between his fingers, he watches with one eye a line of low, magenta monsoon clouds moving down toward the mouths of the Mekong where a lone Huey flutters drunkenly across his vision. He kicks the port tire, grumbling happily, "Let's get this pig in the air. Go find us some Cong."

Reluctantly pulling wheel chocks on the far side of the aircraft, The Operator refuses to acknowledge the gigantic tower of weather boiling down from Cambodia. He ducks beneath the wing, running his hands in a convulsion of hopeless benediction across patches of army green tape. Covering unrepaired ground-fire rents in the Beaver's skin, the temporary fixes are improvident.. He turns, dragging the mission bag, helmet, weapon, and parachute to the port hatch.

"Don't do it!" Foreman, acolyte of fire watches in oil-stained chasuble, calls from the edge of the burned grass. The fire extinguisher, his reason for being, lies thirty meters back of the parking apron.

The Operator regards the seer silently, unmoved. He yanks the door free and mounts.

Sky Queen, nimble as any octogenarian, scampers up the ladder and wedges, then straps himself in the front left seat. In formulaic monotony he sets mixture to RICH and pushes the throttle to OPEN, his eyes fixed on a horizon far beyond the moldering paddies about the airfield.

"The world is flat, Operator. Sky Queen, don't go! Pilot your ship out there, you'll fall off the edge." Foreman's eyes are as sane as his task demands, as mad as his world.

Flinging the long, white silk scarf over his left shoulder, Sky Queen turns away from this presumptive Cassandra, flips him the circular bird, and laughs as he thumbs the starter. An urgent, descending whine erupts, overlying jerky prop rotation.

The Operator cinches down on his harness and leans forward, staring through Plexiglas at Foreman as the old man hits the mag switch and the fire watch disappears in a hacking cough of blue smoke.

chapter one

Bavarian Idyll

Bad Aibling, Germany: Spring 1968

Winter was duty officer the night Electric Man assaulted the Army and killed it.

Truth be told, E-Man did not actually administer the killing blow, but as precursor to the fragmentation that would come — was then already epidemic throughout the Green Machine — he served as understudy to the drama. He brought the message of disaster for those who would hear. And as we are wont, we responded by executing the messenger.

Electric Man was no more myth than was the unfortunate fall from grace which he represented. His raison d'être may be counted mythological to the extent it could never be confirmed, though his corporeality was never in doubt. Understanding the dichotomy of E-Man may prove to be what this story is all about.

Maybe not.

Electric Man, threatening the realm with his infantile, sanctity-of-life death wish, descended on Bad Aibling post in a bewildering attack ominously threatening to the conditioned military mind. There was little lasting impact though, and in retrospect it must be admitted that E-Man was no more than a quirky brush stroke in the still life of Bavaria. A hiccup in the gastronomic process of an army that ingested everything in its path. Entries in a logbook.

Nothing could have been changed in any case. I understand now what Winter meant when he said afterward it was already too late for book burning. At the time, the allusion brought me only images of tax evasion and Ray Bradbury.

But, I speak in riddles — or as Richard Three so disingenuously advises his audience, "I go before my horse to market."

I was Duty NCO that night, reveling in the inactivity of a twenty-four-hour duty shift in the staff office. Nothing lived in that after-hours world in the old headquarters building, nothing but ghosts of its Nazi past, and we three assigned players: myself, Duty NCO; the duty driver, Younkin, a World War Twice and Korea recidivist, as useful as the proverbial; and Warrant Officer-One Winter, Officer-of-the-Day. We had ten hours of duty remaining on an already wasted April evening when the muddled call came in from Headquarters Company CQ.

You expect incoherence from admin types in stress situations. That was not the case with this Charge-of-Quarters. He was one of many bad fits in the Army and consequently not bothered by the concerns of his appointed office. On the phone the CQ's nonchalance bordered on silly, his silently alarmed appeal so incomprehensible I left Younkin on phone watch and drove to the Officers Club where Mister Winter had gone for a sandwich. No point in telephoning the O-Club. The drunks wouldn't answer, couldn't talk if they answered, and anyone who answered unfortunate enough to be sober passed the phone to a drunk.

Inside the O-Club the atmosphere was dismal, the air deadly with tobacco smoke, kitchen vapors, and the ripe fecundity of freshly fertilized Bavarian farmland. Vision was a secondary sense. The tiny bar was packed, as exciting as algae. Stasis gripped our officer corps. A perpetual suspicion among the lower classes, confirmed by the sophomoric antics I encountered when I braved that sanctified space, was that officers just can't drink. They don't know how. They've not been trained in it, forced to it by the despair with which every enlisted man lives. We enlisted swine are suckled on three-point-two.

I spotted a flash of teal-blue armband at the bar and pushed toward it through a dithering of junior officers to where Winter pushed something dark and disgusting about the plate before him.

"Josep!" he called to the barman as I edged in beside him. "My compliments to the chef." He turned toward me and rolled his eyes toward the heavy beams overhead.

Dave Winter was not a mean person, no question, and I knew him well. We'd served together in three previous tours: a year's overlap eight years earlier in Asmara; nine months together in a '64-'65 tour in 'Nam; and up north on the East German border at Rothwesten last year and for the winter deployment to Gartow earlier this year. I'd known him as Specialist, Sergeant, and now Warrant Officer — vindictive in none of those roles.

Consistently apolitical vis-à-vis European politics, he felt no particular enmity toward Yugoslavians; every officer in the bar understood that. His concern for Balkan nationalism — any faction — bordered on the non-existent. If he thought of the subject at all, likely it was with a sense of surreal disbelief. So his remark can be attributed to nothing more insidious than a poignant comment on the O-Club fare, directed politely to the Montenegran bartender.

That expatriate cast-off, a balding, aging, muscular man of impressive stature and rheumy eyes who resembled Lon Chaney with a head cold, moved along the bar, feigning disinterest, swiping in listless wet circles at the stein drippings. I leaned close and seconded the ruin of Winter's meal with the message of the phone call. He turned away abruptly with no comment, and Josep and I watched him depart through the crowd in the general direction of the door.

"*Hah!*" Josep shouted in the face of a lieutenant at the bar, as if that young officer were somehow to blame. "*I, Josep, am the chef.*" He jabbed his own chest with a broad, hairy thumb. The lieutenant allowed as how he believed him and fled to the latrine. I followed the OD into the chilly night.

I found him in the parking lot talking with Mr. Stoneking, another Warrant Officer-One, and offered him a ride to Bravo Company in my car. But Winter, something of a Jesuit and seeking penance, insisted on driving the official vehicle — another of the Army's jokes — that was his for the duty period.

* * *

The MP Jeep dome lights were visible long before I rounded the curve to Bravo Company billets. Like a carnival appearing out of a dark, featureless countryside, multiple electric blue glows strobed eerily on the night air and headlights and flashlights bobbed through the mist, creating a nimbus of cold brilliance against the night sky.

I braked, stopping the vehicle in the street, feeling an anticipation I couldn't explain. Military life is rife with such premonitions, and though exciting, they are often inexplicable, patience the only response. I would learn eventually what I needed to know . . . or I would not. It would all be explained, or I'd live in ignorance.

That's as close to black and white—to absolutes—as it gets in the military.

I waited in the car for the OD and in a few minutes saw the single yellow headlight in my mirror, heard the dysfunctional engine as Winter pulled in behind me. I walked back to the sedan as he turned the key. The engine continued dieseling, the single headlight bobbing like a buoy at high tide. Around us, beyond ground zero, Bavaria lurked quietly in darkness.

Winter allowed a snort of reflection, clicked the key back on, then off again. The rumble slowed, the sedan gave a dry gasp, lurched once, sighed, and was finally dead. Winter wrenched the door open and stepped away from the remains. He seemed offended at the vehicle's attitude and would not look at it. Yet I knew he expected nothing better. Winter was career military, and not a foolish man.

Inside, where I followed the OD, Charge-of-Quarters Blaylock leaned against the Coke machine in the dayroom. Captain Meechan sat on the near pool table among the balls. His uniform blouse was unbuttoned, his collar brass green and mismatched, his shoes muddy. Winter, soldier that he is, wrinkled his nose without comment.

Meechan was talking at Blaylock, leaning into the CQ's face in a pose conveying sincerity. And it was a pose. Meechan, by birth and inclination, was incapable of relating to any subordinate on an interpersonal basis.

Winter motioned Blaylock toward the door. The captain continued lecturing his retreating figure as the SP5 slouched away. Blaylock sniggered silently and positioned himself beyond the door in the hall. I thought to shut the door, but if Winter had wanted secrecy he would have ordered it; he could read Blaylock's little ferret eyes as well as I.

Outside the barracks, bursts of laughter rose in arrhythmic crescendo, fading away to uneasy silence.

The captain swung his head, and I saw him glance at his wrist watch when he first saw Winter. Gearing up for his first mistake. "Well, hell, Mister Oh-Dee Winter, you took your time." He flicked his gaze to me and struggled to raise one eyebrow, a gesture he'd admired in some past commander, but one never mastered. His efforts produced only comical facial distortion. Failing regality, he emanated impatience and irritation at my presence. My evening was better for it.

"Let's have it, Malcomb," Winter said, his voice tired.

Meechan started, began to rise. "Now just a minute —" he blustered, likely at Winter's unwelcome first-name familiarity, though such practice was common among officers below field grade.

"You wait a minute, Captain," Winter said gently. He knew the limits of propriety and spoke to ensure Blaylock, an enlisted Rona Barrett, could not have heard his soft words beyond the door, though the CQ might have recognized the tone.

"Keep your seat and knock off this imperial horseshit act," Winter said. "What the hell? Why're you here? This isn't even your company. Why're all those M.P.s running around out there playing cop? Jeez-us! Billyclubs, ballyhoo, and bullshit. Blaylock!" he bellowed.

"Sir?" Blaylock pushed the door wide and stuck his head around the corner, smirking.

"Find the senior M.P. out there. Send him in here. Sergeant Brenner," he turned to me, "get on the horn to the guard shack. Tell Sergeant Janssen the O.D.'s here and things are under control. He's not to send anymore friggin' cops over here."

The CQ was turning away when Winter called after him: "And Blaylock, do your job. Some troop's got a *Schatzie* up in his room. Above the dayroom, second floor. Brazen young hussy wearing nothing but a field jacket, leaning out the window watching this exercise with her tits hanging over the rail. I don't want to know who he is, who she is — nothing! Just get her young ass out of that issue jacket, into some clothes, and out of the building. Off the post! *Wehrstanden?* OK, then, *Macht schnell!*"

The door crashed shut and there was silence.

Winter stood before the captain, carefully avoiding eye contact. Maintaining eye contact with Meechan demanded you be on his wavelength, and that was a place not of this world. Winter glanced meaningfully at me. Like the good serf the Army trained me to be, I obediently turned and stared into the wall, dialing the phone.

"Malcomb," Winter appealed to the misfit captain, "goddammit! Didn't you understand anything the colonel said at staff meeting? Don't you understand what's going on with the enlisted in this man's army? Right here in B.A. You somehow not aware of the discontent, the hysteria?"

That was too many questions. We waited for a divine intervention that would not come. The captain's mouth opened, and I could see the search pattern behind his eyes as he sought commanding words.

"Captain," Winter began again, softly, "when the C.O. said to downplay little disruptions, I think he meant this kind of event. How 'bout you, Sergeant Brenner?" he asked my back. "Do you think he could have been referring to something like tonight's circle jerk?"

"Yessir, precisely what he meant, sir." The phone still buzzed at the other end of the line in the guardshack, unanswered. "In a manner of speaking, sir, I fear the colonel's plea did not entirely generate the response he might have wished. He—"

"Stop talking like a goddamned dictionary, Brenner," Meechan began.

The OD, hard on the trail of a point, ignored my pinging on the errant captain. "Sshh-sshh-sshh. Jeez-us Christ!" Winter, his face forward in the captain's face, his voice constrained but urgent, swept his arm about in a motion that took in our surroundings: the dayroom and the company, the Military Police, the CQ, the troops. "I mean, is this low key?"

His voice echoed in the empty dayroom, and the blue flash of cop lights flickered across the peeling plaster walls in a syncopated cycle. A *Stars and Stripes* headline, several weeks old, announcing in 96-point Cheltenham the Marines' capture of the Hué Citadel, was taped below a sign forbidding any posting in the dayroom. The voices outside were controlled, mellow, persistent.

Shifting gears, Meechan whispered to Winter, "Dave, the bastard tried to kill me."

I was thrilled with the possibility, though knowing it likely to be only a manifestation of the captain's well-known paranoia.

Mister Winter wasn't too disturbed either. "Yeah? Okay, Malcomb. Tell me." The guard shack phone continued ringing, unanswered.

"Tried to kill me. I never . . . I don't even know who the hell it was."

"Don't tell me what not — tell me what," Winter said.

"Okay! Okay. I was checking the messhall for midnight chow. I left there and came across the street about eleven-thirty or so to stop in B. Company, and —"

"Why?"

"'*Why?*'"

"Why were you checking B. Company, Malcomb? I presume you mean Bravo Company. And the messhall, for cripe's sake; you're not Headquarters C.O. A-*gain*, I presume you meant twenty-three thirty hours," Winter said, implicitly chiding the hapless, unmilitary officer. "Captain, may I remind you, I'm the Officer-of-the-Day. Note the armband. Note my presence here in the middle of this lovely spring evening." Winter pointed to the blue band on his sleeve with large gold letters: SDO. "See. Staff Duty Officer, like it says in the book. New name, same game. S.D.O., O.D., D.O. Under whatever guise, my turn to ride night herd, cowboy."

Winter's voice shifted into harder mode. "You're on my turf, Captain," he said pointedly. "The companies, messhall, guard posts, Ops; everything and everybody. It's my chosen profession. You want to pull this gung-ho, late-night, slink-around shit, the next time I come up on the O.D. roster, I'll sleep with my wife and you can pull my duty. Okay?"

There was frustrated silence. I hung up the unanswered phone and listened.

"Flash for you, Malcomb. When another warm body pulls the duty . . . when a fellow officer's name comes up on the roster, it means you can bag it," Winter continued. "Go beddy-bye. As the Air Guard says, 'Sleep tight. Your O.D.'s alert,' or some such shit. Am I getting through?"

"I'm Alpha Company com —"

"*Am I getting through, goddammit*, Captain?" Mr. Winter stared at the young officer, with concern I thought, as well as with a case of the red ass, his voice demanding but even. "Of course, you're the Alpha

C.O. Of course, you're a commissioned officer and gentleman. You should be out checking your company—occasionally. Whatever it takes to ensure your unit does its job and life in the Army as we love it goes on. *Your* unit! This does not extend to harassment of the troops during off-duty hours. Especially in other companies. Right?"

Nothing. Hangdog.

"Right?" Winter's voice softened. He would avoid pushing too hard, even if he was duty-bound to try to impart some sort of military education to the fledgling officer. The man wore railroad tracks, after all.

"Yeah, sure, Dave. I just—"

"I know. Now tell me about this mysterious marauder. Okay?" The OD was there and had things under control.

But reacting inadvisedly to the verbal spanking, Meechan drew himself up taller than he was. He might have been preparing to remind the warrant officer that he was speaking to a superior officer. He might have been about to take command of the situation. He might have done any one of a thousand things useful and proper, but he did not. Instead he stood glaring down his nose at Winter, his demeanor haughty and distant, attempting to salvage some element of dignity, unsure how to go about it.

I almost felt sorry for the pathetic man. Almost.

His once-patrician nose had been broken and pushed to the side, off-plumb by several degrees. I saw it as a mark of Cain, a sort of biblical warning from early days in Meechan's army travail. It might have proven a reminder to brash young lieutenants not to let butter bars go to their heads and try to separate two brawling, drunken motor pool mechanics releasing garrison tensions on a payday drunk. But it wasn't merely his nose.

Meechan's physical appearance in general did nothing to inspire military confidence: posture like a rubber rat; his physical build the model for Before. Eyes the color of eels gone belly up, a pale brownish-yellow. Strange eyes. Weak, and watery, a fault Meechan tried to hide by blinking rapidly at the person he addressed along with shifting his gaze from side to side. In addition to the calamities of the nose and eyes, an expensive orthodontic correction had been allowed to go to seed by over-indulgent parents who would not enforce bands and nightguard discipline. Now, Meechan's chipmunk smile was only grotesque.

Mister Barnshell, once when the subject had come up at the club bar, so Mister Stoneking told me, had defended Meechan in his own insidious manner, insisting that the young captain couldn't help being ugly. But Barnshell did express outrage that Meechan would take his offensive appearance into public. "Of course," he'd added, "the man's negative appearance is offset by his unique personality, which is even worse. That's something! If I believed in perfection, I'd consider Meechan a perfect asshole."

Still—and both Winter and I were never unaware of it—he did wear captain's bars.

And finally, he got it together. "I was coming up the walk out there," Meechan nodded toward the front entranceway, crowded now with curious, off-duty soldiers seeking change, excitement— something. "About ten, fifteen feet from the door I heard a noise. Saw a flash of movement. I looked up just in time to see this . . . this person crouched in the window. He was in a blue suit of some kind, and sort of . . . ahhh, wearing a cape," the captain whispered.

In the pall of silence that followed, there was felt the expectant sensation of a bomb that had not gone off. A second shoe not dropped. A line not spoken on cue.

"You hear me? A cape. A *cape!*"

"Sure, a cape. Gotcha. What kind of suit? Single breasted, normal kind of man's suit? Or double—"

"No. Shit, no! A suit, a kind of costume. Skin tight it looked. Like Superman . . . sssss." He tried to suck the words back.

"Oh! Sure. Superman. With a cape. Okay, Captain, did he fly out at you? Out the window?" Meechan glared at me, his eyes wild and unfocused. I quit laughing, put on my professional sergeant's face. Winter began to fidget, shifting from one foot to the other.

"No! Christ, I'm not nuts, you know." Meechan grated, utterly failing to convince me. "He wore a costume, and a cape, and a . . . a mask, I think." When he rushed out this last item, the captain seemed to shrink, realizing he'd maybe gone too far.

"Yeah, the mask. Yeah, now, that's what I was waiting for." Winter did seem to be in a particularly unsympathetic frame of mind.

"Damn it, don't you question my word, mister; he attacked me. He jumped out the window and came at me. Right at me, with a knife . . . or maybe it was a hatchet in his hand. He moved so fast it was hard to see." The captain began to hit his stride now.

"What did you do? Why aren't you dead?" Winter asked. I enjoyed again brief flashes of the possibilities.

"Before I could set myself for him — " Meechan said, falling back on some private fantasy, a mysterious martial art he knew nothing of " — he jumped me. He came out the window, through the bushes, and was on me. I was naturally . . . uhh, I was somewhat taken aback."

"Taken aback?" I marveled, my mouth running away. "I should damned well think so."

"Sergeant Brenner — "

"Let's finish this, Captain, if you don't mind. I'll be half the night writing up this silly shit, as it is," Winter said levelly.

"It is not silly shit, damn it. He charged me. Attacked me. Suddenly, there he was. Right in front of me. Not far as from you to me. He just stood there a minute staring at me — "

"A minute? A real, full minute? Or do you mean seconds?"

"Well, maybe seconds. A few seconds, glaring, sizing me up, and then he attacked." Awed by the memory, the captain searched every corner of the dayroom for residual threats.

"With *what?*" Winter demanded. "His hands? The axe or knife? What kinda weapon did he use?"

"I told you, a hatchet. Or knife, maybe. Yeah, I guess a knife." He squinted at the fly-specked ceiling and nodded. "I'm sure it was a knife."

The two men stood toe-to-toe in the lull. The Coke machine by the door hummed and rattled on its uneven mount, copper-tubed indigestion loud in the cavernous room.

"A knife. Jeez-us!" Winter turned away, then back into the breach. "Did you see the knife? Did he cut you with it. Or stab you? How do you know it was a knife?"

"Well, damn it, Dave. He came at me with his arm upraised — like this!" Meechan leapt from the pool table and raised his arm in a move projected by bad movie villains; the classic knife assault; a graceful, photogenic move more likely to guarantee a knee in the nuts than a successful attack. "And I saw it. But I handled him," Meechan assured. Warming to the subject of his own valor, he launched into a colorful rendering of his encounter and incredible personal courage.

Meecham obviously had begun to believe the tale he told. Mister Winter removed his cover and scratched at his head, ruffling the short hair, massaging out the weirdness that beset him. I would have helped if I could . . . but, hah! That's why he gets the big bucks. Besides, you take your fun where you can find it.

Meechan continued talking, staring down at the pattern of tiles on the floor. I could imagine him trying to find there some kind of settling reality, seeing firm substance in the scars from generations of military boots. Seeking some understanding of Nazi Luftwaffe histories in the ineradicable stains, Cold War scenarios in the gouges, readiness alerts in the chipped tiles. The captain's irritating nonsense droned on at the edge of my mind.

When Meechan had exhausted the subject and left for his quarters, trailing an atmosphere of expulsion, Winter called in the CQ and questioned him. He would have done as well pissing up a rope as to try to make sense out of Blaylock. I told him so. He looked at me, sadly, as if I'd reminded him of unpaid club dues.

A few curious soldiers came into the dayroom offering their views, but more interested in expanding the bullshit quotient than shedding any light for the OD. Winter closed the inquiry knowing less than when he began. Dealing with Meechan and the happily conspiratorial soldiers was exhilarating to a point but, like a Kafka story, the experience left one feeling anxious, insecure.

It was past 0100 hours. The sidewalks had cleared, the MP kiddy cars gone. Winter picked up the phone, dialed, and to my chagrin immediately connected with the guard shack, sending Sergeant Janssen and his cops on a bound-to-be-fruitless chase searching for the mysterious attacker. There wasn't a hope in hell of finding him—if there was a him—and Winter knew that, but he went through the motions, every bit the good soldier.

I walked outside, hitched up the web belt and holster, took a deep breath, and gagged. On the street, in the open where night breezes rolled across the ripe croplands, the air of the Alpine meadows held all the fragrance of Korea in August. The stench of freshly spread animal-waste filled the night with a consciousness-altering miasma. I had a sharp memory of the honeywagons during the day, trundling across fields beyond the fence, spewing forth a golden-brown stream collected from the barns where stock was held through the winter. The biting reek of ammonia brought tears to my eyes.

I failed to recognize any greater cosmic significance in the immutable cycle of fertilize-plow-plant-grow-harvest-fertilize. All nature and man seemed only irritants. But the Far East had taught me something about debilitating environments, so I breathed through my mouth on the way to the car. As I drove away, Winter was wrestling with the sedan which refused to start.

I drove by the NCO Club to check on closing, and returned to headquarters believing the green lushness of coming summer would pay us back for the present, temporary wretchedness.

I didn't know then about that summer.

* * *

Winter got there just ahead of me and opened the door into the headquarters building; we walked in together, returning from the Moldavian minuet with musical strains lingering. The stairwell was dark as the inside of a cow.

"*Younkin!*" Mister Winter shouted up the stairs. I knew what was coming, and understood it to be my responsibility. But why deprive the man of a few minutes of entertaining aggravation?

On the heels of rumbling thunder above, the fat PFC stuck his head over the railing. Despite Winter's proximity as we climbed to the second floor, Younkin boomed out in his pseudo First Sergeant's parade-ground bellow, "*That you, Mister Winter?*" He stared into Winter's face emerging into the light three feet away as he asked.

"Fix the stairwell light, Younkin." Winter gestured up into the blackness. I admired his restraint. Younkin was a slug that should have been smothered at birth.

"Sir, what was the trouble at the company?" the driver-clerk asked in servile fashion.

"Now. Do it now, Younkin." Winter did not try to hide his impatience, though he still didn't raise his voice. "And get the stairwell swept." The task of dealing with the enlisted man was beyond Winter's immediately attainable goals, and he realized it. The Augean stables were shits-and-giggles alongside Younkin's salvation.

"But my report, Mister Winter. What about the captain gettin' attacked? The knife and all?" His forty-five-year-old smoker's rasp was an unpleasant factor, even in whisper.

"Sergeant Brenner!" Winter's voice, on the edge, penetrated the wall to the next office where I'd betaken myself.

"You have no report to worry about, Younkin. The O.D. will write his report, as you well know. It's not a function of your duty," I responded kindly, leaning around the edge of the door. "Change the goddamned bulb and get the fucking stairs cleaned, dipshit," I growled. The Younkin Syndrome was working on me. "If the X.O. comes in and finds this place looking as it does, our ZIP code'll be Leavenworth. *But you won't care, you worthless sonuvabitch.*" I realized I was shouting but could do nothing to stop it. "*You'll be dead! Goddamned piece of shit! Is that clear enough for you? Now get it done!*"

The .45 duty pistol was draped about Younkin's middle without any sense of threat, a saddle girth on Sancho Panza's mule. The pistol belt was let out to its final grommet and stretched across a hairy, distended expanse of fat, bare below the fringes of a Tee-shirt that defied reclamation. It was not a pretty sight. The old PFC shuffled away, staring vacantly, no acknowledgment to me.

Winter wrote a long, detailed summary of the evening's mystery flap in the duty log, carefully wording the report. He locked the logbook in the desk drawer, pocketed the key, and headed for the stairs, waving a silent hand as he passed.

Younkin was sweeping the stairs with careless strokes, stirring the dirt of the day's passing feet from one side of a step to the other, off one ledge to the next. He swept in darkness. The stairwell light bulb was still out. Winter wordlessly passed the old retread on the stairs, and with straining eyes I watched him feel his way down into the well of darkness using the railing.

"You're gonna die, Younkin, you asshole," I predicted when the door closed behind Winter.

An unanswering silence overlay the sibilant whisk of the broom.

* * *

When Winter eased into bed it was after two, and it was only later, recalling that night as a sort of nasty genesis, that he realized a sense of disquiet.

Nickie turned and murmured sleepily: ". . . late tonight. Heard sirens . . . wazzit, trouble?"

"Nope. False alarm. Tell you in the morning. 'night."

Her puckered lips held their shape long after he kissed her. She was already asleep again, cuddling back into the curve of his body, settling herself like a warm puppy.

Winter lay, the events of the evening vivid in his mind, not accepting sleep until he had reviewed every word, every suspicion hinted at. *Something* was out there, he was sure.

When he had replayed it all and knew there was nothing more he could have done, he fell asleep. The last thing he saw in feverish re-run before he went under was Captain Meechan, locked in combat with the mysterious creature in the cape. It was a fight to the death. Meechan screamed for help. Headquarters Company windows were filled with laughing GIs who ignored his pleas and leapt out the windows in glee, floating down toward the beleaguered officer under ponchos that billowed like parachutes above.

Winter went to sleep smiling.

chapter two

Involuntary Tour

Bad Aibling, Germany: Spring 1968

Winter returned to the headquarters the following morning, signed off the duty log, and turned it over to Sergeant Major Vinagree. Duty NCO Brenner and the driver had already been released. The off-going Duty Officer was mildly relieved he didn't have to face Younkin again in the early morning.

When Winter came out of the latrine, Chief Warrant Officer Barnshell stood by the window outside the Sergeant Major's office reading the duty log. "So, Dave," he said blandly, "an entertaining shift last night?"

"You read that in there, do you?"

"Fortunate man. Most fortunate. Younkin *and* Meechan, all in one eve. Topped off with a killing freak. Man, man," he shook his head, "how *do* you rate?" TJ Barnshell savored a cruel streak. "And that snide bastard, Brenner, ridin' your flank."

"No big thing, T.J. — all the doings. And Brenner's my cohort."

"Win-*ter!* This's your old WOPA buddy. I learned my A.B.C.s on duty logs. Trick is not to read what's there; one must read between the lines, one must. Ahh, *Scheissen!* Not to worry. T.J., this day's Duty Officer, is ever vigilant. Relax, sleep well. As the Air Guard — "

"Yeah, I know."

"Hmmm. A mite testy. What's a 'hort?'"

"A what?"

"If Brenner's your co-, what's a hort?" Changing gears, "Meechan in uniform?"

"Like an Albanian bandmaster. Sporting his moldy brass and muddy shoes and a set of greens he was baptized in. Jeez-us!"

"I've known worse . . . I think. I just can't remember when." Barnshell did not indulge in pointless flattery — any flattery that did not lead to getting laid — and it was suggested by some that he lacked compassion. Winter had heard him point out that Army convention did not allow measurement of that elusive trait.

"I can't make up my mind if him wearing that uniform all the time, day and night, year round, season after season, pleases me or not. He is such a disreputable misfit, such a piss-poor soldier, such an ignorant, useless lout—not to say a bad commissioned officer, you understand— that I'm ashamed for him to be seen in uniform. God damn it! That derelict reflects poorly on my Army." Barnshell lit a House of Windsor cigar, a taste he'd acquired from WO1 Stoneking in another life. He offered one to Winter who shook his head.

Warming to his theme, "On the other hand," Barnshell continued, "when I change out of uniform myself, and I'm shopping in the PX or drinking at the club or playing with Wendy Rudemacher in the back of her fifty-three Fiat—whatever—I don't want that bleeding asshole infringing on that separate part of my life either." Though others might not have expressed it so vehemently or so readily, it was a common reaction to Meechan.

The depiction of Alpha Company's Commander as pariah was well established. When Winter had unadvisedly referred to Meechan in those terms once within his clerk's hearing, Magic Marvin snapped back that he didn't know anything about fish, but voiced the question, "Who gives a shit?" about the captain's dilemma.

"He's really not an enigma, T.J.," Winter said. "It's true nobody understands him. It's unfortunately true nobody wants to. And that's sad."

"Not to me. Fuck 'im!"

"You gentlemen going to impinge on the Army's business my whole day, venting your spleens on a fellow officer?" the Sergeant Major growled out the doorway. SGM Vinagree, practicing venom and ire for many years, was qualified to recognize it. An officer during the Korean War, he was now an enlisted man again—albeit the highest-ranking enlisted grade on the post—and he took very seriously a regard for military propriety. He personally refused to acknowledge his current rank as downgrade from officer.

"Go right on with your work, Sar'nt Major," Barnshell said. "I'm having my period."

"Sir!" As a captain, Vinagree had been assigned liaison duty with the Brits' Princess Pat Light Infantry in Korea, and some of his more endearing traits stemmed from that brief service.

The two warrant officers walked away down the hall.

"Vinagree's in a class with you-know-who," Barnshell groused.

"Yeah, but he's right. That's a no-no in front of troops." Winter felt a sense of uneasiness.

"Ahh, Davey, lad. Would you lecture himself on the proprieties? You won't ever get Vinagree to agree he's a 'troop.' He still thinks he's an officer. Ought to remind the prick of that sometime. He's a snob. Not the same kind of snob as Meechan, or you'n me. But a snob all the same."

"Maybe, but you can't discuss Meechan's snobbery and his military service in the same breath. Colonel Satterwhite's right. Meechan's condition does not arise from a bare two years mediocre military service. Nothing to build on there. No, it's a trait inherited from a long family line of Meechans, no doubt equally undistinguished."

"That's harsh, David." Barnshell looked hard at his friend. "Maybe it's you having the period."

"Yeah, sure. But not my assessment. Colonel Satterwhite's. Overheard him talking to Major Brewer in the club. Nahh, with me, just . . . you know, Meechan, the Mysterious Marauder and all. Younkin driving. And Brenner, rubbing salt at every opportunity."

"Well, Brenner'd put the pope's hackles up, and Younkin alone could ruin your evening, worthless piece of dog shit that he is."

"There you go again. Give the guy a break, T.J."

"You're a dishonest man, Dave. Worse, you bleed for the world. You just pulled O.D. with the turd, and you feed me that weak shit. Phase out!"

"Yeah, you're probably right. That's one in a row. Give me the Windsor." Winter reached and pulled one of the massive cigars from Barnshell's pocket. "I've got to see the Old Man about last night." What the hell could he say that wasn't in his written report?

"You'll have a wait. Old Man's in Munich, sitting a court martial today." Barnshell stared out the window. "See Satterwhite. Don't forget to genuflect."

Winter reported to the Executive Officer, Lieutenant Colonel Satterwhite. The XO had read Winter's report and had few questions. He would not confirm or deny any rumors about the mysterious attacker that had sprung forth following the incident in the night past. Winter left the headquarters with an impression of unfinished business.

He turned up his field jacket collar against the blustery spring morning. Snow still blanketed the Schlafen Jungfrau across the valley beyond the autobahn. Between the military base and the foot of the mountains, red tile roofs gleamed wetly in the misty air and low gray clouds moved up the valley in serried layers. Echelons of green — pastures, ploughed fields prepped for seeding, bordering pine and fir forests in varying shades — cascaded off into the mountains beyond. It was a country of beauty and romance, and the zany, illogical hysteria of the night past was hard put to mar it.

The World War II *Luftwaffe* hangar that housed Operations stood drab against the gray morning light. Rivulets of moisture made silver streaks like millions of snail trails down the corrugated metal siding. Inside the hangar, Winter's steps rang on the iron stairs. At the second level he looked out across the aircraft bay at the trucks, vans, and trailers lined up, clean and neat for inspection. Beneath the green paint and polished windshields, black-painted tires, and new unit stencils, he knew sixty percent of the vehicles were not road-worthy. They would be unable to perform their allotted functions if the Group of Soviet Forces, Germany, burst through the Fulda Gap. Should an alert sound at that instant, it was a good bet no more than five or six of the rigs could answer the call and roll. Reflecting the general attitude, his only hope was that the GSFG units were equally dysfunctional.

He grimaced. Not a hope on which to build a national defense policy.

Threading the maze of hallways back toward his office, a presence of white noise and piercing manual Morse signals grew more invasive as he advanced. Depressed by disillusionment so early in the day, he sighed, thinking, Don't worry, Winter. It'll get worse before day's end.

"Morning, Marsh," Winter grunted, frowning at the stack of files and memos in his clerk's hands.

SP5 Marsh murmured grimly. "Morning, Mister Winter. Long duty?"

Winter nodded, grasped the pile of paperwork, and went into his office. The clerk looked across into his OIC's space and raised one furry eyebrow.

"Magic" Marvin Marsh — a pseudonym of unique propriety. Imbued with panache and uncanny survival instinct, he was a veritable Falstaff of shifting values without the girth. He skated between officialdom and the soldier at the bottom. He looked out for his boss. He got the job done, whatever it took.

Specialist 5 Marvin O. Marsh was small, grey-brown in color like a field mouse, his bushy eyebrows and hair an appropriately mousey shade. Despite sincere attempts at military conformity, his dun-colored hair flared upward like rays from a pale sun. With undistinguished coloring and washed blue eyes, he passed for a German in Munich and on the streets of Bad Aibling village, where he spent more than casual pass hours. Surrogate homes, Marsh frequented many habitats away from the military post. Working nights at a bar in nearby Rosenheim had brought him proficiency in the local *Bayerischer Deutsche,* and he spoke the language on every practical occasion, establishing a quasi-official, small fiefdom over which he reigned.

Any requirement on the post for local language fluency called for Marsh's assistance. Off-post lodging rentals, telephone installation, fitting Americans among the strange clothing sizes in German stores, any and all; official and unofficial; tasks for the colonel, the Operations Officer, the housing office, the Chaplain, Military Police — they all called on Winter, as the soldier's OIC, to avail themselves of Marsh's magic interface.

And if Marsh as a soldier was in the ultimate business of intelligence collection, he applied first cut of his skills to his own ends. His interests usually were those of the military, though it might be otherwise. Incomparably well informed on every event within the Manual Morse Branch, in Operations, on the base, in the Army, town, and country, militarily related or not, his were the eyes and ears of a personally defined movement to accomplish some honorable end. It made him unique.

Marsh was fiercely loyal to Winter. He made it clear to anyone — those who asked and those who did not — that his loyalty was to the United States Army and to his boss, Warrant Officer Winter, *and*, he stressed, not necessarily in that order. He'd demonstrated the depth of his conviction on several violent occasions. He was willing and quick to back his loyalties. More than a few times fights had erupted in the club or barracks, once on a tourist boat on Chiemsee, when his narrow philosophy came into conflict with the radicalization endemic in the Army.

But Marsh was so transparent, so undeviating in his role, his fellow soldiers eventually accepted him on that basis. Unusually rational for the times and his place in the world, Marsh respected the fact he had signed a contract with the Army committing both to certain obligations. He saw himself merely living up to his part of the agreement.

Winter would not arbitrarily assign Marsh to fulfill unofficial requests for language assistance. He always put the task as, indeed it was, a request in which he, Marsh's OIC, was simply middleman. Winter could not recall Marsh ever refusing help to anyone except Captain Meechan. Magic Marvin's customary response when asked was, "Sure. Who gives a shit!" It was a given on Bad Aibling post that *Who gives a shit!* was Marsh's response to everything. But this morning, when Alpha Company clerk called with a request for Marsh's services on behalf of Captain Meechan, there was not even a question as to the nature of the need. Marsh responded, "I got no time for such shit, Billman. I'm backed up from here to Santa Fe with critical ops stuff. Go fish!"

He slammed the phone down. Winter spoke out through his open door. "Alpha Company owns all the *Deutsche* linguists on post; perhaps they might find one in-house."

"I wouldn't piss on Meechan if he was on fire," was Marsh's diagonal reply. "Sir."

The Wine Troll stood in the clerk's office, awaiting assignment to work detail. He had missed training two weeks in a row and was in the barrel again. Troll observed the unmilitary exchange between officer and enlisted man. Though all military relationships were mysteries to him — horrifying rituals with mystical terminology — he was saved from outright amazement by a perpetual hangover . . . and he was unsure where he was just then.

Troll was an anomaly. His drinking habits would have qualified him as a *cause* for social-minded groups. In polite civilian worlds he might have been the bum one stepped over in the city street on the way for morning coffee. But he was a natural manual Morse operator, a ditty catcher so talented as to foster legend. He came from money, but his family, apparently unsympathetic to his dissolution even before the invidious influences of the Army, had ceased to clasp him to their bosom. The Army provided for him; he provided for them. And it didn't matter for his craft whether he was drunk or sober.

"What do you need, Troll?" the clerk demanded.

The phone rang. Magic Marvin raised a finger suspending response and answered the call, talking in monosyllables. Winter heard the phone slam down, heard Marsh muttering. He looked up to see his clerk standing in his doorway. Marsh said softly, nodding in the general direction of the Operations Office, "He wants to see you."

"Now?" There was no question as to whom.

"Yessir."

"Shit!"

"Yessir."

"Goddammit!" Another one of those days. The Ops Officer, Major West, waited for nobody. His needs and wants took precedence over all; only on rare occasion did he reluctantly acknowledge the supreme position of the Field Station Commanding Officer.

Winter shoved the paperwork back on his desk, grabbed his pipe and pouch, and rose to his feet as if in pain.

"Good luck, Mister Winter." Magic Marvin turned away from the officer's searching gaze, sighted the bewildered Wine Troll where he had left him hanging, and yelled, "What do you want? God *damn* it, Troll, if it's not one thing with you, it's another. Why don't you shape the fuck up? You're in this office, in deep *kim-chee*, every time I look up. Well? Come on. Speak! I haven't got all day. See all this shit on my desk?"

The Wine Troll blinked at Marsh, still working on the first question, as Warrant Officer Winter left the office, picking his coffee cup off the bookcase as he went.

* * *

Winter opened the door of the Ops office. The Operations Sergeant waved him toward West's inner office door and said, "Go on in, Mister Winter. He's on the horn to Frankfurt."

Inside, West motioned to the coffeepot and continued on the phone, spreading his famous charm through official channels across Seventh Corps: "Your ass, Harlan! I don't get no more oh-five-aiches, you can count on me dropping two positions. As of oh-eight-hundred tomorrow."

Winter sat down with a half cup of wicked fresh coffee and leafed through the Read File of incoming messages. He saw West peering at him over his glasses, a strange, melancholy appraisal.

"Yeah, you do that, Harlan. Thought you'd see your way clear. Be a good soldier and keep both our butts outta the brig. Yeah, sure. See ya." He dropped the phone onto the cradle. "Goddamned headquarters pussies. Lean on 'em, they fold everytime." He grinned viciously.

"Morning, Sir," Winter greeted him.

"Hghmm," West grunted and looked down at his desktop. Pushing stacks of papers in no precise scheme from one area of the littered desk to another, he said, "I guess you already know, then." There was an ominous echo in West's voice; he was noted for parsimonious small talk. He pulled a folded teletype tear-sheet from beneath a forty-millimeter-shell paperweight and held it out.

"Know what?" Winter felt suddenly uneasy. Defensive. His hand stopped mid-reach.

"Marsh didn't get to you? Felt sure he'd know. And if he knew, you'd know." He pushed the yellow paper at Winter and looked away toward the tactical map of Europe on his side wall. "Can't make a difference. Here."

Winter, reaching for the telecopy, suddenly froze. He knew! His stomach turned over.

He knew! He didn't just suspect.

As if writ in God's own sulfurous script, he knew the contents of the message without reading it.

He stared at the innocuous yellow sheet that suddenly was not at all common. A rush of sensations assailed him, a flood of memories: burning heat, unbearable humidity; the stench of rotting vegetation and diesel-fuel-soaked human feces smoldering; fear — always the fear — the eternal, racking paranoia of only half sleeping; ubiquitous noise, predominantly the hollow thudding clatter of helicopters.

All the things to be done: battery of shots, re-qualifying with a weapon, clearing Crypto accounts and classified documents register; packing, shipping the car, moving the family to the states, finding a home . . . telling Nickie.

No more Salzburg festivals, no Oktoberfest, no *gemutlichkeit*.

. . . telling Nickie.

How would he tell Nickie? Of this thing that was not supposed to happen.

Queues for flights. The heated frenzy of JFK in tourist season; the long drive south . . . or would they go south? Yes, surely, and with it the dismal visit with Nickie's folks. All this, his mind running away from him in so-far-unconfirmed intuition. The confusing sights, sounds, and emotions raced through his mind, like watching a chatter roll come off the high speed printer with messages too fast to read, just hints afforded, glimpses, and finally, the reality of the bottom line — *Viet Nam!*

Winter knew it was Viet Nam before he unfolded the message. He glared at West, silently begging a smile, a glimmer of humor. Daring his Ops Officer to permit this to be what he knew it was. Maybe this was a joke. Or had he been pegged for some irregular honor he didn't expect? Was West's dour face an act?

No, not West. Winter, old man, it's the sixty-four dollar handjob, the gold-plated shaft.

The one ugliest, unassailable, un-funniest *Gotcha!*

He waited . . .

Nothing.

"Sir . . . ?" The implicit question hung like an accusation between them.

West stared back at him defensively. Apologetically. Neither spoke.

Suddenly Winter had to know: when? where? He forced his eyes down to the page. He said, "Viet Nam again, right, Major." It was a statement; questions were pointless.

"Sorry, Dave. I thought you'd know by now. Got the message this morning. Straight from D.A." Major West launched into explanation, skirting the actual event, listing the steps he'd taken to try to sidestep this particular assault on his personnel roster; his attempts to reverse the orders, including a call to the Department of the Army. Winter heard him only as an echo over meaner images and sounds.

His words were a screen. The major kept talking as Winter unfolded the paper and stared at ordered black etchings spread across the page in neat, blocked format.

Final. Irreversible.

The ciphers blurred before him, everything flowing together into a smudged yellow pronouncement: WARRANT OFFICER ONE WINTER,DAVID D., SSAN 425-60-1896. His vision skipped over the boilerplate, seeking the line that read . . . INVOLUNTARY ASSIGNMENT . . . UNACCOMPANIED . . . REPORT 509TH REPLACEMENT GROUP . . . NLT 06 SEP 68.

The sixth of September! In the late summer. Nearly fall. There was time yet; not this month, or the next. More than four months away. Anything could happen—

Winter found himself back in the Ops office as West said, ". . . and I called in every favor I had outstanding at Frankfurt. No go. Nothing they can do. And man, I gotta tell you, with The 'Nam eatin' up all my junior officers, especially lieutenants and captains, I really cannot afford to lose you. But I guess I'm gonna." He shook his head in perplexity, a faux adaptation, for he'd already had to work through this exercise with others.

"I might be able to wring thirty, forty-five days delay out of 'em. I can justify keeping you until BROWN GANNET's wrapped up." The hot *operation de jure* had occupied the best of West's officers and NCOs for months.

"No. No thanks, sir," Winter said. "I'll have my end finished in plenty of time. I appreciate it, but with this—" he tapped the paper, thinking furiously " — I can move the family home, get them settled, get Jeremy in school with the start of the term. Then, when I return next year — " It got out before he thought; but he had to believe, and he hesitated only slightly " — it'll still be summer and we can make the move to the next station without . . ." He seemed to run down.

"However's best for you."

They sat in silence.

"You want to take the rest of the day? Go home, break this to Nickie?" West offered.

"Unh-unh. Can't do that." He thought for a moment. "Who knows about this?"

"Colonel Satterwhite, for one. I just called him. The old man don't know; he's in München. Let's see, who else? A couple of Comm Center people, obviously. Probably Marsh. Maybe not, since he didn't tell you," the Major said. "Nobody else I can think of."

Marsh. Magic Marvin. *Good luck, Mister Winter.* Oh, yeah. Marsh knew.

"Listen, Tom," Winter said, in his urgency slipping into familiar mode. "I can talk to the X.O. Marsh can handle the Comm Center weenies. I've got to squelch any talk about this until after my leave. I've *got* to. I have to give Nickie this vacation without something like this. You don't know what all's at stake."

"Hghmm. I can guess. Nickie and Cissie . . . They talk a lot, and you know Cissie." West's glasses had slipped forward on his nose and he peered over them at his Collection Officer like some benevolent family doctor.

"Nobody else knows, you say. How about Cissie?" Winter asked, knowing West kept little from his wife.

"Damn! You're right," said West. "She called earlier about going to the crystal factory. I was just reading the message then and told her." He reached for the phone. "I never thought . . ." He started dialing. "Maybe Cissie went on. She was in a hurry when — Hello! Frieda? *Darfe sprechen, bitte, mit Frau West, Frieda.*"

Winter gripped the cold coffee cup so tightly it burned. Please let it not happen like this, he thought. If she heard it from someone else —

"Ach, ja. Gut! Danke schön, Frieda. 'wieder hören." West eased the phone back and looked up at Winter. "She left for Kufstein right after she talked to me. Frieda said she made a call, but didn't get any answer, so she went alone. 'bout oh-eight-thirty."

That fit. Nickie was going early to the commissary. "Thank you!" he said, his eyes flicking to the ceiling. "Tom, if you can get to Cissie as soon as she gets back, you know what to tell her. I'll talk to Colonel Satterwhite, and if he's told Judalon, make sure she keeps quiet. Only three more days and we're away to Italy. After the trip, during the trip . . . sometime later, I'll tell her. I'll have to tell her as soon as I can, as soon as practical. But I will not have this leave . . . spoiled by *this*. If I can help it."

His mind raced ahead, darting off in myriad directions, seeking to ameliorate a situation not yet materialized. The threat was enough. The countless details that went with the transfer he'd worry about later. He couldn't think of the implications of the assignment; those would come when they came. Neither was he concerned with duplicity. Nickie—if he could reach her, get through to her at the right time, if he knew her at all— would know why. She'd understand.

*   *   *

Winter walked out of the Ops office and returned down the shadowed passageway to Morse Branch. It seemed the men he passed in the hall and working in open offices stared at him with an aura of shared secrets, with compassion. Or were those smirks?

Sergeant Winnifer, a Russian linguist, passed him, avoiding his eyes, appearing to read aloud from the copy in his hands: *"Zheet boodyesh, no yet nye zakochyesh!"* It took ex-linguist Winter a moment to assimilate the message; his Russian was stale. He no longer worked transcription, and the pithy expression was unexpected. No, probably not a slam. Likely just something from the transcript Winnifer was reading.

Ridiculous! He was overreacting. Imagination. There were only a few who knew. He walked past the Analysis shop where Sergeant Baldwin grinned at him. Winter could have sworn he heard him utter that overused and insincere nostrum from 'Nam, "Sorry 'bout that!"

In his outer office he passed Magic Marvin without speaking; the clerk was intensely involved with something in his typewriter. Winter sat down at his own desk before the stack of untouched paperwork. He felt a tremendous weight on his shoulders, and called out, "Marsh, get us a cup of coffee, please." He'd left his cup in West's office.

The clerk brought the coffee and Winter motioned for him to shut the door.

"You knew, didn't you, Marve?"

"Of course, sir."

Of course. "How many other people d'you think know about this by now? No, never mind. I don't care. Question is, can you help me keep this from getting to Nickie? Just for now."

Marsh stared blankly into space, rodent-like. "Well, let's see. Coupla' guys in the Comm Center know. Major West. Probably the X.O., maybe the Adjutant. Some of the other guys in Ops . . . you know Comm Center pukes talk . . . it won't go far. I can help with the guys. I can't do much with the officers–"

"No problem. I'll handle that. I have to put the squelch on a couple of wives, too, but I think it's manageable." Winter prayed it was manageable.

"How long you gonna try to pull this off, sir? Goddamn post is like a small town full of widows. Gossip. Bullshit." Marsh had grown up in a small town; nor was the allusion lost on Winter.

"Just until we go on leave. I'll take this afternoon off, take her and the boys somewhere. Just to get her off post in case word gets out. Let's see, this is Friday. Maybe run down to Salzburg over the weekend. That'll cover all but Sunday night, early Monday." He didn't mention when he was leaving for Italy; Marsh knew his schedule as well as he.

"You're covered, sir. Mister Buford will handle anything in the shop, anything routine. The major, everything else." The clerk stood up. "I'll run down the nattering and put a halt to it." Marsh was in his element and engaged.

Winter stood, hearing but not hearing, his mind leapfrogging into other concerns.

"Don't you reckon the C.O.'s wife will call Mrs. Winter?" Marsh said. "It's customary."

"I'll get Mrs. Satterwhite to talk to her. Probably she doesn't even know yet."

"Right. Colonel's in Munich."

"He doesn't know yet either, and if he doesn't personally report activities at court to her, nobody else will bother." Winter's fleeting image of the commander's wife was of a decaying man-o-war, under full sail but in the twilight of her power. Paralleling her husband's declining fortunes within Army hierarchy, her guns were spiked now; she posed little threat, and wallowed in even moderate seas.

Mrs. Ahls had undoubtedly been a terror at teas early in her husband's career, the scourge of officers' clubs from one corner of the globe to another. Now, almost in her dotage at an age short of fifty, she was the object of such pity it was often embarrassing to the officers' wives who had to suffer mandatory military socializing. The decline of the woman's autocratic demeanor, along with her self assurance, could be traced to the trivialization by her self-righteous husband, Lieutenant Colonel Bernard B. Ahls. A chosen-by-God evangelist, bible-thumping tee-totaller. An avenging angel of light and rectitude. A prig, the theater commander had once called him at a command meeting, Winter was told, the first time he'd heard that term outside historical novels.

Ahls' philosophy was, "What's right for me is right for my command," a conviction which the Army's hierarchical practices allowed the colonel to inflict upon his subordinates far too long. A God-fearing man, he called himself. A God would-*be*-ing man, the troops labeled him. And while disdaining his wife's slavish devotion, the colonel knew he must not lose her confidence; she might be his only devotee. He repaid her with gossip and tales told out of school, revealing even the most personal and professional confidences best kept under his hat. Without him, she would be oblivious to all about her.

"Poor woman," Winter concluded, ending the brief silence and jaundiced insights.

"Who gives a shit?" Magic Marvin asked a larger audience.

* * *

Winter couldn't sit still in his office. He left the Operations building, and walked to his quarters, thinking the three short blocks the longest walk of his life. It was almost 1100 hours. The sky was clearing to the east, the air warming. Along the walk before the library crocuses waved gently in the breeze above grass so green it glowed.

He found his wife and youngest son in the parking lot before Building 301, unloading groceries from the VW. Nickie was surprised to see him, but a quick exchange was enough to arrange an outing. Winter's schedule was irregular, and they had developed an ability to adjust to any hours of work, to take advantage of any free time whenever it could be squeezed in.

Upstairs, they put away the groceries. Winter changed into civilian clothes and grabbed his camera bag. They settled Adam into the back seat, picked up the older son, Jeremy, at school, and were on the autobahn south within an hour. They stopped for lunch lakeside on Chiemsee. Over food and wine in the brisk lake breeze, Winter studied Nickie closely. Circumspectly.

She knew nothing! He'd gotten her away from the post, he thought — he hoped — without suspicion. How long could he juggle crisis?

They spent the windfall afternoon at Burghausen, a middle-ages architectural relic, not quite a castle, more than a mere domicile, complete with moat — long dried up — and pea gravel walks, gardens, and enough dank, lightless passageways to interest the most jaded wanderer, and fire the imagination of two small boys.

chapter three

Electric Man

Bad Aibling, Germany: Spring 1968

Ilsa. *That* was her name, Ilsa Dorfmann.

A face like sunrise, a body to make you goofy. The gate guard, musing in memory, beheld the German shopmaiden's image before him, bold in relief against the skyline shapes of nose, chin, breasts, pubis, and thighs of the Schlafen Jungfrau to the west, in shadow now, the setting sun beyond a mélange of fiery orange streaks, roiling pink and purple rays, mauve clouds. A Viking, she was. A goddamned Valkyrie, with that long blond hair, long blond body.

It took several re-writes of his statement, when he was later interviewed by the Provost Marshal, before PFC Waller was able to define anything meaningful about events.

He clearly remembered the bicycle squeaking by him on his right, in the outbound lane at the front gate, cutting in front of the guard shack before Waller realized he was not alone with Ilsa. The figure in orange blended with the last glow of the fading sun against the western sky. The MP gate guard's initial glimpse was construed as a part of his images, then feared it might be a mirage. Torn from the visions of his mythically proportioned *Mädchen*, it did not immediately occur to him that he might be experiencing reality. The bicycle turned, squeaking, and the bizarre figure rode out of the golden glow, back past the guard shack on the other, inbound, side and disappeared from the guard's view.

It took a moment of reflection, but the squeaking could not be ignored. Waller stepped out of the guard shack in the middle of the road in wonder: "What the hell—" The biker, unresponsive, turned in the street before the headquarters building and raced back up the road toward the front gate. "Hey, you . . . hey, stop. Stop there!"

The orange-clad rider paid no attention to the guard, rode out the open gate, wheeled at the fork with the road to *Schloss Maxlrain*, and rode back in again. There was a light breeze and the cape streamed out behind the bicycle, flapping down threateningly near the spokes.

Waller was a combat vet. Fifteen months with the 18th Military Police Brigade, running the Bien Hoa-Sai Gon shooting gallery, assimilating a daily diet of mines, snipers, vehicle breakdowns in hostile vacuums, the gate guard was not unaccustomed to adversity.

The Adjutant, Captain Spears, working late in his office in the headquarters overlooking the road behind the guard shack, had never benefitted from testing in combat. When the fireworks began, he opened the window and leaned out in curiosity. His was the most reliable observation of those contributing to the later incident report: "I have no earthly idea what the hell I saw. A murderous guard. A wild cyclist with a penchant for garish dress. And a cape."

Then the sirens had begun.

* * *

Winter slowed the VW wagon to a crawl. The front gate was closed!

Regulations allowed, even dictated, closing the post at particular times: during alerts; when violence occurred off-post in the immediate area, a distraction often manifested on May Day when the communists demonstrated in the streets of nearby Rosenheim; and for inclement weather conditions. Once, as Officer-of-the-Day, Winter had closed the post following a winter ice storm to keep off-duty troops from the hazardous roads. But now the weather was clear, the roads dry. The only mob he saw as he approached was inside the gate. Winter drove to within three feet of the gate and pulled up, flashed his lights, and switched to parking dim.

Inside the heavy-barred gate he could see revolving blue lights. Two nights in a row!

Seen only as shadowy figures, Military Police were stationed strategically behind the gate. One of the MPs directed his flashlight at the windshield, blinding Winter. Nickie awoke and sat up, shielding her eyes.

"Where are we, Dave? What's . . . is it a wreck?" The afternoon outing among the winding paths and hills around Burghausen — moat, keep, and chapel — had taken their toll.

Someone yelled out beyond the gate: "Open up. It's Mister Winter. Billings, get the frigging gate open."

Another voice, heavy with authority, said, "Sergeant Bloomer . . . mouth! Family in that vehicle."

"Sorry, Mister Barnshell. Sorry, Mister Winter," the MP sergeant shouted through the fence. He stared through the streaked windshield and added, "'scuse me, Mrs. Winter." The gate slid back on its rails screeching like something in a horror movie. It was not often closed, not often serviced, and the rusty squeals, like giant steel fingernails on a cast-iron chalkboard, sent shivers up Winter's back. He drove forward until he was directly between the guardroom at the side and the guard shack anchored in the middle of the road. The gate was quickly closed behind him.

Winter's first thought was that someone had broken into the American Express office in the stone building adjacent to the gate. But that structure also housed the MP station with a soldier-cop on duty at the desk twenty-four hours a day. What kind of simpleton would risk that for the meager sums kept in AMEXCO? But meager was a relative term, he knew.

"T.J. What's going on?" Winter asked.

Barnshell leaned in the window of the bus. "Dave," he nodded. "Nickie." He glanced into the back seat and saw the boys asleep. "Well, since you ask so nicely, I'll tell you all I know. And that, as the man says, ain't much." He inhaled deeply on his cigar.

"Your friend of evening past, the caped crusader, has been on the prowl again. Man, man! I thought since you played Marshal Dillon last night, I'd get a nice quiet duty." He snorted, bit off a scraggly bit of cigar and spat it to the side. "Nothin's ever easy," he said mournfully.

"The midnight marauder?"

"Whatever. Bastard rode right up here to the guard shack, 'bout sundown. Rode around the shack a coupla' times on a bike — right here where I stand — and by the time the goddamned gate guard got his eyes back in their sockets, the mother was halfway down the street toward Alpha Company." He drew carefully again on the Windsor House.

Winter remained silent. Nickie said nothing. He had told her enough of the previous evening's events from his OD tour, and she knew enough of military convention, to realize there were uneasy people afield. Whatever it turned out to be, for now it was under wraps. Winter knew it seemed silly to her. GIs gossiped like bridge club devotees and she would know it would all come out when the time came. The military had a tendency to slap a hush on anything it didn't understand, or couldn't explain to the outside world. It probably didn't sound significant to her, just another GI prank. But this one was getting mileage.

Winter said, barely above a whisper, "Did he hurt anyone? You know . . . attack anyone?"

"Hell no. You're talking about Meechan's . . . nawww. That silly shit in the guard shack must've been playing with himself. Said it was all quiet out here, no cars in or out, despite Friday night and all. He was standing here, 'staring off at the mountains,' he said. Something flies by him, coming from on post, going around the shack. Can't believe his eyes. Stands there, apparently frozen to the spot, dis-remembering the instructions about this mystery clown from last night. Around he comes again, the *Man-on-the-Bike*, as I've been instructed to so un-dramatically refer to him. They'll attribute nothing to him beyond his skill on a bike. *Any*-hoo, so the guard, apparently more afraid to do nothing than to do whatever it is guards do, finally locks down on this clown in the orange tights and —"

"Orange?"

"Yeah, orange. Sure, sure, I know. Your's was in blue. I read the report. Must've been a different dipalong, right?"

"You're excruciatingly funny for an old guy with hemorrhoids."

"Rapier sharp tongue there, you witty devil. Any*how*, this guy has on orange tights and some kind of helmet and goggles and high boots, and a — you're gonna love this —"

"A cape."

"*Shit!* Yeah, a cape. Will you let me finish telling this. This's the biggest thing's happened to me on O.D. since Sergeant Willingham caught his wife banging that ditty-catcher in the gym and burned her Opel in the parking lot during *Fasching* two years ago. Where was I? The cape. Yeah, he had on a cape. Orange cape." He hesitated. "Your report never mentioned a cape last night. Neither did Janssen's M.P. log," he said, playing his one trump card. "I had to hear about it from one-a the guards."

"What d'you expect, T.J.? This outfit can only handle crises is small doses. On top of the attack on Meechan, a cape would have pushed my luck."

Barnshell chuckled. "You know what this dummy did? The guard? He leans out the door of the guard shack, apparently after watching mystery man ride a circle around the shack for half an hour—" There was a groan of protest from someone in the crowd of MPs behind the Duty Officer. "—yells at the . . . this *thing* and tells him to halt. Yelled twice, if you can believe him. Didn't seem to be able to just step out the door here and yank the screwball off the bike while he was pinwheelin' 'round the guard shack. Never tried calling inside the guardhouse right over there, not thirty feet away, where three stalwart young defenders of law and order lay on their asses reading comic books. No! This featherbrain is going to Wyatt Earp the orange Good Humor Man . . . gonna blow his ass away. Gonna shoot him outta the saddle." TJ found the modern Army incredible. He drew deeply on the cigar, smoke wreathing his head as he savored recent events.

"So, anyhow," he drawled sagely, "it musta put the fear of God in that clown on the bike, seeing the guard pull that cannon. He lit for the boonies, straight back down the road toward the companies. Yellin' at the top of his lungs, *'Electric Man! Electric Man! Electric Man!'"* The children in the back seat stirred at Barnshell's evocative re-creation of the orange visitor's battle cry.

"Electric Man. What the hell's that mean?"

"You're asking me, Tonto? What am I, physic or something?" Winter was never quite sure how much of Barnshell was put-on and how much legitimate dumbass. He didn't bother to ask; it might be a question he didn't want answered.

"Deadeye over there—Waller's who it was—levels down on the bike whizzer and cranks off three rounds. Just like he was back in the Capital Military District—shoot at anything that moves. Can you imagine?"

With his own question, Barnshell was struck suddenly by the potential enormity of the guard's actions. He turned to the shuffling group behind him and demanded, "Does this look like a goddamned free fire zone, Waller? Does it?" Encountering only silence, he turned back to the car. "Silly asshole. Probably daydreamin', and when the dude flies by him, he flashes on The 'Nam, thought, *Zip in the open!*, and cut down on him. Fired three rounds."

Nickie's face bore a strained look. Winter was trying to find the serious side to TJ's narrative, but had little to choose from.

"One round hit the wall of the Old Man's house," Barnshell continued. "Scared hell out of the Mrs. One round, we got no idea— into the grass or a tree or over onto the golf course, somewhere. The zinger was the one took the windshield out of the fire engine."

"All the way to the firehouse?" Winter said.

"Don't go bug-eyed on me. It's only two hundred sixteen yards; we measured. Scared the shit out of Dietrich, who probably hasn't heard gunfire since the GIs shot off his pinkie in 'forty-five. But give him credit. The damned old Nazi rang the alarm, started the truck, and laid on the siren. Drove out of the station . . . but that was it. Didn't know where to go from there. Time I got outside Headquarters all I could see was this goddamned big red truck, racing 'round and 'round the triangle with the siren going, bell clanging. Horn blowing. Smoking. Sonuvabitch crushed every tulip in the flower beds around the flagpole. Old Lady Mrs. Lieutenant Colonel Ahls will have somebody's ass for that exercise, for sure."

"Jeez-us! Must have sounded like full alert."

"You ain't wrong. I was resting my eyes when this all started. Hell, *I* thought we had Zips in the wire. I came up off the bunk, scared. Sergeant Bentz said I was screamin' 'Incoming!' and he was under the desk before I knew where the hell I was. And here's this bloody great red truck, racing in circles out here in front of the Old Man's house, siren bustin' my ears, scarin' the hell out of everybody. Got every dog on post howling. Sounded like we were besieged by *banh sidghes*. You can still hear one every now'n again."

He glanced about cautiously. "We chased the kraut in circles for ten minutes before he settled down enough to stop the engine. I'm still shaking."

Winter was bent over the wheel, his face buried in his hands. Nicole covered her mouth and looked away toward the chapel, invisible in the dark.

"Nice, Winters. Thanks a bunch for understanding."

"Take two Löwenbraus and call me in the morning. C'mon, T.J., you got to admit," Winter said, coming up for air, "that *is* a wild scene. Breaks the monotony in the O.D. log, for sure, for sure . . . if you can write it?"

"Yeah, I guess it sounds kinda funny to a non-participant. I'll probably laugh later. About next Christmas. Yeah . . . and that ain't all. Spears was in his office working when the fireworks went off. The silly shit is still hyperventilating. They had the ambulance out here, thought he'd had a heart attack. Took him to the dispensary. He's still over there breathin' in a grocery bag, far as I know."

Barnshell was clearly a perplexed man. "Soldiers shouldn't oughta act like that. That goddamned cape, that takes it. You don't suppose . . ." he hesitated. "No. I guess not."

Winter, anticipating the ridiculous, said, "Superman's not a viable suspect."

"Aahhh, your ass, Winter. You're beginning to sound like one of these commissioned officers. I might have to report your insufferable behavior to the Warrant Officers' Protective Association. WOPA don't allow harrassment of Chiefs. Now be serious. Just imagine . . . 'round and 'round the guardshack, like he was on a goddamned merry-go-round. Cool as you please. Of all the brass — "

A mellow roar rumbled up behind Winter's car. The roar peaked to an ear-piercing screech. The disturbance mushroomed: an engine backfired; brakes squealed; metal, rent by counter-stressed metal, grated. Tinny clinking sounds filled the night air as loose parts fell randomly to the roadway. A VW Bug shuddered to a halt just beyond the gate, one headlight flickering in a spastic series of lurid winks, giving Winter a flash of déjà vu from the previous evening's OD sedan.

"Dim those — that light!" yelled one of the guards. "God!"

"Nope. It's Stallman," another guard added, chuckling.

The VW squatted belligerently like a pug bitch, its one good headlight glaring on the front gate while the other sent spastic, oscillating signals into the void. The guards slid the gate open again. The Bug chugged forward a few feet and stopped with its front bumper against Winter's rear bumper. The Volkswagen was missing its muffler and the driver continued to race the engine, riding the clutch, rocking the vehicle back and forth, setting up sympathetic motion in Winter's wagon. He stepped out to assess the new-found chaos. The boys in the back seat stirred again, and Nickie covered her ears, her eyes wide with question.

In the lights just inside the gate, Winter examined the tiny, battered vehicle whose original color was indistinguishable through the mud and barnyard droppings that coated it. Only a thirty-degree arc was cleared on the passenger-side windshield. Behind the VW a long, ragged tangle of silver net, stiff and glistening, trailed off twenty yards behind the car.

As TJ Barnshell went into his Duty Officer act, Winter walked back and examined the wire mesh fencing strung out from the car's rear bumper. The wire, and the road behind the car stretching off into the moonlight, was littered with pale feathers. A flurry of them spiraled around on the road surface in the light breeze. Several yards behind the car an immobile duck was tangled in the mesh, webbed feet splayed skyward. Not a quack audible. Farther back, the brilliant red of early geraniums decorated the unlikely tangle.

"What the hell's going on here?" screamed TJ. "Where've you been with this tank?"

From where Winter stood, the driver's voice was drowned out by the revving engine.

"'Just down the autobahn, my ass. You're drunker'n a skunk, Stallman. Get outta the goddamned vehicle. Shut it down." CW3 Barnshell stood and waved his arms in helpless fury at the calamity before him. "What the hell you mean you can't shut it off?" He screamed a fresh torrent of abuse at the hapless driver. Winter could hear only muted rumbles and giggles from the driver and an unidentified passenger inside the VW.

"Well, since you're having such fun, and we gotta run," Winter called, "see you later, T.J." Making an instant decision, he said,

"We're off early in the morning on leave. Gotta hit the rack." He climbed into the car.

Nickie's face jerked around. "Leave? What do you mean, 'leave'?" she blurted. "We don't go on leave until Monday." Her voice held an edge of panic.

Barnshell walked toward the station wagon, muttering. In the background an indignant Stallman was being escorted into the gatehouse by two laughing MPs.

"I was just trying to save the two days' leave over the weekend, but I think we should go ahead before something comes up to hold us here." Winter explained.

Barnshell ignored the talk of leave and said, "By the way, Dave, I meant to say something. I just heard, late this afternoon, about—"

"Ohhh, yeah. Sure, we'll have to get together later, maybe after we get back from Italy." He turned his face directly toward Barnshell, away from Nicole, and desperately rolled his eyes back toward her in a silent plea.

"You heard what?" she asked Barnshell. She turned to her husband. "David Winter. What are you two up to? Am I being set up?"

Winter realized she inadvertently linked the two subjects, assumed she was to be surprised by something he had planned, and further assumed his friend knew about it. He was gratefully relieved at TJ's silence, and did not answer.

"We can't go on leave, yet" she protested half-heartedly. We were out today. I've got laundry to do, things to get ready by Sunday night. We haven't even packed."

"A thing of no consequence, woman. We can pack in five minutes, you know that. And don't worry about the laundry. Get Cissie to call Frieda to come in tomorrow. She's always looking for extra work. She can do laundry and get the quarters squared away while we're gone."

"You'll not have to ask me a second time, Slick. As your charming friends so eloquently put it, let's get it on." Then she hesitated. "No, we can't. Janet's not available to keep the boys until Monday."

"Have you asked about the weekend?" He knew the answer was no.

Barnshell leaned in the window, listening. He shook his head, said caustically, "Deliver me from domestic bliss." The disgruntled senior warrant officer's dedication to bachelorhood derived from one failed experiment with marriage, a union dissolved by the untimely but graphic revelation that his shy young wife entertained a preference for female sexual contact. He'd walked in on her and her preference in a back bedroom at a friend's house at Fort Benning during his own promotion party. TJ wasn't up to handling that, being a confirmed heterosexual and preferring to remain that way, and expecting of his wife a similar commitment. They parted company and the experience left him only slightly bitter, a state that manifested itself solely when he drank to excess and fell into a mood of self-pity. It was invariably gone with the hangover.

The self-pity, not the revulsion.

But he took his friend's hint. Mister Winter, wife Nicole, and children drove to their quarters without further comment, leaving behind midnight marauders and VWs that acted with independent powers, and a gruff and caring warrant officer who could see nothing good for his young friend in the situation building.

Major West and Magic Marvin had done their part. Back in quarters, there were no waiting messages, no visiting gossips. No late phone calls of commiseration.

* * *

Saturday dawned dark and overcast in Bad Aibling, threatening with spring clouds drifting down off the mountains across the valley. Janet Cummings arrived while the family was finishing a hurried breakfast. The boys were still in their pajamas and returned to their rooms to play.

By 0730, Winter had been to Ops and confirmed there was nothing afoot serious enough to disrupt his leave. He'd cleared his early departure with a phone call to the adjutant the evening before, with the proviso that nothing of significance was occurring by departure.

Farewells were said, last-minute instructions repeated, and Dave and Nickie Winter drove away from the housing area. Nickie was content that the boys were almost oblivious to their departure, though it caused her an uncomfortable twinge. Janet, childless, a fellow officer's wife, a friend and neighbor, had kept the boys before and they loved being with her. It was all an adventure.

The only disturbing note — and obvious only to David — occurred as the Winters were climbing into the car. Jeremy, with a plastic rifle gripped in his hand, yelled from the third floor balcony, "Dad, is it all right if me'n Adam play down by the stream with Miltie?"

"Adam and I," David corrected him distractedly. "I guess so, Jeremy," he managed, his carefully balanced mood shattered by ugly flashes as he stared at the toy rifle. "Be careful around the water . . . watch your brother. Behave yourselves, guys." Wasted words. He knew Janet would be wherever they went, and the water in the stream that ran through the housing area, in its most extreme pockets, reached the depth of nine inches.

Adam's head popped into view, straining to see over the balcony railing. Janet appeared behind the boys, hands reassuringly on small shoulders. Adam waved a small hand, purple and sticky with jelly. Winter held onto that image as they drove away across the stream, out the gate, and south down the autobahn toward Austria and Italy.

Overwhelmed by conflicting emotions, he switched on the VW's radio, seeking something distracting, and was surprised to find himself in the midst of a bagpipes classic, "The Black Bear." Despite his fondness for the pipes, he suddenly felt an ill-defined anxiety.

* * *

Parris Island, South Carolina; Late Autumn, 1953

Private Winter left his bunk and padded in sock feet across the concrete floor of the Quonset hut. The smell of fuel oil in the spill pan beneath the heater was strong, masking the fug of eighteen young male bodies sleeping, cramped into a space the Marine Corps considered indulgently generous. At the door he stood and listened, this the second night he'd been awakened by the sound. This time he was sure.

Third Recruit Battalion slept; the Quonsets lined cleanly in every direction were silent. Except for recruits on fire watch, there was no movement. He could see the aircraft warning lights atop the three parachute jump towers, so there was no fog. But neither was there a moon. Only lamps sporadically located about the battalion area at each company headquarters, platoon office, Drill Instructor's hut, fire-alarm post, and latrine provided any guide for movement. He couldn't see his watch, but guessed it to be around 0300. He shivered, not from the mildly chilly night, but from the sound he heard. His skin crawled with exhilaration.

The Quonsets spread along the road from mainside, Third Battalion anchored precisely where the road angled some forty degrees, continuing on to the rifle ranges that backed on the sea. Behind the cluster of metal huts, macadam streets, cinder-block latrines, and concrete wash racks, Ribbon Creek flowed through the swamps, brackish and deadly to the dream and intent of escape.

There were two ways off Parris Island: through the swamp, or over the causeway. PI was an island to the extent that it was surrounded by some kind of water, fresh or salt. Mostly swamp, the drowning threat was shallow and tired. But cottonmouths and the occasional alligator — whether mythical or not, the fear was the same — were enough to make the swamp and tidal surge of fresh-salt water an effective jailer.

"Across the causeway" implied graduation from the fifteen-week boot camp for new Marines. True, a few had made it over that passage without the globe-and-fouled-anchor diploma, but traditionally those few would be in a box or a straight jacket. Even so, they were more a part of the mystique than the occasional legitimate "mistake," rectified ex-post-facto by some late-discovered paperwork.

Outside on the macadam, Winter heard only the sibilant whisperings of coastal breeze through marsh grass, and far away the muted, teasing susurration of surf.

Then it started again!

A cry, as of a child. An animal. Keening up in timbre and range, the secondary elements blending tenuously with the clean, clear stab of the first breath. Bagpipes always brought chills to Winter, and he shivered visibly as the melancholy skirl built to ever-higher urgings. The tune was one he knew; he could never remember the names, but he was familiar with more than a dozen traditional pipe pieces, all military in tone if not in origin, sonorous and mesmerizing. The Gloucestershires had their repertoire; the 48th Highlanders of Canada, the Black Watch and other regiments, different tunes.

Except for exposure to the Brit battalion in the line adjacent to his rifle company in Korea—and there'd been little call for the pipes, little opportunity to hear them there—he was as unfamiliar with the traditions as most other Americans. But he was haunted by them.

Was it some reciprocal, visiting highlander here at PI? Or more likely, another Marine like himself who'd served with the lads from Dundee or Skirl-a-Whivaree, Glasgow or Minnieton. Someone else who was drawn to the ineffable shades of the music, the plaintive wail that held all the anguish and pain of countless generations in the barren and stony Celtic settlements of the world? Another survivor who found the pipes the only fond memory of Korea?

Winter stood, recapturing the bitter pain of a moment he thought gone. A momentary stab of pathos, a fleeting flare of hatred for dark memories. The haunting echoes of the pipes were lost for a time, over the distance, as the lone instrument droned into its lower registers. During that few moments, only the sea breeze teased forth the memory of standing deep in snow and ice, Mickey Mouse boots frozen into the mud of a regiment's passing. Saluting with a stiff hand wrapped with the merest rag of a mitten, watching the gunners in the funny kewpie bonnets moving like mechanical dolls around the three stiff corpses while the single piper bore up to the tradition in kilts above blue legs barely covered with ripped hose. The Seventh Infantry Division Army troops straggling through the Marine lines halted momentarily to watch with blank, hooded eyes, shivering in the few ineffective pieces of clothing and blanket they could claim.

Could this South Carolina magician be playing to that same memory? To one like it? He didn't doubt it, but Winter would never know. No recruit had free run of the base—he agonized again then at the incongruous circumstances that put him, a combat veteran, here, just now going through basic training, a 'cruit—and it seemed a foolish thing on which to waste a question with the Drill Instructor. That kind of knowledge, unless it had particular application, presented a pointless and aggravating kind of exercise to the DIs, and would lead to duck-walking and other mindless, punishing frivolities.

Winter would keep the feel for the pipes while he lived, and through the remaining days and weeks of that autumn, straining his ears late into the night, listening . . . waiting . . . hungering for the pipes.

But they were never there again.

chapter four

Age Quod Agis

On the road, Italy: May 1968

Awareness: a state of mind—taut with double meaning.

Though early in the forenoon hours, it was like driving at night on familiar road when sleepy, the lack of alertness dangerous without seeming so. Leagues of road, fraught with history, fled by without significance. Looking back after an hour on the road, David Winter could not remember the landscape passed.

Nickie, tired from six days of walking, had found little solace in the short night before. This morning, on the Grand Raccordo Anulare before reaching the *autostrada*, she had exercised a useful ability to disconnect and dozed off. Traffic was light around Rome out as far as the fork to Terni, and it was three hours ahead to Florence up the Val di Chiana. Traffic picked up at the fork, heavy until they were clear of the Orvieto exchange, then slacked again. David let her sleep, his mind marginally on the road, essentially on the one event that must come sometime before the end of the road. Inevitability was a heavy burden.

It was almost noon when he nudged her awake. Distracted by his dilemma, yet entranced by Tuscany, he could not fail to respond to the soft, pastel skyline of Firenze—misty blocks and spires in sienna and umber, roofs in shades of red—emerging from behind the hills in the valley off to the east. The peaks of the Appennines came down to the rushing Arno there, the *duomo* framed against mountains that formed the spine of the peninsula.

"Nickie . . . Florence," he said softly.

She snorkled and straightened in the seat, wiping the corners of her mouth. Once fully awake, she took his hand, said nothing but watched the gentle mirage, the loveliest of Italian cities, until cut off by the sweep of hills. David thought it likely they would never pass this way again and was saddened by the knowledge. Not another Ponte Vecchio visit, no more Uffizi explorations; Michaelangelo's David a cold image in a cold atrium; the Medicis a mystery.

But after Venice, they would not regret the choice of Rome. They talked now of Rome, then again of Venice and the little jewel of Treviso in a guarded way, as if too close a review threatened what they'd had. With even greater care was his terrible secret guarded. Time running out, he faced the effects of the past six days, living a suspended lie.

The VW wagon droned on, steadily chewing up kilometers. They stopped for gas and David bought bottled fruit drinks and small sandwiches of egg and cheese and finely minced vegetables in mayonnaise at the roadside *trattoria* overlooking an endless curve on the great highway. They swapped off driving. Both ate while Nicole drove and David sought words that would not come.

Late afternoon, deep into mountains and still many miles short, they climbed toward the Brenner Pass. *The Pass of Brenner*. Winter thought wryly of his friend, but lacked inspiration to make a joke.

In a pull-off they switched driving back to David. Inured to the passing panorama, it was hard to realize that less than a week had passed since taking this road south. Now the snow on the lower slopes was melting. Alongside the road wild mountain streams spilled past them, runoff crashing down the slopes before and behind them.

Silence inside the car; the non-act of not speaking was mutually understood, accepted between them as contentment. Nothing more. He managed to keep his thoughts at bay.

But it could not last. Time was running out. The moral impetus to deal with the dilemma was a mounting pressure, urging him to commit. To speak. He couldn't recall when trepidation so paralyzed him.

She'd known this could happen, he rationalized. She *must* have known, though he had studiously avoided any discussion over the months and years that could have dealt with it. He'd gone to great lengths to convince her, as he fully believed, that Vietnam did not continue a viable threat to them. It had been his conviction he would be selected for the special covert assignment, subsequently beyond the reach of the dreaded rotation.

Now with the reality of orders, hope faded. The fantasy of somehow making it through to retirement without returning to the war vanished like the men he would follow there. It was as if he had never believed the fantasy, was forced now to admit it; as if that chance had never existed. He'd been tagged from the start and had known all along. He'd lived with the truth: they just weren't on speaking terms. It could not have been a surprise in the real world, and he felt sorrow for having believed otherwise. Because, like seasonal changes, this had been inevitable.

Inevitable since that day he was wheeled off the World Airways Angel-Flight charter more than three years ago, a partially-used-up man. It was all right though, he recalled his feelings at the time: he was home! He was *alive!*

The long weeks in Letterman Army Hospital. San Francisco rehabilitation and pain. Strengthening exercises. Finally, release with aid of the cane. Then, over the long months through the demanding distraction of Russian language training, the sharp edge of trauma had dulled to a bad memory. Lately he didn't think about that time except with weather-change twinges, or when he put sharp pressure on the leg—stress in running, playing with the boys, occasional demands. And he had believed it was over for him, he wouldn't have to face it again. Wouldn't have to ask her to face it again. He had *wanted* to believe.

Once he and others like him emerged from that returning plane, wounded or whole, he knew that an unseen, impersonal hand had pushed a button in a master control room somewhere in a beige-colored building in the Washington suburbs. Somewhere on the end of a data line a computer card was lifted from one deck, electronically examined, manipulated, and re-inserted into another deck. His name came off the list of personnel serving in Vietnam— or recovering from wounds sustained there or in the skies above or the waters contiguous thereto—and went onto another list. A list of those waiting to go.

There were only two lists for career personnel in that time: you either were there, or you were waiting to go. Having been only created a hiatus in the immediacy of going; it did not change the eventual fact. Being there even offered an ironic relief from the threat of having to go. Because while you were there, someone waited for you to leave so they could put your name on the list to return. Even that was better. As if there was less threat in the realization of it than in the anticipation. The constancy of the process inspired awe.

When he was a child he could not stand to be chased, and it was with great effort he forced himself to run from pursuit; he would almost rather give in, suffer the consequences, to get it over. He still ran with deliberation, though he now understood his conflict.

So, at dreaded last, he had come to the top of that second list. Merely the place he occupied in the cyclical process that sent them all there. He despaired of that process, the entire unstoppable procedure, the forever-clicking-over counter, one more name, one more tour, one more year; three hundred sixty-five days and nights to sweat and pray and hope and curse and yearn at both ends of the link to loved ones and strangers; that irreversible list that existed somewhere in chaff-free tape, punched cards, and electromagnetic bits and bytes arrayed in mathematically sustainable logic, catalogued in the bowels of a vast, indecent man-machine that played Russian roulette with lives and hopes and dreams of fathers, mothers, children, lovers, and friends, people you owed money to, and those you'd never met.

He had come up on the list.

* * *

In the mountains the light had gone beyond the peaks and shadows grew across the land, engulfing finally the road he drove now with headlights. In darkness the sharp fear of his hidden knowledge returned in full force. North of Bolzano, once the glow of the town was behind and there was nothing ahead but hours of dark mountain curves and tiny winking villages on the slopes, he knew the time had come.

"Nickie."

"Hmmm?"

"You not asleep?"

"Hmm, no. Suspended. Want me to drive?" she asked.

"No. Not that." How to start?

"Something I have to tell you." He stared ahead through the windshield. Huge granite slabs formed the walls of the canyon they twisted through, the edges of the headlights picking up bright glints from particles of crystalline schist. He understood Dante's inspiration; all he lacked were the words.

"Okay," was all she said. He would have to do it all.

"Nickie . . . honey . . ." *Get on with it!*

"I got orders. Just before we left B.A." He knew immediately that matter-of-fact was the wrong way to go.

"Yes?" she said, her voice suddenly hoarse, tight. She stared ahead. He knew she could not see what the lights sought ahead and above in the rocks. Her voice was steady but her fingers knotted. Her hands, he sensed, with a life of their own, grasped for something firm, the walls of the canyon and the peaks above beginning to slide away in silent crumblings.

He couldn't see her reaction in the darkness when he said it, but Nickie would know what early orders meant. His crushing grip on the steering wheel reflected a desperate quality.

"I'm on the list," he said in sparse explanation.

She was silent. Forever, it seemed, as dark, featureless crags along the road swept by in a blur. David sought to hear her thoughts; he felt in a vacuum. Even car sounds were absent.

"Viet Nam?" she pled. She knew only one list. A stygian void, darker than the night, seemed suddenly to envelop the VW, a tangential blackness carried along with the car. Her voice betrayed little — betrayed everything. "Again?"

His very word. Again! He heard her, heard the car sounds again.

"Yes."

There was only the angry whine of the engine and the flat percussive wind against the boxy frame for several long minutes — or several hours; neither could have said which. David Winter was afraid to speak, reluctant to shatter the tenuous hold on the mood of the past six days, as if by talking about it, acknowledging the safety in it, he would acquiesce in the loss of it. Allow it to happen.

Instead, without words — ignoring it! — he might hold off the inevitable. He had no words to fix it; there was nothing to be done. As if he had committed some terrible social *faux pas* and everyone of a crowd in his presence knew it and condemned him for it, it was already a thing done, an irretrievable act.

He regretted, now, not breaking the news to her as soon as he had known. He realized he had done wrong, but there was no way back. He could only rely on her wisdom, her love, to see them through.

"When?" She was doing this well, he thought.

"Early September."

Did he dare hope it might come off okay? He could offer nothing more. They'd both seen this happen to friends: junior officers and warrants, a few field grades, sergeants and specialists, married, single, divorced — it didn't matter. The demand for bodies for that distant conflict was insatiable, swallowing them whole, ingesting, assimilating all into its bowels, converting into waste, vomiting out others in a partially consumed state, forever changed. Nickie smiled a sad smile only to herself. David concentrated on the lights ahead, a faint luminescence pulling them up into the rocky heights of the Tirol, leading them home.

He waited for her to say something illogical and untrue. Something like, The Army can't do that! But he knew she would not; she knew better. *They* could do anything, that same ubiquitous *they* who invariably committed acts rational minds couldn't comprehend. She knew that; she had suffered proof of it.

Still, out of frustration and fear might have come a protest, knowing she was wrong but persistently hopeful of finding a crack in that impenetrable and deadly thoroughness. She might have argued the justice or fairness to her of a second tour in Vietnam for him, when she knew women whose husbands had yet to go the first time.

As he might have argued.

Equally fatuously and ineffectively.

But she said none of that. Deep down he really had not expected anything different. She sat beside him and he knew she thought now the things that had overwhelmed him when he first read the message. About time remaining at Bad Aibling. About other officers and men who, along with their wives, anxiously watched daily for the devastating message. That was immaterial. The chaos had little to do with what was happening, but what had already happened.

Whatever his relationship to other soldiers—whatever their relationship with other couples—regardless of fairness-of-assignment doctrines that failed and chaplains who could not find adequate words to blunt the anguish of the Pentagon's revolving door to 'Nam as they preached to empty chapels on Army bases around the globe, when the word came down everything was reduced to one man, his personal chimera, and his loved ones.

No, Nickie was Army enough to understand how useless any argument would be. She might blame him, she might curse him. She might even hate him. But she knew, like any soldier, the inviolability of the sentence. He felt sure of that.

She was silent for fully ten kilometers. When she spoke, it was in a curiously detached tone. "I guess I'm relieved. In a sick kind of sense. Do you know how worried I've been? About you? Since Friday, a week ago. The day we went to Burghausen. *My God!* Nine days ago, and in the past fifteen minutes it already feels like decades." Her face in the dim glow from the dash lights was set: sad, yet vibrant. He felt uneasy but did not respond.

"Things went kind of out of focus that afternoon. I can't ever remember you coming home from Ops early. Tom West wouldn't give you an hour off for brain surgery. I knew something was wrong; I felt uneasy then. I just couldn't put my finger on what . . . there was something reserved in you. That day . . . this past week— though you've hidden it well." A touch of bitterness belied her restrained tone.

She stared into the tunneled headlights a few kilometers more, silent. David could say nothing in the face of either her voiced or silent accusations. He sensed her trembling.

"You always pay, don't you? *For everything!*" Her voice rose sharply. "It never fails. Why was I foolish enough to think I could beat the odds?"

Then she cried.

His protestations sailed into the black void beyond the windows. His attempt at assurance, his plea for patience, his prayer for understanding were pointless exercises in rationality. This was no time for rational. In giving in to tears, relinquishing the discipline that had carried her through all the other years of separation, loneliness, and fear—the needs and the helplessness and the strengths, too—there was suddenly a new fear, David thought. He could see on her pale, drawn face a ripple of some new emotion. A new threat? Anticipating, he knew she was venturing into previously unmapped territory. He thought the new fear might suddenly be that she couldn't handle all the other fears, and the tears were for that, too.

* * *

By the time they reached the Austrian border, high in the pass where the snow still lay in moon-splashed crevices, her tears had stopped. They had begun the unavoidable talk, worrying the necessary decisions: tentative plans for the move, what to tell the boys, when to tell them. But each time David tried to talk about where he should settle them in the states while he served his tour in Viet Nam, Nickie was evasive. Non-committal and vague.

Something was being left unsaid. Something that could not be said. Both were aware of it, and the presence of that unwanted something trailed the VW like another vehicle, always there, just behind, the same distance away whether they sped up or slowed. Both talked as if she'd never uttered those line-in-the-sand words in Monterey when he'd come home that first time from 'Nam. As if no line had been drawn.

She began asking the questions that begged answering.

No, he didn't know where he'd be going. He would learn only upon arrival in-country. He thought it likely meant flight status again.

She didn't know if that was better or not. He would be safer at some relatively secure airbase rather than out in the bush, when he was not flying. But to her there was the lingering horror of him going down in one of those ridiculously small, unarmed reconnaissance playthings. He had tried to keep it from her, but she knew the names of at least one crew gone: Warren Nesbitt and Mister Phillips. There were the pictures in that box in the closet. A photo album of the first time out. Tom Cats in flight suits or jungle fatigues, clustered, smiling and somehow World-War-One-ish around the radial engines, or near the vertical stabilizers so the tail numbers were readable. Those she had come to know from drinking tales of the ones who remained. The stories, like teenaged bragging about drag racing and the number of beers drunk at a Saturday night drive-in, had given her screaming fits, he knew, trembling rages she'd suffered by herself in dark rooms and quiet corners in whomever's home they found themselves when it came out. And it all came out.

There the guys were in the pictures, crowded about the planes like children about a fire engine, pointing at the almost unnoticeable punctures in the fuselage and wings of the craft, cocky and proud. But some of the variously dressed wingmen bore black felt-tip X-es on their chests. On pictures of their chests.

The worst of it, though—he knew her thoughts, and knew she felt no shame for the thoughts: she had, over time, revealed all this to him—were the long husbandless, fatherless, loverless days and months to come. No one to turn to, to laugh with . . . only to cry for. She tried to push her thoughts from that; in that direction lay only chaos. Four months left!

The trip planned for Spain the following year: that was lost now. How much leave should they take? Should they take it here, or save it to take in the states? He sensed when she awoke to what she was doing, letting her mind run with the old pattern. She didn't want that. This was different. The old questions, the usual problems were insignificant alongside this new, frightening reality. He knew she would see it thus.

They talked in generalities with an unspoken understanding that anything was conversational grist, except the one thing both were so aware of, afraid of, and neither would touch on—*them*, her mind phrased it.

All the time as the VW worked its way upward toward the peaks as of its own volition, as if David's hands on the wheel had nothing to do with where it went or how fast or why, toward the pass and the north, grinding toward Innsbruck and beyond, one question she raised repeatedly: Was there no hope of getting out of it?

"No. No chance." He related his conversation with Major West, the fallback on logic, fairness, all the doctrines that doomed him.

Austria slipped by in the darkness, in no way beautiful now. Clusters of lights that should have been fanciful and romantic dropped behind them unmentioned, harsh and garish in the undulating landscape, not even identifiable as villages. Ghostly patterns raced alone in shadows painted onto the snow beside the road.

"Damn it, Dave, it's not right!" she cut into his thoughts. "Can't you find some way around West?" Her voice sounded an unaccustomed shrillness.

"It's not Tom. Christ, Nickie; he didn't do this. And he can't do anything about it. This came directly from D.A., probably because I put in for the special assignment and they flagged my record. They want one more tour out of me before they lose me to the covert work where I'll be out of reach. Tom did everything he could. He doesn't want to lose me."

"*You* could do something," she snapped. "Lots of men fight back, refuse to go. They get out of it, one way or another."

Who was this belligerent woman offering ridiculous panaceas? It was as if he suddenly was debating a stranger, one who made illogical and unacceptable arguments, who battered him with commands he couldn't obey. Suggested a guilt he could not carry.

"I can't just refuse to go, Nickie. You know that. What are you suggesting? You talk like some first-termer's back-home honey. This is the real, military world. I can't just *not* go. I can't—"

"Then get out!"

"Get out? Out of what? This situation? The car?" His mind had lost its facile mobility, but he knew in the same moment that humor was not acceptable.

"Get out of the damned Army. The fifteen years don't matter. Give them up. A bad investment. I've heard you say a thousand times, Dave, playing poker, 'Don't throw good money after bad.' We'll take our children and go somewhere, start new. Put this out of our minds. Behind us." Her voice modulated between a harsh, demanding tone and a plea.

"I can't do that, Nickie."

"You won't."

"No. I mean I can't. All arguments—job, years of service, promotion, patriotism, what-all—all that aside, I can't. Once you're on orders for 'Nam, you go. It's too late to quit."

"Then resign your commission. Your warrant, whatever . . ."

He was shaken by the degree of her anger, her willingness to throw away everything. The desperate, illogical solutions.

"It wouldn't change anything. I'd wind up going as a sergeant or EM. But I would still have to go."

"*No-o-o-o!*" she screamed in deep despair, as if, until that moment, she'd secretly harbored a saving grace. He glanced over at her, began searching the roadside for a place to pull over when he saw her face. But in the narrow winding confines of the mountains, there was no parking.

"You'll go back there, then. Back to the killing and the horror and murder . . . and hate . . . and . . . ." She ran down.

"Nickie, honey, don't think it. Nothing will happen to me. Don't you think I've had my share of risks, Korea and 'Nam? I'm a survivor. I'll be all right," he assured her. Through the long-accustomed relationship, he misread her.

""I won't," she murmured in a low voice.

"Nickie, you will. I promise. You and the boys—"

"The boys need you here. Here—I mean at home, with them. Here, or in America. Anywhere with them. They don't need a hero. They need a father."

"It'll be all right. They'll be fine. You're strong, you've proven that. You're a soldier's wife."

"*Screw that!* A soldier's wife—what does that mean? Does that mean I can't be lonely? I can't be scared, or need help? Does being a soldier's wife take away all that I am as me? As a person? A woman and mother?" She was turned on the seat, almost shouting into his face, and on the winding mountain road he dare not turn to face her.

"I'm not a soldier's wife. I'm *your* wife. And I don't want a soldier. I don't want a hero . . . or a casualty. Or an officer or anything else. I want you! I want my husband! Father of my children—our children. I want you, just as you are. That's what they need, who the boys need."

"Nickie—"

"No! No more! I cannot go back to . . . I can't . . . there's no other way to say it. I cannot go back to the states and sit in some ready-made widow's grove on some military base. Sit and wait for a telegram, for that goddamned green Army sedan with some sad-faced apologist who doesn't want to be where he is, doing what he's doing, to come knocking on my door to advise me on filling out the paperwork to ensure my benefits, and when and where the ceremony will be, and come back to an empty house that I can't even stay in without your service, and find a place to keep the flag they give me. For God's sake, just sitting in that house waiting for that sedan is a horrid kind of public Russian roulette. Every eye in the neighborhood pressed to the window, watching, waiting to see who gets visited today, and a chaplain who can't sustain us losers . . . " Her voice was almost a scream. "I can't. *Damned if I will!* Not anymore!" She moved away from him to the far door.

"Nickie! That's not fair. Not . . . rational." He knew it was feeble. No! Not just feeble: the wrong argument.

"Rational! *Not rational?* Do you think it's rational to go off? . . . Fair? Fair for you to forget your family and join the half-million guys already there to go kill some little foreigners? With a half-million doing it, why do they need one more? You've done that already. In two wars. What do you owe the Vietnamese that you don't owe your family? Or is it that call to arms — "

"You know better. It's my job."

"Your job? Your passion, you mean. Your fantasy. You and those damned books. About the war. About . . . *war!* The movies, the songs, the barroom talk. *All you people — you soldiers — ever do is re-live the war. Re-fight* . . . And it's always funny, heroic — why is it you don't remember the terrible things that happen to you all? You laugh and tell tales about the hilarious and odd things; why don't you remember that landing zone?"

"Nickie, that's not — "

"You tell me, is there anything worth what you went through before? Is anything worth the lives of the guys you talk about who didn't come back? Does that seem noble to you?"

David would have liked to categorize her as ranting, but he realized she was coldly logical, as focused as it was possible to be.

Wrong! he thought. Not that focused, not yet. Merely logical and impassioned.

He felt a furious rush of defensive anger, wanting to overwhelm her with facts of his own, perspectives she now did not acknowledge or had forgotten. Or didn't understand. But he held back; there was no profit in his own reasoned logic; his only hope lay in prolonging the status quo until they had talked through and beyond all contention and could find common ground.

"That's not fair, Nickie. You know me better than that. You know I'm not a warmonger, not some kind of killer freak. I don't *want* to go to war. But ultimately, that's what the military does. And there are things worth going to war for. I know you believe that. Worth killing for. Even worth dying for. Does that make it all wrong?"

"You're living in the past, David," she said bitterly. "It's not that simple. You read books about the so-called *good* wars, times when objectives were clear. Now—especially now—we're guilty of the same crimes we go to war against."

She spoke with a conviction he'd never heard in her before. He did not agree with her, but was moved, even frightened, to find her so adamant, so committed! He knew these specters must have accompanied her a long time

"It's a damned John Wayne movie for you guys who all see yourselves riding off into the sunset on white horses. Well it's not that way, Dave. It's just not. You can't fix the rest of the world. And I don't care about them, any of them. My world is in one place. A very small world. It's wherever you are, and the boys. And where we have a home and are free from fear and—"

And phone calls in the night and unannounced deployments and separation tours, he thought.

"—too many things. You and me and the boys. That's the only world you need to worry about saving. Dave, *Dave!* You are tilting at windmills, trying to right wrongs that won't be corrected." She wrung her hands in the anguish of her vision, knowing her entreaties could have no effect.

"Ahh, Jesus, Nickie. You make it sound as if I choose to go play war as an alternative to staying home to play house. It's not that kind of choice, not that simple."

"It is to me."

"How can you even believe that. Have you never understood what I do? Why I do it?"

"It all comes down now to going or not going, Dave. You force the issue, let it happen, because you never wanted to hear my side.

And for too long, I never spoke up. But there's nothing that's beyond question. I'm just sorry I've been so long waking up to that."

"There is something beyond. There's my oath, my commitment to my career, a two-way street. There're my beliefs. My job and responsi —"

"Killing people? Women and children? Destroying homes and farms and churches? Burning —"

"Jeez-us Christ, have you lost your goddamned mind?" He stopped the car in the middle of the dark road. The wind against the flat side of the little square vehicle rocked it slightly. There was no sound above the low churgle of the engine. The snow lay in zero-degree ripples.

"Sure, now it's me. Wacko! Well, I watch the news. I read. I'm not as unaware as you think, sucking up the pulp they feed us in *Stars and Stripes*, the propoganda. I never thought you'd be a part of it."

"You make it sound like some vast conspiracy. What do —"

"It's not the same now, David, even as it was when you were there before. You know that. It's changing. They say we can't even win."

"They? *They say* . . . Does that mean we walk away? Forget our commitments?" It sounded hollow, even to him. Convinced he was right, he knew too that this was a time of change. There was a look of distress, a self-imposed tinge of guilt on the faces of too many coming back. The media full of vicious acts and ugly, negative things. It all spelled *Guilt!* Things he knew were a part of every war; but somehow, in this one, we'd lost the vision to persevere, the will to bear the guilt and horror and see it through for the larger good.

He tried to take her hand. She pulled away — a child, shunning contact. Her head was tucked down, her chin almost on her breasts. She shook her head at everything he said and murmured, "Unh-unh! Unh-unh! No-o-o . . ."

"This is not you, Nickie," he said as he put the car back into motion. They still had a long way to go.

"Who the hell is it?" she snapped, her head up, confrontation foremost. "I'll tell you who. It's somebody who's had enough. Had enough of waiting. Had enough of cold beds and eating across from empty chairs and holding idiot conversation with toddlers. Had enough of the Army, and army life. That's who it is." In growing resolution, her voice grew firmer, the querulous whine fading.

"C'mon, David, be honest," she demanded. "That first time, in North Carolina, before Jeremy was born. When you were still in the Corps. Three-thirty in the morning they called you out, and you were Johnny-on-the-Spot. You couldn't wait when you found out you were shipping out for Lebanon. You didn't call me until way late in the day, didn't tell me anything then. Wouldn't have come home, probably, except to pack your seabag. Then you were gone."

He hadn't the vaguest memory of what was going through his mind at the time she reminded him of; he was confident he had not been deliriously happy to leave. He wouldn't have wanted to be gone, less than a year after their marriage, awaiting their first. She was flailing.

"Two months you were gone. Oh, you wrote. All about life at sea, about how grand aircraft carriers were. How hot it was later in the Caribbean, and the markets in Saint Croix and Saint Thomas. All the good stuff. But you almost didn't get back in time for Jeremy's birth. The July and August I spent in that little North Carolina town, living in that old, tin-roofed house, shaped like a watermelon . . . and just about that mobile. No air conditioning. The only time I could get comfortable was in the car. I used to go out and drive around, just to use the A.C. And there was nowhere to drive to.

"I thought I was going to have to deliver with that strange doctor, and no family and few friends. Even the other Marines . . . we were so new there when you left we hadn't many friends. Then you came home. And everything was okay. I was so glad to have you back I forgot all the worries, the fears. I didn't know it was to become a way of life, because you got out of the Corps."

Her deceptively calm tone carried more of a threat than when overwrought.

"Then, coming back in the service. And I was all right with that. But part of the reason you changed services to the Army was to be able to have your dependents live with you abroad. But first tour, off you go to Ethiopia for two whole years. Without us. Two years, me and the boy there in Jackson with the goddamn Ku Klux Klan protesting school integration and me trying to get Jeremy into first grade. Two years while you were off, being a good soldier. Never enough money to dress decently, even adequately; never going out to a movie with Jeremy — we couldn't afford it — never eating out or visiting relatives. Both mothers hovering. Always just the child and me. You don't know what two years of that is like."

Where had this ire lain for so many years? She had never voiced such disgruntlement before. He felt it somehow ate into her assumed moral superiority. This put-upon, self-pitying role threatened to outgrow her due.

"Don't you think I know it was a long time? Don't you think it was long for me too?" he argued. "It wasn't war, but it was no picnic. Back, living in a barracks, separated from you and Jeremy, going sometimes a week or more without hearing from you, wondering if you both were all right. I remember whenever either of you got a cold or the flu or anything, by the time I learned of it in a letter, you were over it, and by the time you received my letter with questions about your health, half the time you'd forgotten you'd been ill. In that sense it *was* like the war."

"Oh, yes. The war! That came next. You could have gotten out of that, too. You could have stayed on in school in Milwaukee. The Dean gave you a chance. All it would have taken was his word. The Army was content for you to stay there another six months." She had a return volley now for every serve, playing the net close, aggressively.

"Nickie, we've been all through this . . . in Monterey."

"Exactly! It doesn't seem to have taken."

"That's nonsense. You know if I hadn't gone to Viet Nam when I did, I would have gone later. If I'd slipped that early tour, who knows what I might have gotten caught in later when the war got worse. And it got worse quickly." He had strong arguments; he just couldn't be sure he was capable of winning with them. *Mea culpa!*

"At least you wouldn't be going again this soon. You wouldn't have been hurt so badly . . ."

"You don't know that. I might be dead now." Stupid! Wrong argument. "What's with this second-guessing? Who knows what might have happened, where I might have been? Besides, I had orders. That's my job, Nickie. That's part of being career. I lost the option to pick and choose when I took the oath." *Mea culpa!*

"What about your marriage oath? Doesn't that mean anything to you? What's the protocol for choosing one oath over another?"

David Winter saw lights playing up the side of the mountain as the headlights of a car, somewhere behind and below them, swept into range. He shifted down again as the VW ground slowly up the slope. He fought to keep an eye on the road while watching his wife's face.

"That's crazy. One has nothing to do with the other."

"Oh? Really? I have nothing to do with the Army. And the Army, nothing to do with me. What is it I've *thought* I had to do with for the past eleven years?"

Suddenly, her voice changed. A soft, pleading voice continued the argument, the dynamics different but the relevance even more damning than when conveyed with the cold, shiny luster of righteousness and contempt. "My God! What is it that draws you back there? All of you? Again and again! There's no hope of it ever ending, don't you see. Why can't you see that? Why do you keep doing it?"

She was turned in the seat, the first time she'd fully faced him since he told her. She tried to light a cigarette, but she'd not pushed the lighter in; it was cold; the cigarette broke as she pressed it against the element, spilling tobacco across her shirt, into her lap.

"I can't make those decisions, Nickie."

"You *can*. You can make them by not —"

"No! I cannot. That is not an option. It's certainly not an answer. I go because I've been ordered to go by legal authority." He felt the despair of his pompous response. "Win, lose or . . . I've got to go." *Mea culpa!*

"If you don't make that decision . . . if a lot of you don't make that decision, who will? Is there no one able to stand up and say 'Enough!'? No one to stop the madness? You were lucky last time, Dave. Even with the pain I know you still have, the times I see you dragging that leg in cold weather, trying to make it into the shower.

Lucky to be alive. I've heard the story, even if you wouldn't tell me. You almost died on that L.Z. A lot of your buddies did die, if not on that L.Z., somewhere in-country. You still live with the pain of the wound and I know with the pain of their deaths. And I hurt every time you do." There was no disputing the pain in her voice.

"Isn't that enough? Haven't you done your share?" Her voice began to rise again. "What do they want? From you, from *us?* God, I hate them. I hate them all!"

He had no response, nothing she would accept. He feared he was part of that all-consuming *them* and he dare not find out.

"I wasn't joking when I said 'No more!'" she stressed. "This shouldn't be a surprise to you—I told you that in Monterey."

"I never assumed you were joking. I just didn't think it would ever happen. Surely you understand I didn't have anything to do with this. My orders read "Involuntary Assignment." He felt cheapened, offering such a simple, lame excuse in answer to her many-sided plea.

He felt her continued withdrawal as a physical absence in the car. He heard her snuffles, her attempts to control them. He felt the tremors from her body, saw her head drop, and knew she was crying in silence.

"Honey, I don't want to go. I'm not anxious to return to that place," he said truthfully, his mind skipping the many losses, the pain, the fears and anger and frustrations. "I didn't volunteer before. I didn't this time. You can't just hate it; it's what I do. The Army's my life, *our* life. We chose it." He was talking to the mountains and they were silent. He thought he heard an echo, *You chose it!* but knew it arose from an inner darkness. He let her go; he had to. *Mea culpa!*

The VW wagon continued grinding slowly up the steep grade in low gear, and the high-pitch whine of transmission seemed to scream frustration and helplessness. The fear greater than the going. It was happening and was beyond his control. He felt her slipping away from him.

"Nickie—"

"No more, David. I can't talk about it anymore. Get me home. To my children."

He talked to a stony silence as the VW climbed, up the harrowing curves, and north. After a period of no response, he went silent in concession. He drove fixedly. Blindly.

* * *

At a point nearing Innsbrück, his gnawing guilt gave way to objection. Then anger. He felt sharp flashes of reaction to the pointed accusations, her glossing over of the good elements in their life. He sought perspective: he acknowledged her view of her trials and truly momentous efforts in raising their children and maintaining their family during his repeat absences in *his* chosen career. But his mind, desperate for words, for help, fed him both black and white, good and bad. He could not divorce his absences from his obligations, and her own one-time contentedness with this arrangement. Anger, blossoming, fed on his jejune taint of ineptitude.

But he would not, dare not, respond in this frame of mind. He sought distractions. He turned on the Blaupunkt, good for reception in sketchy atmospherics — like these mountains. He knew nothing about programming in this area and tuned blindly for several moments, the sound turned low. He glanced surreptitiously to his right; Nickie's head was turned toward the far window . She showed no reaction to what he did.

He felt the need for music. Something classical, melodic yet powerful. A brief thrust of fulsome, antiphonal chanting burst upon him; he dialed quickly past.

At the very limit of the band, a swell of emotional chords caught his attention; tuning back and forth he isolated Enescu's *Romanian Rhapsody*. The resonance of the music caught his imagination. Some ephemeral attraction seemed to link the soaring power of the music to the thrusting peaks of the mountains about him, at times only visible as shadows of the uprising earth, but a mounting, soaring presence all the same. His imagination was caught, held, propelled along with the increasingly urgent phrasing of the glorious strains, and in that moment in which David Winter soared alone, above the earth, his battered psyche rose above its quagmire of despair and anguish.

Clasping to his core the evocative melody of the rhapsody, Winter's entire being seemed to take flight, seeking the level he had for long, without conscious acknowledgment, lived with and presumed to be his, a part of him, another one of the many facets of his own *raison d'etre*. He *was not* consumed with the manifestations of war, the pyrotechnics no less than the resultant agonies and exculpations. He *was not* a war junkie, a militant groupie. He never had been, had never thought in those terms. It was not fair that this woman, the one who knew him best, his love, the passionate and willing mother of his children, should suddenly, in her arguably fair anger and fear, describe him thus. Worse, it was presumptive and dishonest to put the burden on him to prove *he was not* of this unattractive characterization.

Images, forceful though disparate, flitted through his mind: proud moments in his life in uniform; terrifying moments, in Vietnam *and* Korea, some with pain, others with mere terror; good times, too, comradeship, laughter — feasts and famines — booby traps, lost comrades, shrapnel and the smell of burning flesh rising on an effluvium of oily napalm smoke; objectives taken, positions lost, the cacophony of firefights and the creeping solace of sunrise on a littered hilltop the morning following suicidal assaults. Like a runaway tape drive he could not stop or fix on any single image, he could not isolate any positive or negative aspects of this exposition of his life.

But the respite this epiphany provided, this interruption to the persistent and despoiling state of mind into which he was first forced nine days before, allowed for hope. He dispelled the coruscating flash of visions and thought of the plus side of what he had done with his life.

He remembered his first combat, and how he responded — scared but in control, effective, taking command when the squad leader went down, and for the lives they said in the citation that he saved; for the smiles on the faces of Ban Me Thuot children at the receipt of food and candy, and for the grimaces with which they paid for those treats by submitting to inoculations by the medics. His work, here in Europe, on the border and at the field stations, helping "stem the tide," whatever the hell that meant, though he knew that his and many like contributions really did carry measurable results.

No, he had nothing to be ashamed of. He would *not* hang his head or be a whipping boy, no more for his love than for the worst of the nay-sayers.

The VW crested a line of hills and Winter saw, far in the distance, the lights of Kufstein. He went still, remembering the excitement and eager anticipation he had felt when leaving the school in Milwaukee in 1964, suddenly on orders for a place where war was a growing reality. He had known then that he was merely fulfilling an ancient pledge of men, and he had gone, not with fear, but with conviction that what he did was right. And now, as soon as he had thought it, he knew, despite all the counter-arguments he could muster, deep down inside and against conscious wishes not to leave his family, he still felt that same elusive thrill. *Mea maxima culpa!*

Why did the Latin come back to him? Absolution was not there. No, but the litany of healing just might be.

Age quod agis!

Across the bridge from Kufstein was Germany. Bavaria. Bad Aibling a short drive, and the children. They'd be home in less than an hour, together for a while. He'd find a way to make her understand. He had to. Tomorrow. One step at a time.

Do what you do!

For the last anxious miles, he found himself reluctantly trapped in that first despair, as it now defined the present furies.

chapter five

Warp Zone

Viet Nam: May 1964

A nuclear sun hangs high in the west. Familiar, as if it has always been there. The mechanic seeks to rationalize the three suns he sees through the Perspex of the cockpit, studying the multiplying effect of refractions through the Mohawk's front screen. As if he came from a distant solar system in which this might not be an anomaly, he would think of home. But he knows of no such place.

Heat, like visual images, seems multiplied by the triptych in glass at conflicting angles, though he senses it is only an impression heightened by the smothering claustrophobia of the cockpit. White, motionless heat. It no longer works its greatest damage on the skin or consciousness, but is etched somewhere beneath, eroding life.

Nothing moves in the heat. There is awesome presence in the heat's power to immobilize; something that is real, hostile to the touch of flesh on the instrument panel. Bare surfaces know the hidden power of the sun.

A sky like washed bunting arcs over the field. It is devoid of clouds, other features, offering only a bare expanse of emptiness. A buzz with a piggybacked hum is persistent on the air, reminding the mechanic of insects, but might have been something else, something distant. Away from the sun, in another quadrant of the vault, the sky burns with a blue-white intensity.

The mechanic, trapped in this anteroom to hell, flashes on a vague memory of some elementary art teacher's confident words: "Blue is a cool color, Frank. And green. The warm colors are—" He knows the warm colors; they include blue.

A smile would surface, but his lips are dry, the sting of chapping present. The shimmering diamond-luster world of runways and white sand, white and silver aircraft create an unmistakable but elusive incandescence, drying the creases around his mouth.

Beyond the dazzling white taxiways and ramps, a single tree without leaves droops lifeless branches toward the earth. A forlorn rebel, it is independent from the scorched land of concrete; a Picasso tree, unsuited for shade. In the compound beyond the fence hangs a flag the yellow of quarantine pennons bearing three scarlet stripes horizontal to the earth. It is limp and still.

Only late spring, yet. Afternoon Viet Nam.

Beyond the hangar, louvered-board huts structured like coops for tall chickens waver in the heat, mirages that disappear into the ground on the periphery of vision. The roadway of crushed white rock and dust circling the hooches might be smoking slag drawn off a surface of molten steel. Vegetation that somehow survives along the roadway and between the coops is a whited, brittle parody of grass.

In the silence, a *sque-e-a-a-al smack!* of a screen door against a loose jamb that rattles after. A grunt as a fragile pale figure, wrapped at the waist in an OD towel, moves into the glare of the street, shower clogs flip-flopping through the scrabble, raising comma−shaped spurts of dust. A second distant flat slap, then another−two more screen doors opened and shut−carries through the stillness with the sharp report of gunshots.

Beyond the tennis court stacked with supply pallets, across the packed and oiled dirt road that circles Davis Station, a chorus of shouts erupts suddenly from the ARVN Ranger training compound: sharp excited yelps of mock-combat paradrops. Vietnamese versions of *Geronimo!* as trainees leap into space on spidery ropes− the screech and rattle of cables on pulleys The excitement of training kills, the dry, rattling clatter of bayonets slammed into rib cages of dry sticks, as difficult for the rifleman as the real thing. Grunts of effort in three languages.

In the opposite direction, unseen behind high corrugated metal fencing, giant blades chop a slow *whhuup! . . . whhuup! . . . whhuup!* as a post-mission gunship idles on the pad. In the distance past the motor pool, barely visible through the runway haze and the distortion of tropic mugginess, a flight of dragonflies angles in from the green world of paddies ripe with new rice and muddy green rivers and fields of grass where water buffalo graze like dun-colored stones. The sawtooth growth, waved languidly by some ghostly volition in the absence of wind, stretches away toward mountains invisible from here, toward the big river, toward Cambodia, Thailand and Burma beyond. The dragonflies fall into line for the landing pattern, their buzzing sounds only irritating at this distance: the heat defeats even metal insects.

The shower door closes silently behind the solitary figure. A splash of water. A touch of imagined cool.

Down the row of huts another *scre-e-e-ak . . . slap!*

It is the way it should have been, somewhere in southern America in some Faulknerian idyll. But it is too much that way. Faulkner would have blanched at this fierce, indolent climate.

Summer in May. Viet Nam!

* * *

The quick, muffled explosion of a CS cannister, out among the parked gunships beyond the metal fence, caught Winter bare-assed between the hooch and the showers. Before he recognized the significance of the hollow *fpop!*, the prop wash of the idling chopper had stirred the fumes over the fence into the 3rd RRU's compound. Like acrid smoke, it burned eyes, throat, and nose tissue, choking, itching. Laden with threat — what might it mask? — and no breeze to dispel it.

Winter turned and, shouting *"Gas attack! Gas attack!"* raced back toward his hooch for a helmet and gas mask. A mutter of irate voices arose about the compound, some rising from the depths of midday sleep, sluggards caught in the near-awareness of drugged slumber in sweat-soaked bunks. Winter heard a cry from the far end of the company street, and he remembered all the off-duty troops sacked out, Swings- and Mids-baggers. Being naked made him feel more vulnerable, and he repeated the cry as he ran: *"Gas! Gas attack!"*

As if awaiting Winter's confirmation, Master Sergeant Tseko burst out of the Senior NCO hooch in skivvies and boots, shrugging a pair of fatigue pants over his skinny, white, hairless legs as he ran, his old man's blue veins standing out in his frantic charge. His face was red, his eyes bulging, wheezing before he got the first whiff of gas.

Soldiers crashed out through the screen doors along the walk of Mids Trick platoon, hugging ponchos and weapons and helmets, tearing open gas mask pouches, pounding across the crushed rock and dirt pathways. Clerks fled the Orderly Room. American mechanics dropped their tools and abandoned the motor pool in search of a weapon and a gas mask; local hires, Vietnamese, had no issue masks. A squad leader grabbed SP5 Wilmouth, demanding in an outraged scream to know why the soldier had returned to his hooch when he already had his gas mask, weapon, and equipment.

Wilmouth held up a book of chits for the NCO Club. "Hell," he said with an attempt at nonchalance, "never know how long this thing's gonna last—how long we gonna be holed up. Gotta be prepared, man. Gotta be able to get a *brew*." He wrenched away from the screaming sergeant and, limiting himself to a trot, ambled toward the bunker. SP5 Wilmouth disguised his terror well to the untrained eye—alcohol did that for you. Others did not bear the burden so well, and there was an element of panic in the alarming events, a panic mandatory during alerts.

The alarm sounded from the direction of the Orderly Room as the morning report clerk held a gas mask over his face with one hand and pounded a 155-millimeter shell casing with a length of pipe. The alarm signified air raid or gas attack. It had seen extensive use in jest, never in earnest: Charlie didn't fly, and obviously had not thought of using gas before. The sharp metallic frenzy added a certain urgency by its tone alone, the air charged with anxiety, with fear.

Soldiers looked to the skies, eliminating the threat of air attack immediately; and as they encountered the gas, those who had them crammed the black rubber masks over their faces. It was the odd soldier whose mask fit properly; there was never a reason to check and adjust them. They'd known mortar attacks, random and mostly ineffective. Artillery, rockets, even sappers were not uncommon. But gas!

Inside the loosely fitted masks the soldiers of the 3rd RRU coughed and choked, their eyes streaming, as the barely visible cloud insidiously worked its way across Davis Station. Some ripped off the ineffective masks to vomit.

Tseko lumbered up and down the walk between the Orderly Room and the fence, flapping his arms like an overloaded C-130 that couldn't effect lift-off, screaming in a whiskey-cracked voice, "Get out! Get out! Incoming! Gas! Outside . . . in the bunkers . . .

in the trenches . . . with . . . your gear . . . helmets . . . gas masks, wea . . . pons . . . out . . . side . . . *wheeze* gas . . . attack . . . *whheeezzz* . . . move. . . ."

Like a toy drummer winding down, the overaged, overweight NCO's arms flailed slower and slower, pacing his wobbling legs, until he stopped suddenly in the midst of his scramble, grabbed his left bicep and winced in pain, gasping, dragging in deep sucking breaths. Troops ran around the old soldier as he stumbled along the walk. He collapsed to the gravel and Barnes leaped over him in a dash for the sandbagged bunker. Above the chaos of doors slapping and boots pounding, the loud flutter of chopper blades added impetus to the strident clanking of the alert signal. Shouts of alarm, queries couched in fear and anger—some muffled by masks, some obscured in incoherence—echoed off the metal fencing.

A rash of hacking coughs rippled across the compound. The gas was a viscous, cloying cloud wafting slowly across Davis Station, and without wind, hung in the billet spaces, shrouding the sad bushes and lone tree.

Tseko had run out into the gas to spread the alarm, forgetting his own lessons. Now he was choking to death on the ground, unable to catch his breath, strangling in his own mucous and vomit, while his heart pounded and threatened to burst, the pain in his chest unbearable. He lifted his head from the scorching ground and inhaled deeply, dragging the stinging cloud down into his chest. The gas burned down his throat, blistering the tobacco-scarred sacs in his lungs. He lay on the ground, tears streaming sideways across his cheeks, coughing in wrenching spasms. He raised one hand in a begging gesture and let it fall back loosely.

Lieutenant Zwick lurched out of the Orderly Room like a frightened stork, carrying an undersized carbine, loping toward his Jeep in long, ungainly steps. He saw the old NCO lying on the ground, dropped his weapon, and grabbed Tseko under the arms. He yelled an order at a Security Guard, but it was muffled by his gasmask. He ripped the mask off and repeated the order, and between the two, they dragged the first casualty into the captain's office. It was one of the few walled rooms in the compound, and an air conditioner hummed in the wall. Zwick grabbed a gasmask off the weapons rack and clamped it over the old sergeant's face.

Tseko was still gasping, his cough growing weaker. His hands twitched feebly.

With the mask in place—Zwick did not know if it was the right thing to do, now that he had the NCO inside with AC— Tseko's thrashings subsided after a few moments. He grew calm, quit fighting the mask that Zwick held in place by force. The air conditioner was not a firm deterrent; it merely meant colder gas.

The lieutenant, now without a mask, held his face near the floor to avoid fumes, but he coughed continuously and was nauseous. He periodically raised his head, expecting at any moment to hear gunfire, explosions, to know the shock of sappers in the compound. He waited for the shout of "Dinks in the wire!" Tseko finally lapsed into unconsciousness and his breathing shallowed out. And still there was no further sign of attack. Zwick, watching the rise and fall of the NCO's chest, pulled the mask straps tightly into place and rose.

Outside, the defensive squads had established positions. They awaited orders. Soldiers in underwear, in flak jackets and trousers alone, some fully dressed, crouched behind the sandbags that walled the Orderly Room by the motor pool fence. Behind the movie theater they awaited orders.

Nothing!

Captain Rucker, the CO, was out of the company area. The Executive Officer had not been seen for days. No one cared. The latter was known to be shacked up downtown, drunk; the former, merely ineffective. No soldier who valued his life or sanity looked to Captain Rucker or Lieutenant Peche for leadership. First Sergeant Whiteneir assumed a tenuous command of the company defenses, but he was as confused as the ranks and remained huddled in a corner of the bunker. And the men waited.

Still nothing!

They did not know what they waited for. The gas was presumed to precede . . . what? A barrage? An assault by ground troops? Something . . . The enemy didn't practice urban control with the use of gas alone. The uncertainty of this new phase of the war was unnerving.

After the armorer had been found, and used his key to access the company's weapons kept locked in the armory, when the defenses were as good as they could be made, and after the squad leaders and trick chiefs had cleared all the hooches of sleeping troops, a deep silence fell across the compound. Voices and laughter could be heard from beyond the metal fence.

Within Davis Station, nothing!

No rockets fell. No bursts of automatic fire zapped in through the wire or the metal fence. Mortars were not an unwelcome surprise. The defenders looked again to the skies, but they were empty of all but an omnipresent buzzing from afar. There was nothing.

The gas slowly dissipated. The sun inched down the sky, holding the compound fixed in a harsh glare. Another cackle of laughter rose beyond the fence. No orders, no word came down.

"Hey! . . . I mean . . . what the fuck? Over." The lone voice carried its own message of despair. There were greater threats than the enemy.

A babble of voices then. A call for the First Sergeant.

No response.

The men of the 3rd RRU hunkered in the sand-bagged bunkers and ditches and crumbling trenches for half an hour, awaiting incoming. But gradually, as the gas dissipated, as nerves grew ever more taut and knuckles ached from the white grip on weapons, as breathing became more difficult in 98-degree heat in the musky, ill-fitting masks and still the perimeter was quiet, the alert began to come apart from lack of interest. Heads popped up like curious tortoises. The response to squad leaders' warnings was a finger to the sky in a universal gesture of contempt. They craned their necks, eyes peering cautiously in ever-increasing arcs across the grass of the airstrip where it could be seen at the end of the fence, across the ARVN Ranger compound now deserted, down the dirt road toward ARVN dependent housing, back at the fence shielding the airstrip.

The men crept out of the defenses; then the squad leaders, the armorer; finally, the First Sergeant.

As awareness of the silence seeped through their caution, the soldiers grew more curious. They emerged and saw their hooch mates and poker pals and co-workers from Ops with the same questioning faces. They grew restive.

No leaders! The First Sergeant had again disappeared. Marching out of the orderly room bunker, he'd stared around in relief and hurried off in the direction of his hooch, ignoring the questions and demands for guidance on every side. No information filtered down—there was no one at the top to provide that commodity; the platoon sergeants and trick chiefs and squad leaders looked about blankly—and the soldiers grew angry.

During the alert the bunker grapevine–the latrine telegraph–had identified the assault, variously and ignorantly, as everything from a single tear gas grenade lobbed at the First Sergeant's hooch by a vengeful soldier, drunk or sober, to a new kind of Soviet rocket carrying a lethal, slow-acting nerve gas masked by the commonality of CS tear gas and vomiting agents. Some soldiers, new to the makeshift war, were convinced they were already dead. The older, hardcore, Sai Gon bar commandos fed their fears with speculation and highly suspect stories. A few banded together to make demands, but couldn't settle on a common objective. Convinced on the one hand there was no time for remedies, on the other that they were the victims of a hoax, their fear and anger as they stormed through the company streets might have been laughable if it had not been so compulsive. If the prospect had not held very real possibility.

Medics from the 68th Armed Helicopter Company dispensary, in response to a clerk's phone call, came in gas masks, the driver hunching over the wheel of the field ambulance like an alien green being with a grotesque black insect head, though by the time they arrived the gas was pretty much gone. They grabbed Tseko off the CO's bench without a word, deposited him onto a stained litter, and raced out into the street. Tseko, comatose and better for it, was launched into the back of the three-quarter-ton truck-ambulance, the doors slammed behind him. The brindle-colored vehicle roared away in a cloud of dust, blue smoke, and lingering tear gas fumes.

Winter stood in the middle of the street, watching the disappearing vehicle. He felt useless. The compound seethed with frustration and anger. The peak of adrenalin that prepared them for the enemy attack now drained away, and an echo of post-coital depression set in. Winter felt it with others, and to emphasize the uniformity of sentiment, he had to laugh when a mechanic from the flight line went by, wiping his streaming eyes, cursing in a curiously mixed litany of born-again youth and frustration: "I know the Lord's just gettin' his own back for my sins. Thank you, Jesus . . . Fuck me!"

Still, there were no orders, no indication of the nature of the attack. Mid Trick's Assistant Trick Chief was on the phone, seeking information. Beyond the confines of Davis Station nothing seemed out of sorts.

Winter heard the rattle of tin and turned. CW3 Self, one of the 3rd's pilots, came through the door in the fence from the helicopter ramp. In the midst of the alert, it was from that direction laughter was heard, other sounds inconsistent with attack. Soldiers milling in the street saw Mister Self and, since he seemed the only soldier in sight doing anything with a purpose, they crowded toward him. Widespread belief that Self would have answers served an urban myth purpose. Soldiers shouted, cursed, made accusations, as if the warrant officer were responsible. Somebody — some part of the establishment — had to take the rap.

"*Break it up!* False alarm," Self shouted. He spoke to those nearest him, answering to the anger and fear in their faces, their gestures. "It was just some gunship hooligans loading gas to fly a crowd-suppression mission downtown. There's another coup a-building. Somebody dropped a case of CS and a couple of the canisters broke. Blade wash carried it over. That's all."

"That's all?"

"Crowd suppression?"

"The Sixty-eighth? Those assholes did this?"

"How d'ya think they'd like it if my fuckin' Swedish-K misfired through their magic wall."

"Bastards! Smart ass, flight-paid, don't-give-a-shit bastards!"

They crept out from bunkers and gun pits finally, those most cautious who had waited. The word spread like the gospel.

Embarrassed at their own fear and panic, the angry soldiers sought an outlet. There was a scuffle near the fence as an NCO argued with a vigilante squad who were armed and on their way toward the fence and the careless helicopter crews beyond.

"Chief," Specialist Five Winter said, addressing the warrant officer pilot, "what's up, here in the war zone?" He knew Self, knew his droll humor, and he wondered now at the sad, angry look on the pilot's face. Self stared at him fixedly. Winter was suddenly aware of feeling exposed. He looked down, realizing how ridiculous he must appear. He took off his helmet and, trying not to be obvious or appear self-conscious, held the steel pot casually over his crotch and stood, naked except for a towel about his neck, a flak jacket, and shower clogs in the middle of the company street. The stream of GIs flowed about him without notice.

Winter thought the pilot had not heard him. "Chief?" He reached to drape the towel about his waist.

Self's voice came out of some tired, hidden reservoir of bitterness, a well of old anger and hatred that should have been used up by time and experience, but was not.

"*Warp zone*, Specialist. Warped . . . Mort Brill. C.W. Three Morton T. Brill—old buddy of mine I flew with at Wolters—he's dead. Caught a faceful of that shit close up. He was trying to push the busted crate of gas into a *benjo* ditch. Too old. . . ." Self had tears in his eyes and he stared blindly at the black rubber mask in his hands. "Old bastard should have gone home months ago. Should-a never been here." He brushed at his eyes. "Three fucking wars, and he's killed by some nonsense that don't even . . . A seizure of some kind," he mumbled lamely. He slammed the mask into the green canvas case and walked away. He looked an old man too, Winter thought.

There was a feeling of loneliness in the street. The compound was deserted. He heard the slam of the metal door at the rear of the club. He knew that's where they would be, washing it away, talking it up. The fears real; the valor imagined—reviewing it all. He thought about Tseko, another old man, and what he'd been trying to do. And what it might cost him. Like Brill.

He didn't know if the gunship crew ever got the gas loaded, whether they flew their mission. Helicopters were pulsing in and out for an hour after the alert, but it was the time of day for sampan strafing and the activity could have been regular ops. You couldn't tell one lift-off from another; it didn't matter. Coups came and went, and it was impossible to keep track of the local players. But one good man was dead, another maybe on his way. It didn't seem an acceptable balance, somehow.

Winter walked back to his hut. He rubbed his eyes and sneezed; his nostrils still burned, and he felt slightly nauseous. He dumped his helmet and gear by his bunk, cinched up the towel, and headed again for the showers. He crossed the open, empty street, chasing with flying hands an elusive itch that seemed to scurry from one hard-to-reach spot on his body to another. Tear gas effects were acquired far more easily than they were dispelled.

The young housegirl who worked his hooch was sitting on the steps of number 17. Winter saw she was suffering from the gas and didn't know how to deal with it. "Hey, Mama-San," he shouted, addressing her with the ubiquitous term for all local national females, regardless of age, "gas got you?" She didn't answer but continued rubbing her eyes, swinging her head from side to side, coughing, moaning and talking rapidly in her sing-song language. He walked over to her. "Hai, you okay?"

She sniffed and continued rubbing. She was called Hai—number two in Vietnamese—because she was the second house girl hired by the 3rd to make bunks, sweep floors, shine boots, and perform menial household tasks in the billets. She shook her head finally in answer to his question, but she obviously could not see him through burning eyes.

"Numbah huckin' wan. Hai o-kay!" She had been with the 3rd RRU for months now, long enough to learn a selective smattering of GI vernacular. Unfortunately, it was mostly the obscene and scatological phrases she had retained, but they did allow her a level of communication with the soldiers. She might have been twelve years old, or thirty. She was a slim, quiet cipher, a depersonalized serf in a world of barons. But she was a good worker, and she sat now on the steps of the hut, surrounded by boots and polish cans, waiting for the pain of the gas to clear so she could continue her work. Civilians had no masks.

Standing over her, Winter tried to stop her rubbing her eyes. She fought his hands but after a few futile gestures, gave in to his strength. He held her hands from her eyes. She whimpered and flung her head from side to side with the pain, the long black hair whipping like a dancer in frenzied ritual, but she did not fight Winter. In a few moments tear flow washed the offending agent away and the pain eased. She looked up at Winter through filmy eyes; tears traced twin paths down her cheeks. Her eyes widened.

"Choi oi!" she giggled, covering her mouth and looking away in the manner of Vietnamese maidens. Winter looked down and realized he had dropped the towel while struggling to hold her hands—his naked organ hung inches from her face—and he jerked the towel off the ground and whipped it about his middle. He backed away, trying to cover more than just his crotch—all of himself—as he went,. The girl wiped her eyes again and kept her head to the side.

"Hell, Hai," Winter blustered. "You see naked GIs everyday. Why the shy act all of a sudden?" His embarrassment annoyed him more than his nakedness.

She giggled again and would not look at him. She just sat and stared down the company street, blinking and wiping her large, dark eyes.

The lines of hooches baked in the late afternoon, soaking up heat to hold long past sundown, ensuring an unbearable night. Even the prop wash that had spread the gas through the compound and was steady now as the Hueys lifted their skids and fluttered down the yellow-striped corridors, served only to stir the muggy air about. It did little to relieve an atmosphere that was like entrapment beneath a sodden blanket inside a steam bath. Winter could imagine a hundred pairs of eyes focused on his nakedness from behind the louvered walls, watching his discomfiture.

"Ser-gent Win-tah . . . you numbah wan. For soor . . . numbah wan." She spoke softly and Winter could barely understand her, but he felt his face flush. He snorted and flip-flopped away toward the latrine. She giggled again behind him, a soft tinkle across the dusty space. Winter refused to look back. He slammed the screen door of the latrine.

It took a long shower to rid himself of the itch.

chapter six

Nothing to Recommend It

Viet Nam: June 1964

Winter snapped awake. Fully alert without fumbling through intermediate stages of confusion and disorientation, he lay trembling, halfway out of the bunk, waiting for the second round to fall . . . the second burst of automatic fire. The next scream — whatever!

Quickly focused, he relaxed from alert mode. Something had brought him out of a sound sleep, a luxury not enjoyed since the false attack several days before, but there was only silence all around him. He lay for a moment, gripping the rail of the bunk with sweating hands, shaking from the sensation of being yanked back into the world of the living, seeking to recapture from his dream what it was that woke him. Was it a dream?

Winter could distinguish shapes in the meager light in the hooch. The ceiling fan had stopped turning, though he heard a strained buzz. It wasn't a power failure; he heard the hum of generators and saw at the back of the hut the lights shining through from the motor pool. The fan was probably again caught up in the shroud lines of the cargo parachute suspended from the ceiling.

There was only stillness. It must have been a dream, a nightmare that came too close. He closed his eyes.

Then it began again. A blasphemous litany, louder this time, closer: *"Winn-terrr . . . you fuckin' lifer puke. Show yourself! Get out-side, you miserable goddamned half-assed ex-gyrene strac-shiny-boot-white-side-walled mo-ther-fuck-er!"* The long drawn-out blasphemy echoed off the bare plank louvers and filtered through the mosquito screen. The war shuddered to a halt.

Great God! That had to be . . . oh, no! *Jeez-us!* Pray it ain't so.

"Ratty Mac?" Winter screamed and leapt from the rack. "Mac, that you, you foul bastard? Mac?"

"Where are you, Winter? Quit hidin' that overrated career ass of yours. I can hear your whimperin' shit now . . . show your bod."

Winter stood in the door of the hooch and searched the dark street. Black within the perimeter, pole lights were directed only out into never-land. In the company area, only the orderly room, latrine, mess hall, and motor pool were lighted. And in the boundary of light from the latrine door stood a familiar, shabby figure— Algernon A. MacGantree. Terror of the Horn. The Nemesis of East Africa. *Ratty Mac!* He stood in the street, swaying, one hand thrust skyward, social finger probing the heavens.

"Fan-fuckin'-tastic!"

Winter could smell the whiskey fumes across the distance, radiating outward from the derelict being. Ahh, the erudition of the man.

"Fan-fuckin'-tastic!" Mac repeated and Winter, homing on the sound, crashed through the door toward him.

They stood in the street, one shadowy figure in olive drab skivvie shorts and dog tags, the other in beer- and sweat-stained khakis, their bodies entangled in a crushing hug.

"Jeez-us, Mac—"

"You no-'count shit!"

"—where the hell'd you come from? What—"

"Can't seem to get away—"

"—the hell're you doing here?"

"—from goddamned lifer pussies, no matter—"

"You assigned here?"

"—how hard I try. Assigned here? Yeah! *Yeeaahhh.* Assigned to the good ol' Third Rusty Rifles," Mac said, employing one of the randomly applied euphemisms for 3rd Radio Research.

Both tried to talk, to listen, shake hands, and erase the years, all in an instant.

"Jeez-us," said Winter. "Man, you are a sight. You are really just about all this war effort needs," he roared. His voice was thick.

"And you, you bloody asshole. You too. You mean that?" MacGantree asked, lagging the conversation by a measurable span, and only slightly garbled.

"Like shit, I mean it," Winter laughed. "You bastard!" He stared into the beady eyes that glowed red even in the semi-dark. "We don't have enough problems with friendlies who aren't, the steady coup parade, the Vee-Cee, typhoons, short supplies, rusting equipment, crotch rot, runaway V.D., and other good things . . . now we got the Terror of the Horn. Jeez-us! And it's not 'ex-gyrene,' you ignorant man; once a Marine, always a Marine."

"Well, fuck you very much, G.I."

Winter stood back and examined the tattered remains of what had never been very much of a soldier, at best. "What the hell you doing here, Mac? You *hate* the Army. When I left Asmara two years ago, you still had a year to do. Every breath out of your mouth you preached you were gonna finish your hitch, hunting the Zula every break, then get out of the Army, go home and screw every white woman you missed in your misspent youth. What happened to all that short-timer shit? Where'd the hate-Army campaign go?"

"Aahhh, man . . . you know," Mac muttered. He stumbled backward, almost sat in the street; Winter grabbed him by the sleeve and pushed him toward steps.

They lurched over to Winter's hooch and sat. They were still slapping each other's backs and sides and shoulders, laughing, both trying to talk. A growl from inside the hut next door offered them a choice of silence or crushed gonads. Mac leapt shakily to his feet, but Winter held him. "No, no, bad move. That's The Linebacker. C'mon." He coaxed Mac across the street and into the enlisted mess where a galley coffee pot perked around the clock for trick workers and other aspiring warriors. He pushed Mac into a chair and filled two cups.

"The Linebacker?" Mac said thickly. "Who's that?"

"Guy name of Perkins. Never played a day of football in his life, but he's a big mean sonuvabitch, and if he likes to live in fond memories that never were, who am I? . . ." Winter smiled wryly, dismissing the growler.

He looked Mac over in the weak messhall light. No evolution: beady eyes, red with booze, squinting; unshaven, that same long, scraggly mustache too blond for effect; skin that would never tan, sunburned even in the mildest climate, already burnt dangerously red from the fair sun of tropical Asia. There was nothing to indicate he had changed at all.

Mac made an effort to focus his eyes, and picked up on Winter's last question. "And what about you, you bloody Lifer? You left Asmara for college. Suckered Uncle Sugar into a freebie." The black coffee had no effect on Mac's condition, but he drank it as if it were good, as if it contained magic powers to bring him back to earth. "You ain't due outta that school yet." It was a statement; any question was implicit.

"Yeah, well, turned out engineering isn't my thing. Y'know?" Winter grinned as if that explained everything, and sat down at the shiny table. The cockroaches fled to other seating.

"Your ass! Goddamn, Dave. You're the only Lifer I ever met I really wanted to see get somewhere in this miserable fuckin' Army. You had a chance for a commission out of that school. Here you are, still an enlisted puke like me." Mac had gone suddenly serious, sober or not, and Winter was touched by something he didn't try to analyze.

"Birds of a feather, Mac. Birds of a feather." He tried to reach Mac with a grin that said it was all for the best.

Mac seized the moment for madness. Seriosity, he used to tell Winter, was not his bag. He shouted, "Sheee-it! Who gives a fuck! Two E-Five honkers, together. We'll shape up this mama-humpin' war, killer. We'll polish our boots and dazzle the shit out of 'em. Drive the bad guys back into the paddies with footlocker inspections. Blow the little yeller swine away with Sergeant Sulzer's rollcall. Hey-y-y, shit, man. Give 'em hell!" He threw his arm around Winter's shoulders, splashing coffee from the cup in front of him. Mac's eyes had a shifty, wild look and he would not meet his friends's searching gaze.

Winter, averting his eyes, watched the movement of the coffee, the black pool inching toward the edge of the table. He watched Mac from the corner of one eye and knew he wasn't as drunk as he pretended. It gave Winter a warm feeling. The Terror of the Horn never could come right out and admit to feelings about anything. It might be sentimental bullshit, Winter thought, but this unkempt, misbegotten misfit and I have logged a lot of klicks together. And now, it looked like kilometers to go. He smiled.

"Hell, I just got in today . . . yesterday," Mac explained, as if the subject had changed. "A couple guys from the plane 'n me went down the road to that Howard Johnson's—" the facetious reference directed at Vietnamese vendor carts set up on street corners, military bases not excluded, that sold noodles and vegetables, soup called *phô*, and *Ba-nui-ba* beer " —and got blowed away. Don't remember how your name came up . . . bullshittin' about hunting I think and I was re-galing them with tales of Africa. I was sayin' — now I remember! Tellin' 'bout that time you tracked and killed the vicious, wild klipspringer beast, and it turned out to be the Agordat game warden's fuckin' Chihuahua. Remember?" Mac bent over the mess table, hysterical with the memory. Winter could chuckle too; he was finally over the embarrassment of the tale.

"Anyhow, this guy from the Third was there, havin' a brew, 'n' he heard your name and said there couldn't be more'n one of you in the entire Yew-nited States A.S.A. Told me you were here and where you bunked down. And so," he said expansively, throwing wide his hands to accept the plaudits of a repressed people whom he'd pledged to save, "here I am."

"Jeez-us!" said Winter. "Here you are!"

"So where's the fonkin' war, killer?"

* * *

The galley pot was almost empty. Mac's eyes were several degrees redder, but clear of fog. He and Winter had been at the table for nearly two hours, except for the times when Mac stumbled to the latrine to payback the Vietnamese beer. He'd cleaned the table of the spilled coffee a half dozen times, but still he rubbed at the spot.

Mac wiped his eyes and suddenly, in a fury, flung the Bakelite cup across the mess hall to ricochet off a large, squat kitchen range. Coffee dregs rained down, brown and cold, dirty on the table surfaces, puddled on the floor.

A tall white hat with a small brown face attached peered around the corner of the kitchen. There was no expression on the face, and it withdrew without comment or change to the lack of expression.

"That old joke," Mac continued with a wry smile that held no humor, "the one about gettin' a 'Dear John' from your mom, ain't really much of a joke." He shivered slightly, as if a chill had passed over his bony frame. It was an unmentioned, open acknowledgment that Mac's disillusionment with civilian life need not extend further. His mother had spoiled him for civilized women, he said, and he felt no need to explain anything else. Winter did not object.

"There just wasn't nothin' for me at home, Dave. Nothin'! My school buddies gone for a long time. Or married," he added in a tone that intimated they were interred in some callous ground. "I had to get away. Had to. The Army was all I had left," he said, rationalizing his traitorous reenlistment. Excusing his degradation, though he knew Winter was not one ever to accuse him of that. "All I'd *ever* had, if I'd known it. And ain't that a great big, sad bitch!"

They sat a few minutes more in the pre-dawn hush. A vehicle drove by, down the helicopter ramp unseen beyond the fence, tires whispering on the humidity-damp concrete. A slurred voice, strong with indignation, echoed across the flat spaces of the airfield. *"I hate this fucking place!"*

Mac looked up, smiling. "He here, too?" No answer required; none provided. The day cooks began rattling pans on the stove behind the kitchen wall.

Good morning, Viet Nam!

The conversation took a sharp turn and began again. Mac asked about mutual friends. Winter named a few, some in Sai Gon — some a few yards away in one hooch or another — others in Phu Bai up north with Det J, a few more scattered in Nha Trang, Can Tho, Bien Hoa, Da Nang, one on Can Son Island off the coast near Soc Trang where the Vietnamese government interned their political prisoners. Many he had no knowledge of, and knew they couldn't all be in Viet Nam.

"Stefkovitch is here," Winter said. "But he's short." Both soldiers collapsed suddenly with laughter. Stefkovitch, at five-five, *was* short and the men who'd worked with him had used that to good effect; he was, after all, a lifer, a career non-commissioned officer. "Yeah, laugh," Winter said, "but the truth is, I'm hoping to get his slot when he leaves. I'm next on the list for Staff Sergeant."

"Christ! 'bout time. What's this make for you, total time, Marines and Army?" Ratty Mac had effectively lost the harrowed appearance and physical results of his recent carousing.

"Little over eleven years. Long time to make Staff, though. Don't think I'll do it this way, next time around."

They laughed easily together. One day they were going to do this entire career thing over: it was a standard plea for understanding—

among themselves as well as outsiders, civilians—and from those who thought they understood them.

"Well, the war should speed things up," Mac said.

"Oh, yes. And that's just *wonderful* for us military types," Winter said in mock thanksgiving. "Wonderful to get a chance to serve . . . *et cetera, et cetera, et cetera*." He snorted.

"Mac, you won't believe. It's so goddamned boring here most of the time that guys from the Third are volunteering to fly door gunner on the new Hueys . . . which they never did on the Flying Bananas." Winter's incredulity was obvious, and Ratty Mac was surprised at the vehemence of his friend's comment.

Winter had written to Nickie, in one of his rare references to day-to-day conduct of the war, about the incongruous servitude of volunteers in the UH-1B armed helicopters. Volunteers out of boredom, impatience, dissatisfaction with a half-assed war that was not living up to their expectations. Some wanted to fly, all wanted the hostile fire pay which they could not draw while on their present duty; some even wanted to kill—a thing basically denied them by the passive nature of their intelligence work— but most of all, everyone wanted *to have been there* when it was over. They wanted certification of participation, verification of their contributions. They wanted their ticket punched.

Still, there were many who volunteered for the Hueys, even for Viet Nam, out of a sense of willingness to be a part of what they believed the war meant. What the American soldier still stood for.

Most could not have said what that was.

Winter was a professional, he would argue. A job was a job within his chosen field; a mission was a mission. The war was just another in a sequence of assignments. If he'd been ordered into choppers, he would have gone with a sense of mission and a dedication to give the best he could. But the volunteering was illogical to him. Wasteful. Stupid that it was even allowed.

"No kidding, Mac. The volunteers pick up an extra sixty-five bucks a month hostile fire pay—which is more than we get, of course, unless we happen to be out in the field for six days or more in a month, and you get it for any month in which you get wounded or are recovering from wounds—and they get an Air Medal or two, provided some clerk in the chopper outfit remembers to put in the paperwork for them. But they don't even draw flight pay, since they're just volunteers and don't have an M.O.S. rated for flight pay. They're risking their ass for a few bucks and kicks. Or worse."

"Well, sufferin' snakeshit, Winter. Didn't you just tell me a while ago you'd like to transfer into the Air Section? What's the difference?" Mac got up for more coffee and found the pot empty. He held up the pot and shrugged.

Winter shouted for the galley swamper. In the background the KPs were arriving, Vietnamese day workers who chattered in a harsh rattle above the clatter of pots and pans, firing the stoves for the morning meal. It was still dark out, but off toward the horizon, east of Ben Cat, a tinge of mauve and pink — titty pink, Mac observed without disturbing the flow of his challenge — ate away at the rim of sooty sky. Sporadic flashes came from there, preceding deep, weatherless rumblings, as early morning cannoneers held reveille in their unique manner.

"It *is* different, Mac. I'd just be doing my job, only in the plane. I'd like the air job, is all I'm saying. If it was offered to me or if I'm assigned to it. Comes with another stripe. If that means getting shot at, so be it; it's part of that job. But *they* have to do it. Like me being here in the first place, I didn't volunteer. Army has a million personnel people with a billion dollars worth of computers and dart boards to make those decisions." Mac just looked at him, as if the difference was unremarked.

"Out of school in Milwaukee, when I dropped the engineering gig, this is where they sent me," Winter continued. "I was offered no choice. Okay! So, I'll do my job — that's the name of the game when you wear the green — and I'll do it well. But I'm not looking for medals. I could use the extra money, but my wife would hate to use the S.G.L.I., she says, and I believe her — that she'd rather have me , have a father for my child rather than the insurance. I've seen better country than this, and flying ain't the biggest kick in the world for me. I spent some time on flight status in the Corps; the job was okay, but bor-r-ing! It'd be okay for a change, I guess, and it would mean the slot for staff sergeant in the Air Section. But in our own birds, not a goddamned mixmaster."

Winter shook his head to clear away any doubts about his attitude that might linger in his subconscious. "I'm not sure how I

feel about this war, yet. I believe we're doing the right thing, and
I'll sort it out in time. But there're a lot of things wrong with what
we're doing, or *not* doing here. In a lot of ways they're all pretty
much alike — wars — and I guess I've seen worse. I wasn't looking
for a crusade, but I do think it's right we're here. Whatever," he
mused, "I lost any right to dispute an assignment when I signed on
the dotted line, you know, the —"

"The wearin' of the green! Yeah, shit!" The distinction Winter
tried to make was lost on Ratty Mac, but he did not argue the
point.

Sensing Mac's skepticism, Winter added, "Look, for these guys
to volunteer for door gunner — where's the sense in that? Any G.I.
can squat behind a machinegun and burn Zips. I can train an ape
to do that. But every one of these guys I'm talking about — oh five
eights, nine eight twos, linguists, three-ninety wire benders — all of
them school trained in tech skills. The Army's had some of them
in school for a year. Longer. We've been lucky here so far, but I
wonder what happens when we have our first casualty from that
shit, when we lose one of these highly skilled machine gunners.
How's the C.O. going to explain to Arlington Hall what a Traffic
Analyst was doing riding shotgun on a frigging heli-chopper?
Shit's gonna hit the fan, Mac. For soor, G.I., as the bargirls say . . .
for soor!"

"Yeah, but 'til it does, those dudes are havin' the best time of any
of us. And drawin' extra pay for doin' it." He leered at Winter.

"Somehow, Mac, in the midst of all this half-ass soldiering — and
this isn't a real war yet, though it's going to be, mark my words —
with all this military grandeur —" he gestured about at the shabby
surroundings " —I cannot convince myself we're here to have a
good time."

"Aahhh, screw you, Winter Man," Mac said easily. "You
wouldn't if you could. You think Santa Claus drops in in a T-5
chute. Your trouble is you really do believe in this shit. You think
this place is another Korea, for whatever argument that is. You
think we can help these slopes, think they *need* our help." He stood
up and snorted. "Fuck it, anyhow. Forget that shit! Where'm I
gonna bunk down?"

"Come on, you ratty bastard. More ricky-tick! There's a free bunk in my hooch. You got about twenty minutes before Day Trick reveille."

MacGantree grinned and threw his arm about Winter's shoulders. "That's about twenty minutes more sleep'n I usually get, Tiger."

* * *

The Yin and Yang of ASA service — in the guise of two Spec-5s with a common history in distant lands — ate breakfast with the Day Trick, and Winter caught the duty truck to WHITE BIRCH Operations. MacGantree reported in at the orderly room at zero eight-ten hours and promptly ran afoul of First Sergeant Whiteneir, known locally, nevertheless without affection, as "Whitesnake."

Whiteneir was a dyspeptic malcontent, a master sergeant who had remained in the service past his time, though impossible to say when his time was. He had entered the Army in nineteen thirty-seven, rose to master sergeant during World War II, and reverted to staff sergeant during the great Reduction-in-Force following the war. He rose to master sergeant again in Korea, and reverted to sergeant first class in another RIF after the hostilities ended there, the legions no longer needed to guard the realm. He got out of service; he came back in.

By the time he arrived in Viet Nam in 1964, Whiteneir had risen finally to permanent grade E-8, master sergeant, acting First Sergeant. No one could convince him it was simply the war/non-war cycle that had thwarted his career — a fortunate gap in credibility, since the man himself *was* primarily responsible for his roller coaster progression-regression. He was adamant, convinced that he had finally, by sheer perseverance and the connivance of an ultimately just God, gotten the best of the Army and the system. He never knew that his last promotion, for which he had waited so long, was an error; that he was carried on another roster in the Pentagon as having died in Panama of blackwater fever in 1959. Whiteneir was never in Panama — in 1959 he was assigned to Fort Benjamin Harrison in Indiana — and had never had the fever, but he was a dead man on someone's list.

The clerk who eventually discovered the error could not comprehend there might be discrepancies in his two lists and threw both away. Whiteneir, along with other unfortunates relegated to non-existence, had ceased to exist for the Army on the one level, while they were assigned, paid, rated, and promoted—sometimes, demoted—through equally erroneous administrative actions of a self-generating nature within their career branches. Such was the insidious propagation of ever-spiraling confusion within the bureaucracy that it was not in the Army's, or any individual's, best interests to find and correct the errors.

The reigning spirits of short hair and starched fatigues decreed it inevitable that Whitesnake should take exception to Ratty Mac. The Terror of the Horn's Viet Nam service suffered a rude initiation when, bristling, he took exception to the First Sergeant's assessment of his unsoldierly appearance.

"Specialist MacGantree," Whitesnake snapped finally, terminating the heated discussion, "until I release you to report to Operations, you will honcho details for me here in the billet area."

"But First Sergeant, I thought the Third was short of oh-five—"

"Quiet! I care not one whit what it is you thought, soldier. Since when do specialists perform thinking duties? Do not answer! I regurgitate; you will take the three enlisted persons who await your grievance in the outer reaches of the orderly room, lead them forth to perform munificent enticements upon the uncomplete structure which stands adherent to the arms room, close-by. Refer to the Field First for complicit instructions."

"Enticements?"

"Dismissed!"

"Adher—"

"Dis-*missed!*"

Whiteneir talked that way. No one knew why, for sure. He was, as Winter later told MacGantree when Mac was giving him a play-by-play dump on his welcome to Viet Nam, an abysmally ignorant man whose oral erudition, liberally laced with malapropisms, was exceeded in atrocious misapplication only by his parallel piss-poor efforts in the written arena. Ratty Mac understood Winter's spiel little more than he had understood the First Sergeant. But had he known of the confusion in Whiteneir's service, he would have said that the Pentagon clerk who'd destroyed the records was right: either Whitesnake was dead, or by all rights should be.

It was Lieutenant Zwick's caustic opinion that Whitesnake had been frightened as a child by one of the Bard's more pretentious productions, sponsored and performed by the South Corvallis Women's Goat Roping Club and Parachute Riggers' Union number 11. Lieutenant Zwick could speak with authority; he effected a somewhat similar manner of speech. Legitimately, he felt, since he had the heritage of old money and family decadence of long standing behind him. Lieutenant Zwick was born the day Corporal James J. Whiteneir landed on New Guinea in War number two.

* * *

Sergeant First Class LaMaster, a section chief from A Branch, was acting Field First Sergeant, a meaningless title tantamount to interface between the First Sergeant and subordinates engaged in doing his bidding. Ratty Mac held his comment about "zebra-striped flunky" when he read the zeal in the man's eyes. LaMaster marched the four-man detail down the road from the orderly room, introducing himself to Ratty Mac as they went. It was already a wonderful day, Vietnam at its most picturesque, tropical paradise that it was. And it promised better. Early hours yet. The Field First halted his reluctant command before a low, boarded-up building which stood, starkly unfinished, unpainted, and unused at the end of the company street.

"There it is, MacGantree. The new orderly room. Yours to shape and make. First Shirt wants it opened up—here are the keys—and cleaned out. By noon, the engineers will deliver a load of plywood and some sheetrock and paint." LaMaster relayed only what he was told.

"Sheetrock! In this climate?"

"Roger that, MacGantree. Don't look to me for rationale." He held his hands up in protest. "The man wants sheetrock, you put up sheetrock. Of course, you could put up drywall, instead. 'kay? Get my drift?"

"Sure, Sarge. I'll pound fuckin' sand up the goddamned chimney too, if he wants it. My achin' ass!" He looked back at the privates in the detail and found a total absence of interest in the three. He turned back to the door, shuffling the keys musically. "Here we go, up the yellow-fuckin'-brick road. Hi-di-ho!"

LaMaster fled back up the company street to the safety of the supply room, where he could commiserate with the Supply Sergeant about the qualities of the modern soldier.

Inside the soon-to-be orderly room, the half-finished structure was one huge, wooden oven, the air musty, heavy, unbearably hot. To enhance the glory of MacGantree's punitive assignment, the stench of something rotten pervaded the stifling atmosphere. The soldiers opened all the windows and both doors in the hope of circulating the air. It was equally hot outside, even more humid, and there was no breeze; but eventually some of the foul atmosphere leaked out, dissipating in the open, leaving a gag index of no more than 7. It took Private Mallows less than a minute to locate the source of the odor under a pile of two-by-four studs: three large, grey rats. Very dead. Very recently dead, just beginning to decay.

"Yeah, LaMaster said they put out rat poison around here early this week. Effective shit, ain't it," Mac grinned. He stood for a moment, head cocked to one side, surveying the rats with something like fondness. "Let me see now," Mac said, reaching for the roll of blueprints. "This here's the new orderly shack . . ." He scanned the blue sheet, his finger following the white veins along joists and walls, studs and sole plates . . . his finger stopped.

"And here's the First Sergeant's new office," he exclaimed, as if surprised it should really exist. "How 'bout that, sports fans!"

MacGantree set his men to work.

* * *

The new orderly room was completed eight days later and occupied in turn. When First Sergeant Whiteneir opened the door into his new office, he was staggered by the smell. On a level with corrosive gases, it seemed to emanate from the very walls of the cubicle that was soon to be called "Whitesnake's den." Inside his private room the stench was unbearable; in other parts of the building only terrible.

The CO, Captain Rucker, issued a mandate: Top would keep the door closed between their offices at all times. When the senior

NCO became frustrated to the point of distraction — when he'd had all he could stand of the stench, and tried to sneak the door open while the company commander was out — the two clerks threatened both instant mutiny and to report to the captain the First Sergeant's disregard for orders. Sometimes, on the rare occasion when Lieutenant Peche graced the company area, the XO would order the door closed and locked, giving the order with his hand on the butt of his .45.

The First Sergeant assigned details of men to search, some crawling beneath the building where it stood on pyramidal concrete pillars, some digging around the edges of the structure, all seeking the source of the malodorous irritant. They could find nothing.

Engineers, at the First Sergeant's demand, came and drilled holes along the baseboards and used long, snake-like cables that thrashed and racheted around inside the walls. They inserted pencil flashes and small, angled mirrors on handles into the walls.

Nothing!

They came again and put brighter lights, larger mirrors into the walls through holes they cut; they searched and searched, holding their noses the while. One wore a plastic conical surgical mask until the First Sergeant ordered him out of the way. But they found nothing.

After more than a month, the pressure became too much for Whitesnake and he caved in — "'round the bend" according to Johns. "Bonkers," by the British Attache's definition — and was shipped out in an elastic shirt. There were those cynics who pointed out that it only happened after some unkind soldiers in the 3rd had run the ad in the *Saigon Daily News* under "Positions Available," urging applicants interested in a job as First Sergeant to apply in writing to Commanding Officer, 3rd RRU, PO Box 1632, APO San Francisco, 307. Like a bank in Kalamazoo seeking to fill a cashier's job, or a supermarket in Palm Springs.

Sometime after that, SP4 Dann, one of the clerks, was heard to comment, apropos of nothing: "Hey, you know, with Whitesnake gone, I don't smell the rotten shit anymore."

"Nope," echoed the other clerk, "not since Whitesnake left."

It could have been coincidence. The captain said nothing and kept his door closed. The new First Sergeant who replaced

Whiteneir—a grizzled veteran who was as much a cliché as that description applied to him by the troops, who came to the 3rd RRU by MilPerCen assignment, not in answer to the *Daily News* ad—refused to acknowledge a particularly bad odor. He said the entire Far East smelled like that and he couldn't credit his predecessor's problem.

Ratty Mac would only infer obliquely, even to Winter to whom he was closer than anyone, the true cause of the ripe mystery. Winter took that meager hint, pieced it together with an intriguing comment by one of the privates who had worked with Mac on the new building, and discerned the truth. Or as much of it as he really wanted to know.

MacGantree had cut three sections—there were three dead rats—out of stud braces in the outside walls of the First Sergeant's office-under-construction. He took the removed segments of two-by-four, split them lengthwise, hollowed them out with a chisel, and drilled a number of holes all the way through the sections. He separated the split segments, deposited a dead rat in each of the hollowed spaces, cemented the split wood together, and glued them back into place in the wall. Then he put up drywall, careful not to nail into the weakened joints. Drywall could not discourage the miasma that spread through the First Sergeant's holy space, and the rats served their purpose.

Rumors in the military are, by their nature, sourceless. They spring full blown from dreams and wishes, hates, fears, and loneliness. They spring also from truth—quite often from truth. Ratty Mac, who, after finishing work on the orderly room, was moved into his proper slot at WHITE BIRCH, never asked who squealed on him. He knew it was not done maliciously; no one who knew what he'd done held any brief for the departed First Sergeant. The story, essentially as it had happened, spread as a rumor. Mac was content with the results. Word was out about the specialist's revenge, and that served Mac's purpose.

Mac wanted so little out of life, Winter told Sergeant Biggs one night in the mess hall not long after the rumor began, that it seemed a shame not to humor him. It was like a relationship with a snake: one need not necessarily be afraid of the snake . . . but perhaps, as long as it didn't get into the henhouse, it might be better left alone. On its own, it might even do some good.

The company commander, when his sneak squealer passed on the story to him, said he thought such rumors in poor taste, and he judiciously avoided snakes around Davis Station.

* * *

Something to be said for getting up early. The streets in downtown Sai Gon-Cho Lon were no less filthy that time of day, but the heat had yet to build. The stench was less debilitating. Vendors and shop owners sloshed cans of filthy river water over filthy sidewalks to give the illusion of freshness; the efforts were poorly rewarded.

Winter sat back, enjoying the cyclo ride in the relatively cool morning air. Many of the shops and sidewalk vendors were not open for business yet, but that was easily amended simply by having the driver pull over. Vendors would materialize. The customer is always right.

His early morning, downtown mission was a stretch, at best. Likely nothing he mailed now would reach Nickie and Jeremy in time, anyhow. He had only six days before their joint birthdays, one day apart. But he was, after all, in a combat zone. He'd had no opportunity before now to get downtown during the day.

Sure, tell a six-year-old that.

"Go to Cho Lon," old hands advised. "Best shopping around, and cheaper." So he found himself in that Chinese section of The Paris of the Orient, and when his driver brought him to the markets, he saw his work cut out for him. The stalls and stands, stores and outlets, all of a kind, stretched endlessly, and where there was a gap, a vendor seated on the sidewalk offered any item in the Sears and Roebuck catalog. Plus some. But the format of the markets was unusual, something that had eluded Winter's western-oriented awareness before now on his few trips downtown.

There was no supermarket effect here. Each product was designated its own area for display, bargaining, and sales. Different products were separated into different venues. The first section he came to offered bread. Mostly standard french *pain*: *baguette* and *avion*, but some enterprising bakers offered rolls, cakes, delicate cream puffs and *éclaires*. It was a busy market and as many as thirty different vendors of gustatory delights.

As they rode slowly beyond the baked goods, the product line shifted to cloth and household linens: bed sheets, pillow cases, throws, curtains, towels—the world of fabrics occupied the stalls and booths for half a block. After that, it was hand tools, then a full block of vegetables. Winter wondered why the vegetables were not located nearer the baked goods. Looking closely, he recognized a pulpy green succulent which he'd seen boatmen harvesting from the opaque, chocolate-colored Sai Gon River and tributaries; his question regarding propinquity took a back seat. Still, he could discern no logic in the disposition of goods, except that integrity ruled within a product line.

His eyes widened, his senses heightened, when his driver peddled around a corner and there, stretching to the edge of the market area, were stand after stand of ice-cream-colored Honda motor bikes. Pale mint green, pink, aquamarine, sky blue, yellow, almond —a pallette of soft, pastel machines for the Vietnamese-on-the-go. Winter dismounted, walked among the bikes, his driver pushing the cyclo along behind. The display was a treat. The contrast with red dirt, green jungle, and murky waters of the inhospitable countryside was remarkable and tantalizing. He might have shopped for a special prize here, under different circumstances. He almost envied Asian buyers their tendered opportunities.

He climbed back in the front-end seat of the cyclo, and rode on, past another section with material goods; but here rolls of cloth: silks, cotton, rayon, and totally out of scope, one bolt of corduroy. He'd never seen corduroy on a Vietnamese, male or female. Some Chinese Slickie-Boy likely had done a number on the shop owner. The colors here were almost as startlingly varied as the Hondas.

Then they turned another corner.

Pale, honey-colored woods. Whited planks, and the dark tones of mahogany. A hundred shades of brown, some reddish-tinted exotic sculpture, and very commonplace, un-peeled timber that offered the bottom line for the very poor who yet had to honor their loved ones with a proper burial. The coffins—some on trestles, others up-ended against a brick wall, others economically displayed wherever space allowed—stretched as far as he could see. One very large, bulky affair represented someone's wait for fat Uncle Vinh to die. Most were of a common one-size-to-fit-all. There were some tiny boxes that could only be for the stillborn and very early victims of Oriental life. Some were obviously of high quality, the results of careful selection of materials, lined with silk or satin — prizes of the coffin maker's craft. Then a wide selection of the commonplace. Beyond that, very basic boxes where the bark had not been removed from the boards used for the sides.

Ugly flashes assaulted his consciousness. Winter could see the coffins filled, each with its honorable assignee, though there were no clear features. He had instant visions of tiger-stripe-fatigued Viet privates, exploding beneath the soil; the boxes collapsing, imploding as had the wall lockers in the NCO hooch crafted by these same artisans. His head swam with a dark, dismal presence. He incoherently tried to urge the cyclo driver to turn around, to drive him from this preview. He realized the first faint stirrings of panic.

Huffing out a deep breath, he gained control. He signaled the driver to a halt, stepped from the seat into the street littered with fine, curling wood shavings, and directed the driver in a circle. Without speaking, foregoing the search for presents, he was driven away from the sad market, reluctantly he thought, discerning the driver's attitude. Even the myriad colors of the Honda bikes now seemed subdued beneath a film of mist rising from the river.

chapter seven

Paris of the Orient

Viet Nam: July 1964

In July, Specialist Five David D. Winter was magically transformed into Staff Sergeant David D. Winter. Though changing his rank, the Army let him keep his name. He was promoted as Non-commissioned Officer-in-Charge, Air Section. The Air NCOIC slot was a paper exercise, used to promote the next candidate on the list when stripes came down. The NCOIC function was retained by another NCO; Winter continued at WHITE BIRCH as assistant to the Operations Chief on Day Trick, moving up from Trick Chief. He understood the Army's workings and made no complaint, though he would have wished it otherwise. He did his job at WHITE BIRCH and, exercising his assumed Jesuit strictures, did not bitch about missing out on the flying job.

Ratty Mac appeared on the roster at WHITE BIRCH as Assistant Trick Chief on Bravo Trick, filling a position Winter had once held, vacated when he moved up, replacing a sergeant who had completed his tour and rotated to the post at Vint Hill Farms Station, Virginia, to replace someone who had been transferred to Fort Benning, Georgia, to the 11th Air Assault to fill in for a sergeant who *et cetera, et cetera*, on and on in the ever-widening ripple of life in the military pond.

Winter and MacGantree worked together, and spent off-duty time together. It was the bond of their service together in far places, Asmara being as far as could be imagined. From anywhere! No one ever questioned that Eritrea (Ethiopia) was the end of the line, and regarded the two friends as survivors of some particularly debilitating banishment. Viet Nam, on the other hand, still possessed enough flavor of the new and different, the as-yet unknown, and the two men so concerned themselves with the mission, that the assignment did not even appear in the same light as other remote areas. And unlike Asmara, the one-year tour in Viet Nam assured a constant and rapid turnover of personnel. In Viet Nam the number of troops was twenty fold that in Eritrea

(Ethiopia); and it would be years and battles and extensive political and diplomatic shufflings later before the hazards of the one-year fixed tour became unarguably evident.

American soldiers at Tan Son Nhut Air Base outside Sai Gon lived under relatively crude conditions, according to complaints filed with Army Inspectors General–the IG. But the complainants were men who had fought no other wars.

For the Americans who found themselves in the Sai Gon or Da Nang areas, or in other large cities in Viet Nam, there were compensations. One holdover from French colonialism was a selection of fine restaurants in the city, another, the number of decent hotels, and moderately passable bars.

It is not in the nature of Oriental cultures to assemble gaggles of people in order to make public fools of themselves; it requires the influx of westerners to bring about that phenomenon. These watering holes—the bars—under the influence of increasing American presence, quickly lost their original, quasi-genteel European ambience and assumed, instead, the brash, hard, commercial atmosphere of American dives. It was straight to these slum salons that Ratty Mac, along with thousands of other young GIs, were drawn. Drawn by cheap beer and cheap sex with bargirls and "hostesses."

Winter had no interest in the bars, particularly as constituted in Sai Gon. After a few trips into town with Mac shortly after the latter's arrival, Winter announced his reluctance to accompany his friend downtown. The bars, named The San Francisco, Diamondhead, The Golden Gate, Frisco Lil's, The Blue Moon, The Casino, and other nostalgic titles, were memory tags in name only. Reminders of San Francisco seemed to be particularly alluring to the lonely young soldiers: it was the most common port from which they'd embarked from the United States, and it was the place they would first return to when the nonsense was over.

But the calculating appeal to his loneliness held no attraction for Winter. It was an atmosphere of tawdry, juvenile revel, and the new sergeant hoped he'd outgrown that. He certainly had no interest in the girls, with Nickie and the boy waiting at home. And VD statistics in the southeast Asian port were "top-o'-the-chart" horrendous.

But Winter did enjoy some of the restaurants. Over time, a custom of sorts sprang up involving him and MacGantree and one of the cafes. Sometimes, shift mates and hooch mates from the 3rd accompanied them, but for the most part it was Ratty Mac and Winter.

The custom came into being late one night when Mac stumbled into Winter's NCO hooch after an evening of boozing and grousing in the NCO/Enlisted Club. Winter lay on his bunk reading, after spending two hours scratching out a long, frustratingly impotent letter to Nickie. Loneliness his sole roommate, he welcomed the unexpected boon of Mac's company, questionable as it might be.

"Dave, my man, let's go get a beer. They closed the club on me. 'Inventory' they said, or some such shit." Mac was only mildly drunk, a sorry situation in his judgment.

"Can't drink then, not if the club's closed, Mac," Winter said, laying aside his book, making the next move in the farce by tilting his frosted Heinneken up and drinking slowly. Ratty Mac was so predictable.

Mac's move: "The hell you say! Town's fulla bars. Le's go!" Winter could read rampage in Mac's rodent-red eyes.

"Tell you what, Mac. I know a place downtown — Broddard's — has the finest French pastries in Indochina, as much an anachronism as that might be, and an espresso that will stand! you! up! You've seen it, the place with the plate glass windows on Tu-Do, on the corner up from The Casino. I'll go down to Broddard's with you. For pastry and coffee."

Winter read the startled look on Mac's face, and was surprised when his tipsy friend agreed. He was immediately suspicious. While he dressed, and later as they took the *dzong* cart across the base to the front gate, a thinly veiled contest of wills developed over their destination.

"C'mon, Dave. You don't hafta drink more'n one. Le's have just one." When Winter reminded Mac of their agreement, the soldier shrugged it off, growing more insistent about the bars. Finally, in the tiny Renault cab bouncing down Kong Ly toward the city center, Winter put an end to the game.

"Dung lai!" he shouted into the cabbie's ear. When the cab screeched to a stop, he opened the door and turned to Mac. "Who gets the cab?"

"Aw, c'mon, Dave. Don't be an asshole." Mac rubbed his long nose and turned away, motioning for the driver to drive on.

"If you want the cab, take it. I'll catch one going the other way, Mac. That's just the kind of asshole I am." He started out of the cab.

"Wait a minute. Wait . . . just a goddamned minute. Shit, Dave . . . c'mon. Don't get out. We'll go to the . . . you know, what you said." He effected a crushed look and slumped back in the seat.

"Hey, Mac. Buddy. If you want to go drink, go ahead. No sweat. I'm not making a judgment. I just don't care to go. I'll catch another cab back to the base. You — "

"Get in the cab, you pious asshole. I guess I've had enough today anyhow," he grumbled, pulling Winter back into the cab by his shirttail. Winter kept a straight face and motioned the cab ahead. They pulled away, the driver jabbering, shaking his head.

"Ba mui lam! Ba mui lam!"

* * *

Broddard's occupied a street corner with a plate glass wall fronting on Tu Do Street, the main thoroughfare in Sai Gon. Still called Rue Catinat after the French by old time residents, it was both the bright, bustling, commercial center of downtown Sai Gon with airlines offices, restaurants, and bars, yet maintaining much of the delicate influence in architecture and pace of the French colonial period. Broddard's fell somewhere between the two extremes.

After his first halting taste of the *petits-four* and the scalding, black coffee, Ratty Mac sent back for the dessert cart again, selecting a variety of fancy cakes and sweetbreads.

They sat on twisted-wire-back chairs at spindly legged tables. They ate with white cloth napkins in their laps, the silver service gleaming with polish in the soft light; the china was quality and unchipped. It was a touch of unfamiliar elegance in lives that saw only olive drab and khaki, regimentation, and multiple-copy sameness.

Outside, late night pedestrians and aimless wanderers passed close by the windows. Through the spidery script lettered on the glass, the two American soldiers watched peddlers and money-changers, thieves, flower girls, whores, sellers of whores, front men and ad men for whores, mothers of whores, brothers and sisters and aunts and uncles of whores, even children of whores who offered "... my mother — she cherry" in the bland enticement that drew more takers than was likely, and a montage of Asian domestics, plying their trades — some legal, most illegal — along the still-busy sidewalks of the nighttime city. Winter could not avoid the conviction that some measurable percent of the passers-by were certainly allied with the underground revolutionary government, the Viet Cong–the enemy.

It was past midnight but there was no curfew, though there was talk of one to come. The Cong — anti-government political and military action workers, terrorists, and soldiers — floated as inconspicuous minglers in the sidewalk crowds. They were not conducting all-out war. They did not attack the bars and restaurants, so long as the establishment paid them VC "taxes" and did not take an active role against them. The American and Australian troops were not long in ferreting out which bars did and which did not subscribe to the Viet Cong's extortion. Those that did not — those who made a point of flouting their contempt for the guerillas — did not survive in business. They were inevitably targeted for their revisionism, and because they were targets, they did not enjoy the patronage of the soldiers who sought refuge from a regular diet of targeting.. The pace of the war was dictated by overriding economic factors.

It became a habit and a convenience for Mac and Winter to visit the restaurant in the late evening hours, once Mac knew he could not entice Winter into the bars, and they traveled from their quarters on the compound of Davis Station, across sprawling Tan Son Nhut base on a *dzong* cart to gate 2. There they paid off the cart, then walked another seventy-five yards beyond the guard shacks and traffic baffles to a pickup spot along "100-P Alley." That innocuously titled passageway was a filthy strip of street that fronted bars, barber shops, and whorehouses whose nominal price of 100 *piastres* for a short time gave name to the region. From there they took a cab six miles into the city.

Dzong carts were proscribed by law from operating in downtown Saigon. Inconvenient to make the change from cart to another mode of transport at the actual limits the administration had set, GIs from Tan Son Nhut always rode the cabs the full distance.

Winter commented on how much more comfortable it would be in the sultry nights to ride the open carts, but the law was harsh and cart drivers would not risk taking GIs into the city — unless the financial inducement was worthwhile which, of course, was the name of every enterprise in Viet Nam.

At work, collecting and processing intelligence raw data through the black boxes, was a challenging enterprise. Work in the WHITE BIRCH facility was noisy, hot, and sweaty, and in bad weather frustrating to a fault as build-up of invidious atmospherics, lightning, thunder, and the steady drumming of heavy rainstorms on the tin roof made the chasing of elusive, shifty radio signals a matter of sorting ant farts from among bassoon concerti. And without feedback as to significance of any particular bits of the product they produced, the manual Morse ops and analysts labored on in a vacuum that, in a circular fashion, just made it all that more frustrating to keep on doing it. But if something happened, some military event of the enemy's making that impacted negatively on the forces of the good guys, then the WHITE BIRCH team was the first target of headquarters ire.

Enemy attacks, though a real fact of life, were not common enough on the large base at TSN to constitute a daily or nightly threat. Night was by far the likeliest time for them to occur, and when they occurred they were serious. Then, no matter the casualties, attacks were the overriding determinant of life in the succeeding four-to-five days. But boredom crept back in and the same slow pace became standard once again. A greater threat to stability were the disruptions to the Vietnamese government process occasioned by frequent *coups d' état* and counter-coups, as one general or another struggled for power.

There was little or no sense of an army in support of national interests; instead, loyalties were marked by dedication to individuals who controlled some segment of military and/or political power;

loyalties that were bought, not with zeal for a *people*, but for a family, a village, a district at most. Associated with them were colonels and generals whose military careers were begun with purchased commissions and a system of open, recognized nepotism, fostered by influence and extortion, blackmail and blackmarket. Outsiders failed to understand how any hope could be had for a government controlled by such men in such conditions.

"Tay Ninh Province is going VC," Winter remarked one night to Mac.

"Shit, it is now, I don't care what the stats people say," Mac said. "Nobody can work with Marvin the ARVN up there. How many advisers we lost with those assholes, anyhow?"

"Just the one. In Tay Ninh City. The other one, the one on the road up to Nui Ba Dinh, was an accident."

"Yeah, shit, accident. I don't want no part of their accidents. Friggin' Zips have too many accidents, especially involving our people, for my taste. And we almost lost a Beaver up there two weeks ago, 'count of their lax airstrip security. So Sergeant Sheldon said."

"You can't just *not* take chances in war, Mac. The crew knew it was chancy when they went in there. But it was important enough to get the tapes from the team on the mountain to take the chance."

"Bullshit, Dave! Nobody asked the operator if he wanted to take the chance. The pilot, okay. That's his job. The op is supposed to be operating, not acting as a fuckin' courier coolie." Winter listened in frustration to Mac's eternal refusal to recognize a war scenario as different from parcheesi. "Why can't they fly one of those friggin' eggbeaters up to the top and make the pickup. They got time and fuel enough to hop all over Three Corps, buzzin' sampans, showin' straphangers the countryside, takin' generals to cocktail parties. Grab-ass!"

"Can't draw attention to the mountain."

"Mountain's ass . . . that fucker sticks up outta the flats of Three Corps like a size forty-four tit. We can't draw attention to it? Shit, you can't see anything *else* when you look in that direction. Hell, we step outside right here, on a clear day I can see the sonuvabitch."

"We can't draw attention, dip-shit, to the fact that we got somebody on top doing something important enough to fly choppers in there. Don't ask me to explain the difference . . . that's the explanation," Winter said defensively.

Still, the war did not touch them directly, though they both felt it was merely a matter of time.

"It's gonna happen, Dave. You watch. Ten years now these assholes been on the loose, since they booted the French out. If we ain't awww-ful careful, old Camelot Jack, even dead, will turn out to've dragged us into shit over our boot tops."

"Could be something of a surprise; I don't think it's a trap."

"Man, I felt trapped ever since I joined the goddamned Army. The first time. And I don't see the difference — surprise or trap."

* * *

Winter felt himself spiraling into a downer when, going into June, it seemed the summer would never end. Then some scholar revealed that they were not even *into* summer yet. He finished a set of days and dropped off the duty truck at the club on the way into Davis Station. He was beginning a two-day break, and it felt like a beer. Maybe two.

Inside the club, Spec Four Reese and several other 058s, manual Morse ops who worked for Winter at WHITE BIRCH, were gathered about one of the tables. On the table in front of Reese stood a bamboo container resembling a large birdcage. Winter saw the little spider monkey inside the bars as he walked past, but did not stop to stare as others were doing. He'd heard of Reese's monkey; he recognized the significance of the cage there in the club.

"Hey, Sarge. You seen our buddy?" shouted one of the soldiers at the table, a day worker from the headquarters platoon.

"Yeah," Winter answered evenly. "I've seen him."

The soldier, sensing disapproval, leapt to exploit it. An opening . . . "Hey, Sarge, you wanta —"

"Yeah, hey, Sarge . . . come take a look," Reese intruded. "This dude's a real swinger." He laughed wildly at his own wit, and as his companions worked it out, the uproar became general. Winter, standing by the table in silence, saw it did not scare the monkey; the monkey was too numb; the monkey was out of it.

The monkey was drunk.

"How'd this sick shit get started, Reese?" Winter demanded.

He could not share their laughter; it was a brittle, vicious barking that had little to do with humor. Winter stared at the tiny creature lying on its side, curled against the bamboo slats in a stupor. Its human, baby-like claws twitched and the animal whimpered in its pitiful state. Winter felt pity and sadness, not just for the monkey; but mostly he felt anger; he wasn't sure why it was suddenly so violent and pervasive.

"Awww, Sarge, hell. Ain't nothing but a monkey. You don't believe that Darwin shit about some kinda kinship, do you?" Reese laughed and looked around to the others for encouragement. Their ready cackles were mocking.

Winter leaned on the table, his fists tight, white-knuckled. His voice was low and even when he spoke, but it carried through the noise in the club: "Reese, if I recollect properly, there's a USAR-Vee regulation about pets in the facilities. Nobody pays much attention to that, normally. But if an NCO were to take it into his head . . . well, you take my point, I think. And that," Winter added pointedly, "along with your sterling record in this outfit, should just about — "

"Yeah, yeah. Okay, I read you," Reese growled. An unaccountable intensity of hate was in Reese's glare. The sergeant knew he was merely a focal point for the frustrations and fears of a group of unguided men, unwillingly doing something they would rather not be doing in a place they'd much rather not be, and for all the wrong reasons. If asked, they would have had no explanation, no rationale, no understanding, and for that reason alone they were doubly dangerous.

"I got him downtown on the Street of Flowers for a carton of Salems. *PX* Salems," Reese added defiantly, challenging Winter to try to deal with *that* problem, the overriding curse of black marketeering, for which there were also command regulations. The weak light in the club made the ring of faces around Winter appear alien in their anger, and the faces of the men bore the aggression of their distorted allegiance. The room beyond the table thrummed with talk and laughter and the sound of slot machines slamming, coins spilling, the crunch of crushing beer cans, and the tinny clank of their impact on walls and ceiling.

"When I brought the monk back to Davis," Reese continued, pushing his disdain for regulations in his sergeant's face, "I kept him in the motor pool for a couple of days. We all fed him, scraps from the messhall, C-rations, so-forth. Whatever we could find. One night we were sitting out back of the huts, having a brew. The monkey was there, doing his time like the rest of us. Someone, one of the guys, gave him some beer when his water bowl was empty. The monkey lapped it up. When he got stoned, we almost busted our ass laughing. And you don't think that's funny," he said accusingly.

Winter did not. He said so in a manner that indicated the ridiculous nature of the question.

"Well, after that," Reese continued, chuckling in a vaguely challenging manner, "word just got around. Next day when I got in from work, the monkey was stoned again. The mechs'd been pouring beer in his water bowl all day. After that, whoever was around kept the monkey juiced. Monkey was happy like that; we never mistreated him or nothin'." The righteous tone in Reese's voice grated on Winter's consciousness. "Wouldn't you rather stay blown away if you was Vietnamese? A Zip soldier or a monkey, don't matter. Just Vietnamese. I know I would," he added in a burst of redundant information.

Winter did not reply.

"So, now we got a First Monkey who's a boozer . . ." he hesitated, then slammed his hand on the table and laughed aloud, "and a boozin' First Sergeant who's a fuckin' monkey." The illogic of his non-sequitur critique did nothing to diminish the hilarity around the table.

Winter could feel hostility in the brutal laughter. He said, speaking as softly as he could, holding himself in place, "Reese, I don't want this to come as a shock to you, but a lot of people don't give a rat's ass if you complete your tour here at WHITE BIRCH, or spend the rest of your three-sixty-five in the stockade. You might find duty in some less pleasant place a possibility. Even a likelihood."

The Spec Four glared at Winter with hatred.

"Now I suggest you find some other means of amusing yourself."
Winter glanced around the table, into the eyes of the other primate
tormentors. "Get started on it right away." He turned and walked
away from the table, away from the bar, toward the door. A beer
wouldn't taste very good right now. He heard muttering around
the table behind him.

"What the fuck's *he* gonna do?"

"Hell, Reese, he can't make you do nothing you don't want
to. This's a free country," one of the merrymakers groused in a
patently false pronouncement. Despite the turmoil in his head, the
fluttering in his stomach, Winter almost smiled at that ludicrous
myth. They'd forgotten what country this was.

"Listen, Reese, if he turns you in, the Old Man—"

"Winter's no fink. He won't do that, despite what he said. I
give him that much. He could make it pretty tough on my ass at
work, though. Give me shit details out the wa-zoo."

"Screw 'im!"

"Yeah, easy for you to say, Kleinschmidt. *You* screw him. I
think I'll find another home for the fucking monk. I'm tired of
smelling monkey shit in the hooch anyhow."

One voice came to Winter as he crossed the sticky floor, a
loud, aggressive challenge: "Hey, Sarge! You wanna *make us* get
rid of our buddy?" All the soldiers in the club, those beyond the
table where the monkey was imprisoned, and those at the bar, the
waitresses and bartenders, had turned toward the rising voices.
The barber stuck his head through the door from the adjacent shop
in wonder.

Winter ignored the unidentified voice. The conflict implicit in
the challenge was meaningless and childish. He chose not to make
it a disciplinary matter on the basis of a barroom taunt.

Winter left the club and crossed the quadrangle to his hooch.
He seethed with frustration; he was angry, disgusted with the
soldiers, disgusted with himself for not handling it better. When
Charlie Forbes passed him in the street and spoke, Winter found
himself incapable of speech and he passed by the linguist without a
word. Forbes stopped and stared at Winter's back until the hooch
door slammed behind him.

Inside, Winter ripped off the fatigues, threw on slacks and a shirt, and jammed his feet, without socks, into civilian loafers. He slammed back out the door, headed for the front gate. Ratty Mac was just coming in past the guard.

"Where you headed, Super Sarge?"

"Downtown! Somewhere! Away from here."

"Hey, what's up? You pissed off about something? At me?"

"No, not you." Winter kept walking, through the gate and up the gravel road toward the Vietnamese soccer field. "It's nothing," he called back to Mac, "not your problem. See you later."

Mac spun about, caught up with Winter, and began walking backward up the road in front of the angry sergeant. "Give me a coupla' minutes to shower and change. I'll go with you."

"I don't want anyone with me, Mac. I won't be good company."

Mac stopped walking backwards, put his hands up to halt his friend. "You better do as I say, Dave. I'm going with you." When Winter attempted to step around him, Mac moved to block him. "Okay? Five minutes?"

Winter could read MacGantree, all right. He knew what his friend was doing, and he knew Mac was right. He was in no mood to go off downtown alone. "Yeah, sure," he said, caving. "I'll wait. Come on, you ratty bastard." He turned and led the way back toward Mac's hooch.

The sergeant sat and let his anger run out of him while leafing blindly through a tattered *Playboy*. It did not matter that he could not see the pages in front of him—there was "Not one bare tit left in the whole rag!" as Mac had so succinctly phrased it, the girls all gone, cut out and dispersed to grace private walls and lockers, how many of them a surrogate stimulus, companion in lone-love in a late night latrine stall? It was a measure of his disturbance that none of that seemed to matter now. The pages blurred together and he looked beyond.

True to his word it took Mac only five minutes to shower, a couple more to dress. Neither man said anything on the way to the front gate of Tan Son Nhut. In the taxi on the way downtown along Kong Ly Boulevard, Mac said only, "If you wanna talk about it, do it." He let the matter lie when Winter did not respond, and they sat in silence through the rest of the ride.

chapter eight

A Transient Imperative

Sai Gon, Viet Nam; May 64

The taxi rocketed down the center of the broad tropic avenue lined with palms and mangroves and improbable growth, and white sidewalks where nobody walked anymore. Along the left side of the boulevard, between the partially destroyed palace and the Catholic cathedral, stretched a lush putting green of lawn bordered by a tangle of exotic trees, bushes, and vines enfolding pulpy shrubs. Startling frangipani blossoms decorated the branches of banyan trees, as if part of the same growth instead of merely thrust together in symbiotic competition for the sun and the cracked, red soil. Bougainvillea, a deceptively attractive parasite, masked tall tree trunks and hung on bullet-scarred stucco walls. In shadow, the pock marks resembled vicious acne. In the sun and sticky closeness of the fading afternoon, greenness was a tangible, measurable presence.

Winter gripped the back of the seat before him and stared down the street ahead of the taxi, warding off oncoming cars by an act of will. Unwittingly scouting ahead of the cab driver, he watched a mass of people in the path of the taxi spilling out of the John F. Kennedy Plaza in front of the cathedral, overflowing the square and edging across the boulevard. They didn't seem to be doing anything or going anywhere; they were just there. A lot of them. Perhaps bearing consideration, he thought, as they bore down on the crowd on an unwavering track. Surely the driver would slow his mad dash, ease through the mass without incident.

"Sweet Magee . . . it's a goddamned quorum of slopes," MacGantree offered.

As if resenting Mac's ethnic slur, the driver wrenched the taxi to a halt in the middle of the street a hundred yards short of the crowd. But the driver hadn't a word of English, Winter was sure; there had to be another reason for his untimely stop beyond Mac's homily.

The driver stared at the two GIs in the rearview mirror as he shouted, eloquent in Vietnamese, gesturing with limp, flailing wrists. His face, bearing the scars of the pox wars of the disenfranchised, was a yeasty façade that Winter associated with billboards and blank walls. It made him imagine the driver was smirking because he didn't sweat, and there *was* something inherently superior about that in the tropics. Graham Greene characters never seemed to sweat.

The driver's jerky, impatient motions were the result of anxiety, if not fear. He did not waste time with courtesies or argument, but held the door open, urgently gesturing the passengers out.

Mac, offended, began to argue but the driver wheeled the cab in a screaming U-turn and pulled up on the opposite street side, the nose of the Renault directed back in the direction from which they had come. When he jerked once more to a halt, Mac scrambled out, yelling. "You sonuvabitch, I ain't payin' nothin' . . . *nothin'*, you hear! Dave, don't give the bastard a centime. Not a sou. Man, this ain't *even* the Street of Flowers by a long shot. Fuck 'im!" Ratty Mac slammed the door and it bounced back open. "Don't you give 'im nothin', you hear." He leaned toward the open taxi window. "You hear me, Zip . . . you bastard, you get fuck-all!"

Winter followed Mac onto the street, quietly. Uneasy. Senses alert, he dug in his pocket for the fare. Mac danced around the cab in anger. The driver, ignoring both efforts, rammed the shift into gear and roared away, back down the street toward the palace that shone in late sun with the particular purity of alabaster tainted with gold. Winter, staring after the retreating vehicle, noticed that the state house–nothing but rubble since the overthrow of Diem the previous November–looked, from his angle, singularly pristine in the late sun.

". . . and don' ever let me catch your ass around Tan Son Nhut again, you goddamned Zip asshole!" Ratty Mac's impotent, screamed taunts attracted no more attention in the traffic than did the loose door of the taxi, rasping noisily on broken hinges as the cab shimmied off into the glare.

MacGantree continued shaking his fist in the air, yelling incoherently. Winter was silent. Mac's invective ceased in mid-threat. It occurred to both of them at the same time to wonder why they had been dumped so far from their destination with no explanation. Even more unlikely, they'd been deposited without paying a fare. They turned toward the crowd.

Winter was apprehensive of crowds. Especially crowds in Southeast Asia. Crowds never augered good in 'Nam. They were attendant to terrorism, assassination, execution. Nothing good. Crowds could topple governments, had overthrown Diem here only seven months before. Well, sort of . . . Crowds did not necessarily constitute a threat because one was for or against something: the determinant was proximity.

"Mac, I don't like the looks of this. Let's walk back and pick up a taxi by the palace," Winter said, his eyes searching the streets. They were in a dead zone: taxi pickups were made beyond this area, nearer into town or farther out toward the base; here they only passed through. No taxis were in sight and no busses; *dzong* carts were forbidden here, and the cyclos could have been on strike for all their presence.

"Aw, shit. C'mon, Dave. Let's find out what the hell before bugging out. Since we're here, man." Mac made a tentative move toward the crowd. "Look. There's other G.I.s here, in the crowd. Some guys in uniform. Must be a show or something." He moved in earnest toward the gathering. "There's an airdale with a camera."

After a moment of hesitation, Winter reluctantly followed Mac into the square.

Celebration seemed imminent in the gathering, a mood almost festive. Banners, flags, twisted streamers bright in multi-colors hung from flimsy wooden racks that had been erected along the walkway. The two men moved nearer, Mac leading, waving and speaking to those in the crowd he knew or recognized as westerners. Winter followed, less enthusiastic.

The crowd noise grew to an ocean's murmur, swelling and hissing away in breakers, then rising in a swell of excited chatter, a babble that drowned out the hum of traffic moving about the square, along the boulevard. It squelched the drone of a Mohawk, stringing out his pattern from Tan Son Nhut Two-Five, far enough out on the downwind leg to carry his aircraft over the edge of the city. Winter did not look up at the plane, did not wonder what it was like up there, though the thought had often crossed his mind that it was cooler and cleaner.

Small children, tattered and careless, raced through the crowd, delirious beneath the stares of parents who disapproved but would not shout at them in public, shaming them. Squeals and giggles of their chase carried above the tide of voices. One old man stood in silence in the midst of the bustle as if in religious meditation, his stringy white wisp of beard and cone-shaped hat creating a caricature so exactly like the *Pocket Guide to Vietnam* booklet cover, he might have been labeled a *venerable ancient*. The old man watched the children but did not smile. Neither did he ever quite frown, though it seemed likely he would at any moment. His expression never changed. He seemed frozen in a stance of cautious disapproval.

Winter was held by the old man's difference, and he recognized that the expression was sadness on a face that was not inscrutable. Winter, though curious, could not share in the old man's private vision; he had no hint of the crowd's purpose.

The atmosphere brought back to Winter those October carnivals of his youth, state fairs that came each year with electric air and the promise of two-headed freaks, dog-faced boys, and fat ladies with mustaches and a hint of beard. The weather here was different, not like those chilly Mississippi autumns, shockingly frigid after barefoot summers. He maintained only a blur of memories, images from an album of nightmare and fairytale. Just after the big war, seedy con men with flat straw hats and canes, hawking untitled but unlimited landscapes of the dead at Dachau. Auschwitz, with its improbable heaps; the wire at Buchenwald hung with grinning, striped Jewish wraiths, awaiting deliverance with no hope of anything of the kind. As a kid it had taken a close look to determine that the expressions were not grins at all, but the rictus of dying — starvation, and death.

The small people here about him in this square conjured up all the bibbed and overalled, tousle-headed, round-eyed farm kids, their post-depression, post-war faces thin, snot streaming green and yellow, crusted on their fuzzy upper lips and weak chins as they stiffened against the crush of the midway in the October night. Around Winter in this carnival plaza, with the cathedral spires rising to European heights above, alien in the skyline of temples, he felt the same mood of daring — of naughty adolescent, touch-me-if-you-can, ten cents a head to get in, kid; a quarter to go behind the curtain; see some bare ass for only a quarter more. Psst! Ever see a beaver talk, kid? Come right in! Show's just starting! There was that same distorted gaiety here in this Asian carnival that held a touch of madness, an alien frailty of wonders that could not survive the viewing.

Back then, reality could be discarded with the myriad attractions; and now, without the sawdust under foot, he could still smell it. Sawdust here in the rank, steamy streets of Sai Gon, and fleeting wisps of cotton candy, the rancid scorch of ground beef and suet, long before he came to realize what the main attraction was and why such associations.

Winter shied away from the body of the crowd, but the Vietnamese, recognizing him and Mac as Americans, moved aside and with courteous gestures opened a passage for them toward the center of attention. A murmur preceded them and the gathering parted; strangers urged them on, insistent, bowing, smiling in that gentle way they had. The two GIs felt a sense of being propelled forward, though not a hand touched them.

In a moment of alarm, remembering his first days in country and the exaggerated alarms against murder and abduction, Winter searched about him but could find none of the white-uniformed civil police. He did not know if that was bad news or good. Following suit, he referred to them as White Mice, a typically American disparagement that seemed to have no particularly offensive racial texture — maybe social or political. He would have been reluctant to admit he thought of them in the same terminology. Some said they were so called because of the design of their uniforms: thoroughly white accessories over khaki, right down to the glossy white patent leather holsters and cartridge belts with whited webbing and bleached gloves. Others merely reminded you of the color of surrender flags. As a joke it was tasteless, but the symbol was unforgettable — agonizingly so if you had ever suffered the need for one of the para-military lawmen in a moment of crisis.

Uniformed officers and soldiers of the Army of the Republic of Vietnam — Marvin the ARVN — Rangers in tiger suit fatigues, Vietnamese Special Forces with red berets — the elite of the land war, gathered in a madhouse of disunity, vicious children with smooth young faces—gawked and shuffled like the peasant farmers and shopkeepers and prostitutes whose sons and daughters they were. Winter was aware of them all, each and every subtle difference, and yet they possessed a sameness that ensured anonymity in alien western eyes. *How do you tell one Zip from another; they all look alike?* he heard echoed in his mind, and realized the truth of the damning solipsism.

Alienation was not in the eyes of the Vietnamese; it was not that simple. It could be argued there was nothing in their eyes, a blankness, a mirror, a vague acceptance of some older reality that Winter knew nothing of and accepted that he would never understand. But he could feel alienation seeping out of their souls like a vapor. And though he could rationalize that he was in no danger here, still he wanted to run. His unease was not definable, but was distinct and powerful. He found himself scouting about, cautiously, marking avenues of retreat. The Vietnamese smiled shyly at him, he smiled back openly, and they both stared at the ground and moved continuously apart.

But MacGantree maneuvered him on. He pulled Winter forward through a cluster of young ladies, dressed in the fashionable *aow-dai*. They clung to one another like delicate insects, collected by nature and necessity on the same trembling branch where their voices formed a soft, chirping chitter. Winter was awkwardly amused at his own imagination, but they seemed unaware of his interest. He could never catch their eyes on him.

"Mac, this's got all the marks of something we can do without. Let's go somewhere and get a beer," Winter said, making the ultimate concession.

"Aahhh, bullshit, Winter Man. The *Ba-mui-ba* will keep. Let's find out what's going on first . . . then the beer. Might be a naked broad up there, or something like," he laughed. Ratty Mac was onto game, and he was an indefatigable hunter of sorts.

"Mac, dammit . . . I'd rather . . . Mac!"

A swelling sound like rushing wind or water, a loud *whoosshhh!* from the spectators drowned out Winter's plea. The crowd began chanting in a soft sing-song that quickly, insidiously grew in volume but seemed to contain no element of music. The pair continued moving, thrust forward, a part of the swaying movement and the chant.

Abruptly MacGantree and Winter stopped, brought up short by the space that opened out before them. Some twenty feet away a young Buddhist monk sat on the tiles of the plaza walk. In the closeness of the crowd Winter felt he stood immediately over him. The monk's legs were folded beneath saffron robes in the manner of the Lord Buddha himself, his hands laid palm down, loosely on his knees like hands carved on the arms of period furniture. The monk's eyes were closed and he rocked slightly, to and fro, while his lips moved in a soundless invocation.

Neither man ordinarily would have been moved by this picture: a monk, no different from the many — neither older nor younger, leaner or fatter, better dressed or not — sitting in the middle of the broad walk, late of an early summer afternoon in downtown Sai Gon. Honoring their vows of poverty, they were commonly found clutching the allotted bowl, begging along city sidewalks, resting from meager labors on the boulevards about the residential and government-office neighborhoods, along the edge of country roads and national highways. Uniform in habit with shaved heads, they could not be distinguished, one from another.

But all similarities aside, Winter had the feeling this young postulate was no ordinary run-of-the-temple priest. Poston had said they were called *bonze*, but Poston was a Burmese linguist; what the hell did he know? But for the first time, without knowing why he felt it, Winter thought Poston's word somehow appropriate.

The *bonze*, if such he was, sat, rigid and immobile, a jade carving cast yellow in the late sun, brown skin as wet-shiny as peeling paint blisters on a chalk idol, a surface disdaining earthly smudges and streaks. Like an outsized doorstop that had been hoisted from its place, dragged outdoors during renovation of some failing house, he had been left to weather away.

The chant of the crowd grew louder. A prolonged wailing, punctuated by isolated cries sharp and disparate, was audible above the chorus. Winter was remotely aware of a gentle breeze that stirred the limp air and riffled the fronds high in the skinny, dusty palms around the square. Above the trees, thin pale smudges that might have been clouds shared blue and gold and lavender reflections from the late sun, shifting and blending colors indiscriminately over the palace, temples, churches, bars, and the squalid shacks fronting on the river.

Around the *bonze* the crowd pressed in a circle up to some invisible boundary. A cleared no-man's land forty feet in diameter remained at the center of the circle. Almost a no-man's land — the young *bonze* was there. And one other, a middle-aged monk with horn-rimmed glasses and a blank, disinterested face. Like the walls, Winter was reminded. The older monk exhibited a fastidious manner in the way he handled the familiar red can with only his fingertips, as if passing a chalice of profound reverence. He walked with a mincing step, toes in like a balletomane, his sandaled feet flashing brown and sanctified beneath the yellow hem of his robe, and he glanced repeatedly at a large, silver wristwatch he wore beneath the loose cloth of the robe's sleeve.

Winter watched him set the can on the ground at the edge of the gathering. He heard through the crowd noise the slight, hollow, tinny *clank*, and was struck in a rush by understanding.

He imagined himself back at the fair again: *desperate, the wheels of colored lights that climbed circling and whirling into the night sky above the fairway, the ozone smell sharp to frigid noses, sweet and brittle to the bite and red-hots and peanuts and burgers on the air and taffy candy apples and sawdust; the fairgrounds cattle shows freaks rides girly shows and above the fairgrounds the city, hovering, watching like a distant but tolerant Oz.*

Seeking alternatives, he thought of Charlie Maris and Beeks sliding down the long, shaded, green-grassed hill behind the old state capitol on Great Northern cardboard sleds before the October winds browned the grass. The hot summer Sunday memory out of nowhere with Charlie, racing his bike down the hill on the way to the Jackson Senators ballgame, daring the others to make the jump when they crossed the double railroad tracks bounding high, front wheel coming down hard — the fork coming down hard, rather; the wheel heading off on its own course, the fork finding the August-soft asphalt arresting — and Charlie, flung forward from the rigid and wheel-less inefficiency of the bicycle, parroting a stringy Superman flying leaping faster than a speeding projectile through the summer heat, and for a moment he almost managed the transformation, until suddenly — the inability to crash through barriers of steel. The stifled humor and manufactured sympathy for the walking scab that was Charlie for two months after that. Not too much sympathy; Charlie Marris was a bully and a crud. A scab!

Winter, coming down as from a spate of madness, disoriented and spent, shivered.

Even as he thrust himself away, grasping for Mac in the sea of writhing, moaning bodies, the breeze brought the piercing odor of gasoline to his nostrils. He could not move in the jam of bodies who had begun a spastic, hysterical muttering, low-voiced and intense. A counter-litany. The crowd continued to press in tighter until their shoulders crushed one against another. Winter watched, unable to do otherwise, frozen by the inevitability of the horror he realized he was witnessing, ashamed of something that tied him to all those around him. He sought escape. Between desperate glances behind him, he saw the older monk bend and hand a book of paper matches to the seated monk. Only then did Winter realize that the bright orange robes were soaked through, almost uniform in a darker gold, and he knew the wet glistening on the monk's smooth, youthful face and shaved head, down his hairless arms and hands, was not perspiration.

Winter reached a hand involuntarily toward him as the young monk, in one calm, deliberate move, peeled one match free from the book, closed the cover in some reflexive ritual of safety, and opened his eyes to stare straight ahead. There was no focus to his gaze and Winter stared directly into his eyes, finding no sign of life. The *bonze* faced south and might have been seeing equally well the Mekong Delta beyond the river front at the end of Tu Do Street, or the icecap of Antarctica. But Winter knew what he saw was far beyond either: a short cut to nirvana through expedient political necessity. In a swift but deliberate movement the monk scratched the match across the sandpaper strip on the cover; a flame sprang from the tip and was carried.in the same continuing sweep of his arm to the hem of the monk's garment.

Someone behind him pulled Winter back. Hands held him as he struggled to reach the sacrifice. He heard a voice in English and realized it was Mac. He had forgotten Mac.

"Dave . . . oh, God! Dave! Jesus, Dave . . ."

The flame, yellower than the robe, redder than the sunset on the bricks of the cathedral, banked off the clouds above, licked upward, burst outward and around in one air-sucking, gunshot-quick inhalation, spreading like a gushing main of molten light over the whole of the seated figure, drenching him, surging and washing over him in a flood of hellish, all-consuming combustion.

The crowd watched, mesmerized, as the flames immersed the body, ravaging, teasing the life within the framework, and crawled farther upward, creating a brief nimbus of blazing radiance around the monk's head, and enveloped that finally in flame. His features remained composed. His hands, seeming to jump in a furious, soundless reverberation of knuckles on searing skin effecting a silent drummer's tarradiddle, were now laid palm up on his knees. Winter could not remember seeing the monk turn them over.

Then, as if more new fuels were added in a roaring flush of re-ignition, as if even more unlikely sights self-generated out of the spectacle, the *bonze* was burning—not just his robes, not just the gasoline on his body and the ground around him, but his revered person, all over— throughout, his entire being shot through with shafts of flame and light. To Winter, the horrifying rush of events seemed to have occurred in the blink of an eye over an agonizingly drawn-out, slow-motion eternity, one climax building on the previous.

Beneath the shock his mind tried to shut out, what his eyes by closing tried not to see, Winter faced multiple visions, barraged by images of fatty hamburgers and roasting franks on the open grills at the fair across from the snake tent. He shielded his face from the heat, but his own body was burning.

Flashes—intelligence briefings: the rhetoric of religious persecution, pledges of graphic extremes and fiery suicides, political solutions, the insincerity of promises never kept—swept his mind, but he could not block out the roar of the fire and the crackling, parchment-rustling sounds, the skin bursting as it roasted away from the bones, splitting open, searing to ash and vapor. The stench was like nothing he could name: cooking meat and gasoline, scorched damp air of the fetid city, nauseous reek of diesel smoke on the air where trucks passed, the stink of the unwashed, summer-ripe multitude around him in the close evening heat. His senses in overload, Winter noticed most damningly a stifling sweet, nauseous effluvium of jasmine garlands, worn at the neck, pressed to the noses of the delicate to mask equally the incredible stench of sacrifice or the reek of the open sewers.

His mind in a parody of stream-of-consciousness, impressions seemed to settle on him, did not linger, but ran in torrents. Even as the fuel-anointed body and the robes were engulfed in the purifying flames — as if the penitent had willed his total being, body and soul, combustible with piety, into the earthly conflagration — the flames, like a backfire set by cautious forest rangers, were feeding back on the horrid pyre, burning the skimpy fats and oils of the rigid corpse, producing a roar like a small blast furnace that went on and on, constant, overwhelming every other sound in the spectrum, drowning out the crowd and the traffic and the aircraft above, until Winter knew with a start the roaring was within his own head.

Twisting free as he could, turning aside from the horror in the scorched circle, fighting the press and frenzy of the crowd, he sought some measure of respite from the ritual madness in front of him. He grasped briefly a glimpse of a face across the space to his right. The face seemed to exist alone, floating, without attachment to a body or the crowd about it. In that instant, he knew it was an American face, surely an Occidental face, and it was a face he'd seen before . . . somewhere . . . sometime. A face out of . . . he lost it.

Find it again! He had the rapid sensation that there were horrid associations with the face, too, as with the present.

No, it couldn't be that. And the face was not merely accepting this . . . this idolatry! He *must* find it. He searched frantically, but the crowd was a shifting, living organism. Focus . . . there! There it was again. He *did* know that face. Where from?

God! It was on the edge of his mind, like a forgotten word on the tip of his tongue. Right there . . . unreachable. And he felt a sameness with the horror on that face, as with the scene about him.

His mind careened back on the crowd, and the moment was gone.

In the space where he'd seen the face in the crowd stood a Vietnamese bargirl from the Manhattan Bar. A Sai Gon tea queen.

He jerked his head, side to side, startled, seeking the face from the past. He looked back. The bargirl closed one eye in a lewd, grotesque attempt at coyness, and the gold of her smile flashed in the sun. Winter looked away, desperate. But the face was gone.

He found instead an old woman, one eye clouded with the muddy milk of neglect and disease, and he wildly imagined in that moment how blessed she was to have been witness to only half what he had seen. Something about the old woman mimicked the face in the crowd that was now gone. And she was a survivor. Winter could not take his eyes off her, as if she held some spectacle in her repertoire for his salvation.

Her face quivered, her eyes widened; the wrinkled skin drew tight around her mouth. Jesus! he thought, she's going to be sick. Thank God! Thank you, strange and mysterious and dispassionate God in this goddamned herd of godless freaks. At least one here has the compassion to feel revulsion. He stared gratefully at her working mouth, committing his own anguish and nausea to her act of contrition; and as her lips pursed and twisted, with jaws spasming, masticating with relish a reaction she could not contain, he saw her head bob back once, twice, and snap forward futilely. He felt a flash of kinship, a surge of love for this old, ugly, dirty woman — this mother of hordes who littered the streets and roads and battlefields of Asia — and she turned her head to one side, swiftly, puckering her stained and wrinkled lips and spewed forth a broad hot stream of blood across the curbing, into the street, staining the bright scrubbed whiteness of the stones; and he was stunned out of his own horror for a moment . . . until reason did a backstep . . . he hesitated, sickened and enervated . . . and then he recognized the pattern of the betel addict. The blood was only spit after all. He was fixated as she looked back on the smoldering remains, twitched her nose, hawked and spat again, and discreetly slipped another of the narcotic nuts into her mouth.

Winter felt betrayed. He felt lost, felt the horror, all over again, re-doubled, and the sickness that had momentarily fled with the promise of compassion now returned, more visceral than before.

The flames died to a low, eerie flickering. Tiny ripples of blue scampered along extremities of the residue. A man in street clothes at some hidden signal stepped forward from the crowd and spread a cloth over the black, smoking hulk. Winter recognized the shroud as one of the banners he had seen earlier, a Buddhist flag of orange and yellow and peach and cream colors, angular in geometric design and unearthly symbols. The mere touch of the cloth caused the fragile, charred mass to crumble forward to the concrete with only the slightest whispering. Ghastly, unspeakable remnants scattered to the edge of the crowd. Onlookers remained unmoving and stared and swayed, moaning in a low sound of summer thunder.

Winter, drawn by a subconscious need for quantification, looked at his watch. The entire sequence of events had taken less than fifty minutes, from the time the two unsuspecting soldiers alighted from the nervous driver's taxi, until the civilian threw the final cloth over the smoldering remains. It seemed hours to Winter that he had stood and stared, trapped by the crowd and this hell, while MacGantree, who professed nonchalant acceptance of the worst the world could offer, screamed and cried and fought the hands that held him.

In the silent, hypnotic aftermath Winter shuddered and looked around to see MacGantree's face frozen in stupidity. He moved quickly, grabbed Mac's arm, and ripped free of the convulsive clutching around him. No one moved to stop them.

There was a sense of aimless hysteria in the square. As the two GIs pushed through the dense throng, wanting only to get away from that place, they shouldered aside a cameraman, a westerner trying to push his way forward to the immolation, photographing the while over the heads of the crowd. The newsman, with the disdain of *Paris Match* written on his worldly face, sniffed at the two white faces and said, *"Excusez moi, messieurs!"* He laughed and turned away, intent on his own version of newsworthiness.

"Fuck-ez vous, you goddamned vulture!" Mac screamed through eyes blinded by tears, and he leapt for the sardonic journalist. Winter held onto him and kept pushing, elbowing aside men, women, and children, hobbling old mama-sans, soldiers, and nursing mothers, struggling to get out. To breathe. Neither of them dared take a breath, inhale the gaseous remains of the unholy pyre, until they were beyond the range of the nightmare, though they did not stop to consider the limits of that influence.

In the wake of the fiery demonstration, the Vietnamese ignored the two Americans who fought through spectators and stumbled across the boulevard to the paths among the cool shadows of the evening park. Mac slumped down on an oddly square stone and wrapped his arms tightly around his body. Winter watched him as if his friend's actions were incomprehensible. He himself was physically drained, but so charged emotionally that had he touched anyone beyond the influence of the square they would have drawn an electrical arc of industrial proportion.

Winter was still clutching MacGantree's shirt, and he bent suddenly, leaning away from Mac toward a bed of carmine-bright flowers, and tried to vomit. He felt great, gushing purges begin in his stomach, quaking and coursing up through his body . . . but nothing came. He gagged until his heaving stomach knotted, and still the convulsions continued — dry, retching, racking sounds that tore at his throat, spasms in his guts he could not control — but no product. He had a momentary fright when he thought his stomach and intestines might come spewing forth, dragged up on the tether of shame and horror along with the vomit, when it came. But his eruptions remained limited to emotional wrenching.

When the dry heaves finally subsided, he slowly straightened to find Ratty Mac holding him around the waist, preventing his fall into an anticipated puddle of bile. Mac's head was pressed against his back. For a moment, struggling for breath, Winter thought he was hearing an echo of his own reactions to the madness in the square, then realized it was Mac, crying like a child with a broken heart. A thing Winter had never before heard.

Together, finally, leaning on one another like two aged drunks, the two soldiers shuffled away down the boulevard, stumbling aimlessly toward Gia Dinh, leaving the place of sadness as rapidly as their rubbery legs would carry them.

They were thankful to be clear of the crowd which still milled around the littered, scorched tiles of the plaza. The crowd was utterly silent at last, stilled.

Winter, in the vacuum of after-affect and in his own quest for reason, searched the square for a sign, a visitation even, in a land that specialized in the form — a cliché: some small, half-naked child, perhaps, playing an idiot's game among the tall, fixed legs of the adults, chanting a tinny rhyme. Some wild-eyed hack, politicizing on the moment, or some entrepreneur of social or religious orientation.

But there were only the dark, oily clouds that the dying breeze could not dispel.

The light was going, rapidly now. The crowd began breaking up, but the two soldiers ignored any final dissolution as they fled toward the bars in Gia Dinh.

* * *

Winter came awake with the reluctance of one pulled, in a reverse process, back from a black purgatory into a vivid red hell. His reluctance was legitimate: his head split open the first move he made; he felt his brains and eyeballs, tissue and bones and liquids, spilling about him in the gritty agony of total disintegration. Every subsequent move, however slight, was a downhill plummet into greater destruction. Ever greater pain.

He lay in the narrow bunk, trying not to move; he dare not move. Gradually he became aware of a grating insistence, as if something from his tortured dreams remained to torment him, crushing his body, tearing at his organs at the same time he acknowledged he was still among the living. Something soft but threatening raked across his face; a movement of silky-legged spiders; a whispering suspicion of black, ragged vultures high above him, waiting, sweeping languidly back and forth across the sky. And through lids that were tightly closed he finally realized it must be a cloud of bats, whirling across the extremes of his inner vision, strafing his pain-wracked body. A horrible weight pressed down on him.

After an eternity of fearful anticipation and pain, he managed to open his eyes fully, and he saw the black blur closer onto him. It gradually came into focus as a cascade of raven hair, swishing to and fro, brushing his body, and thus he found he was without clothing of any kind. The weight pressing down on him was a body. A small and naked body. He had no understanding; he could not connect the dissimilarities.

He grabbed and pushed, and the housegirl, Co Hai, fell onto the floor. She was up in a scramble and back onto the bunk beside him.

He tried to back away and was run to ground against the wall. By God! She was naked . . . so was he.

Why was she naked?

She smiled at him with child-crone confidence as she thrust her smooth pelvis against him. Before Winter could orient himself, back from the world of fiery, black devils she had bent forward and thrust the hard, swollen nipple of one youthful breast into his gaping mouth. She moaned slightly as she rubbed her erect bud across his lips. Despite his swirling head and the nausea that threatened him throughout, the first real truth that penetrated his alcoholic numbness was how sweet she tasted.

He shook himself, experienced his skin rippling like the glossy coat of a stallion shaking off the flies that buzzed black and persistent over its body, as if he would so easily free himself from this thing feeding on his body. He drew back as far as the wall would allow and clamped his mouth shut. She squealed in pain, or passion, pulled his head forward, and bent over him, rubbing the tender-hard protrusion of both nipples alternately across his tight lips. He became aware, at the same instant, that her hand — the one that did not hold his head against her breasts — held his traitorous, erect member in a vice grip.

He pushed at her, but he was unbelievably weak, and the explosions in his head were chain reacting, magnifying, echoing and amplifying down into his vitals.

The housegirl pawed at Winter, kissing him across the back as she leaned forward over his face and shoulder. She leaned back, grabbed his hand and placed it between her legs. Again, despite himself, as he struggled weakly — gingerly, lest he make too violent a movement — he felt with a burgeoning flush of eroticism the moist softness of her hairless mound. Before he could react, she crossed her legs, trapping his hand, and reached again for his erection.

She was moaning, a ludicrous broken-language replay of the Taiwanese love stories she had rhapsodized over in the theaters of her youth: "Win-tahhh. You numbah wan . . . for soor . . . numbah wan . . . for soor. Do me, Win-tahr. Huck me. Numbah wan."

Winter, in a frenzy of desperation, thrust violently and threw her off him. She rolled onto the floor, undaunted. She crouched there, looking up at him with aroused adoration, but there seemed a lack of focus in her gaze. She crouched, ready to spring. Winter pushed her back, but even in his pitiable state, when she swung her head forward, leaning toward him, he smelled, above his own saturation, the sour reek of whiskey on her breath.

The girl — the child — was drunk!

It was at the edge of his intentions to ask who had gotten her drunk, when suddenly without any precognition, any warning sign, he vomited on her. All the trauma and the sickness of the day before, the horror and shame and guilt that had led him to the bars and the drinking with Mac after the square, came spewing forth. The cheap formaldehyde-laced beer, and bile generated by the adrenalin-charged arousal of untimely sex and promise, futility, and the final degradation to find she was drunk, gushed over her smooth nakedness. Into her black hair where it hung in long, glutinous strands, and between her tiny hard breasts and over her stomach. The foul, hot fountain washed over her olive skin and pooled between her legs before she could move.

Co Hai stared in shock, frozen in disbelief as Winter's body heaved and bucked. She could not have understood, even had she known the magnitude of his catharsis.

She squealed and leapt to her feet, scrambling away down the length of the aisle in the semi-dark hooch. Holding her hands in front of her in supplication for an end to the flood, she ran screaming from the hut. Her slim buttocks glistened in the early morning sun as she raced across the compound and into the showers. Winter fell back onto the bunk, dimly aware of the commotion and catcalls from early day-trick workers in the latrine.

He slipped into a sour but deep and dreamless sleep that may have lasted only moments. When he jerked awake, he knew he would live.

He was disappointed.

chapter nine

Sinh Loi

Viet Nam: August-September 1964

Staff Sergeant Winter was transferred without preamble to the Air Section in mid- August, to physically occupy the slot he already filled on paper. A new aviator, Captain Vernon Pyburn, had assumed command of the aviation mission. His first act of command was to issue a decree: *All personnel would have a specific job; all jobs would have a man filling them; the right person would be in each job.* On the day he was transferred, Winter was ordered to report to the CO's office in the aviation shack across from 3rd RRU headquarters. He reported and saluted.

"Sergeant Winter," the captain said, without preliminaries, "you occupy a slot in my Air Section. You will work it or lose it. If you lose it, whether you keep the stripes or not depends on the colonel; and it is dependent upon yours truly as to how you fill that slot, *if* you work it."

On his first day in the 3rd, Pyburn had picked up rumblings of discontent. He chose to determine for himself the degree of disinterest of the men in the Section. Since he was a flyer, and thought nobody in his right mind would choose to be anything else, he made the immediate assumption that it was by his own choice that Winter was not working his slot, enthusiastically or otherwise; had in fact avoided flying because of a reasonable interest in preserving his health and welfare. Not an unusual concern, considering the frailty of the unarmed reconnaissance aircraft with which Airborne Radio Direction Finding air section performed its mission.

"Sir —"

"I don't know how you've managed to slack your job, but that shit is out of scope. End of story. You'd better —"

"Just a goddamned minute, Captain!" The day had been crunch-ridden: the rush to find a replacement for himself at WHITE BIRCH when peremptorily ordered into the new job, angling for transportation to get to the hangar headquarters within the short time allotted him, and other Army misdirection. "Excuse me, *sir.*

You're new here, *sir*, and I don't think you quite have your ducks in a row . . . sir."

"The old boy network, that it, Sergeant?"

"That is *not* it! Sir, I've been here for five months, here in the Third. For five of those five months I've wanted into the Air Section. I'm a good oh-five-eight, I can do a good job at that and a good job as NCOIC . . . as soon as I learn the fly-boy shit."

"Where you going with this self-promotion?"

"Call it what you will, Captain, I *am* good. But I'm also married. I've got a family. For me to fly — for any oh-five-eight to fly in this program — requires a six-month extension of tour. I'm not about to extend in 'Nam for six more months just to go wheeling about the sky, bagging Air Medals. I'm career Army, but —"

"Now there's an admirable notion."

"You're right, sir. It *is* sort of a big deal. I'm kinda proud of the fact, and I'll tell you another big notion," Winter said forcefully, his temper building. He knew he might lose it in the face of this unwarranted abuse from a new officer, an officer who walked in, took a look at things, and without any solicitation of input proceeded to make his own uninformed judgment call. "I have nothing to do with this unit's application or misapplication of slots. You want to talk shit about manpower utilization, talk to the colonel. It's his personal policy, so I understand, that controls this job . . . sir."

Captain Pyburn glared at the sergeant before him. The air in the room was close. Beyond the building — built on the order of billets: screened, without solid walls, and thus not insulated in any sense — an angry buzz marked the progress of a T-28 as it sped down the strip and struggled into the air.

"You've got a hot head, Sergeant. Those stripes are not so firmly fixed that they can't be removed, you know."

"Oh, yeah, I know that, sir. Eleven years is how well I know that, Captain. But when they told me I was promoted to Staff Sergeant, I'd have taken that rocker if it meant latrine orderly instead of Air Section N.C.O.I.C."

"No doubt —"

"And the last thing I have to say, Sir, while I'm letting my ass overload my mouth, is this: if I am N.C.O.I.C. of this frigging section, the first thing that's going to happen — with your concurrence, of course, *Sir*—is that your goddamned pilots are going to start making briefings. The mission briefs, not just the airplane driver shit where they puzzle over Shell road maps and tell tall tales. They're going to know what the hell they're out there for, playing von Richthofen, thrashing about over this Land of Oddz. Bus drivers don't do us shit for good up there, honking some piece of laughable trash about the sky. We've got to have pilots who understand what the mission is directed at." There was a deadly, pregnant silence.

Winter then plunged ahead: In for a penny, in for a piastre. "Your pilots, most of them, are cleared for the mission. The rest are awaiting clearance; that was the plan when they were assigned to the Third, I understand. The cleared ones *must* come to mission briefings, learn what the operator is doing, so that when the op tells the pilot he needs to hang around an area for five or ten minutes longer to work a target, they'll hang around, and not give out with this 'schedule' bullshit, or start worrying about low fuel soon as they go wheels-up. This unit was not set up just to let these clowns log flight time and Air Medals.

"You want an N.C.O.I.C., Captain, you got one! You wanta get this shit together, we'll do it. Or you can bust my ass back to WHITE BIRCH where I will still do my job and do it damn well. Sir!" Winter maintained the full brace he'd assumed when he first reported in.

There was silence in the room. Another small aircraft brazened its way off the strip, outbound in desperation for anywhere else.

"At ease, Sergeant Winter. How is it you've just today come into this section, and you stand there and tell me things it's taken me two weeks to learn?" the captain said through tight lips.

"Like I said, Sir, I've been here five months. Sir," Winter leaned forward, the emphasis in his voice at one with body language, "who do these flyers think they are flying for? I've been working the ground mission at WHITE BIRCH. WHITE BIRCH ops, by radio, tip off the ops in the planes on skeds and freqs; we know the air ops, work with them, bunk with them. Air operators come right out of ground operations themselves. These guys talk. I've heard the reasons missions are aborted, reasons why they come back empty-handed. It cannot continue."

He glanced at the chair to the side; the captain motioned with his head; Winter sat.

"Laughable trash, huh? That what you think of my airplanes, good sergeant?" the captain asked straight-faced.

"Sir, I'm no wiseass. Sorry 'bout the blow-up—" Pyburn waved off the distraction "—and you should not mistake me for a problem. I am a good N.C.O., and I can run you a hell of a good section. But I must have cooperation. I know, for one thing, that I'm not alone in understanding the deficiencies we live with because of lack of interest and cohesion. We don't need prima donna pilots who wish they were flying gunships or fighter planes—they have a job to do here. And we don't need snobs for ops, guys who extend for Air and think they're somehow above the common herd. We need teams, ops and pilots who can get it together and do what's necessary to win this sucker and get us all out of here."

"Eleven years, huh? Korea?" the captain said.

"Fifth and Eleventh Marines. You?"

"Seventh Infantry Division. Want a cup of coffee?" Before Winter could respond, the captain yelled, "Phillips!" and stood up from the desk, extending his hand across to the startled sergeant.

* * *

Winter knew many of the Air Section personnel: eight operators, not counting himself, all enlisted, and nine pilots whom he mostly did not know, consisting of the captain, one lieutenant, and seven warrant officers, W-1 through W-4. The mechanics, supply, admin, and avionics people worked out of the line hanger; they did not have security clearances and, to a man, never entered the Operations building.

Among the pilots was a triumvirate of strange beings who had developed in just a few short months a reputation for erratic behavior. It seemed erratic to ASA personnel; it was not so unusual among pilots, whether because they were really different as a breed, or because they believed that wearing wings represented an obligation to be different. Whatever the motivation, the three, all young, known collectively as the *International Brigade,* exhibited all the reckless abandon of their predecessors three wars removed, in flying or in pursuit of less lofty goals on the earth.

Warrant Officer-One Helmut Stoetzel, hometown Cleveland, had grown up in Mexico where his father was the sometimes

American representative for a fertilizer firm in Ohio. Stoetzel, at fifteen, had learned to fly with a barnstorming four-man aerobatic team drifting around south of the border, shilling crowds where they could draw them. Supplemental jobs included the odd gun running, illegal-immigrant-into-US insertion, moving untaxed and non-duty merchandise about, and various opportunistic schemes to earn enough to keep the aircraft together. Stoetzel had worked his way up from gofer to fill-in pilot, flying an eclectic mélange of antique and decrepit craft, and he'd never flown a plane he didn't love.

Flying for a last-ditch Panamanian freight outfit at the age of seventeen, having finally shucked the rigors of school in the States and the control of his parents in Mexico, he had just survived a near-fatal crash in an aircraft that was neither certifiable nor serviceable when he heard about the US Army's warrant officer flight program. It sounded heaven-sent. At least different. To prove his American citizenship, both to the border guard in El Paso and the Army recruiter in that same town, he'd had to sneak into his parents' home and dig for hours for his childhood passport.

For all his time in the Army, with basic training, ground and flight schools, and a short tour with an armored outfit at Fort Bliss, Texas, when he reached Viet Nam Stoetzel was still only nineteen years old. He spoke good, serviceable English with a solid Tex-Mex border-Spanish flavor.

In contrast, WO1 Juan Batiste Orozco, Mexican-American by descent, had grown up in Germany where his father, a US Army NCO, managed to homestead for twelve years in Kaiserslautern Military District Housing Office. Orozco came by American citizenship legitimately; there was nothing even marginally damp about his back. His father, Mexican born, had enlisted in the US Army while visiting a dying sister in Puerto Rico; he had earned his citizenship before the boy was born. Growing up in Germany as he had, Orozco spoke better *Deutsch* than he did Spanish, far better German than Stoetzel, who had forgotten whatever he had ever known of the language of his parents.

The third member of the band, another newly crafted warrant officer, John C. "Giancarlo" Travaglia, was a naturalized American, having come into the world by way of the Neopolitan suburb of

Posillipo. He spoke fair American English and, surprisingly, gauged against his two companions, spoke his native Italian impeccably. The International Brigade had picked up their collective alias in Ground School at Fort Rucker. They reveled in the association and the title.

The first day in his new job, Winter struggled with the arcane improbabilities of flight mission schedules, tasking the Vietnamese Air Section for joint operations, a failure in concept and in fact. It was a job he had been warned of when told he was going to Air, and one he did not relish. He had worked with Vietnamese ops in SABER TOOTH Operations. He knew they were individually as good as anything the Americans had. He had also heard them talk about their own pilots, so unreliable that the ARVN ops taunted them openly. ARVN ARDF pilots were uniformly scorned by American and Australian flyers. As Winter worked his way skeptically through the unfamiliar task, the International Brigade stormed in the door of Ops, targeting the coffeepot.

"Glad you weeth us, man," said Stoetzel, holding out his hand to Winter.

"Hey . . . yeah, good show, Sarge!"

"Aahh-h-h, Signor, we do great theengs in thee air . . . *Avvocati delle cause perse!*"

"*Herr Leutnant* Zwick," Orozco called, first in the door. "You hear what happens up in Two Corps?" When he addressed Air Section's Operations Officer and XO, the Brigade burst into laughter.

"Yeah, peecture thees . . ." Orozco said, spreading his arms wide in popish splendor before the startled Zwick could answer, "got thees little coun-try, known as thee asshole of the world. Vee-et-Namm! 'bout to get her stuff blow away by thee bad guys. So, 'long comes thee guys in white hats, shit-stain sneakers, and — get thees now; thees important — and their *hal-lies!* Don' for-get, das important to thee story.

"So-o, this hal-lie, thees big humpin' mamacita Proosha — now known of an alias, wheech shall remain unmentioned but eet ees spelled with a capital *Deutschland* — shee comes to the haid of thee good ol' hyou-hess-of-hay who has, by thee way, already come to the haid of thees little asshole coun-try. Got thee peecture?"

He did not wait for confirmation. Zwick's face held the look of a man with a kidney problem, stuck in a queue, number three at a one-urinal relief station. "Well, let's say thees hal-lie goes as far weeth haid as they dare; dey won't send any good ol' boys, what we reel-ly need—no stormtroopers, you know . . . I mean, where are thee fuckin' *Standartenfuhrer*, the Hess-Hess, when we need theem?—so, rather, they send . . . guess what? What? Ri-i-i-ght! Bow wows. *Hunden.* Guard dogs!"

"What is this crap?" Lieutenant Zwick demanded in a strangled voice, irritated by the obvious send-up. Zwick liked quick solutions, quick punch lines. Zwick also deplored, to a fine degree, his enforced attachment to a desk at anytime, something he was committed to as the second ranking officer in the Air Section, an Executive Officer, of sorts. He was also Flight Operations Officer as well as, in the opinion of most, a spontaneous jerk by way of cultural proclivities, genetics, and schooling. An Air Force Academy washout, he was a thoroughly rejected would-be fighter pilot, Errol Flynn mustache and all and, having found his way into the Army's sorry substitute for an air *force*, thus allowing him some kind of flight—slipping the bounds of earth, as it were—he continually pushed the envelope.

"*Dos* hondred. Two *cientos.* Count 'em!" Orozco continued, glancing around at his audience, holding up two fingers. "Two hondred blooded German shepherds, prime condeetion. Guard- and attack-trained. Thees to support our lates' brillian' strategy, thee Stra-teg-ic Hamlet ploy, of course." Orozco's border shuck- and-jive immediately morphed into a cleaner brand of Anglo, to no one's surprise. "And the Zips can really use the dogs, don't you know. I mean, these hamlets are being shit upon something fierce. So, the Krauts shipped the guard dogs to the land of the big experiment—Two Corps."

Winter tried working through the voice-over, but was caught up in the tale. Several enlisted men drifted into Air Section's space to listen, drawn to the Brigade's latest exploits and stories, knowing their predilection for the bizarre. Stoetzel stirred his coffee with a survival knife. He shook his head and glared at the greasy slick on the surface of the brew.

"Well, the beasts arrived in country, off-loaded in Nha Trang. They were all shipped to Than Quan Song District for distribution.

McNamara must have creamed his shorts . . . means to help implement his silly-ass scheme. The goddamned Zips were ecstatic. They couldn't believe a bunch of alien strangers—a redundant repetition for you —with absolutely no ties or obligations, would do them a number like that. So the big cheese, the District Chief, who's a Zip infantry colonel, calls all the people in his region together to throw a party. Celebrate their new friends and good fortune. They invited the *Deutsch* ambassador, flew him up from Saigon with his entire staff; the Thirty-Fourth Group choppered them in from Nha Trang to Dalat. Red carpet, torches, full dress military honor guard. The real razz-ma-tazz." He smiled enigmatically, ending his story, nodding to himself, satisfied with the outcome.

"And?" Zwick frowned and looked around in panic. Had he missed the punch line?

"And, what?" said Orozco. "Mothers had a big feast, is all. No big deal."

"No big deal! *No big deal!* You fucking clown, what's with this . . . this shit? What about the celebration? What's . . . why'd you tell this . . . this *nothing!*" Zwick sputtered. He rose and came around the desk, his expression pissed-clueless. "No big deal!"

Winter squirmed, uneasy. There was an air of suspense in the room, and he felt the same left-out indignation that irritated Zwick. Oh, man! he thought. What kind of squirrely outfit have I fallen prey to?

"Oh, yeah," Orozco added, his liquid brown eyes calm over the rim of the coffee cup, "did I mention . . . the menu? At the feast, they served the dogs. I don't mean they *fed* the dogs; I mean they *served* the fuckers. They were the meal. Ate 'em. Two . . . hundred . . . German . . . shepherds. Almost had enough to go around, too, but they had a lot of guests. Betts in the Thirty-Fourth told me that's the best dog he's had since Korea. And the Zips sure seemed to appreciate the Krauts' thoughtfulness. "Man," he mused finally into the stunned silence, "where *are* the S.S. troops when you need them?" He smiled into the coffee cup. The grease slick was still there.

Winter thought of the long days ahead, the empty skies, the notion of being trapped for hours in tiny craft high above the earth. He moaned and put his head down.

* * *

It was a five-day-a-week war, Monday through Friday. Saturdays were given over to soccer, whoring, drinking, and bitching about the illogical persistence of the war . . . as were Mondays through Fridays. What the hell, the GIs argued, why're we over here, risking death and destruction, crotch rot, and venereal disease when the Vietnamese government won't even draft their own young men to fight the war? Sundays never came around; if they existed, they passed in a haze of hangovers and sunburn.

Life in the hooches did not improve. The GIs lived well enough, with locally hired servants for cleaning, bunk-making, menial-labor obligations. Mama-San, the ubiquitous title for all female hootch and messhall workers, came and went in the various jobs like turnover at a cheap drive-in. The 3rd RRU became a training ground for these low-skilled workers. The 3rd paid the least of all local American military units, which was good as far as it went; only it meant that when the local hires had gained a modicum of skills requiring the intellect of plant life — daubing black polish on boots, swirling a filthy rag through filthy water and across filthy floors and steps, raising mosquito netting, and stretching damp, sweat-stained sheets to a tension that would not encourage anything to bounce — the girls would forgo their labors for the GIs of the 3rd and seek increased wages elsewhere.

Because of her shocking treatment — her spurned offerings — his hooch maid, Co Hai, had departed the day of Winter's barbarous rejection, and had shopped the helicopter companies, 39th Signal Battalion, various ordnance groups, and other labor markets until swallowed up in the maw of American military growth, never to be seen again at Davis Station.

Though it might be argued that, lacking these minimal functional responsibilities, GIs lived well, they did not live well. They were, until proven otherwise, still in Viet Nam.

After his transfer, once the pecking order was established with accompanying qualifications, Winter began flying immediately. He privately began a journal for later use — what, he didn't know — after his first couple of flights, or as they were commonly known, "frights." His notes, incorporating abbreviated and later-found-to-be-almost-incomprehensible English, sometimes made their way into his letters home, where his wife, shaking her head in resigned confusion, ignored them, assuming them to be a means of downplaying tensions.

* * *

"*Sor!*" I barked, holding a brace the envy of long, gray lines. "Specialist Fifth Class Luther Emanuel.Brenner reporting to the N.C.O.I.C., Air Section, as ordered, *sor!*" The messhall grew quiet and heads turned toward our little tableau at his table.

Winter stared like the naive twit he is. Likely couldn't believe his eyes. No more could I: he wore Staff Sergeant's stripes. Too early in the ay-em for that kind of shock.

"Jeez-us Christ! Has it come to this?" Winter boggled.

"It has, sor! And I'll be bloody well damned if it's not a poor showing. How are you, shitbird?" Other than smelling a little gamier than normal, my man David was . . . my man David. Beyond crushing the breath from me, he showed no excitement at my presence.

"You don't look Filipino," Winter sagely observed as we sat down at the greasy table.

"Didn't take," I explained. "May have to go back for another tour. But before we launch into this long-lost-buddy routine," I said, watching his eyebrows rise, "I've a query? Coming through the gate, I saw Air Police in those new jungly fatigues I been reading about, the ones 'all the men in Vietnam are wearing.' Well, looking at you, that's obviously bullshit, but why A.P.s? I mean, here's old Joe the G.I., slovenly and unlovely as always, wearing old-style fatigues — starched, of course; it's always smart to wear starched garments in the world's worst climate, in the jungle — while these slackards, who never get farther than fifty feet from a flush toilet, are outfitted in the latest fashion? 'Splain me that, my man."

"Spare me, Brenner," he said. "Don't start your three-sixty-five here tiltin' at windmills. OK? I mean, the friggin' Air Force holds political trumps over us all. But tell me . . . Jeezus, it's been two years. More. How ya' been?" My man appeared to be adjusting well to surprise.

"Been the same. You know me. Managed not to get busted for two years in the P.I.," I bragged.

"Musta' been dull duty."

"Like Two Rock Ranch. When do you read me on board?"

"In Viet Nam?" When he said it, Winter looked as if he meant Neverland.

"Here. The Air Section."

"When'd you get in country? I assume, since I haven't seen you, you just arrived."

"Yesterday. Landed here at Tan Son Nhut, where some geek major came on board before we deplaned, told all A.S.A. and M.I. troops to remain on board, the rest to go. Gave us a brief security brief. Mostly emphasized we remove our A.I.S. collar brass before going public. Said there was a bounty on our elite heads, M.I. and A.S.A. True?" Already, I thought, the myths abounded.

"True enough, far as it goes. We haven't actually lost anyone to a bounty, far as I know, but it makes the boys careful about where they go at night around here. For starters, don't let a cyclo driver take you over the Bien Hoa Bridge. As for Air Section, you gotta spend six months in the mission, on the ground at WHITE BIRCH or SABER TOOTH, and then you have to extend for six months in 'Nam to go Air."

I must have registered a lack of enthusiasm. Winter added, "Yeah, I know. That's so much pig shit. And no, I haven't lost my reason; I did not extend for this job. I got promoted into it and didn't have to extend. Why? You interested in flying?"

"Seems like where it's at. The rest of this magic kingdom fails to attract."

"Wait until you visit the fair city beyond."

"Sai-Gon? City of Lights with sampans? Yeah, I can imagine, especially with Frogs as role models. Went downtown with some dude last night to eat at an Indian restaurant—good chops, by the way—and what I saw did not leave me clamoring for lots of time off work. Place is all shot up, screwed-over something terrible. Was that from last year's coup? Or just the way they like it?"

"Mostly coup. Ever since the coup, and Kennedy's assassination three weeks after, this place has looked like a movie set for some bad double-U double-U two movie."

"Kennedy's assassination?"

"Those ubiquitous rumors, my man. Too close in time not to be linked."

Another myth? Solid as soup. "Not what's in the travel books, my man. How's Nickie? And the urchin?" I had never met Winter's wife, but the pictures he'd kept on his desk in Asmara were enough to entice one to consider the matrimonial state.

"Good. All good," he answered lamely. I could tell he had a million questions—tough shit. "Where you gonna be, do you know?" he wanted to know.

"Here. Sai Gon. This place called WHITE BIRCH, I guess. Is that the Ops Center?"

"Collection site. Yeah. You're a fast study, Luther; three-four months at WHITE BIRCH, you'll probably be up on the mission enough I'd support your transfer into the Section. But you'd still have to extend the six months. You up for that?" He stared at me as if he thought it unlikely I would answer "Yes."

I wasn't about to commit to that yet. "Maybe by the time three-four months passes, I'll know. Where you living?"

"N.C.O. hooch by the office," Winter answered resignedly. "The First Sergeant's office. The C.O. don't count in that arrangement. Veterans are allowed to refer to it as Orderly Room. Second hooch from the fire bell. Can't miss it."

A pair of warrant officers and a couple of loud enlisted guys, all wearing flight gear, stomped into the messhall, making sounds about 100-mile-an-hour green tape and depressurized fuel tanks and how bad Charlie was in the shit. They all nodded toWinter.

"See you later, Dave." I nodded at the newcomers, shook my head when he rose as if to introduce us. "Later."

"Where you bunkin'?" he asked as I got up.

"I don't remember the hut number. Right next to a guy named Axelson."

"*Sinh loi!*"

That was the first time I heard the term. "Come again."

"*Sinh loi!* Sorry 'bout that!" Winter said.

"You're sorry about what?" Out to lunch there for a moment.

"That's what '*Sinh loi*' means: 'sorry about that'," he explained.

"Axelson, you mean?"

"Just kidding. He's okay. How about we dine at the E.M. trough after I get off? About eighteen-thirty?"

"'kay," I agreed. And just to jangle his bells, said, "Couldn't we make that nearer six-thirty?" Choking off his response, I said, "See ya" and headed off through the maze of tables.

"By the way," he said while I could still hear him, "if you think the Air Farce's wearing of the new, comfortable, well-designed jungle fatigues is anguish, note the weapons these guys are carrying," directing me toward the old M-14s the operators leaned in the corner—both warrants carried .45s for sidearms—"and know that the airdales also carry the new M-16. La-di-da!" Someone at the next table laughed.

I left Winter, thinking of the phrase he'd used. Vietnamese for "sorry about that." The Viet was new to me, but in just over twenty-four hours in-country, I'd already heard, probably a dozen times, the utterly trite and insincere "Sorry 'bout that!" A common Vietnam-service expression, I concluded, picked up by GI linguists and used for everything from Gee, it's regretful that only one night's bliss resulted in your pregnancy to So your mother, wife, and seven children are dead in an alley, along with the village dog and your leprous uncle. I checked it off: one more indicator I probably wasn't going to want to retire in Viet Nam.

* * *

At Sea in the Atlantic ; July 1958

The long, sweltering afternoon of September 17, 1862, produced the bloodiest statistics of an already record-breaking conflict of horror. The campaign that led to this infamous tribute had begun a few days earlier when General Robert E. Lee's forces, driven west from the Catoctin Mountains of Maryland, came to bay near Sharpsburg along a creek that rose that day from obscurity to glorious infamy: Antietam!

Desultory engagements at first, sharp cavalry scraps, and probing that filled the next few days until the 17th, a day when insignificant names became etched in the annals of military conflict: The Irish Brigade, losing 540 men in the first hour of battle; General French, a Union commander, losing 450 men killed in the first five minutes of a hapless assault on Confederate regulars at the Sunken Road, known thereafter as Bloody Lane. The Cornfield, Dunker Church, Middle Bridge, the West Woods—Antietam!

That first day claimed 2,108 dead, 9,540 wounded, and 753 missing among Federal forces; 1,546 dead, 7,752 wounded, and 1,018 missing Confederates: a total of 22,719 total American casualties in one single, bloody day there at Sharpsburg.

* * *

Sergeant David D. Winter of MATCU-64, a disparate element of the Marines' cobbled-together Marine Air Group-26, had discovered the bronze tablet on a pedestal at the aft edge of the hangar deck the first morning aboard ship, learning details of the battle for which the aircraft carrier had been named. It was all new to him. Thirty-six hours before, he'd been unaware of the existence of this particular floating arsenal. But a dustup in Lebanon brought him and his unit, from NAAS Edenton, together with other squadrons from Cherry Point and New River, all North Carolina Marine air stations, to roll-call on the USS Antietam (CVA-36). Scuttlebutt foretold eventual insertion into the biblical country in a manner inimical to the interests of the bad guys.

Whoever the hell that happened to be this week.

The ship commanded Pier 12 in Norfolk for two more days as bombs, bullets, and beans were crammed aboard, along with the aircraft of four fighter squadrons, one observer fixed-wing squadron, and two helicopter units, all crane-lifted aboard. Some 3,000 Marines infiltrated passageways and a few billet areas; the majority of the squadrons' enlisted personnel slept on cots and blanket rolls on the unyielding surface of the hanger deck, beneath aircraft–their reason for existence–jammed wingtip to wingtip in some esoteric logic of combat loading.

The ship had operated off the Florida coast out of Mayport, training navy and Marine pilots in carrier landing procedures, before dispatch to Norfolk for embarkation. As a training prop, the Antietam marginally functioned with less than fifty-percent normal personnel complement.

Norfolk sweltered; still, the ubiquitous bitching was surprisingly contained. Any degree of tolerance could be ascribed to standard

Marines' hyper-anticipation, heading as they were into the unknown with the likelihood of a scrap. What with last-minute inoculations, cramped spaces, and uncertainty, the Marines and sailors produced a satisfactory number of fisticuff encounters to take off the edge. The ship sailed on the third day after Winter's midnight boarding.

Later, he would recall the entire episode with a detached sense of novelty, a measurable remove from the daily boredom of barracks life and endless training. He would remember few things with relative clarity: lounging on the hanger-deck fantail below the lip of the aft flight deck, mesmerized by a gently rolling, empty, gray-green Atlantic beneath scudding clouds; moving tentatively along passageways in the meager red glow from safety lights; performing a benediction of hands on 250- and 500-lb. bombs anchored to the bulkheads where Marines slept on cots stretched inches above. One frustrating memory was of working without success to repair the ship's hopelessly inoperable radar and communications equipments. At the time, it had left him mystified as to how the Marines might be able to implement GCI concepts without GCI equipment, should it come to a shooting war there in the Monte Carlo of the Middle East.

And he would remember Red Borders, diesel mechanic, veteran of the Canal and a cold walk home from the Changjin Reservoir, in that soft whisper of his, apprising Lieutenant Stein of a basic fact: in combat, possibly in the offing, unpopular officers sometimes suffered a high probability of casualty, even death, and the threat did not always come from the enemy side of the MLR. After this frugal bit of wisdom was examined, there was an amazing attitude adjustment in the previously arrogant young lieutenant.

Just a matter of getting the word out.

But whatever the explanation for the crisis that had precipitated embarkation, it came undone, chaos averted, and the ship and its destroyer escorts heeled hard to starboard and dashed off at flank speed to play about the benign waters of the Caribbean, leaving the Med and the Atlantic to fend for themselves.

When Winter, in September, had disembarked in Norfolk and convoyed back to Edenton, it was to a ghost base, tenant units packed and, for the most part, gone, moved south to merge with their parent 2nd Marine Air Wing at Cherry Point.

Winter took that—along with very nearly missing the birth of his first child, a son, there where his new wife had languished in despair while he cruised the seas—as an omen, and severed his relationship with The Corps.

chapter ten

Don't Mean Nothin'

Viet Nam: October 1964

Just past 0700 Winter was walking off the effects of messhall breakfast and Brenner's surprising appearance, strolling up the flight ramp past parked aircraft toward headquarters, when a Jeep roared up from behind and squealed to a halt. A Spec-4 he recognized from the S-3 shop peered at him over the top of sunglasses. "Sarge, you gotta go back to the Orderly Room. See Top."

"What now?" As close to a snarl as he would allow himself.

The specialist threw up his hands in mock fear. "Hey, just bearin' the message, Sarge. But I think you been tapped to honcho fam-fire for some new guys." He smiled without a trace of humor. "Top held a drawing. You're the newest N.C.O. You lost."

"Great." Winter turned and started back down the line past the broken, the bent, the disenfranchised aircraft of the Army's TWA — Teenie Weenie Airlines; the 3rd's birds — and then the sleek, deadly looking Hueys, gunships of the 68th Armed Helicopter Company.

"Doncha wanna ride?" the specialist taunted. It was all of fifty yards to Davis Station.

Winter strode along without reply. The Jeep's clatter faded beneath the thunder of a Mohawk's engine run-up on a stand behind him.

At the company, First Sergeant Jonach informed him he'd have to pull detail for part of the day. As the Jeep driver had indicated, it was to shepherd a group of men, new in country, out to the makeshift range for familiarization firing of their TO&E weapons. The only NCO in the armory was on sick call — third time this month, same complaint: pissing broken glass. "And *this* First Sergeant," spoke the First Sergeant, "isn't about to let a little incidental V.D, mess up the training roster." Winter remembered his own trip to the *range* when he'd first come in country. An exercise! A waste of time, gasoline, ammo, and patience.

Sorry 'bout that!

The First Shirt had already telephoned regrets to the Air Section for Winter's untimely absence.

He walked past his hooch to the motor pool, found the PFC designated as his driver, and instructed him to check out a six-by and pick up his fares at the Mail Room. Winter went back to his hooch, grabbed his web belt with canteen and first aid pouch, and walked to the Arms Room, where he drew his weapon. As he checked the bore and trigger housing group of the M-14 for mold, dirt, and spider eggs, he noticed a rack of old carbines, circa WWII-Korea. He searched for a Garand M-1, in his mind still the best infantry weapon ever built, but seeing none he asked the private behind the counter to sign him out an M-2 carbine, the one with automatic fire capability. He didn't know the status of the weapons, whether assigned to someone or not, but the armory clerk couldn't have cared less. He took back Winter's issue M-14, returned his weapon card to him, and snatched one of the carbines at random from the rack, scribbled the serial number on a greasy sign-out sheet, and thrust it at Winter for signature without ever meeting his eyes.

There were nine new guys with weapons milling about in the street before the Mail Room, grab-assing, conversing in John Wayne dialogue. On the steps sat two Spec-4s with rifles, one of them Winter recognized from WHITE BIRCH from months before. The man had been gone from the unit for some time now for some reason Winter couldn't remember. Was it up country to Det J at Phu Bai? Didn't *seem* right. Who knew?

The second soldier, a stranger, had the palest skin Winter had ever seen short of an albino. Jailhouse pallor. The thought struck him as funny, and everyone stopped and stared at him curiously when he laughed out. Impatient, he waved them into formation as the deuce-and-a-half pulled up. Winter stepped up on the passenger side step of the two-and-a-half-ton truck and leaned over the bed, saw the open ammo box partially filled with the .30 cal. ball ammo he expected, and waved everyone aboard. With his borrowed weapon, he wore a bandolier of .30 cal. carbine ammo slung around his neck like a *pistolero* in Emiliano Zapata's marching band. The two Spec-4s, tantalizingly slow in mounting up, Winter saw, were letting him know that they were only tolerating him.

Considering the recalcitrant soldiers, he suddenly recalled the story on the one he recognized: SP4 Moncrief. Of course, *that* guy. Moncrief had gone home on emergency leave—someone in his family died or the mule was sick, some crisis—and while back in the states had pulled political strings to get reassigned out of the combat zone. But here he was, back in town.

Sorry 'bout that!

The PFC driver drove like any local national, getting into the swing of things as soon as the last man boarded. Winter, riding shotgun, felt a momentary flicker of compassion as he listened to yells and curses from the passengers bouncing around in the truck bed. But empathy passed, like a flickering warning bout of bowel gas presaging worse afflictions.

When the truck left the surfaced road west of the airbase, the rough ride began in earnest. The route continued west from Tan Son Nhut toward the Song Vam Co Dong, a colorful name for a river which was only a muddy ditch. The VCD owed any distinction to the fact it was one of the few streams in the country that did not empty eventually into the Mekong.

Shortly before they would have reached the Vam Co Dong proper, they parked on the edge of a scattering of bamboo and stucco huts at the edge of a small stream, an assemblage too mean and forlorn to be called a village. The only other structure visible above the ubiquitous palm trees was a square stucco tower some two hundred yards away from the stream. Its function was unheralded, its demeanor scrofulous and battered. Winter could not tell if the scabrous appearance was due to weather and neglect, or shellfire. Insulators on a wooden plaque at a top corner spoke of a French electrical heritage: ancient history—there were no wires attached now.

The soldiers piled off the truck, dusting themselves, cursing the driver. Moncrief, the appellate transferee, got into the PFC's face and made noises about doing him bodily harm, at which the PFC invited the Spec-4 to "take his best shot." A business-as-usual interlude in the daily life of thrilled-to-be-here GIs. Winter, ignoring the histrionics, set the soldiers about their tasks of burning up perfectly good ammunition in a meaningless drill.

The space that served for a firing range was merely a flat, treeless, open area flanking the stream, with no water buffalo or rice paddies at risk. There were no targets, no range safety officer, though it could argued that was the purpose of Winter's presence; that and keeping the exercise on track. Beyond Winter's hapless admonition to keep all firing down range, there were no rules. Down range had no meaning beyond *away from each other, the truck, and if convenient, the scattering of local nationals* that had quickly gathered. Mostly children, they'd seen this drill before.

Winter did attempt to impose a minor bit of beneficial guidance by instructing the firing party to practice loading and unloading magazines in quick exchanges. No one seemed to think he might ever need such a skill. The firing consisted solely of pointing and pulling the trigger–at an attacking clump of brush or a threatening muddy spot on the ground. It served no purpose other than possibly exposing the soldier to the visceral sensation of actually pulling the trigger. Everything they had learned in basic training was months or years behind. Unlike Marines and some few combat-oriented Army troops in the Rangers, Special Forces, or the better grunt outfits, soldiers — especially ASA troops — were not inculcated into the combat rifleman mystique.

As his twelve charges — the driver included, who took an M-14 from the cab and joined the new guys — ate up taxpayers' money, Winter fired off two clips of carbine ammo. Nothing new there, and having no banana clips to incite sustained bursts of frivolity, he lost interest and ceased firing. He put his weapon and remaining ammo back in the truck, after inserting a full magazine, and waited for the process to come to a halt. It did within ten minutes when the ammo was exhausted.

Winter noted that none of the troops had retained even one full magazine to sustain them, should they be attacked here or on the way back to Davis Station. He and his trusty, rusty carbine would have to do it all. And he knew it was exactly the kind of thing some observant little commissar might have noted of the Americans' behavior. Winter thought such shortage of vision particularly stupid of the driver, as he must often have made this run. But he'd never been attacked; therefore it could not happen. When he mentioned to the driver what he thought should be obvious, the

PFC jumped into the cab, started the truck, yelling for everyone to board up or miss chow, and made some obviously smart-ass reply which Winter could not hear over the roar of the engine.

When the last new man was part way over the edge of the bed, the driver rammed the shift lever into gear and the truck shot forward several yards before skidding to a halt, practically in the door of a ramshackle house. Winter spoke sharply, "Hey, hotshot. Give it a rest, will you. There're people all around us." He glanced into the side mirror just as the truck, jammed into reverse, shot backward. Winter saw her an instant before there was a dull, insignificant thump.

"Stop the truck!" He leapt from the cab and sprinted toward the back where the men in the truck bed were quickly gathering, looking over the bed to the muddy ground below.

A tiny girl lay like a disjointed doll beneath the edge of the bed, one leg caught below the huge, nubbly tire of the six-by. Several men jumped from the truck bed. One of them quickly took in the scene and ran forward to the cab. He grabbed the PFC driver by the jacket, jerked him from the truck and threw him aside. He mounted to the cab and put the truck in gear, eased the clutch out, and pulled slowly forward. As he did, the first screams erupted from the child and, at the same time, they heard screams from a young woman scuttling forward awkwardly from the dilapidated house on grotesquely twisted legs.

Winter, yelling "Get back, everybody," knelt down and examined the child. She was terrified and obviously in pain, but he saw no blood. He noticed quickly that the tire imprint in the mud ran over her leg below the knee; and the leg was covered in mud and bits of straw from the ground; no protruding bone splinters, no ruptured flesh. Where she had been overrun, the ground was muddy and soft beneath her leg.

"God—" Winter intoned into a void, invoking the wish that the child might have been the beneficiary of a bit of a break, along with her misfortune. He put his hands under her body, fighting the screaming woman, who attempted to wrap herself around the child for possession. When he lifted the casualty carefully from the ground, the broken leg dangled at an unlikely angle. But there was no sign of the wheel having run over her body. He felt a flush of thankfulness.

"You, driver, what's your name . . . Cantor? . . . you get back . . . away from everything." The PFC looked stunned, immobile. "Bailey," Winter, looking at one soldier's name tag, spoke tersely, "give me a hand here. We need to get her in the cab. You get in, take her when we lift her in." The soldier jumped into the passenger seat, and Winter motioned to a couple of the others. "Let's lift her, *carefully* . . . onto Bailey's lap." The two men moved reluctantly forward, took the child gently, and Winter moved, running interference for them toward the open door.

"Moncrief, get around to the other side. You drive," he spoke to the Spec-4 before him, at the same time motioning him out of the way. "You know the way back from here?" He didn't look at the man as he spoke, assuming compliance.

"Ahh, fuck this. Ain't nothing but a goddamned Zip. She don't—"

His teeth clacked resoundingly together when Winter's fist smashed him in the mouth. The sergeant didn't bother following up, leaving Moncrief to spasm on the muddy ground, but ordered, "Everybody, get on the truck. Help that woman into the front seat with Bailey" he nodded toward the hysterical Vietnamese cripple earmarked as mother. "I'll drive." He turned toward the driver. "Cantor, you get behind the cab and give me directions. To the Thirty-second. Now!" Winter gave him a shove.

Two men helped Moncrief off the ground and pushed him roughly toward the truck, leaving it to him to clamber into the back. One of the men, who claimed to know a little French, turned and spoke a few words to some of the nearby Vietnamese. When Winter gave him a questioning look, the PFC shrugged and said, "Hey, I don't know if any of them speak French or not; I just told them we're taking her to a doctor. We are, aren't we?" Winter nodded jerkily and jumped in the driver's seat.

"Can't hurt," the soldier mumbled.

There was no conversation at first, the soldiers consumed by fear for the child. More likely, Winter thought, they were astounded by the speed with which it had happened, with which calamity had overcome the child and her family in the midst of a clear, cloudless, otherwise non-threatening day. But after a couple of miles, Winter could hear the rumble of conversation behind him in the truck bed, one voice increasingly louder, more strident. Then, above Cantor's occasional subdued instructions for turns, the voice rose clearly, screaming into the wind.

"I'm gonna have your ass, Winter. You're going to Leavenworth, you bastard. Punch me, will you. I'll have your stripes in a shoebox." His pronunciation was amazingly clear.

Ignoring the bombast, Winter heard after a few moments another voice in reply. "Moncrief, you asshole, I suggest you re-think everything after reveille. We all saw you attack the sergeant, and I don't think it would take the captain long to decide where charges might be pressed." There was a long, silent moment. "You follow my reasoning, don't you?"

Winter, still ignoring the voices from the back, couldn't avoid thinking that Moncrief's past sins—trying to parley his body from harm with political overtures—sat well with no one. And it was obvious that his history was known, even to these new guys.

* * *

Didn't take me long to get the feel of Sai Gon. Tan Son Nhut. WHITE BIRCH. Operations. The mysteries of this esoteric assignment were not necessarily related to enemy engagement.

Winter was right: the Air Force had a lock on priorities, though they had far less people in 'Nam than the Army. Altogether, best I could determine, we had about sixteen thousand troops here, mostly advisers, Special Forces, logistics weenies, Air Force, Navy, and intelligence spooks. Even then, early days, we had every alphabet outfit in existence setting up shop, posturing for power and control, each one convinced they were the entire effort. ASA, for starters, though shrouded in euphemisms. CIA Asian legends, carrying exotic weaponry, drifting menacingly in and out of the scene like wraiths. State in their seersucker suits; NSA in nondescript, unmarked, shiny new jungle fatigues; DIA, DoD, ONI, AFIS, Tic-Tac-Toe, Riki Tiki Tavi. Like a medieval court, the jesters flailed for attention around the king's throne, downtown in the Embassy.

The Army was handling the bulk of the would-be war, doing it with outdated weapons and equipment. Always the case, taking a whole new war to catch up with the last one; always fighting a war with last war's weapons.

On the black market GIs bought personal weapons, ranging from anything resembling a model 1911A1 .45 caliber Colt semi-automatic pistol, to Swedish K submachine guns — everything in between. Within a few days of the Air Force issuing the M-16 to Air Police, gate guards, and their own internal perimeter, the new weapon began showing up on the black market, where we bought them back. Every wall locker on Tan Son Nhut held one or more illegal weapons. But, as the man said, you do what you gotta do. Some grand thinker's asinine policy dictated that trained Army troops, living and working in a combat zone, must exist without immediate access to their issue weapons. Those were kept safely locked in the company Arms Room; keys were held by the armorer and the CO, either or both of whom might or might not be available come attack time.

Downtown, Slickie boys on motorbikes and motorcycles — mounted bandits and hit men for whichever faction paid them — were called Cowboys for their emulation of movie screen antics. Prostitutes, in addition to walking the streets dressed as people, worked in bars and practiced their trade in a full range of venues, from a thin, dirty mattress on the ground in an alley, to exotic digs in the best hotels. Some had even taken to working the streets on motor bikes. The logistics of that enterprise challenged the imagination.

Indian and Chinese nationals cornered certain trades: restaurants, tailor shops, and money-changing. Whatever the legal exchange rate was for dollars converted into piastres or dzong, it was always at least double that on the street. Then troops discovered the locals wanted cigarettes more than dollars, so GIs bought their full ration, whether they smoked or not, and everything they did not use themselves they sold on the black market. GIs paid one dollar a carton for cigarettes in military exchanges. That was upgraded an unreasonable percentage by inflation, swelling the benefits of illicit exchange, and troops could realize ten-to-fifteen times their expenditure in local currency. They were authorized to buy six cartons a month at the PX.

American dollars were forbidden to be spent on the local economy, which of course ensured they were not. Right! Greenbacks flowed like Ba-mui-ba through the bars and markets, whorehouses, restaurants, and tourist trash shops. Everybody—and I mean everybody—was on the get-well-on-Uncle-Sam wagon.

Brenner, Luther E., SP5, one each, I thought—you're allied with the forces of darkness.

* * *

A screen door squealed and smacked shut. A pair of bright orange Ho Chi Minh sandals *squinch-squinch*-ed along the damp concrete floor of the latrine, slowed, and a stall door clunked shut. Judge Monaghan, seated on the throne of his adjacent kingdom, cleared his throat and rustled his newspaper to let the new occupant know he wasn't alone.

"Who's in my house?" asked the newcomer.

"It's me, Chef. Judge. Saw your clogs, knew it was you."

"Yo. Wha'cha doing?" he asked facetiously, considering the meager list of options.

Staff Sergeant Jerry "Judge" Monaghan didn't usually go out of his way to cultivate friendships, even acquaintances. The man in the bold shower shoes was an exception.

Sergeant First Class Benjamin "Chef" Biggs, mess sergeant of the 3rd RRU, was a surprisingly erudite soldier. An anomaly, considering most mess sergeants were considered ignorant as brick mortar, perpetrators of mass soldier-cide and indifference. But Benny Biggs, the Chef, was a good cook and a good manager of institutional food services. It was those qualities that made him important to Monaghan, rather than erudition. Leave the latter to Brenner.

Chef made do with what the government prescribed, fed the 3rd RRU with what the Army provided him, within budget, and managed always to offer good chow and generous with it. Along with an honest mail clerk and a friendly medic—one with a blind eye toward unreported/unrecorded dispensation of various VD treatments—an accomplished mess sergeant was one of the most highly regarded soldiers in any outfit. Not to overlook, of course, a larcenous but friendly supply sergeant.

Being erudite alone did not ensure an enduring sense of humor. Neither did it preclude it.

Monaghan spoke above the rustle of paper and assorted bodily functions. "Just reading here in the *Saigon Daily News* about the attack on the officers' wives' tea party last Friday. This is a hoot." Monaghan viewed officers' wives as a military affliction.

"Didn't hear much about it. Just some cadre flipped a Mark-two into their garden party," Chef replied over the sound of a solid, rushing stream into the bowl.

"This Salmagundi clown, whoever he is, writing for the *News*, gets to the crux of matters more ricky-tick. The attack story is sub-tended to an article about the government's belated removal of dependents from 'Nam." This was an opening guaranteed to catch the interest of any soldier assigned to the 3rd RRU.

Seven months earlier, in February, 1964, President Johnson had ordered all unassigned American civilians out of the country. But implementation of LBJ's edict lagged.

In the early days of America's presence, under the two contradictory efforts of impressing the world with her peaceful intent, and propping up a series of unpopular and shaky Vietnamese governments, senior US civilian officials and military officers had sent for wives and children. They still resided in Sai Gon in villas of the departed French. Life went on in the colonial vein, with or without the tricolor.

Their inexplicably continuing presence created unwarranted demands on the soldiers of the 3rd RRU, who, during what was supposed to be their off-duty time, were required to man guard posts at the dependent school, along with equally put-upon troops of the 39th Signal Battalion.

Whatever Cook County shenanigans within MAC-V allowed the tardy departure of these disinvited dependents, a random terrorist attack had now occurred that emphasized urgency.

"Yeah," Monaghan continued, "'an afternoon tea party for senior officers' and officials' wives was underway in the garden of Mrs. (Colonel) Abernathy,' I'm reading here. She, whose husband apparently 'whiles away his time between the Air Force's Seventh Air Division Headquarters on Tan Son Nhut and a–'listen to this '–a chic little *pied a terre* off The Street of Flowers, containing an equally chic little slut named Patsy whose favors, unknown to the colonel, are shared by a roster of Australian pilots. Mrs. (Colonel) Abernathy, at the time of this breach of decorum—' the grenade attack, I assume he means '—was in the act of pouring something stronger than tea into the frosted champagne flute of Mrs. (General) Conners when an irreverent young idealist, apparently given over to fancies of cadre life and the glory of sacrifice, rolled along the sidewalk outside the sumptuous grounds of Abernathy Acres on a bicycle–' listen to this shit! '*–with a bent front wheel,* and casually flipped an American-made Mark-II fragmentation grenade—' minus spoon, and with fuse advancing, I have to presume '—over the wall. The attacker then decamped, and watched the arrival of American M.P.s and Vietnamese Q.C.s from one of the many branches of 100-P Alley—flashing lights and young troops of two governments primed for action.' This guy, Salmagundi . . . where's he get his inside shit? *A bent bicycle wheel!* 'One of the Quan Cong N.C.O.s spotted the youthful adherent, made the association, and not only shot him down in a hail of gunfire, but took his bicycle. The V.C. was identified as fourteen-year-old Vinh Ho That of no known address, Cho Lon.'

"'The following morning news briefing at the American Embassy did not play up the incident, as it was not the first such: its event was noted and low-keyed. The Air Force dispensary on Tan Son Nhut recorded the admission of Mrs. (Colonel) A., the administration of a local anesthetic, and removal of a sizeable fragment of good, American labor-union-crafted steel from the abundant left buttock of the outraged and embarrassed dependent.' Goes on to say Headquarters, Mac-Vee, announced four V.C. killed in a terrorist attack on a civilian house." He paused. "An added threesome of complimentary Vinh Ho Thats, no doubt."

There was no immediate reply from Chef's stall. Following a sustained grunt and a splash, the master cook said, "So I guess we got Mrs. Colonel Abernathy and her achin' ass to thank for getting our troops off guard duty at the dependents' school, and tea parties, and such shit. If I'd known that would do it, I'd've arranged to have her fragged before now. Why weren't the goddamn camp followers shipped out six, seven months ago when L.B.J. ordered it?"

Indignities were anything but mundane. Both NCOs understood the enlisted men's aggravation. Not only did they face guard duties at the schools and villas and at civilian functions during what should be their off-duty time, but the presence of dependents created other inequities.

"Look at the exchange on Tan Son Nhut, and downtown in the Brinks B.O.Q.," Judge complained. "Except for cigarettes and skin magazines for the warriors, stock's given over to a dazzling array of hair sprays, sanitary napkins, scented soaps, mouth washes, panty hose, over-the-counter remedies for the treatment of yeast infections and various other vaginal disturbances, diapers, baby formula, sewing accessories, canned and bottled ecstasies for canapés and mixed drinks, and a host of other civilian-, female-, and child-oriented products." He took a deep breath.

Chef thought he might be getting off the hook, but Judge had built a head of steam. He wasn't anywhere near finished. "A popular brand of canned diet food substitute—drunk cold, shaken first—covers a third of one entire wall of shelves. I think you'd agree, you'd have to be desperate for weight loss to chug-a-lug one a' them chalky-tastin' shit cocktails."

Judge had additional concerns. "And I can't buy ammo for a personal weapon in the P.X. Since command wisdom specifies personal weapons are outlawed, they find no logic in providing a source of ammunition for them, despite the fact that every star-bearing patriarch in the command who contributes to that collective wisdom, himself carries everything from a .357 magnum to a Walther P.P.K.

"I have to risk my ass downtown to obtain such illicit items, forced to buy them on a street corner. Though it's true that while there I can also replace my climate-rotted skivvies, pick up the new jungle fatigues, so eagerly sought but unavailable through Army supply channels. Buy Tetracycline tablets to self-treat a staggering array of venereal diseases. And acquire quinine pills that are easier on the digestive tract than the remedies issued and decreed prescriptive by the command and our medics.

"Anything, *everything*, is available on Tu Do Street or Tran Hung Dao. When something's unavailable through channels, we shop the V.C. market." It was so called from the common knowledge that many enterprising salespersons, if not VC cadre, were, at a minimum, funneling profits into Ho Chi Minh's coffers. It was a Machiavellian subtlety that invested the GIs in their own destruction.

Chef flushed the toilet and said, "Sorry 'bout that!"

* * *

"Hey, Red. Send the duty clerk out here, wouldja," the guard yelled through the screen.

"What the hell was all that carryin'-on out near the gate?" The duty NCO managed to rouse himself from a Shell Scott mystery long enough to inquire after a confused episode of shouting and screams just past. He looked out through the screened wall of the Orderly Room at the guard standing there, exhibiting boredom.

"That's why I need help. You may have to call the Thirty-second for an ambulance. Dumb-shit Krebs," the guard, Mollinson, related, "and his dumb-shit counterpart, Nesbitt, just attacked the Zip Ranger *Kaserne.*"

Across the oil-soaked dirt road that by-passed 3rd RRU's Davis Station compound lay the training facility for fledgling Vietnamese Rangers. During the day the compound echoed with the screams of young men—both enthusiasm and pain—as they underwent physical and pre-parachute jump training to qualify for one of the premiere Vietnamese Army outfits, the Rangers.

Even within the confines of Tan Son Nhut, individual tenant units maintained their own integral security, some with barbed wire, others with simple strand wire or concrete walls, some with electric strands atop—all with their own sentries. The Ranger training grounds were not especially well secured, for what could an enemy want there? There was no equipment, no aircraft, no radios—nothing to provide valuable, accessible, easy targets, and if you did assault those grounds, you were going in the teeth of the best troops the ARVN had.

Still, the Rangers had established defensive positions for use in case of attack, or for show—whichever came first. At each corner of the Ranger compound and flanking the gate into the 3rd RRU were sand-bagged positions for the emplacement of machine guns, mounted and manned only under alert conditions. To enhance the positioning of these defensive weapons—American .30 cal. Browning light machine guns—the Vietnamese had sunk two-inch steel pipe into concrete, roughly three feet of pipe extending above ground. During alerts, defensive gunners deployed to these positions slammed their machine guns, already prepared with a mounting sleeve, onto the open pipes and instantly had a maneuverable, stable gun emplacement.

SP4 Warren N. Nesbitt and SP4 Archie (NMI) Krebs, both flying operators from the Air Section, had returned to Tan Son Nhut after a night's revel on Tu Do. They had borrowed a Jeep from in front of BOQ Number-1 while the driver was taking a leak in a nearby alley—Krebs acknowledged later that they ". . . *had* to drive; we were too drunk to walk!"—but shortly abandoned the vehicle in the triangle before Gate 2, dimly aware they'd never get it past the guards. They walked through the gate. Then later, getting out of a cyclo a quarter mile down the road from Davis Station, as far as the driver would take them in their condition, the two drunk soldiers ambled unsteadily down the dirt road, their intention toward mayhem growing more intense the closer they got to home.

They stopped in the middle of the dark road, discussed who might be on guard duty at the gate into Davis Station, and decided to attack. Ill-advised from the start, sober men—even Krebs and Nesbitt—would never have offered themselves up to such level of risk. They didn't know who was on guard. They thought it might be some pussy who would flee screaming toward the Orderly Room. They ignored that it might be one of the relatively old soldiers— anyone who had been in-country ninety days or more—experienced in combat, who responded to attack with counter-attack.

But they weren't sober.

The two drunks charged the gate of the Third, silent until they reached the nimbus of light from the pole-mounted security lamp, then broke into banshee yells, effecting a pseudo-Asian threat from movies of wars gone by: "Amelican, you die!" "You die tonight, Yankee dogs." As their screams escalated, they veered off the road and made for the machine gun emplacement across from the guard shack . . . just in the unlikely instance that the guard might indulge in the act of guarding. Krebs' contribution was truly overboard, though not worthy of memory in the events that followed:

"Amelican imperialists, running dog capitalists, all die—" The two soldiers flew with grace over the sandbag walls.

Nesbitt smashed head first into the back sandbag wall of the emplacement. Krebs's sincere effort to bend the steel pipe with his right knee resulted in an unaffected pipe. The GI guard, watching the entire sequence from across the road with mild disinterest, took his time reporting to the Duty NCO.

"Bring the asshole on in," the NCO said, "I'm calling the Thirty-second." He dialed for the nearby Air Force Dispensary that did, on rare occasions, dispense medical aid to US forces on Tan Son Nhut. "Shut up, Krebs, you wimpy piece of shit. It's only a leg, for chrissake." Sergeant Lesser, unimpressed with the chorus of screams and moans emanating from the specialist's knotted form on the floor, let him lie where he'd been dragged by the guard and duty clerk. Nesbitt still lay in the gun emplacement, unconscious from his half-gainer into the sandbags. No rush; he wasn't going anywhere.

* * *

Korea: Spring 1953

They came upon the mules first, early that morning. All those dead, dumb animals, slaughtered there in the open—the mules no one could explain. Cold that morning, cold for early springtime, with frost in the air. The animals were shod but bore no US markings; so, unlikely they were ammo or pack-howitzer humpers. But there were so many, scattered there where the artillery had found them. Blown to meaty chaff and fragmented white shards, the ground about them soaked dark. Beyond the kill circle crouched the village.

A tiny hamlet, barely noted on the map, it consisted of a dozen mud-wattle huts, some stone enclosures where animals had lived, a quagmire for a street, and the road passed on beyond, uninterrupted. The orderly desolation of the village seemed somehow consistent with the find of the mules, and the rifle squad passed through the quiet, deserted spaces without curiosity, until the scout sent back for the lieutenant. North of the village, the point man had found another corral, a separate place of slaughter. The Marines shambled forward.

A sturdy wire-and-stake enclosure, this pen had been built by some farmer to keep his hogs, long before he would have been adjudged North Korean or South, if the worn troughs and oft-repaired gate were any measure. Any domestic stock was long gone, but the fenced space was not empty. A number of crumpled heaps that seemed at first a part of the filthy, crusted wallow were not animals the pen was built for, but remnants of some displaced order.

Human bodies, frozen into the solid mud, as cold as the ground they occupied; the blue and white diagonally barred striations on the shoulder patches scoured to a solid grayness by the elements, spoke to long exposure. They were dead only days now. Herded into the tiny enclosure, likely back after the autumn fighting, they had been left for the duration, somehow surviving the incredibly harsh winter when the mud they slept in became sharp-ridged ice and there was no shelter from the open sky and all its ruinous elements, and the little straw there was festered with hibernating lice and fleas. And then, for these few sad-season survivors, times had gotten hard.

When they pushed north and found the five Army infantrymen, the Marines were scouting newly taken ground that had previously formed a bell-shaped kink in the front, a place where the enemy previously pushed south in a bulge of the main line of resistance across the peninsula of The Land of Morning Calm. A coordinated air and ground effort had straightened the boundary, bringing it into configuration with that to the east and west in anticipation of the upcoming cease fire, expected sometime later in the spring or summer. The land within the bulge, like the rest of the MLR, was held by Chinese troops, but CCF forces commonly contained North Korean elements, remnants of the armies routed and destroyed two years before, following the Marines' landing at Inchon. It would have been the Koreans who had, in the last moments before fleeing, taken retribution, a final, savage affirmation of their vacuous ideology.

But their vengeance had been hasty.

One lived.

One man — one face, rather — alone in the icy horror, unconnected to a body, floated like a seance vision. It peered through the squares of wire at the riflemen and waited, knotholes for eyes, burned-out vacancies with no life, no light. What face it had was blurred, indistinct. It made no sound. No movement.

The living said nothing, but stared in speechless dread at the thing occupying the pen.

Something needed to be said. Corporal Winter longed to say something . . . to comfort the soldier, to welcome him back, acknowledge the end of his torment — anything. But like the rest of the squad, he stood, dumbly staring at the haunted face, until Bramlett lurched forward and began ripping at the wire, cursing, and Winter and the squad, like the pack of savage animals they felt obliged to be, dropped their weapons and tore the structure to splintered fragments.

chapter eleven

Metaphors, Conceits, and Bad Dreams

Vietnam: October 1964

Winter was right: I was a quick study. In just over a month I had the mission at WHITE BIRCH down pat. About mid-October, the Third Rusty Rifles mushroomed. The force in Phu Bai in the north was upgraded from Detachment J to something larger, aspiring to field station, not there yet. The Air Section, finding no more planes, did acquire several pilots. They still needed operators. When I told Winter I'd take the extra six months to fly, he shook his head in amazement, and said it was a done deal. It didn't take him long to make it happen.

I was flying as soon as I could finesse a flight physical. I spent a couple of interim days on the ground, looking over Dave's shoulder as he drew up schedules, learning the logic of Airborne Radio Direction Finding, observing how he scrounged and threatened and cajoled to get men and flights — and that was the easy part. Tasking the Vietnamese in what was supposed to be a mirror-image operation was a whole other ballgame, the mirror a funhouse glass.

The small air section of the VNAF ARDF was notorious for not completing missions. Always some excuse: engine malfunction, no available pilot, weather. Dave showed me a returned tasking slip from a week before. It was the piece of paper which 3rd RRU daily sent to the VNAF giving them targets and sked times. Following missions, it was normal for the slip to be returned to the Third with locations fixed for the various targets worked. The slips also came back when the mission was unfulfilled, as the one he showed me. The writing, in English, was quite good and read, "No go fly. Propelow no go round. 33. Nguyen." In essence, "We didn't fly the mission. The aircraft was inoperable. Gone to drink beer. John." Out.

After those slack days, and the results of my physical having come through with a pass, I followed Dave out to the flight line one cloudy morning and clambered aboard an Army RU-6 "Beaver" aircraft with him and a pilot. I sat right front seat, the spot designated for a copilot. Since we hadn't enough pilots to fly more than one per sortie, and since that was the only spot open in the aircraft, it offered little choice. I'd given up wing-walking.

As Warrant Officer Stoetzel went through pre-flight, Winter, flying as operator, briefed me on the physical set-up in the bird. "Sitting front seat, Luther, you can't watch the radio manipulations. But no mystery there: today, a standard R-three-ninety HF receiver, an R-two-twenty VHF receiver, and a generator, stacked. Usually, two R-three nineties, no two-twenty. Basic oh-five-aich equipments. If you watch, you can see how the pilot goes about the esoteric and questionable business of plotting relative ground locations of the aircraft from each signal intercept—each shot—taken and plotted on enemy transmitters by azimuth." His voice had taken on a pedantic tone; despite that attraction, I wasn't greatly impressed.

I did feel excitement, listening on the headset Winter plugged in parallel to his own, knowing the enemy radio I heard was somewhere close. Winter, realizing where my mind ran, said, "That's right. Charlie can hear our engine, probably watching us even as we listen to his Morse transmissions." I didn't dwell on the metaphysics of that shit!

Dave warned me: "It will quickly become irritating, then frustrating, as we work hard to obtain targets and have no rapid way to transmit the information to anyone who can do anything about it. Certainly we can do nothing assault-wise; we carry no ordnance. You might have noticed," he added dryly. "We have no secure comms, and since our source of such intelligence has to be closely held, we cannot transmit in the clear. A little caveat here that might have some meaning, maybe not. About three weeks back, working the Vung Tau area, we rolled in on a transmitter—I was the operator—and before we got within five klicks, the transmission was interrupted, and the Zip op sent 'R.D.F., R.D.F., R.D.F.,' in Morse and went off the air. 'splain me that. Was he alerting his net to radio direction finder at work—us—or was that the initials of his girlfriend?" He pouted into the blank 'Nam sky for a moment. "I personally can't believe Charlie doesn't know what we're doing up here, thrashing about the sky, diving on his active transmitters . . ." He didn't pursue it.

"We do have code books we could use to encrypt short messages and broadcast to our people on the ground, who would then decrypt and, theoretically, act upon our report. But it's awkward, slow, and generally a pain in the ass, so ops often ignore the need to act in a timely manner on what might be critical intelligence. We simply log the data, return to base, compute the fixes on better maps, relate them to identity, and telephone on a secure line to the embassy, where some faceless voice will put the 'target' into the pipeline."

My response, commenting on that as a No shit! proposition, did nothing to improve Sergeant Winter's day, but what the hey? Not my function.

"To get fire brought or airborne ordnance dropped on one of our targets often takes days just to clear the ARVN Joint General Staff headquarters maze. By then, when three rounds of one-oh-five high explosive are expended on the site, it's only monkeys and palm trees that suffer. Sometimes, maybe a water boo. The ARVN chain of command is riddled with subversives, so bad that word of imminent shelling or air strike is illicitly and quickly communicated to the target VC, who will be kilometers and/or days away, before the allies can bring hurt."

A slip of the lip sinks ships . . . and it don't do diddly for us good Christian lads, either. But it seemed to me a hell of a strange way to do business.

* * *

Three days after my initial training flight, I was scheduled with Lieutenant Zwick. The ides, subsequently, did not auger well for my march to operator glory. I walked out to the ramp, found the proper aircraft tail-number, and threw my chute inside along with mission bag, helmet, and weapon. The bag and helmet were the only things I planned to use. No one in 3rd RRU Air ever relied on the parachutes issued; they were used only as seat cushions. Some wit explained to me at the end of my first training flight that the most one could hope for—should he be forced to exit a failed aircraft in failing flight, yanked the D-ring, and looked skyward for the telltale blossoming of the pilot chute—was a swirl of moths, spiraling upward in a disturbed frenzy.

I also regarded the weapon as excess baggage. This was Teeny Weeny Air-lines.

I was in the bird, cinched in and suppressing claustrophobia when Zwick hopped off a Jeep driven by one of the ramp guards. He yanked the door open, put his boot up on the step fixed to the landing strut, and vaulted into the plane in a devil-may-care manner. He paid no attention to me in the back, assuming, I guess, that some proper op would be present. He wasted no time getting us up and away. Some short time later I realized something about his arrival and our subsequent departure that did not set well with me. We were near Tay Ninh in angry storm clouds before I realized what it was: *He had not pre-flighted the aircraft!*

Not trained to do it, not qualified to do it, not required to do it, and too new to have picked up the pattern on my own, I still knew enough to walk around the aircraft, exercise the flaps to ensure free movement; same with the vertical and horizontal stabilizers, check the fuel port cap for overfill or leaks; look over the prop for cracks or other tragedy-producing evidence—kicking the tires and smelling the upholstery, as it was known. But this clown didn't offer even that service.

The Beaver gave a convulsive lurch in the storm, and Zwick's hands flew to his head. I imagined him exclaiming, "Oh, shit! What to do now?" but he was merely tightening the headphones on his head so he could hear over the engine and the crash and rumble of the storm. He must have sensed my discomfort; I heard the intercom click on, and he twisted his head half about and said, "What's the matter, Specialist? Don't like our weather up here?"

I keyed my mike. "Makes a shit to me, El Tee. Just wondering if there was anything disquieting you might have discovered on pre-flight, had you had occasion to perform one. Something, say, that might significantly affect the outcome of the mission."

There was silence on the intercom.

"You a wiseass, wiseass?"

"In the current context it would seem so . . . sir."

"Wiseass!" He jammed down on the right pedal and cranked the yoke hard to starboard. The aircraft fell away from the thunderheads in our path, plummeting us toward a black carpet of jungled mountainside below. Zwick came on the intercom as he pulled the yoke back into his belly and brought the false horizon indicator level: "We'll have to scrub that first sked over the Black Virgin."

"Black Virgin?"

"Nui Ba Dinh." He nodded, indicating for me to look down.

I looked. Nothing but a mountain.

"She is a black, evil looking bitch, ain't she?" I guess he meant the mountain.

I could barely see the forested lower slopes from where we were now at about three thousand feet because of intense weather build-up. But she didn't look like a virgin to me; more an old syph-ridden hag of a massif, riddled with broken aircraft and the bodies of lost patrols going back to Foreign Legion days. I'd read the campaigns of that war, none of them encouraging.

"We own the top," Zwick continued. "Got a Special Forces A Team up there, along with some signal corps people, some Viets . . . and their dependents, chickens, goats. A freaking zoo." He wrestled the Beaver across an undulating landscape, the turbulence — a Devil's brew of rising hot air currents and the edge of the storm — conspiring to wrench us from what was not our natural element, and dash us to pieces where we legitimately belonged. "Charlie owns everything from there down, all the slopes, trails, and approaches. We can only get people in and out, and resupply those there, by chopper." He was silent a moment. "Man, she is a bitch!"

We ambled on across III Corps airspace, the bird yawing and torquing itself threateningly. I was sure the noises I heard were rivets popping, struts giving way. But gradually, as we left the Black Virgin behind, the air smoothed somewhat. The Beaver took a deep breath, shook itself, and settled into smooth flight. This was an early mission, the day not hot enough yet to generate the vicious heat updrafts I would later come to know and love.

We overflew Cho Lon, the Chinese quadrant of the city across the river from Sai Gon, continuing southeast. I checked my sked sheet and saw we had almost forty-five minutes before the next sked. I continued to scan the bands and heard trash and tribulations: nothing worth setting up a DF shot over. The pilot cranked us back toward the east, waiting.

I heard El Tee mutter something, but he hadn't keyed his mike. I looked out the cockpit and could see we were on a heading for the peak of a tall hill, far smaller than the Virgin. I leaned up and forward, keyed my mike, and looked down at the map spread open on the copilot's seat, asking Zwick, "Where are we?"

He didn't acknowledge right away; then without looking, he stuck one gloved finger onto the map and jabbed generally at a set of whorls and elevation numerals which might have been the geographical mass before us. "I think I have a visual," he said casually.

"A visual what?"

"A visual sighting. An enemy antenna mast."

"*Where?*" What are you saying, Brenner? I thought, after the moment it took for the truth to penetrate: it doesn't matter where, it's not where we should be. Where there are antennas there are communications; communications serve military units; military units consist of soldiers; soldiers carry guns. Ergo, from our low-altitude, we don't do visuals.

El Tee disagreed. "It's on the peak of the hill," and he pulled the nose of the aircraft precisely in line with the peak. I have remarkably good vision, but I saw nothing alarming. Nothing but brush-covered peak with brush-covered slopes below that, fading into brush-filled jungle farther below.

Then, as we closed on the crest, I saw it materialize: a thin, rigid mast. A pole. A bamboo pole, sticking out of the bush on the designated military crest, and as we overflew the location just then, I could see some fifty feet below us human shapes darting about a small clearing near the base of the mast.

"Yessir," he said contentedly, "got us a visual. Now if you'll take a couple of D.F. shots, real close in, maybe we can stir somebody off their ass to come do something about it."

His face was a mask of delight. Hell, maybe he would have made a fighter pilot. Sure wasn't his eyesight flunked him out.

"Uhh, El Tee, I don't think we're supposed to seek out visuals; only report them when we stumble over one. Gives us away. Hell, that close they can see our antennas. They must know what we're doing. And we don't know how many troops are there. Or how they're armed."

Logical to me. I do my thing from a distance.

"Ahh, shit, what's your name? Brenner? Brenner, what we got here's an observation post, a few guys stuck up there to count ARVN traffic on Route 13, along the coast. No more'n three, four troops." As he coaxed me along, I watched with growing unease while he made a tight, spiraling turn, and I saw the peak of the hill come gradually into my line of vision again.

"Don't do this shit, El Tee. I can't even take D.F. shots this close. Physics are all off. We can't get a null," referring to the absence of signal that occurred when the source was directly in line with the aircraft's orientation. "Get us about five, six klicks away, then put the nose on them." Fifty or sixty klicks would be better.

"Hang in there, Brenner. Take another look. You verify it too. Then we'll go get some shots."

I started to register further objection, something about just reporting the hill mass which had a numerical designation. If someone was there, they couldn't be more than twenty-thirty feet from the antenna mast — that's all the space there was on the crest. All we have to do, I thought, was to report the hill's occupancy. Running down this attractive menu, my attention was drawn to an erratic, pale-green line that rose lazily from the top of the hill . . . then another . . . several . . . many, attempting to marry up with our trusty Beaver. Tracers! My incoming in-country brief had informed me: where American tracers leave a red path, the Cong use Russian ammo which produces green. That was old news; the Koreans and Chi-coms were customers of the Russkies, too. Christmas insanity ran through my mind: a red and green overture.

"Uhh, op to pilot. *El Tee get us the fuck outta town!*" I heard my own scream in another voice. The seeking green web had not found us, and as he dropped the nose and we sledded down the slope of the hill behind the antenna mast, I thought we'd made it. But far down the slope, approaching the end of our descent, something wracked the aircraft with a terrible smacking sound and violent wrenching. I had visions of the engine exploding, the entire ball of wax continuing to follow the slope of the hill until it bottomed out and became flat land, and we would then merge with the ground and become one.

"*Tree!*" he shouted through the intercom. "Took a branch off a tree. We're O.K." He was scanning the panel. I did the same thing in a controlled panic, with no idea what I sought.

"O.K., my ass. Home. *Home.* We go home. Go somewhere, away from that fifty-one . . ." for I was sure it was a .51 caliber machine gun that sought to exploit our defenselessness. Looking out the side window so low to the ground we appeared to be making about three hundred knots ground speed. In reality, driving a Beaver, we may have been making ninety. Zwick was pushing it, but the silly mother had already pushed it.

And the pilot didn't head for home. He accepted my argument to simply report the hill, but as we departed the hill he asked me about skeds. I told him I had two others listed. He asked where the first was, and off we went, blissfully happy to be in a state of asses intact.

When we banged her down on runway zero-seven back at Tan Son Nhut just before lunch, I was mentally furiously working on schemes to renege on my extension and transfer back out of Air. Zwick strolled off, as calmly as if we'd driven down the autobahn a couple of klicks, sightseeing.

* * *

"Dave, no shit. You have to do something about this yo-yo," Brenner insisted. "I don't think it's just my new-guy status that contributed to my . . . well, panic's as good a word as any, I guess. The silly asshole flew us down the barrel of that fifty-one. We got no armament, no armor, can't even fire out the window past the equipment rack. Oh five eights are not kamikaze-committed. Can't you go to the captain, make him do—"

"I will, Luther. I will, I promise. I had complaints before, but nothing this . . . bizarre. Scary!" Winter agreed.

"Scary? *Scary, my ass!* Fucking death wish, has our boy Lothario. Read me, good sergeant. *I'm* not flying with that wacko again. He can play Tom Terrific and his electric fucking assault rocket if he chooses; I opt out." Brenner, still high on adrenalin; was pale, his breathing labored. He appeared close to shock.

Without regard to Brenner's legitimate concerns about Zwick, the sighting and the automatic ground fire rated a priority report downtown. This time, for whatever reasons unknown to anyone, ARVN reacted expeditiously. At 0530 the following morning a platoon of infantry, far down the pecking order of the ARVN 9th Division, strolled up the hill toward the reported communications site.

The platoon never came down again. Two bedraggled Vietnamese soldiers, both wounded, were all that made it out of what was — apparently, surprising them — a meat grinder.

ARVN Command, in an embarrassed dither, ordered up a company from the same battalion, and they fought a stand-up engagement for about half a day. When their command could make no further contact with the company, the general ordered up an entire battalion. Took half a day for the 34th Group to ferry them in by chopper. When the smoke cleared and the dust settled, Marvin the ARVN had ninety-three dead, two hundred and sixty-six casualties total; they recovered eighty-four VC dead, took seven prisoners, and counted hundreds of blood trails where Charlie vanished in a rain storm like night mist on that great gettin' up morning. J-2 reckoned Zwick had uncovered a VC assault battalion, sequestered on the slopes of the hill in the brush, monitoring traffic on Route 13 and waiting to attack a major convoy. J-2 disdained identification of the enemy unit. Like jealous kindergartners, they never shared.

Captain Pyburn, set to slam dunk Zwick's erratic career, was loathe to do so after the accolades began pouring in. No medals for Zwick, though; only a severe ass-chewing. That, instead of being grounded, which for him would have been the ultimate punishment. Short-handed in pilots as we were, he even piloted one of the birds flying missions during the battle, though there was little to work under those circumstances. The VC operated from pre-laid plans, and when they got themselves into trouble, it was up to them to get themselves out of it, falling back on training and discipline. No calling home for instructions and a Western Union money order. There being no communications, there was little for the Air Section to contribute, not for lack of trying. Zwick was comfortingly compliant with his directives from the Captain, but Winter still had to order operators to fly with him.

* * *

Brenner, beset by irritation, aggravation, angst, and frustration, felt an overwhelming need to vent. It was a few days after his visual sighting adventure with the mad lieutenant, and while he had held himself in check — his temperament, his invective-fashioned mouth, and his bowels — it had not been easy. And days later there was no sign of it ever getting easier. Winter and Ratty Mac had left him in a deep funk in his hooch and gone to the club, where it was nearly an hour before Brenner was mentioned..

"Better get Luther downtown, Dave . . . steam job and blowbath . . . some kinda' relief," Ratty Mac advised, "or he's gonna off that bozo with bars. The lad's festerin' for a fight."

"You ain't wrong. Matter-a fact," Winter considered, "when you're right, you're . . . no, not so, what I almost said. Even when you're right, you're wrong, you mangy bastard." They were eyeing the improbably lush breasts surmounting the chest of the skinny new waitress in the EM club, trying to decide whether to engage in another beer — Winter's second, Mac's . . . well, he'd lost count — and thinking that tomorrow, being Sunday, wasn't all bad. War don't work on weekends. "But this time, Terror of the Horn, you *are* right. That's the start of a string," Winter chided his not quite sober companion. He let a silence settle that was far too short.

Mac broke the quiet spell with an inexplicable *non sequitur.* "Remember after that hunt down south of Massawa when I missed every goddamned thing I shot at, and we went back to the CIAAO Hotel and partook of some spirits, and I went to sleep in Balence's room, his bunk, and the fuckin' rat bit me on the finger? Remember that?" Mac wheedled, flashing from the fulsome delights of present-day endeavors to reflections of past glories.

"How could I forget? You've told that story every opportunity for three years now. Mentioning the Horn set you off, didn't it?"

"Naww. Hell . . . maybe. I was just thinkin' . . . I had to take that series of miserable shots in the gut. They never caught the rat and didn't know if I had hydrophobia or rabies or whatever, even whether I *needed* the fuckin' shots . . . and you know what?"

When it became obvious Mac expected an answer, Winter said cautiously, "No I do not know what. What?"

"That wasn't my rat nohow. That was Balence's bunk, his rat. He's the one shoulda' got bit. *He* shoulda' had to get the fuckin' shots." He glared at Winter, then said, owlishly but with vigor, "Damn the whole damn Army Medical Corps. They owe Balence twelve hurtin' shots . . . and I wanna watch him get 'em."

There was a sudden envelope of silence about the table, the taped elevator music faded into a dull thrum, and the tide of voices from the room packed with sweaty soldiers ebbed, as Winter stood, waving off the waitress with the enhanced breasts and two cold-beaded cans of Carling Black Label. "That'll take some doing, Mac. Frank Balence's dead two years now."

Mac concentrated on his scraped knee sticking through a rip in his fatigue trousers. "Yeah, that's right," he said distantly. "Drowned on a fishing trip back home, after Asmara. Up in the U.P."

Sounds grew around them once more. Movement took on meaning. Mac looked up, said wonderingly, "How'd I forget that?"

It was months before either one learned that Balence was still among the living.

Foregoing additional rejects of the brewers' arts, the two found Brenner still in his hooch, and with surprisingly little effort, cajoled him off the base.

* * *

The *dzong* cart was full. Rumor was that you could get a baker's dozen Zips in and on one of the small motor scooters with the wire cage back—four down each side bench, one on the floor with his back against the cab, two seated on the floor with legs hanging out the rear, and two more up front, one on either side of the driver, squeezing tight cheeks onto non-existent seating, a sort of skyhook for the ass—along with an unknown number of ducks and chickens, depending upon whether they were live rations or cold. Mattingly claimed he saw a cart on Plantation Road just that loaded, and with three dead ARVN tied like awkward luggage on the roof rack.

But this cart was otherwise configured. There were only three Vietnamese aboard, one of them, a VNAF sergeant, sharing the driver's seat where the two yammered incessantly. The other, an army private about fifty-or-so years old who had a grotesque, liver-colored wen that covered half his right jaw. The private wore an immaculate set of freshly washed-starched-ironed khakis and a set of full-dress military medals, among which was the French Croix de Guerre. He sat in the back passenger compartment. He wore no socks, but his broad, spatulate feet were elegantly shod with a pair of shocking-pink *gummi* shower thongs.

Esquire, eat your heart out!

Winter, Ratty Mac, and Brenner occupied one side bench of the passenger compartment. Winter, farthest in next to the cab, had maneuvered Mac to the outer end of the bench in case he should choose to puke, an enterprise in which he was known to excel. Brenner was left in the middle to stabilize Mac in the event of that indelicate likelihood.

The opposing bench on the right side of the conveyance also held three passengers. On the outer edge, opposite the unrepentant Mac, sat the geriatric Vietnamese warrior with the whimsical footwear.

The other two figures, toward the front, were cast in shadow, since all the street lights — *both of them* along the six-mile stretch between 100-P Alley and Gia Dinh — were on the right side of the street, putting any light on their backs. But Winter could tell they were not Vietnamese. One was tall, and even in the absence of good lighting it was apparent he was cadaverously thin. His hand, gripping the bowl in partial light, looked like a claw with long, unkempt yellow nails. Talons, almost. His upper body was hidden in shadow, but from the man's knees down, Winter could see military fatigues. And something uncommon about them. He was directly across from Winter, but never presented a clear impression to him. Yet, something about his uniform seemed out of place, out of time . . .

The man wore no headgear. And carried no weapon. Admittedly, neither did any of the three ASA soldiers, but if the man was, as Winter suspected from his unorthodox dress, an adviser to some ARVN unit, just come to town from the field, he would expect him to be armed and wearing a cover. Even a field cap, fatigue cap — something. And Winter could see no indication of rank. The only thing of note was the metal bowl he held in that skeletal hand, a scarred, yellowish pan, shaped like something he remembered from childhood on the farm. Back when they still had the well pump and there was such a bowl on the back porch for hand washing. Maybe brass, or nickel plate, that bowl, wearing thin. Dented, unprepossesing in the elusive light.

The other passenger, similarly dressed, was much shorter, much broader through the body. So much for physical conditioning requirements of the modern army. But he did wear a hat, an old-fashioned WW-II-era fatigue article called a KP cap: soft, no stiff, blocked crown, crumpled brim all around. And he was a walking armory.

Winter could not make out the pedigree of the weapons, but he smelled Cosmoline and gun oil, and the cart's passage along the darkened road was accompanied by the clatter of loose operating rods, the jingle of brass sling frogs against brackets, the musical clink of belt-linked, magazine- and clip-fed rounds.

The two men conversed very little between themselves, and then in muted tones so that Winter could not understand them. Almost as if they spoke a foreign tongue.

The *dzong* cart stopped in a lightless stretch of road, where the verge was dense bamboo and tall sawgrass. The aging ARVN soldier hopped nimbly from the bed, said a few sing-song words to the driver, and vanished in the gloom. There was not a house or building in sight, and the last thing Winter saw of him was a flash of pink, kicking up dust in weak light from the distant, second street lamp.

As he looked about, he noticed the driver was alone; the VNAF NCO had disappeared from the cab. Winter had not seen him get off, had not a clue when he bailed out, but felt a sense of disquiet about the surreptitiousness of his disappearance.

The only sound, above the sibilant conversation of the pair before him, was the blanket of peeps from a gazillion tiny paddy frogs.

Winter knew this road. Not far ahead, it would course back into the northern suburbs of Saigon, if such an unstructured mélange of houses, factories, businesses, and ditches and streams, and burned-out, bombed-out, blown-up places of temporary occupancy could be labeled the 'burbs. But as they approached Gia Dinh, they would be once again among some semblance of civilization. And when they reached the imposing structure housing the ITTA offices, he could find his way from there, should he have to. He would know where he was. Musing, uneasy, wondering why he even thought in such terms of crisis, he suddenly realized he was not alone. Beside him, Brenner hummed an obscure operatic air. Ratty Mac burbled and snored softly. Winter thought of the errant rat who had got it all wrong on the Red Sea coast and smiled. The muted discourse across from him, for unknown reasons, made him think of the music of Albéñez.

* * *

Before the route edged back toward the city, the cart pulled to a stop on the dark road. The odd soldierly duo alighted, the fat one stumbling and clattering, fighting the load of weaponry and equipment, while the tall one stepped lightly off the rear of the cart seemingly without effort, almost floating.

Winter, leaning forward to look between the slats of the cart side, noted that the short, round one had at least two rifles and a submachine gun slung about his neck. Several bandoliers of ammunition criss-crossed his chest, and his waist was hung about with a sagging web belt anchoring a number of canteens, first aid pouches, messkits, and what appeared to be a couple of old, World War II-era gasmask bags. Who could know what was in there? Those bags had become popular for carrying all manner of treasures by soldiers who seldom had treasures.

A soft expression that might have been a farewell drifted back on the night air as the two disappeared quickly into the brush along the road.

* * *

Winter sat quietly, watching as they were passing among houses.

Brenner spoke up: "Whither?"

"'scuse me?"

"Where are we bound? The Manhattan? San Francisco? The Tiny Tits Teepee?"

"Hell, I don't care. What difference does it make?" Winter knew Brenner understood what the trip to the sinkholes of Gia Dinh was all about; that if there was any choosing to be done, Brenner should do it. "Wonder where those two were going," he said elliptically.

"Who?"

"The two who just got off. Were you asleep?"

"No, just . . . I didn't see whoever you're talking about." Brenner sounded defensive. Ratty Mac sounded asleep.

"You didn't see . . . how could you not see them, Luther? They were the only two other people on here with us, after the Zips got off. The tall, thin one and the short, round one. They got off five, six minutes back. Whadda you mean you didn't see them? They stepped over you."

"Hey, Sergeant," Brenner bristled, "I didn't see any Mutt and Jeff on this buggy. All right?"

Winter caught himself before blurting out something silly. Brenner must really have his shit stirred, he thought, wondering — If flying, even with that dipstick Zwick, was going to take so much out of him, maybe Luther needed to re-think the whole flying gig. He'd have to keep an eye on him. Jeez . . . didn't even see the pair of them. He felt a need to change the tone of the evening. He said the first thing that erupted into his mind.

"Luther, without regard to some internal problems in the Third," he ventured loftily, "how do you feel about being over here? About us doing . . . well, what we're trying to do?" He felt awkward with the drift of his questions; these were personal issues.

"It's a living."

"No, really. Nicole writes she's starting to read editorials in various papers questioning our whole position. 'course, we're always going to have dissidents. If we weren't here, there'd be a faction lobbying to get us here."

"Professional assholes in any endeavor."

"My, aren't we loquacious tonight. Where's that famous Brenner bon — "

"Hey," Brenner burst out, "I got the shit scared out of me the other day. I didn't react well to it. I realized, later, I even looked pretty goddamned silly. I'm chastising myself for it. So cut me some slack while I do the beads." His voice tailed off, exactly as it would if he had been telling the truth, Winter realized.

"OK, we'll have the fucker assassinated," he offered.

"Zwick?"

"Who we talkin' about?"

"Listen, Sergeant Rock. You lay a hand on that zoomie prick, I'll have to take you out of my will. That's my cross to bear . . . my little red wagon," he tailed off again.

"Gotcha. The Manhattan, then. OK?"

"Where the *Ba-mui-ba* is brewed with the finest of mountain waters. From the shit-filled streams of Da Lat."

"That's the place." Winter felt the tension trickle away.

After a short stretch, while both admired the Mesozoic architecture of Gia Dinh's elegant bar district, Brenner said, "I don't know why you ask me to qualify myself about this not-to-be-mistaken-for-a-war dust-up. But you obviously have strong convictions about being here. Saving this ragged remnant of cast-off subcultures from themselves. It's a calling with you. You can't help yourself."

To Winter's silent astonishment, he went on: "But with me, it *is* a living. It's a job. It's the job the Army pays me to do. Even though I'm here by choice—you do know I volunteered, right? I mean, I'm sure you figured that out, knowing me for the stand-up Templar Knight I am —even so, I'm here because this is one of the places the Army chooses to offer me to do my job. I chose to come back in this regimented nest of vipers, so I have little to say about how and where I do that job. I knew what I was getting into; it's not in me to quibble over small issues, such as whether or not to kill women, children, and domestic livestock. That's part of the wondrous scenario, one of the great opportunities of the wearing of the green."

Winter was not fooled by the caustic assertions. He knew his man. But if it was a pose, it was one that was only for the disinformation of the proclaimer. It was only to soften the otherwise uncontrollable, wracking circumstances that controlled every waking moment of every day of every one of their lives.

"Yeah, you're right. I am a self-righteous do-gooder," Winter confessed.

"Just so long as we know who the players are," Brenner amended.

They smiled un-self-consciously at each other in the garish lights of the bars as the cart came to a final stop. When they grabbed his arms to wrest him from the cart, Ratty Mac jerked erect, smacked his lips, and said, "We home? Let's set out on th' porch and have a brew."

* * *

"Sam, my man, you were in error to doubt me when I said we could safely leave the cycles at that peasant's home. They were as safe as with the custodian of the Officers Mess."

"Yes, sir," the short, round soldier responded to the tall lieutenant. "It is true they were still there, though likely because no one would ever expect to find anything of value in such a deserted and wretched shelter. But, sir, if we could . . . if we could just stop for a moment so that I can off-load this gear onto the bicycle. Get it from around my neck and waist, I mean, so that I can maneuver better."

The tall officer pedaled resolutely forward in the murk of the empty countryside. They had emerged from the *dzong* cart at precisely the point they had entered another one a few days before and, as the lieutenant had predicted, found the two bikes where they had hidden them in the abandoned shack. Lieutenant Dan Dewey had immediately stepped astride his bicycle and, pushing down on the rusty pedal, moved off with a series of tinny squeals. Private Sam Fellows, who would have removed the sling-borne weapons and ammunition bandoliers from about his neck, and even the extensively burdened web belt from his waist, if he had had a basket or some other means of containing the gear, was forced to mount the vehicle and push off. Awkwardly wrenching and tugging at various unbalanced elements in order to stay aboard, the private was not given time for even such small graces.

The officer stopped in the road and looked back. "Sam, having lately been delayed by the chaplain, and those two harridans at Cho Lon Hospital, I feel the need for dispatch. Resolve and Dispatch, the twin engines of leadership." The private listened to this smarmy pronouncement and wondered what had happened to yesterday's twin engines, Courage and Honesty, but he did not ask as the officer talked on. "Those two days in bed, forced into inaction, while those . . . *women*" he spat, "took issue with my personal effects, destroying my books, categorizing them as 'antithetical and unwholesome,' a characterization more fitting for that loathsome cleric."

Ayee, Dios, would the man never cease? Private Fellows wondered. He'd had about enough of this. If it weren't for the promise of the island, he would leave his leader to his mad schemes. Let him carry his own weapon and gear, the extra ammo, the excessive water ration. Even that silly pan. Like we're going to need more than just a messkit to handle all the rations we're apt to be able to scrounge up out here in this nether land. Sam worked quickly to balance the gear and weapons across the handlebars and on the shaky fenders of the ancient bicycle. Soon, he was forced to mount again and ride on to avoid losing his charge.

They were only two hundred meters beyond the road where they had exited the cart, but already the terrain about them was given over to rice paddies. They had to proceed with caution to keep the creaky bicycles on the dikes between the pools of growth-filled water, universally avoided as a shit soup. The Holy Mother knew he didn't want to fall off into *that* stuff.

"Now, see. As I said. There they are. Just ahead." The officer spoke in an awed, husky whisper. He had stopped again, and pointed forward.

"There are what, sir?" The round soldier pedaled up beside the lieutenant, who looked down at him disparagingly, searching terrain to their front where the officer pointed.

"There. Surely you see them. Vee Cee cadre. There are several of them, just there. There are maybe thirty or forty that I can see, all across the horizon, though the light is not good."

The light is non-existent, the private thought, and the lieutenant's eyes were wondrously bad. "But sir, I see nothing but rice paddies. The only thing, except for a few palm trees and some brush, are the foot-pump stations on the paddy dikes. There are nowhere near that many of them within my view." It had been only a couple of days, but already he had begun to suspect that his spontaneous acceptance of the officer's offer to accompany him on adventures to enrich themselves while doing their duty, was not the favorable contract he had imagined.

"I will attack. Pass me my rifle, and take refuge."

"Where do I take refuge?" the private enquired, looking frantically about at the featureless landscape. "And what will you attack, my officer?"

"The enemy. Those thirty to forty cadre ahead, there in bold relief."

"Look, your mercy. Look you, that what you see there are not Vee Cee, but only the foot pumps where peasants stand and power water from one paddy to another."

"Get behind me, private." The lieutenant jerked the operating rod handle back, jacking a round into the chamber of the M-1, and pressed down on one pedal, launching his attack run, propelling himself forward as fast as the clunky bicycle would allow. Straight down the dike he wobbled, the rifle extended out before him over the handlebars, the gleam of the brass-colored pan on his head barely visible in the starless, moonless night. A shaft of radiance from some unknown source seemed to bear upon his eminence.

When the lieutenant fired the first round, the bullet struck a piece of angle-iron in the vertical structure of the VC cadre-foot pump before him and ricocheted back, whining dangerously close. His weapon jammed, thus likely saving him from a further malevolent spraying. His violent reaction to the near miss dumped him from his bicycle. Climbing creakingly to his feet, he took a fragmentation grenade from one of the deep cargo pockets of the old fatigues, grabbed the ring with his teeth and yanked, jerking himself off his feet. He fell in a tangle of bicycle, rifle, metal pan, and anguish, howling in pain and grabbing his jaw that was nearly broken, surely dislocated. That had never happened in the movies! Nor, indeed, in any of the books.

Not to be distracted, as from amongst the tangle of metal he reached again, pulled the pin with his left hand, let the spoon pop free and, hearing the affirmative hiss of the burning fuse, flung the small, lethal, ovoid sphere toward the gap in the dike where the pump stood erect. The grenade struck the muddy embankment twenty feet from its target, burying in the soft ooze, and in a matter of seconds exploded with a muffled crump, blowing mud and water and shredded new rice stalks and one piece of loose rock over the landscape. It was all an inconvenience but for the rock, which proved to be a visitation of the most ill-fated sort. The rock struck the officer on the metal dish rocking loosely on his head, and dented it sufficiently to convey the message, knocking him to the ground again amidst his downed cycle's framework.

Private Fellows rushed forward as fast as he could ride and leapt from the bike. "Lord, have mercy upon us. Did I not tell the lieutenant to be careful what he was about? Did I not assure you that what you saw as Vee Cee were just tools for the rice farmers to pump water with? Now see—"

"I pray you, hold your mouth, Private. You know nothing of war, and do not understand the many confusing elements that can overtake one when engaged in such an honorable calling. Ohhh, though I do admit, my body feels sorely used and most abominably bruised and stiff." When Fellows had helped him from the tangle of the bike, and had searched and found the metal basin, staring at the severe dent in one rim, the officer remarked casually, "And you were right, of course. How could I have mistaken such a common enemy? It is from reading too much. I must prove my own existence." He tucked the basin under his arm and asked, in a querulous voice, "But are you not deceived? Might those . . . *deceivers* not have had to do with the milling of grain?"

The private stared at him in awe, hearing nothing of relevance in the words..

The lieutenant brushed the mud from the front handguard of the Garand onto his trouser legs absently, and said, "This, the second sally of our passage, I fear, has not begun in good fortune."

* * *

The pilot entered the pattern over Cho Lon, broke out of downwind short over Sai Gon near the cathedral, held the yoke forward cranked left, his left heel hard down on the pedal, rotating the Beaver to port onto base leg, lined up on the shell-splintered bell tower. Warrant Officer Orozco, overflying his mark, looked down on the remnants of the church, ugly up close. He banked smoothly and lined up on final.

"Shut her down, Mac. You're on overtime," he growled into the intercom, checking his way through landing procedures. Alert for Vietnamese pilot trainees cutting across the pattern, and cautiously watching Colonel Momsley's would-be bad-asses skydiving from a Huey platform on the north fringe of Tan Son Nhut, it always irked him to fly with Ratty Mac. The specialist kept at his business as long as they still had airspace. Unduly long. Regs dictated that the op be shut down, his receivers zeroed out before touchdown in case of a crash. Wouldn't do having crash crew reading the meaningless radio dial numbers. But the pilot always had to talk Mac through shutdown while he should have been dedicated otherwise. No two people in the Group could agree whether that was because Mac was such a hard charger . . . or if he just liked to yank the chain of airplane drivers.

Even worse was the pitter-patter Mac invariably went through on touchdown, a kind of praying, jiving, meaningless exhortation to the world at large. And it was at large: Mac always keyed his mike out as he reeled off the threats, real or imagined, major or minor; a soliloquy both silly and sincere — happy to be back, frightened of getting back, cautious, mean, and momentarily quasi-religious.

"Ohhh, shit! We got one shot at it. Look at Two-Five-Left, look at that blistering white whore. Just put it there! Over the Zip truck park — over, fucker — keep it in a glide, past run-up . . . watch those two scrambling Phantoms . . . oh, shit, Chief, you got an Aussie in a Caribou, ten o'clock, skyside. Don't! Don't! Don't hit that mother Phantom; she's loaded for bear. Dear sweet Jesus, holy Christ, help us now, Lord. Jeep! Jeep! on the crossway, Q.C. Jeep. She's sli-i-ip-ping . . . grass, oilslicks, rubber, bad rubber, burnt rubber . . . benjo ditch to port . . . con-n-n-crete, baby, and we got this hummer down. Yeah!" Mac almost never felt the tail wheel make contact.

"Army One-Five-One on the active, Tan Son Nhut tower. Are you transmitting in touchdown?"

"Uhh, tower, Army One-Five-One. That's a negative," Orozco replied while they rolled, glancing sideways at Ratty Mac who was zipping the mission bag closed. It wasn't even worth mentioning; Mac appeared uninvolved, merely along for the ride.

"Army One-Five-One, Tan Son Nhut tower. Uhh, that's a no-no. Communications wise, so-to-speak. Exit Two-Five-Left on the central, cleared to Army ramp. Out."

Orozco keyed the mike twice. Mac hummed something from Ella Fitzgerald, undistinguishable in the engine noise.

Orozco taxied the olive drab U-6 down the row of assault helicopters, feeling as out of place as a Belgian hare in a kennel of mastiffs. He followed the mechanic's arm waves into a tie-down slot, announced to ground control he was clear, shut down the radios and nav-aids, chopped the power on the mech's signal, and began shucking harness. Seventy seconds back on earth and already he was saturated with sweat. "Where's the band?" he asked, eyes sweeping the barren concrete.

Ratty Mac un-assed the bird and stood, staring across the apron at a C-123 that seemed to have collapsed there at the taxiway intersection. Foam residue, like dried soap suds, crusted the starboard engine and that entire side of the fuselage. The ramp was down; the cargo bay looked gutted.

Mac walked into the shade of the cargo plane. An Air Force Tech Sergeant wearing a beret sat on a 55-gallon drum beneath the wing. The sergeant looked tired, and his fatigues were stained and torn, all vestiges of military propriety faded.

"Your bird?" Mac asked.

"Yeah."

"What the fuck, over?" Mac murmured, his eyes roving over the puncture wounds in the dirty, stained skin of the bird.

"Little ground fire." The sergeant did not seem anxious to make conversation. Liquids dripped onto the tarmac beneath the plane: oil, hydraulic fluid, fuel, others more viscous in consistency. Rainbow colored.

"What kinda mission you been on?"

"Classified."

Mac stared at the sergeant, guffawed. "'Classified?' My achin' ass, classified. See that little piece of shit there I just got out of? That Beaver? That sucker's mission is so classified, you and me both could go to the brig for just thinkin' about it. But you're American. You're G.I., like me. I could tell you. That one-twenty-three ain't nothin' but a cargo plane. What kinda classified?"

"So you could tell me all about your mission, huh?" the sergeant said, eyeing MacGantree with interest.

"Yeah. No sweat. What's that patch you're wearin'?"

"RANCH HAND."

"Say what?"

"RANCH HAND. That's my outfit, Ace, my mission, too. So what's the story with the Beaver, all the antennas and shit?"

"Sorry, classified."

"Get out of here, asshole. You're on restricted turf."

Mac saw a Jeep load of Air Police approaching. He eyeballed the aircraft and counted eleven holes in the fuselage and along the flap and trim tab.

"What's that orange shit leaking out down the ramp?"

"Kool-Aid. We took a round in the galley. Now hit it!"

"Kool-Aid's ass. Don't smell like no Kool-Aid to me." He stared at the pool of bilious, cloying liquid.

"You'll never know, dip-shit."

The AP Jeep pulled up with a squeal of brakes. Mac shouldered his mission bag and followed Orozco's distant figure toward debrief.

chapter twelve

Point Taken

Viet Nam; October 1964

Major Alfonso, Personnel Officer, walked the new officer around on his introductory tour. The lieutenant was boot officer material, *shavetail* to borrow another war's euphemism: the epitome of undisturbed ignorance at play. Brenner said later he had looked at the nametag, expecting either Jesus Christ or Pollyanna; what he read was Chaldano.

"This one," the major pointed to Brenner, whose uniform was without indication of rank, "is an airborne operator, *not* a sergeant — he just mimics one. This one, Staff Sergeant Winter, is N.C.O.I.C. of A.R.D.F., Airborne Radio Direction Finding. The fly-fly people. Maybe the only sergeant here who won't carve your balls off, given a chance. But no guarantees." The major only nodded at Sergeant Lessor, assuming the new LT could read a name tag, and muttered, "Traffic Analyst," looking away before Lessor got started. "Monaghan around?" he asked the room at large.

Three incurious pairs of eyes registered blank.

"Sonuva...*mumble, mumble*..." The major's comment dissolved in the ether. He placed his hand on the stranger's shoulder. "Lieutenant Chaldano, new Ops Officer. Your boss!" he addressed them collectively. Jerking a thumb dismissively at the threesome: "Sergeants Winter, Lessor, and the missing sergeant, Monaghan, who's Mission Management N.C.O.I.C. — Sergeants Three. And Specialist Five Brenner, acting — Sergeants Four. Do yourself a favor, young sir. Do *not* allow yourself to become distracted in your dealings with them. Any of them. Even Winter. Enjoy your tour! Just don't lose sight of who the enemy is." He stomped out.

Brenner started in on the new officer immediately, but quickly lost his taste for it, all challenge gone when he recognized terminal naivete. They went to lunch instead.

Flight crews and 3rd RRU staff regularly found it pleasant to take lunch at the civilian air terminal on Tan Son Nhut. It was close to Air Operations and the food was good and inexpensive: a small steak, fried rice, green weeds, french bread, and a beer was a dollar and a quarter. More than two beers, meals could become prohibitively expensive: if Alfonso learned of it, the cost was a stripe. Or, as had happened to a visiting specialist on the IG team — who'd drunk too much *Ba-mui-ba* and chose to walk it off, ambling back to Operations along the flight line — you could lose your head to a spinning prop.

Monaghan joined them as they left the hangar, and Sergeants Four and the new lieutenant rode in a single Jeep to the restaurant. They suggested his lunch, ordered for him. As he was engrossed in trying to take in the new cultural experience, he neither demurred nor considered Alfonzo's admonition as he grossly exceeded the major's two-beer limit.

After lunch, they poured him in the Jeep, nodding knowingly, witnesses to a limited-distribution truth. Back in Operations, they kept him erect but allowed him to ricochet at will off the hallway walls. It was the singing that attracted Alfonso.

"You stupid shit!" the major screamed at the hapless lieutenant who, with unexpected resolve, held himself vertical against the oscillating wall of the passageway. Sergeants Four found they had pending duties and disappeared. "What kind of kiddie-clutch jerkoff have I inherited? Young sir, I told you the goddamned sergeants would eat you alive. You don't get over your jet lag and inbound airsick before you fall right into it. Lieutenant, mark my words: learn to drink . . . or don't drink! *Pitello!*" he bellowed.

Another young lieutenant leaned around the corner of the S-1 Shop. "Pete, take this poor sap over to B.O.Q. Number One and put him to bed. Greg," he directed at the new officer who was not quite perpendicular to the floor. When he spoke, Alfonso's voice bore more than a trace of resignation: "Greg, go to bed. Catch up to your body. Come back here tomorrow and convince me that's all it was. You're no good to me or to the Army once you lose the respect of the N.C.O.s. Their respect is worth shaggy-dog shit, but if you ain't got it, you're in trouble out the gate. Go!"

Lieutenant Chaldano for some weeks thereafter treated Sergeants Four as lepers, no closer would he get. He was formal in language, addressing each as "Sergeant," or, in the case of Brenner, not at all, though it was common in the camaraderie of the 3rd RRU staff to address one's hired help by their first, or war, names. "Sergeant" was reserved for senior administrators, serious admonition, requests for extra-channel favors, or when visiting firemen were present. Enlisted swine were treated as someone's failed social experiment: employment for the masses.

Judge Monaghan never called the new lieutenant – in reference, or to his face – anything but "Kid." Chaldano did not know how to handle that flagrant abuse, ignoring the regs, but could not bring himself to ask Alfonso to intervene. It became the status-quo, defined by Judge's brazen abuse of military propriety.

Alfonso was aware of the cards being played, but he stayed out of the game. There were more ways than one of divining leadership capacity.

Weeks went by while Chaldano found his place in the world of the officers and the even more confusing world of the Third. He had no luck with the warrants; if anything, they were worse than sergeants and enlisted types. Warrant officers he understood to be some semi-exotic, bastard breed of creature-rank, a diversion along the enlisted-to-noncommissioned officer-to-commissioned officer path. Promoted – "Warranted," Mister Bellingham liked to say – from the ranks of NCO with vast experience, the warrant officer routinely rejected the social and ambition-bound career path of the commissioned officer. Enabling the unbalanced system to work was the fact that warrant officers, for the most part, *were* as good as they believed themselves to be. Chaldano hedged his career bet by avoiding them when he could.

* * *

Two days' flight operations went astray, unfulfilled, during a period of heightened ARVN coup activity. Generals Nguyen-Han-Minh-Long-Ding-Dong-Dell called up their own personal cadres of troops – battalion, regiment, brigade, division, or Military District, depending upon their aspirations and realistic expectations of just how much they could get away with – and made a play for some higher command. This was an old Ring 3 act in the ARVN circus, and often the coups eventually flittered away from disinterest, or became enmeshed in some other, more senior general's parallel coup efforts. Some led to quick, sharp bloodbaths, and *then* they went away. Some coups became state policy. But while in progress, processing "The War" was pushed to a back burner.

In this instance, Gen. Khanh, rotund little mandarin on the General Staff, went for the whole enchilada. Moving his armor onto Tan Son Nhut, he blockaded roads and brought in aircraft from nearby Bien Hoa airbase, flying A-1Es low and slow over TSN to prevent his opposition from launching their own aircraft. The field was closed, by order of the ARVN high command. And Americans, avoiding taking sides, stood by and played pocket pool, watching the Skyraiders tooling back and forth over the field. 3rd RRU-Air stood down along with *almost* everyone else.

On their way to lunch, Sergeants Four stopped to watch from the edge of the parking ramp. They noted a C-21, a small, civilian type jet with indifferent markings, sitting in the run-up area at the eastern end of runway two-five-zero. Black exhaust from the jet in idle contributed to the noonday pollution that hung in a stifling fug over the field. "Wha's the haps, major?" Lessor asked, casually saluting Major Gibbs, the S-3 who'd stood on the ramp for over two hours now, smoking his pipe and taking advantage of the slowdown.

Gibbs, taciturn by nature, continued his part of the pollution project for a few moments, and then said, without turning, "That Lear's C.I.A. , and they've declared outbound for Vientiane. Zip in the tower tells 'em they can't take off. Spook says bullshit, he's going. Zip calls the A-1Es to orbit and ensure he doesn't. Waiting to see it play out." He puffed happily.

Didn't take long. A black cloud boiled up behind the C-21 as it turned onto two-five, and in a turning-roll-launch, throttle balls-to-the-wall, the little jet scooted down the strip, the pilot yanked the yoke into his belly, and they headed for the heights, passing through the flight of three VNAF fighters attempting suppression, scattering them wildly to the winds. Before the fighters could get their ducks in a row, the military Lear was a smudge in the wild blue.

"So much for containment," Major Gibbs murmured around his pipestem. "Spooks playing in a different game."

* * *

In the last week of October, SP4 Archie Krebs hobbled into Air Section operations. On light duty for almost three weeks, Krebs had not flown since the night he and Nesbitt had attacked the front gate of Davis Station. Still in pain, his kneecap the color and size of an eggplant, he considered himself in dire straights.

"Sergeant Winter, you gotta get me a flight."

"I don't 'gotta' anything, Krebs. You off light duty?" Winter tore his gaze away from the tactical map where he was furiously plotting daily mission tasking, taking time he didn't have to hear out the sad tale of his sidelined operator.

"Shit, no. They keep—Sarge, I gotta get my flights in. This is the last week of the month. I barely got enough days left to make my six. I can't afford to lose my hostile fire pay again this month, man. You know I send money home to my mother."

"Krebs, you lying sack of shit. Your mother's in Vacaville, doing five to eight for grand theft-auto. You don't send her diddly. You spend your hostile fire pay the way you spend the rest of your pay—on beer, Saigon tea, and whores." There was no venom in the accusation; every outfit had its Krebs.

"Aww, man, Sarge. Cut me some slack. Get me a flight. I'm a good op. You know I am. I give you honest work . . . for honest dollars." The specialist had the *chutzpah* to smile.

"Honest work, my bleeding ass." Winter turned back to the map, looked down at the lengthy list of sked changes yet to be implemented, and told the imploring soldier, "I'll regret this, but . . . tomorrow, oh seven forty-five. Take my mission. I'm up to my ass in 'gators here. You fly with Stoetzel, U-6 mission. Pick up your sked sheet at half-past . . . *but only if you can walk from the hooch to here, to the flight line!* Hear me? No hitching rides. You gotta be able to walk. I'm going way beyond my authority to do this, just because of your sad story, and I'll be damned if I'll risk it if you can't even walk."

"No sweat, Sarge. Don't hafta walk on the mission anyhow, but O.K. You got it. Thanks." The specialist hobbled out of the section, moving faster than upon his arrival. Brenner, sprawled back in a chair with his boots on the table, reading a SITREP, said, "You soft touch mutha, you'll let that asshole leverage you into Leavenworth yet."

"Hey, guy's gotta make a living. Right? Third's never lost a bird. Like he said, cut me some slack."

* * *

The following morning, after a night of indecent revel among the ops welcoming Krebs back on the roster, and a slow start to the day's work, Winter was bent over the map, worrying too few ops, too few pilots, too many targets — a daily tribulation — when Lessor stuck his head around the corner from the Analysis shop and shouted, "Dave. Ring-a-dingy."

He grabbed the phone and stared it down as it chirred and rustled, settling in: "Sergeant Winter." He stared up at cobwebs between the hanging light fixture and a vent that didn't.

"Sarge, Lieutenant Brill, A.S.R. You guys have an aircraft, tail number one-five-one, anywhere in Three Corps? Say, 'round about Tay Ninh?"

"What's the reason for your query, Lieutenant?" He didn't want to know the reason; he said a silent prayer it *wasn't* the reason. But why else would Air Search and Rescue be calling?

"We got a MAYDAY in that region. Ten-oh-nine hours. Pilot squawked a dead engine, said he was going to try to make an emergency strip. Gave his A.C. number as one-five-one."

"Yeah, that could be ours. Can you give me more details? Exact location — "

"'bout all we have, Sarge. The pilot sounded rushed on the radio; well he might. But it almost sounded as if he didn't . . . I don't know, maybe I'm wrong, but it was almost as if he didn't want to give his location. Why would that be?" The lieutenant's puzzlement was obvious.

"We fly classified missions, Lieutenant. Just being cautious," Winter assured him.

"Might cost him his ass," the Rescue lieutenant observed.

"You're not wrong. Thanks — " and pressed the receiver, released it, and immediately dialed Pyburn's office number. Warrant Officer Travaglia answered.

"Mister T., Sergeant Winter. Give me the captain, quick!"

"Ho-kay, Sarge." Winter heard him speak off into the ready room.

Another click. "Captain Pyburn," the voice clipped, impersonal.

"Sergeant Winter, sir. Just got a call from A.S.R. One-five-one's down in Three Corps somewhere."

Momentary hesitance. "No coordinates?"

"No, sir."

"You got their skeds?" Pyburn's voice was urgent but contained.

"Yessir. I thought I'd get Mister Orozco—he's here in the building—launch another bird and go look for them. From the sked." He held his breath; he knew the arguments.

"Why don't you just give the info to A.S.R.? Let them do their job." Brusque.

"Yessir, I can do that, too. But you know ops don't always stay right on the sked plan. That's Krebs and Mister Stoetzel, and—"

"Krebs is back on duty?"

"I'll talk to you about that, sir. Krebs and Mister Stoetzel work together a lot, and Archie is a . . . an *inventive* op, let's say. They might be anywhere in the region. I can't say on the phone, but I have an idea where they might be. A.S.R. said Stoetzel was looking to make an 'emergency strip.' I know three in the general area they were working. Okay to launch?"

"Go! And if you have any more birds out who can help, divert them. Keep me informed."

Winter, given *carte blanche* to do whatever he could, was grateful to an officer who wasn't sidelined by bureaucracy. He'd have to pay the piper later about Krebs, but he grabbed his .45 and shoulder holster, shrugging into it as he grabbed his flight helmet and went up the hall. He leaned in the S-1's door, found Orozco and CW3 Self sipping coffee.

They looked up and, making an instant decision, Winter said, "Mister Self, one-five-one's down. Mister Stoetzel and Krebs. Captain said we should go look for 'em."

CW3 Lee "Bob" Self was dressed for stress—he wore his sidearm. He set the cup down and said, "I'll get my helmet. Find us a bird." He was out the door. Orozco looked as if he would speak, but he knew better than to volunteer. The Third's Air Section hadn't enough pilots to risk losing two on one flight, especially to search for another who might already be lost.

Winter found a crew chief, got clearance to use -866, an RU-8. When Mister Self sprinted across the apron, Winter was doing a walk-around . He was wasting his time. Self would do his own pre-flight. Every pilot did his own. *Most* did. This time, Self made it a running check.

CW3 Self climbed in, belted in, plugged in his helmet intercom. He primed the pumps, started both engines, and immediately brought the radios up and called Ground Control. Winter was locking into the co-pilot seat, storing the flight bag, pulling forth maps, and did not have his intercom plugged in. As he slid his helmet plug into the cable from the panel, he heard GC give Self clearance to taxi. Within seconds, swiveling his head, the old warrant was clearing the clutter of aircraft in front of the hangar. As they made a quick turn from the taxiway onto the active, Winter heard GC turn Brown Shoes 866 over to the tower controller, who diverted an Australian Caribou on downwind, and gave Self immediate clearance for takeoff.

Self never slowed, but pushed the throttles forward, already on the active, and though the engines could not be fully warmed up, within seconds they broke ground. Self was busy with the tower, his eyes swarming over the panel; he reached down, changed radio frequency. Winter, half listening, smoothed out the onionskin paper copy of Stoetzel-Krebs' skeds for the morning. He looked over the callsigns and times, unfolding the map in his lap. He checked his watch: the MAYDAY had been at 1009, just nineteen minutes ago. He found the sked entry for the nearest time before 1009, checked the grid refs, and began searching the map, all the while listening to ASR directing search operations. The coordinates for the search area were centered just west of Tri Tam/Dau Tieng. From his own flights in that area—an area worked often because of proximity to Black Virgin Mountain and its resident cadre of bad guys—he knew there were at least three airstrips on nearby plantations, grass runways previously used by the resident French in flying about their holdings and back and forth to Sai Gon. Any of those strips might serve adequately for emergency purposes. Winter began searching them out, uncomfortably close to prayer.

He waited while Self made contact with Air Search and Rescue and informed them of his intent to join the search and, based on classified mission knowledge, try to pin down where the aircraft may have been when it squawked. He had already called -275, another 3rd RRU mission bird working farther to the southeast. Two-seven-five had finished their mission after six sorties, and was inbound to Tan Son Nhut. They had an hour's remaining fuel and readily diverted to the search.

When the warrant officer clicked off his mike, Winter keyed the intercom and said, "My first bet would be the strip on Don Bien Michelin, here northeast of Dau Tieng. It's the best strip . . . we don't know he had that choice, of course." He stabbed his finger on the large tract of colonial largesse.

Self nodded, asked no questions, but added, "One's as good a guess as another. We'll check there first." He adjusted their heading and said, "What's your second bet? We'll send Zwick there." Lieutenant Zwick was piloting -275, the other bird joining the search. With him was the op, Nesbitt, the ill-fated Krebs' cohort in crime. Nesbitt had only recently re-joined the ranks of flyers, riding the "head injury/ache" following the attack on the bare gun pit as long as he could.

"Probably here, southeast of Tay Ninh. About . . . hmm, N.C. forty-eight three, at zero sixty-three, one twenty-four."

"*Where?*" Self queried anxiously, glancing over at the map where Winter pointed.

"I still don't have the hang of these damned charts; they're not like artillery maps," Winter said, blanching at his own excuse. "About one-oh-six degrees, ten minutes east; eleven degrees, thirteen minutes north. Or thereabouts."

"Yeah, I'll tell Hot Shot to fly 'thereabouts,'" Self said, smiling grimly as he noted the site.

"Well, hell—"

"*Break, break,*" crashed into their ears.. "A.S.R. alert! A.S.R. All aircraft in vicinity Dau Tieng, now exit the area for rescue operations. I repeat, all aircraft in the vicinity of Dau Tieng/Tri Tam, northeast of the town, stay clear until rescue operations are secured. A.S.R., out."

Self clicked his intercom: "Well, providing that's our boys, that'll save us embarrassment of trying to find some mythical map reference." Self grinned broadly. Winter wriggled in his seat.

The pilot keyed his mike: "Brown Shoes two-seven-five, this is B.S. eight-six-six. You copy A.S.R.? Over."

"Uhh, roger that sixty-six, this is seventy-five. Wilco. Out." He cut short proper radio etiquette.

Another voice came up on the air: "Army eight-six-six, Army two-seven-five, this is Magic Control. Please observe proper protocol in on-air communications. Over."

"Uhh, Army two-seven-five. Uhhh Roger that, Tower Man. Wilco. Okey-dokey, G.I., darlin'. Will do, Control-san, and assorted other bullshit. Way-y-y out."

Self did not bother to respond; Zwick had pretty much covered it all. Zwick, having suffered the indignity of being forcefully evicted from the Air Force Academy, delighted in yanking Air Force controllers' chains.

A call back to ASR elicited no information on status or condition of the pilot and operator. Winter asked ASR to relay to the recovery team instructions to have the pilot and op take "security precautions," if they were in a condition to respond; if not, the recovery folks were to ensure that any radios in the crash were recovered or set to zero and any flight and mission bags, maps, and papers were recovered and secured, to be turned over to the S-2 of the 3rd RRU. Just before breaking contact, ASR informed Winter that both men were alive, but there was no word on their condition. And no word on compliance with his security request.

* * *

Winter skidded the Jeep to a halt in front of the 32nd Air Force Dispensary, and yanked the hand brake. Lieutenant Bland, unit Security Officer, jumped from the passenger seat and Winter followed him into the building. Bland asked the first enlisted man he saw, "Where would they bring emergency cases?"

"Emergency? Well . . ."

"Krebs, Army, just brought in by Rescue from a plane crash," Winter expanded.

"Oh, yeah. Probably the guys back in pre-op. Straight back—"

"There's more than one?" Winter said, surprised.

"Yeah, an E.M. and an officer. Brought in together." The medic went away.

Bland was wringing his hands. "I thought A.S.R. told us they only brought Krebs, the op, here. They said Stoetzel was Jeeped back to the unit."

"Who knows, El Tee? Second thoughts? May be a reg that says he has to be checked out or something, even if he's not injured." Winter was legging it down the corridor as he spoke. Spying the Pre-Operative Suite sign above a swinging door, he pushed it open and walked in.

Warrant Officer Stoetzel was seated on a stool, with a medic bent over him winding a stretch bandage tightly about his bare chest. In the far corner two men in whites were bent over a figure on a steel table. Winter heard Krebs, his voice slurred and uneven, griping about pain. He walked up close as he could get, and one of the attendants raised up—a Captain doctor—and said, "You can't come in here, Sergeant. We've got open wounds." He motioned Winter back and reached for a curtain.

"Sorry, Sir. I'm this man's N.C.O.I.C. and I have to question him immediately."

"You'll have to wait. I've given him pain medication and he wouldn't make much sense . . . even if we weren't busy with treatment," he said pointedly.

Lieutenant Bland—bless his perky little self, thought Winter— spoke up from across the room. "I'm afraid it's a security matter, Doctor. We won't take long." He was conferring with the injured pilot who, it seemed, had at first thought he was not injured, then collapsed on the recovery chopper. He had a couple of cracked ribs and his entire upper body was badly bruised from slamming into the yoke upon impact. They didn't have details of the flight termination, but it must have been unorthodox, at minimum, Winter knew.

"Stand to the side, then, and let us get on with it. And put on a mask." He nodded to an enlisted assistant who produced a white gauze surgical mask. The doctor was gruff, being a captain and all and overruled by a mere lieutenant who played his Security trump.

"What're his injuries, Doc?" Winter asked.

"Doctor, please. For one thing he's got a severe concussion; for another, we think a broken clavicle — collar bone — from what he says was equipment falling on top of him in the crash. We're waiting now for the X-rays. Beyond that, we're still looking. He seems to have an older trauma to his right knee." His voice held question.

"Thank you . . . Doctor. Krebs," he said in a forced, low voice. "Archie, can you hear me. It's Dave Winter."

"Hey-y-y, Sarge. How ya' doin', man?" His voice came from far away.

"How're *you* doing, you flakey shit? Told you it was too soon to fly. You probably caused this whole flap."

"No doubt. No doubt. Got my gimpy leg caught in the throttle . . . or whatever makes those crates stay aloft." His eyes were open, then closed. Then open again.

"Archie, quick now. Where's the mission bag? Did the recovery team get the bag?"

"I think so, Sarge." There was a long period of silence, and just as Winter was about to speak again, "I told them to get it. After we got clear of the plane, after Mister Stoetzel pulled me out from under the rack. I think I was unconscious for a minute. Then we came under fire and the chief left me behind the fuselage and took my rifle . . . but it was broke. My gun was broke. Broke right at the . . . But he thought he could still . . . He'd dropped his forty-five getting me out." He took a quick intake of breath, expelled it followed by a deep, shuddering inhalation, then continued reporting in a higher pitched voice. "I didn't think about the fuckin' bag 'till the chopper came." He seemed to lose the thread of recital for a moment, but labored on. "I remembered then . . . told a Spec Five gunner to get both leather bags from the wreck. There was . . . still some fire then, though . . . don't know what happened. I was in and out." Winter leaned closer as he realized Krebs was mostly out.

"They got both bags," Stoetzel said tiredly from across the room. "I think they're somewhere here, in the dispensary." Warrant Officer pilot Stoetzel sounded done in. "But Krebs is fucked up. Wasn't me pulled him outta the plane."

Winter looked around, spotted another medic moving bottles about on a gurney and asked, "Where would I find these people's gear? Weapons and flight bags?"

"Check in supply, up the hall," he said, never raising his head from his shell game.

Winter left Bland talking to Stoetzel and found the supply room. No one was in attendance but the door was open. Two still-packed parachutes, an M-14 with a broken stock, one flight helmet, and two scuffed leather flight bags were piled in the corner. Winter confiscated the thinner bag, took it back to Pre-Op with him. Away from the eyes of medical personnel he pulled the contents from the bag and checked. The maps were there, and a blank, lined note pad.

Nothing more!

"Archie. Archie, can you hear me? Where's your sked sheet?" Winter asked urgently.

There was no answer. He tried again, and after a long pause devoid of response, Krebs' arm raised slightly and he pointed to a pile of fatigues on a chair, the jacket ripped and bloody. He didn't speak.

Winter found in a pocket the rice paper onionskin with bare numbers and letters, without security classification or caveat stamps. "OK!" he breathed a sigh of relief. "Now, where's the BINGO pad?" He slipped the sked into his own pocket.

There was no answer. The doctor looked up: "He's out. He'll be out for a few hours, at least. Check back later." He bent back to his task.

Winter went back up the hall and checked Supply again, but the thick pad of one-time message blanks, encrypted for sending secure traffic over a clear radio channel, were not in the pilot's flight bag. Only maps and flight esoterica. He gathered up all the items and carried them out to the Jeep, piling them in a heap with the broken M-14 on the bottom, and went back to the pilot.

Before Winter could speak to the possibility of the missing BINGO pad, Lieutenant Bland saw him coming and said to Stoetzel, "Here's Winter. I want you to tell both of us what happened. OK?"

Laboriously, each breath causing him obvious pain, Stoetzel told his story.

"The aircraft—Beaver one-five-one—was just out of hundred-hour . . . engine change. Run up for the prescribed time . . . declared fit for mission use. . . . It was test flown for twenty minutes. Today's mission . . . was the first extended flight in that bird . . . since engine change.

"We launched on time, oh-seven-forty-five . . . worked our target area for over two . . . hours. Then . . . moving from one target area to another, I sud . . . suddenly found myself flying a glider." He looked over at Winter as he used the unlikely term. Winter knew exactly what the pilot meant; he had been exposed to this phenomenon during one of his early flights. Stoetzel, in a personally contrived "welcome aboard" stunt, had cut the power to put a little scare into his passenger. It was at this time when Winter threatened to kill him. Just a little "gotcha" pulled on every new operator.

But it *was* an awesome sound—the sound of sudden silence. And that when Winter instinctively knew they had the means to resurrect their failed options, continue powered flight. But it must be truly arresting when it happens for real, he thought. The plane *had become*, effectively, a glider. The Beaver only had one engine, and when that one stopped, cause existed for concern.

"I immediately went through . . . every emergency procedure since the Wright Brothers' original mistake." The pilot suddenly seemed to catch his second psychic wind, sounded stronger. "I'd already switched tanks earlier, so it wasn't fuel starvation; we must-a had at least a couple hours' juice left. So I squawked a MAYDAY. I tried to pinpoint where I was. I knew there were those three . . . grass strips in the immediate area. All I had to do was get myself oriented to one of them," Stoetzel continued. He was into the flow of it now.

"I chose the nearest, naturally—turned out to be the best and the longest. I made a careful bank to port to line up the bird for a straight-in . . . thought we had it made. Dead stick—I'd have to do it in one—I couldn't go around. The turn was hairy without power, 'fraid we'd fall out of the sky, but once on final I was . . . *wuhoahhh*" Stoetzel caught his breath ". . . able to squawk another MAYDAY with better coordinates. I even mentioned the emergency strip—they apparently never relayed that to the Third—and then rode it in." The lieutenant and Winter, along with two medics who were drawn to the recital, stood mesmerized as Stoetzel rambled on, sounding tired and in pain, still recalling the events in detailed order.

"We had plenty of strip. I needed a shallow descent, and used most of it. As I reached the altitude where I'd normally chop power, a loud clinking sound caught my attention. I checked and saw . . . there were holes where a bullet had come through the left side of the cockpit and gone out the right . . . fortunately missed both of us. I looked out, and I could make out a dozen or so fuckin' little Gooks running out of the brush along the north edge of the strip. They had rifles and sub-machineguns . . . every goddamned one of 'em firin' on us. I didn't dare set it down yet; had to take it as far from the V.C. as I could." The pilot rolled his eyes and took a deep breath.

"Managed to keep it airborne with rudder, flaps, and some severe puckering until I ran out of strip. I touched down; we bounced and rumbled ahead, safe on the ground —" Winter noticed the sudden shift from singular to plural, as if the pilot had only then realized he had a passenger " —still making some sixty-five knots ground speed. And then, oohhh shit! I saw a wide drainage ditch right in my face, running diagonally across the strip. If we went into that, I might as well have flown that pig into the side of the Black Virgin. I stroked the rudder and yanked back on the yoke, and that glorious mother Beaver responded —Thank you DeHaviland," he bowed a tiny obeisance toward Canada " —became airborne again. For a split second. Then I pushed the yoke forward and jammed us back onto the sod. But I could tell I'd cut it too fine. The end of the strip was coming up fast and the bird was still bouncing."

No one dared break his spiel.

"I rode the brakes —" and Stoetzel tried to mimic the action, jabbing his foot into a non-existent pedal, the sudden movement wrenching him sideways with pain, as he described the rubber trees, in stately alignment, rushing at him and he knew he couldn't stop in time. At the last instant, just before engaging the orderly grove of trees, he'd nudged the rudder, directing the fuselage between two rows of whitewashed tree trunks, consigning the wings to the trees, one either side of the aircraft fuselage. When the crash noises and shock of impact stopped, Stoetzel was surprised to find himself alive and conscious. ". . . but there were little, tiny tinkling and crackling noises everywhere, and I could hear fluids — didn't know what; probably a bit of everything: fuel, hydraulic fluid, oil, blood. I probably pissed myself . . ."

The audience took a short respite while Stoetzel dealt with a spasm of coughing, and the subsequent pain that resulted.

"Gotta get out! It was all I could think of. I didn't even remember my op in the back."

It did not demonstrate a lack of caring, Winter knew. A pilot's training instills in him the instinctive notion to get clear of a downed aircraft; worry later whether or not there's a fire or further danger from the crash site. But, evacuate the premises. Stoetzel did.

"The fuselage came to rest on its left side, the port landing gear strut torn away so that my door was jammed into the ground. Couldn't get out that way. Then I remembered Krebs, and called back, asking if he was all right. He said he was buried under the rack of equipment that ripped loose from the floor on impact." Stoetzel's voice was growing weaker. Winter understood: in the Beaver, Krebs had been buckled into his seat on the back left side. The stacked equipment was mounted on the right in floor brackets where a right seat would have been. Gravity-borne inertia had brought the two hundred-or-so pounds of communications equipment crashing down on his right shoulder.

"When I asked again if he was O.K., Krebs answered. Said he hurt all over, but thought he was not injured — just trapped. I got out through the right door, opening upward. Scrambling across the canted cockpit, my forty-five slipped from my shoulder holster — musta come unsnapped — and fell into the broke bird." Stoetzel fell silent for a full minute, then took a deep breath and went on. "Just as I got up through the door, getting oriented, I heard rounds snapping overhead and into the wreckage I had no time to fish my sidearm out of the litter. I managed to reach back in the open door and get a grip on Krebs's hand, but was unable to pull him from beneath the rack."

A break for pain.

"About then," he continued, "I remembered why we were in this shit. The V.C.! I looked back up the strip, checking where they were, how close, and saw most of them still about a hundred and fifty yards away. Their fire was beginning to find us, though. I thought, Oh, shit. It can't get worse than this." Stoetzel looked up at Winter and Bland and grinned through his pain.

"Then, out of the corner of my eye I saw another bunch-a peasants in V.C. uniform: black pajamas and cone-shaped straw hats, coming through the rubber trees from the opposite direction." After a brief pause, as if suddenly understanding all that had occurred, Stoetzel said, "Holy shit! Not only do the bad guys have reinforcements, I thought—as if they really needed them—but I *really* broke my plane. I worried more about that than the friggin' Gooks."

No one spoke. How could the two men have escaped that pincer movement? But, like movie serials of years past that left one spellbound for a week, the hero tied to the railroad tracks, or launched into space over a cliff edge, you knew that he would make it . . . *they* would make it. For here they were.

"I'd lost my forty-five in the crash. I reached back in for Krebs's M-fourteen, but it was broken. Snapped right at the small of the stock like a matchstick. It's all up, I just knew. But when this second mob got closer—all of 'em armed, but none of them firing—I spotted one guy in khaki. No hat, but obviously the leader, waving his arms, urging on the whole damned bunch of them. A squad of Ruff-Puffs." Winter understood he meant Vietnamese Government home guard troops. The good guys. More or less.

Stoetzel told his spellbound audience that when they broke into the clearing near the aircraft, most of the Popular Forces had hit the ground and opened fire on the VC, who were still firing on the downed aircraft as they attacked. The enemy assault stopped; the VC went to ground. Then Stoetzel, who was having trouble breathing by then, watched them as they got to their feet a few at a time and ran, in a very disciplined manner to hear him tell it, back to the cover of the trees along the far edge of the strip.

The man in khakis, a Regional Popular Forces lieutenant, directed some of his men in extracting Krebs from the wreckage, and helped Stoetzel, who by then was wheezing and in wracking pain, and they all took cover in a triangular concrete defensive position a couple of hundred feet from the crash site. Some army's leftover fort. Stoetzel said he'd not even seen it through the rubber trees.

The pilot continued relating events, but it was obvious he was minutes, at most, away from unconsciousness. Soon after securing themselves, he related, and as the enemy fire began picking up again — the VC becoming bolder, working their way ever closer — they heard the sound of choppers. Two UH-1s, flying gunship cover for a CH-37 recovery ship, broke over the near edge of the tree line and from within the fort area, Stoetzel watched M-60 fire ripping along the far tree line, into the brush and darkness under the trees. From there, tiny winking points of light flashes defined the VCs' positions. And then the CH-37 had touched down and GIs, one wearing a flight helmet sprouting headphones, ran toward them.

Stoetzel went quiet. He had taken them through it and now, exhausted, was unable to speak further.

Someone — Winter hoped it was a surgeon when he looked back to confront some ugly sounds across the room — was cutting on Krebs.

* * *

Lieutenant Chaldano was holed up in the latrine when the two soldiers reported to the Orderly Room. They elected not to join him there, but awaited his pleasure in his official den.

When he returned and was duly seated, composed and officer-like, he addressed them jointly: "Ser — uhh . . . Gentlemen." He knew immediately that was wrong, but he was begun. "I have a job. For one of you. Uhh, either . . . umm . . . one of you."

"Yessir, you said. That would be, then, just one of us," Brenner ventured.

"That is correct, Specialist mmm . . . Brenner?" Chaldano, with a fifty-percent chance of getting it right, had struck the gold.

"Yessir. Brenner." The Spec-5 looked down, checking his nametag.

"And you are . . ." the lieutenant consulted a sheet of paper before him, "Val-da-pee-no, right?" He looked up with pleasant mien at the other soldier.

"No, *Señor*, sir. Valdapeño."

"Oh. Oh, of course. Doesn't show the tilde on military records. Hmmm. Well, here's the thing. I have a need for a squared-away soldier for a period on Friday. This week. You were both suggested . . . or either . . . to fill the bill. I have to decide which to use. Who to use. Whom to use." He bobbed his head in time with the pronoun do-si-do. It made sense to choose for himself, and the two supplicants looked no worse than most enlisted men. Though he vaguely remembered he'd had some history with Brenner.

"What is this job, sir?" asked Brenner. "On Friday."

The lieutenant shuffled the single paper back into a stack on the desk before answering. "We have a distinguished guest arriving here in the Third, Friday at ten-hundred hours. Brigadier General Easy, Deputy C.G. of A.S.A., will be visiting us, the first stop on his in-country tour."

The men waited.

The lieutenant, feeling he had explained sufficiently, waited.

"And? . . ." Brenner prompted.

"Oh, and we need an enlisted assistant — call him an aide — to attend the general's needs."

Another wait, but that was it.

"The general's . . . needs." Brenner would have it spelled out. "You mean, handle his baggage, open doors for him, get him a drink? Shine his shoes? Fetch whores? What . . . sir?"

"Whatever the general needs, Specialist," Chaldano snapped testily. "I'll explain all that to the individual selected." Neither man could swear the lieutenant uttered *Harrumph!* but the climate was right for it.

"Now, which of you is senior?"

"I am the *señor*, sir," said Valdapeño.

"No, no," the lieutenant exclaimed quickly. "The senior man. Who has been a Specialist Five longer?"

There was no response.

"All right, you're both Spec-5, E-5s. Valdapeño, what's your date of rank?"

"June fifteenth, nineteen sixty-two."

"Brenner?"

"How odd. Fifteen June, 'sixty-two." He smiled at Valdapeño who smiled back.

"Uhh . . ." the lieutenant said, stumped for the moment. "Right. Both promoted on the same date. Interesting. So, time in service. Brenner, what's your date of enlistment?"

"Twenty-six Feb, 'fifty-eight, sir."

"February the twenty-sixth, nineteen fifty-eight," Valdapeño echoed without waiting for the question, his brows arched at Brenner.

The officer's gaze was one of amazement. His eyes shifted from one man to the other, then back, seeking at first some sign of playfulness; failing that, some obvious, distinguishing military factor between them. Nothing was apparent. "Well, date of birth's got nothing to do with it, so we can't use that. I doubt that G.C.T. scores —"

"I think we have the same scores, sir. It's the weirdest thing . . ." Brenner began.

"Yes, but I am smarter than you, *señor*," Valdapeño said, turning toward Brenner.

"Not according to the scores, you frigging wetback."

"*¡Es muy stupido!*"

"Exactly what I'm saying."

"Ey, behave you fuckin' mouth. I can dreenk you under the console, *Señor* Brenner." His voice rose with choler.

The lieutenant's eyes grew larger, his gaze flickering from one to the other.

"But I'm bigger and badder. I can whip your ass, Valentino." Brenner's demeanor notched up in aggressiveness.

"Ahh, your mama, she wears the combat boots."

"Gentlemen, gentlemen. Let's —"

"Yeah! Size ten, Beaner. So fucking what?"

"Brenner. Valdapeño. Stop this. Immediately!" The lieutenant rose to his feet, pointing a finger somewhere between them. He looked stricken.

"I will tell you this 'what' —"

"Men. *Knock it off!*"

The two leapt to rigid attention, their boot heels loud in the office. With a brief flutter of hands, Chaldano dismissed them.

"Forget I called you in here. I'll work this . . . I'll get someone else." He would not look back at them. "Go. Out. Back to WHITE BIRCH, both of you. Leave."

Outside, as the two strode through the hot, white dust toward their Jeep, Brenner, his face screwed up in anguish, said, "Seemed the silly shit would never grasp the obvious."

"My initial concern. Wonder who his next chump will be."

"Better go over his protocol guide, first." Brenner glanced over at his companion and said, "When did you come in?"

"Shit, I don't remember. Sometime in 'sixty. "

"Fuckin' new guy."

chapter thirteen

Bamboo Junction

Vietnam: November-December 1964

Winter waited until Staysail finished relating his adventures, then spoke up, "It's not there, Captain. I checked both Mister Stoetzel's and Krebs's recovered gear. The book's for sure missing."

"How bad is that?" Captain Pyburn said, not previously having run afoul of security matters.

"A blank BINGO pad of message forms for encryption, with no pages used, no messages filled in, is classified CONFIDENTIAL," Winter intoned mechanically. "It must be accounted for, though it's of the lowest security classification. If it's been used, information written and encrypted with it, it could be TOP SECRET, with further caveats, depending on message content and source. Krebs can't tell us now. It's impossible to determine just how grim the prospects are. But in matters of security, one rule rules: Assume the worst!"

The loss of classified material was feared by commanders and security officers, alike. In the arcane world of super secrets, truncation of budding military careers could easily become the order of the day, and careers and lives were commonly ruined without ever understanding why or how. Lieutenant Bland was horror stricken, suddenly contemplating a security investigation so early in his career, though he might be blameless in this instance. Neither did Captain Pyburn relish the notion of explaining to security people at Group, or higher—invariably unreasonable goddamned Nazis—just how his unit, one of his people, had come to misplace sacred scripture.

"We don't even have a clue how many pages have been used in the missing book, though it's a resource seldom relied upon," Winter admitted. "BINGO pads are issued daily to ops on the flight manifest; no one operator's responsible for the entire contents of the book, except on the day and during the time he's signed for it. Books are carried on missions and returned, often unused, intact; others remain in a safe, never seeing the light of day. They're inventoried monthly. Due soon on the first of the month, but no help now."

All understood that other copies were used as intended, and thus constituted security threats if compromised. If the one Krebs carried *had* been used, it would still contain all previous encrypted messages, and if Charlie got his hands on it he could back-track to any transmissions, using his own records—no one doubted that Charlie read 3rd RRU's mail, as 3rd RRU read that of the Asian enemy—and, by relating to corresponding pages in the book, could then decrypt/decode all previous messages sent using that book.

"This is shaping up as a major chapped ass for everyone even peripherally involved, sounds to me like," Pyburn predicted.

* * *

"Lieutenant Bland, Winter, we gotta get out there, see for ourselves," I heard Pyburn as I walked in the door when he was ringing off the sound-powered phone. "The Sixty-Eighth offered us a chopper. They're holding for us on the ramp." The captain headed for the door, snatching his helmet off a wall peg. Winter, looking like the hapless knight in "The Wizard of Id," still carried his weapon and flight gear and fell in behind Pyburn, while Bland went to scrounge a flight helmet. Bland, as far as I knew, had never flown, in country.

I was standing to the side in the CO's office. "Sir, all right if I come?"

"Don't have room, Brenner. We already got straphangers from the Sixty-Eighth. Gotta be me, Bland's gotta go, and Winter. And a photographer from S-2." He turned to the S-2. "Who you got for that, Bland?"

"Sir? No one, sir." He looked startled.

"Gotta have somebody, Bland. Your security investigation. And pictures for the crash board." He turned to me. "Brenner, can you find your way around a camera?"

"Born to it, sir." God's truth, a long-standing love affair with photography.

"Get the gear, Bland. Meet us out front in one minute. That chopper won't wait."

I grabbed my helmet from the wall, took a carbine off the rack, and followed out the door. We piled in the captain's Jeep. Pyburn had already started the engine when Bland ran out wearing his sidearm, threw a camera bag to me, and jumped in the back, holding a borrowed flight helmet on his head. It rattled around like a bucket on a fence post.

The 68th had drawn new ships in the past few months, transitioning from H-23 "flying bananas" into the new UH-1s, called "Hueys." None of us had been aboard one of the new birds, but in the moment I couldn't get excited about it. They resembled beefed-up locusts. Loud, beefed-up, sleek, mean-looking locusts.

The captain drove us along the flight line in the direction of our billets. The 68th's ramp was just beyond the corrugated metal fence, across the benjo ditch from Davis Station in the far, back corner of Tan Son Nhut. Their area, located on the periphery of the field, gave the helicopter company direct flight access to and from their pads without interfering with fixed-wing air traffic on the base. The captain pulled us up at a ship that sat alone in a rectangle of painted yellow lines. A gaggle of people stood about, body language showing impatience. We clambered aboard. A crew chief- gunner handed Pyburn a headset, while the rest of us resigned ourselves to ignorance of developing events. Immediately, a whine began, growing quickly louder, and then a choppy flutter which rose steadily into a throbbing tornado.

So what's the big deal with Hueys? Mother's loud, like any chopper, more crowded than most, though they had told us a "slick" — a term I came to understand meant a UH-1 without integral or protruding weaponry — could carry twelve troops. Must have been thinking Lilliputians; twelve human people packing gear in that cargo bay and we'd all have hernias. It was a short flight in the Huey, though. Pilot had the thing flat out and, as close to the ground as we were, we seemed to be making about a hundred and fifty knots; probably doing more like half that. It was only twenty-eight, thirty minutes to the crash site.

The captain did a lot of talking on the way but, lacking headsets and over the noise of the rotors, none of us had a clue what he was saying. The 68th pilot made his approach along the length of the rubber tree corridors amongst the circuits of two other Hueys, both gunships, flying escort. They were primed for trouble, but nothing seemed to be happening on the ground; they stayed aloft, kept circling. There was another Huey already on the ground, shut down and empty. When we landed and un-assed our bird, a small Vietnamese officer in khakis ran from the trees and waved. He carried a US Army .45 automatic, and in his child-size hand it looked enormous . . . a ridiculous, dangerous toy for a child.

I was surprised to see, first thing, the Commanding Officer of 3rd RRU, Light Colonel JT "Junior" Meador, out here in the real world. The colonel probably had no idea his name was Junior; but since we hadn't a clue what the J stood for, Junior served. I was further surprised that I recognized him. He ran with the big dogs, at JGS and downtown, and hardly ever played with us pups on the porch. He didn't know me from Adam.

I had taken a couple of photos on our approach, when we broke over the clearing and I first spotted the wreckage in the edge of the rubber trees. It was, indeed, wreckage. "We won't fly that one again, I dare say," I dared say, but no one heard me over the landing noise.

The fuselage of the Beaver seemed to be more or less intact, not ruptured . . . whatever benefit that might imply. The fuselage lay on its left side. The right landing gear was still intact, sticking up in the air with the tail assembly, though the left tip of the horizontal stabilizer was chewed up. The left landing gear had sheared off and was trapped partly under the fuselage. One wing had spun off into the next corridor between trees; the other, the left, was two rows over on the other side. Both wings seemed relatively whole, though detached from the plane. No, I was relatively confident we wouldn't fly one-five-one again.

Now, working around the ship, taking the shots the captain wanted, I realized something was seriously catty-wonkus. I mean, besides the freaking bird being strewn all over Southeast Asia. Didn't take heavy analysis to work out: the Beaver had a short fuselage. The front of the plane ended on the outside of the firewall. I looked about, and up the row of trees, and spotted a mass of aircraft engine half-buried in the dirt, some ninety-to-a-hundred feet away from the rest of the remains. I quickly imagined the crash itself: the sudden application of a full stop — interrupting momentum at the instant the plane impacted the trees, stripping the wings off — had ripped the radial powerhouse loose and it crashed forward all that way. It left a path. One of the helicopter people was standing, puzzling over it. I walked beyond him and took a long shot, showing the distance back to the fuselage.

I was fumbling with the unfamiliar Pentax SLR, wanting a wide-angle shot of fuselage, wings, et al, when I heard a series of pops. I hit the dirt as bullets flitted through the upper branches of rubber trees. Pyburn yelled, *"Hit the dirt! Enemy fire."* He knew the signs, but it was wasted breath: everyone was down or behind something.

The helicopter crew chief, likely from Southern California and still living in la-la land, was hunkered down as on a surfboard behind the tail section of the plane. A nice secure spot, that, given the thickness of the aircraft skin of about one-thirty-second of an inch aluminum. Silly asshole. Once I dug the lens out of the dirt and dusted it off, I got a quick snap of him, in case I ever needed a favor from the 68th.

I glanced around, checking where the colonel had gone to ground. There he was, old infantryman, blooded in Korea, wearing a Combat Infantry Badge pinned to his starched fatigues, eating dirt behind an equipment rack, his ass protruding a foot above cover in a stance even I knew better than assume. I grabbed a shot of him too, just for shits and giggles; I had no notion of ever letting it see daylight.

The Ruff-Puffs got into the game and, with two gunships active, the VC fire quickly slackened, died away. Those of us with prescribed duties continued doing what we were being paid to do. Winter checked both radios, the R-390s just so much trash now. Frequencies on both were set to zero. Krebs had done his job before the crash, all right. But even with everyone searching, there was no sign of the BINGO pad.

I was standing by the ARVN Regional Forces lieutenant when I noticed the .45 stuck in his belt line. A corner of the checkered grip was broken off — just like Mister Stoetzel's pistol. I asked him about it, but suddenly the lieutenant spoke no English, though I'd heard him in halting conversation with Pyburn earlier.

Yeah, right!

I jerked the .45 from his pants and walked away, expecting him to raise hell. And I saw him look at Pyburn in appeal, but he said nothing.

Pyburn came over to me, held out his hand, and though I hadn't a clue, I gave him the pistol. He walked back, handed it to the militia LT, who smiled broadly through broken teeth. The captain then arranged for the militia to secure the crash site until a recovery chopper came for the remains. That would only be done to prevent Charlie from making booby traps of metal and loose parts; none of the equipment—certainly not the plane—would ever be used again. Well, maybe some spares.

We piled aboard the chopper and headed home, satisfied in some respects, but there was an air of heightened suspense over the missing BINGO pad. Well, screw it! Not my worry. If they would put dangerous toys in the hands of clowns like Krebs. . . .

* * *

After the intoxicating thrill of riding in a mixmaster, and being shot at, back on base I felt a decided need for emotional sustenance in a quiet atmosphere. Winter declined to accompany me, his furrowed brow indicating his concern about the possible violation. I commiserated with his concerns, but sought my own relief. The club was the best I could do. I found Judge Monaghan there, holding court, explaining to Lessor, who had been on emergency leave in the States the previous two weeks, the effects of cascading activity while he was absent. Monaghan only nodded at me when I walked up, not about to interrupt his own bombast.

". . . wasn't long back. Thirty October. At night. Halloween next day. Silly buggers could have waited one more day; would have made a hell of a fright night."

"Any night's fright night with Sir Charles," Eddison commented.

Ignoring the peanut gallery, Judge plowed on. "So this company of Viet Cong, carrying mortars and R.P.G.s, filters through the countryside twenty miles northeast of here." He fatuously pointed to the ground beneath his feet. "Situate themselves into firing positions around Bien Hoa airbase. Probably pre-prepared sites.

210 ~ Bamboo Junction

No one sounds the alarm, though locals are standing around like union pickets, watching Charlie set up. Same ol' shit."

Monaghan held a jaded view of Vietnamese national probity. Well, actually, everyone felt that, but Judge had a compelling need to comment publicly on it. His didactic delivery and enveloping facetiousness was both his main draw and a factor of disparagement.

"Picture this. On the airfield at Bien Hoa, arrayed like toys in nice, neat rows, is a squadron of B-fifty-sevens. These are old bombers, people, not a verifiable threat in anyone's war, but the V.C.'s hackles are raised. Transferring the jets from the Philippines into Vietnam has crossed some elusive political Rubicon, and the V.C. feel obliged to respond to this unwelcome presence. The perfection of this line-up echos General Martin's deployment of B-seventeens at Hickam, which led to their remarkably efficient decimation by Jap airmen when they struck Pearl Harbor."

"Where you going with this shit, Judge? I know 'bout Pearl Harbor," Lessor demanded impatiently. He wanted another beer so he could, once again under the influence, begin to forget this place, but the waitress who was waiting tables on the early evening shift wouldn't come near Lessor's table; he kept pinching her ass. And Lessor hated being lectured to by Monaghan. Thus aroused, he didn't even acknowledge Winter's presence when he walked up.

"No! Now listen. You weren't here; you gotta catch up. At Bien Hoa, in the present, nineteen hundred and sixty-four, these little people attack the base. In the ensuing bombardment that lasts several hours without, I am forced to believe, any effective response or defense, American troops and Vietnamese civilian workers and other hangers-on rage and dash about pointlessly, while the mortars pour seemingly endless fire on the nicely arrayed aircraft." Monaghan, catching his breath after that run-on, held up his hand, imperiously forestalling interruption.

"Six B-fifty-sevens completely destroyed. And some twenty other aircraft, including additional B-fifty-sevens damaged. A loss of five American, two South Vietnamese military personnel killed, a number more wounded.

"It's a slap in the face for our government, who still has—we all know, seeing daily the results of this Armenian gang-bang—no cohesive policy regarding American intentions or goals in this wayward, backward mudhole."

Sweet Jesus, the man could talk.

"It is also the stimulus that enables Ambassador Taylor, without fear of censure, to urge Johnson to bomb North Vietnam in retaliation. You'll recall how our President avoids making decisions, anguishing over political and career implications of such a move. But Bien Hoa apparently finally establishes a mindset that may provide, in the near future, a basis for some serious attention to North Vietnam."

Despite that I did admire the Judge's loquacious talent, Lessor was not an adherent.

"Where you goin' with this shit, Judge? Gonna be a test? Where's that waitress slut?" Lessor demanded in quick, triplicate succession, looking at me as if I might jump in with answers. I kept my mouth shut and offered the floor to Winter. He declined, remaining mute.

"Harken to me," Monaghan said in a stentorian tone. "This pertains. It would not surprise me if the intelligence needs to support such new, though long-overdue, American strategy should drive Third RRU's efforts for the rest of this conflict, albeit short-lived. I believe, gentlemen, we are going to find ourselves key players."

Monaghan's lecture was thus concluded with what might have been a bombshell, if anyone had thought he might be approaching veracity—not necessarily on the right page, but at least in the right book. But no one believed such. He and Lessor, in mutual silence, agreed the subject was exhausted. Lessor expressed himself fed up with the slipshod management policies of the EM/NCO Club, vis-á-vis attention to duties by employees, and wanted to move on; the club's ephemeral attractions had worn quite thin. If Lessor couldn't pinch the ass of the club waitress, he knew an ass in a downtown bar he could fondle.

* * *

Monaghan, after boring everyone to tears in the club, proceeded to bitch our ride from Davis Station. Drunken ingrate that he is, chastising the *dzong* cart driver for picking up ARVN soldiers, he embarrassed us all. Thinks the taxi service is run for himself, alone. After that cart driver demanded everyone un-ass his machine, there were no other carts, no cyclos available. So we all five walked to the front gate.

Coming out Gate 2, Lessor argued for the barbershop. We knew that was a lie; he always got his burr cut in the NCO club so he could yell at the barber when he yanked his hair with the hand-powered clippers. The NCO Club barber was always inept, if not always drunk.

No, Lessor, primed by his strike-out with the waitress, was opting for a run down 100-P Alley, and the rest of us had our sights set on greater things. Glencannon was in town from Can Tho where he'd been promoted to sergeant first class and was wanting to party big city. But he and Winter offered no opinion.

I motioned to one of the carts lined up in front of the Violet Vulva supper club. The driver bounded into his seat and kick-started the one-lung engine. Nominal struggling got Lessor into the back wire cage and we fled down the street in a cloud of exhaust. I leaned over and yelled in the drivers ear, "Bamboo Junction."

The cart driver yelled something back with a question mark on the end of it.

"All right, you goddamned V.C. asshole, Gia Dinh. You know Bamboo Junction as well as I. Play your games. Gia Dinh! The Dingo Bar," I added, pointing him toward our favorite hangout on that seamy side of town, named by the Australians who favored its meager attractions. I cannot imagine why the term "seamy" might have attached itself to Gia Dinh, or as we had designated it, Bamboo Junction; it was no grungier than any other part of the Sai Gon/Cho Lon Greater Co-Prosperity Sphere.

Cho Lon I don't want to discuss with any seriousness. Belongs to the Chinese and the VC.

"Monaghan, sit up, you shit," Lessor grated at the raconteur who had turned drunk on us, going silent after evaluation of Southeast Asian politics, "You look like you're gonna puke. Don't you puke on me. Lean out the side. Puke on the driver. Better . . . *Dung lai!"* he screamed at the driver. When the cart whirled to the road edge, Lessor grabbed Monaghan and propelled him to the open rear of the cart where he left him, his head hanging tantalizingly near the road surface. "There, puke off the tailgate. *Di-di! you fuckin' V.C."* The driver pulled back onto the road, the tiny engine pulsing, straining with five large Americans in the back. It could have carried a dozen ARVN with less strain.

We were past JGS compound, past the crossroads with the stop lights. From here on, until we came actually into Bamboo Junction — the main, built-up part of Gia Dinh — we were off on our own in the countryside. The White Mice didn't even patrol out here. Nor the MPs. I had the sudden feeling I should be armed. With that first tense realization I was again confronted with the extreme degree of silliness operating: that here, obviously in a war despite what the political smoke and dazzle artists called it, a trained soldier was forced to go about unarmed. Not as if we were considered behind the lines of battle, or away from the front. There was no front in 'Nam; the line of battle was where you got caught with your ass hanging out.

But Pentagon Willie Wutz decreed we be targets until diagnosed as dead targets, rather than offend some subculture wannabe by carrying a weapon. Replay of the Puritans' test for truth, ferreting out witches: ask the question; when the individual denies witchcraft, dunk them underwater for a period; if they drown, they were telling the truth. If they survive, they were lying, and it's out of the pond, straight to the burning stake. Our own No Right Answer scenario, carrying a weapon in town off-duty, was a gigantic No-No, especially in the bars; it could get one in immense doo-doo.

But then, being without could get one killed, than which there is no deeper doo-doo.

"Truly a quandary of epic proportions," I pondered aloud.

"Brenner, why d'you talk so funny?" Glencannon said to me suddenly. "I mean, why do you use such big words, say shit I don't understand? I'm no brain trust, I know that, but I can usually hold my own with most G.I.s. I'm afraid to start a conversation with you."

It was a fair question, but I thought back and couldn't remember anything particularly erudite or esoteric this evening. Besides, our new inquisitive sergeant was drunk.

Winter injected a salient observation: "He's an asshole!"

"No, besides that. Why's—"

"'cause he's edjicated, you dumb shit." Winter seemed particularly perverse tonight.

"Educated?"

"Yeah, you know what that is. It's something you and I and all these other enlisted swine lack in spades." That was a lie. Besides Glencannon, there was not a man on the cart who had not been to college. Maybe not as long and as specifically as had I, but—

"Yeah, Luther here's a regular study in irresolution," Winter went on, dead-pan. "Drafted. Voluntarily extended for A.S.A., spent fourteen months in Korea, then got out. Used his G.I. Bill and got smart. Then, somewhere along the line it wore off, and he got dumb again. Came back in." My friend looked at me across the dark of the Asian night as he spoke, moonlight and the occasional lamp from a roadside hut casting him in a ghoulish light.

Sporting an attitude tonight. What was his attitude? Was that smirk? Gloat? Or just a sort of sad query? Knowing Winter, likely the latter, but it provoked my response. He'd known it would.

"That's about it. Yet . . . not half the story," I acknowledged.

"You went to graduate school, didn't you?" Winter said in an accusing tone. "Before you came back in. Before Asmara." He wouldn't let it go, taking me to task for . . . what? Like demanding a mentally deficient child recite his lessons for disinterested cousins.

Lessor, not as drunk as he wanted or planned to be, volunteered his succinct appraisal: "Jeezus-Christ! College! That's fucking worse than the Army. Talk about bureaucracy."

"All that G.I. Bill money," I said. That didn't bear up; no one offered a response.

"Where?" Winter pushed. "Where'd you study?" He knew I'd attended Brown.

I found my eyes wandering. I didn't want to go on with this, and the other three were not exactly hanging on every word. Well, except for Monaghan, now sitting up at the tailgate with his disdainful expression. But then, he just might finally have been going to fulfill his obligation to puke.

We were coming into a built-up area where huts and tin-roofed, tin-sided shacks grew in scattered disarray. I watched sly shadows of night people, flitting between the houses and palms and encroaching jungled growth, edging toward the road but never arriving. It was an unstable environment, indistinct but threatening. Unsure. Like something from South Sea tales.

"Well . . ." Winter urged. And I knew where he was going. ". . . you didn't finish the Ph.D., did you?" I could hear the implicit You didn't finish the story.

"No," I said, "Fuck 'em,'" Winter knew what I meant; it was off the board for the rest.

I realized, for the first time as I said it, there on that dark road in north Sai Gon, years after the fact, that I had always meant that. Fuck. Them. All. I'd had enough of the academic bullshit. After more than a year in grad school following the Master's in American Lit, focused on what I thought was a well-defined Ph.D. agenda, a tenured waste-of-space withdrew his approval of my thesis. Told me to start over. Fuck 'em!

There was only the muttering of the straining engine and a noxious susurration of oily breeze stirred by our passing.

"Walked out of my adviser's office, drove straight to the recruiting station, *et voila!* Here's the boy." Yes, indeed. Here is the boy!

The question of further revelation was a moot one, in light of our progress in the cart. Like a well-scripted movie, any need to expand on my tale ended when we pulled up before the Dingo Bar, with its elegant plywood façade bracing a shattered-but-not-removed plate glass window, a yellow-red-green electric sign buzzing a protest after its missing letters, so that the only indicator visible in the night sky was ". . **ng** . **B** . . ". I never understood that sign: neither the gaseous physics of the partial display, the metaphysics of the implicit but lost message, nor the fact that it had been that way since Lot's wife turned salty.

* * *

Bland and Winter returned to the Air Force dispensary the following morning and found Krebs in a white bed, conscious, awake, and pissed off.

"Krebs," the lieutenant greeted him, "can you talk?"

"Sir, these goddamned Air Farce medics —"

"Another time the diatribe, Krebs," Winter said evenly. "We have to know about the BINGO pad."

"What pad?" He winced, writhing in what could have been contrived pain as he answered. "Lieutenant, you the one told the doctors not to give me any pain medication?"

"I am. Until we've gotten this straight about the pad." Righteous indignation on Bland's face overrode any tendency he might have entertained toward humanitarianism.

"What about it?"

"It wasn't in your mission bag. Not at the crash site," Winter said firmly. "Did you do something else with it, or can we assume Charlie will now be sending encrypted messages compliments of the Third?"

Krebs' pale face blanched, then colored in a blush.

"Well?"

"Hell, Sarge. The pad's in the bottom drawer in the small safe in Flight Ops. I never carry that piece of shit on a mission," he blustered, but he would look only at the floor.

A long, pregnant silence ensued.

"You never carry it?" Winter said quietly, unsure if he'd misheard. "How, might I ask, did you plan to pass information to the ground should you have inadvertently encountered something of significance out there, Krebs? *How the hell* —"

"C'mon, Sarge. If we go down out there, I can eat that dinky rice paper sked sheet. I *can't* see myself wolfing down an inch-thick pad of paper. With staples. As for using it when I need to, who're you kidding? Nobody wants to hear from us. In real time, anyhow. If they do, it don't do 'em shit for good, 'cause if there's something out there worth bombin' or shootin' at, then some V.C., masquerading as an ARVN officer, will sidetrack the target plot in J.G.S. anyhow . . . if it got *that* far."

As bizarre as it sounded when expressed, Winter could not fault the man's conviction.

"What do you mean, Specialist?" Bland asked, already shocked out of his preppie blasé.

"You know what I mean, sir. Our own goddamned government is playing games in this sometimes war, and I'm not all that sure we're hanging our asses out over Indian Country for any reason other than to make nice on paper. Nobody, *nobody* goes after our target fixes."

The lieutenant, apparently unable to refute Krebs's heresy, stormed from the dispensary and drove away, leaving Winter to fend for himself. Winter later related to Brenner the story, confirming Krebs's heretical disregard for operational dictate: "Archie was right in everything he said. The pad was in the safe."

* * *

Lieutenant Zwick sat in the Beaver, engine turning over, his eyes roving the panel, hands slithering over the yoke, trim tabs, radio switches, and flap controls in anxious impatience. He glanced at his watch: 1210 hours! They were to have launched at 1200. Where the hell was his scheduled operator? He shut down and waited.

He felt the change in the cabin when the rear door opened. The craft rocked slightly, and he looked over his shoulder to bust Nesbitt's chops when he mounted. But it was not Nesbitt. A Spec-Four, whom Zwick recognized only from having seen him about the 3rd RRU headquarters, climbed into the rear seat and began buckling in. Zwick checked him out: proper helmet, mission bag, chute, weapon; and he watched as the new guy swarmed on through the pre-launch sequence, belting in, plugging in the microphone, and storing the weapon so it wouldn't smash him in the face or break equipment when the aircraft was in violent maneuvers. Which was all the time.

"Who you?" Zwick asked, clicking the intercom.

"Specialist Five Herbert Dann, sir," the op replied.

Man, he was a big sucker, Zwick observed over his shoulder.

"You ready, Dann? We'll talk when I've got this piece of crap airborne."

"Oh, sure . . . sir." His demeanor and expression gave away his unbridled enthusiasm for what was about to happen.

Ahh, well, thought Zwick. He, too, shall bear any burden . . .

"Let's do it." Zwick went through start-up, waved off the firewatch—who then dragged the chocks clear—and sat watching the instruments. Channeling Dann into external comms, he said, "Sai Gon ground control, Army Two-Six-Six. Request taxi instructions from Army ramp, active."

Within minutes the aircraft was cleared of Tan Son Nhut airspace and en route to its first scheduled tasking of the day. Zwick grilled the new op, learning that he had flown five check flights with other ops and been passed for mission flying. Dann had been in country a while, working the WHITE BIRCH ground site and consequently knew the mission well. What Zwick did not learn, but was known by Winter and the other operators in Air, was that Dann had asked for Air, and extended six months to get it, when after nine months in the Third, he'd received a letter from his fiancée, telling him she was three months pregnant, and asking him how soon they could get married. "Not soon!" was his two-word postcard reply. That same afternoon he extended. With extension and the flight physical passed, the transfer was assured. There was still a desperate need for Air ops.

Dann gave Zwick coordinates for their first target of the day, and Zwick drove them to the Fishhook area of the border. The target was found, DF-ed. "Still resident in The Elephant Kingdom, I see," acknowledged Dann.

Zwick could recognize Cambodia. He keyed his intercom and said to the new op, "Working cross-border targets is always a tricky scenario: pilot's got to be forever alert to location, vis-á-vis the border, and we must, under no circumstances, violate that border." The *border*, sounding tangible and ostensibly separating the two countries, was a myth and all knew it; there were no natural geological demarcations such as a mountain chain, a river, or a regular dotted line inscribed down the surface of the terrain. That Cambodia was *neutral* was also a myth, merely given lip service by the media and several governments, most enthusiastically by the government of the Democratic Republic of (North) Vietnam. The North used that enforced myth to enable unhindered movement of troops and supplies along trails from North Vietnam, through another myopic player—Laos. Zwick keyed and spoke again,

"Monaghan describes Laos in terms of horse racing: 'Laos, ten-year-old filly, out of Indo-China by Marx.'"

The region displayed the neatness of overcooked spaghetti. Hundreds of strands of trails and roads and pathways that went to make up the so-called Ho Chi Minh Trail meandered in and out of North Viet Nam, Laos, Cambodia, and back into South Viet Nam, when- and wherever circumstances most favored.

Dann had been told that Lieutenant Zwick habitually dragged his feet on the Intel side of the mission; he flew whatever he was ordered to fly, but often without bothering to learn why. Dann knew the mission and wanted to share. "It's important to keep track of certain radio targets, El Tee, like the one first worked today. It's one of a score of logistics monitoring and air defense groups in the Fishhook that protect the passage of tens of thousands of agents and troops infiltrating into the south, and the flow of thousands of tons of supplies, weapons, ammunition, vehicles, and fuel that come with them down the Trail. Keep track of, but do nothing to upset its mode of life."

Zwick did not reply. .Having reconfirmed the location of the first target, he moved the aircraft on to an orbit near where they expected the next target.

They worked three targets with good results, all out of reach of any kind of reprisal, even if they could have reported their findings. They could not do so, lacking any secure comms other than the BINGO pads, which were inconvenient. Zwick kept them near the border country, lazing about the mid-afternoon sky, while Dann fiddled with the dials. As the aircraft suddenly went into a tight, spiraling turn, holding in the turn through several full rotations, the new operator experienced for the first time a nauseating pressure, a subtle attempt to extrude his stomach and bowels out his ass, while rendering him dizzy and disoriented. G-forces working their inimitable magic.

Dann looked to his left, looking straight into the ground . . . and directly at some odd, very precisely regular, round formations below. They were at 2,200 feet altitude. He stared for a moment. Dann had no field exposure in combat, but he was not stupid, nor was he blind.

"Sir, those look like gun pits," he pointed out to Zwick, whom he saw was looking also down toward the same area.

"Think so?" He kept them in the tight turn.

"I didn't know the Zips had any defenses up here, along the border."

"Which Zips you talking about?"

"Zips. You know, ARVN. South Vietnamese." Where'd this boy lieutenant earn his magic decoder ring that he didn't know the term *Zip*?

"Ah, yes. With that caveat, I'd have to say you're right. They don't."

"Well, who—"

"Those are, no doubt, Cambodge gun pits. Logical, since we're at this red hot moment in the air space of Cambodia. Yessir. Triple-A gun pits. An-ti-aircraft guns." Zwick spoke in a lyrical ditty, as if lecturing a child, an accompanying element to WC Fields phrasing.

"Great jumpin' . . . *get us to hell out of here, Lieutenant. We can't be here! We're not allowed in Cambodia. Get moving, man, before they open fire.*" Dann's body, already large at rest, seemed to grow, his bulk swelling the rear compartment with the flood of adrenalin.

"Let's see what they're going to do," Zwick murmured placatingly, nudging the yoke tighter into his chest as he handled the plane to keep an eye on the guns below while endeavoring to avoid falling from the sky.

"*Get outta the fucking country!* Jesus! Lieutenant, move us."

As if he was only then aware of Dann's alarm, Zwick said, "Oh, O.K. If it bothers you. Gee. You guys act like nobody ever committed border incursion. Shit, FACs are over here all the time." He brought the aircraft back to level flight, headed east. "See." He pointed off to the side. "There's a Forward Air Controller now. See the O-Two? Where d'ya think he is, Kansas?"

Zwick adopted a lecturing tone. "They work over here regularly. They have a special outfit called RAVENS, recruited just to fly FAC in Cambodia and Laos. They fly Hmong or Nungs or some of the border hill people as ops. Call them ROBINS."

"Don't need international relations lessons, El Tee. We're not FACs. We got another job." He began to mumble.

"Say again, all after 'Shit!'" Zwick requested.

"I said, I already heard rumbles about you. I guess they weren't wrong." Acknowledging, reluctantly, that he was talking to an officer, Dann's comments faded into the ether.

"Probably. Don't believe everything you hear, Specialist. And don't sweat even what you believe. It's all just goddamned nonsense. Everybody dies."

"What?"

"When's our next sked. Where?" Zwick angled away.

They worked one more target away from the border, farther south toward Tay Ninh, and flew home. Back on Earth, Dann fled the bird with his gear and weapon before the lieutenant, who sat, unbuckled, writing up trouble reports in the cockpit.

After Dann reported to Winter in anger, the two crossed the street to Flight Ops and confronted Captain Pyburn. They'd barely completed the incident report when Zwick sauntered into the ready room. Pyburn glared at Winter and Dann in turn. "O.K. Get out of here, and keep this to yourself. I mean, *to yourself.* Not just among the allies. You got me, Winter? Dann?"

"Yessir!" in chorus. They saluted, about-faced, and passed Zwick without greeting as they went out the door. He strolled into the captain's space, a wan smile fixed on his face.

Despite the admonition of the captain to no-speakee, Zwick's border crossing was the talk of the mess and billet area, and every office in the headquarters. A hundred troops expressed wonder as to what Zwick's Officer Efficiency Report would look like. But OERs don't a war contain. The Third was short pilots; and Zwick continued to fly. It was a more contrite Zwick who now yanked his craft around the unfriendly skies of South Vietnam, and South Vietnam only, but he continued to be held in awe and fear by operators who had no death wish.

* * *

"Hey, Mister Travaglia, d'ja hear? Lyndon Baines Johnson defeated General Goldwater for the office of President of the United States," Specialist Burke informed the pilot. "Ain't that right, Brenner?"

"I can hardly dispute it, Burke. It's old news," I confirmed.

The expatriate Italian flyer blinked, sniffed, and said in a disdainful tone as he turned away from any possible confrontation: *"É troppo presto per cantar vittoria."*

"Fuckin'-A well said, Mister T.," I commented to his back. Whatever! Perhaps Johnson was too complex for the time, I thought, then knew better than that. Without doubt he retained that Texas bully about him that wanted to swat down that "little pissant country" who had dared stand up to the right and might of the champion of the free world. But I'm not sure any of us were overly thrilled at the election's outcome. At least General Barry knew where to put the ordnance.

In any case, Johnson never had a clue what Vietnam was all about. And if what Travaglia said is what I thought he said, he avoided ambiguity. He was dead right. But Burke, a product of apolitical upbringing, seemed mightily excited, and I hadn't the heart to pop his balloon.

* * *

By December, the pace had become horrendous. The Third was building up in manpower, but to volunteer for ARDF still required a nominal six months in country, so new guys weren't available for the Air role. The flying schedule was brutal, and in addition to his other duties as NCOIC of the section, pulling Duty NCO, and assorted other requirements, Winter made more scheduled flights than his hostile fire pay requirements called for.

Winter was scheduled to fly an afternoon mission, launch time 1235. As one of Sergeants Four—now, finally legitimately titled since Brenner had been promoted on December 1st—he had been accustomed to making lunch every working day, along with the kid lieutenant, Chaldano, and the other three sergeants, at the small restaurant in the civilian terminal building of Tan Son Nhut at the far end of the ramp from Davis Station. "Accustomed" after Lieutenant Chaldano overcame his distrust of the NCOs.

Only officers had Jeeps, the major reason for Chaldano's popularity. This day, though, Winter had hopped a ride back to the billet area and eaten early chow in the NCO mess instead, because of imminent mission launch.

Walking up the flight line, returning to Operations at twelve hundred hours, Winter felt minimal effect of a distant concussion, but knew it was a telling explosion. He watched a cloud of dust, smoke, and debris lift into the sky beyond the line of aircraft before him. It looked to be somewhere on the civilian side of the airfield, and he heard, quickly, a chorus of sirens and indistinct PA announcements.

No one in Flight Ops knew anything; they'd hardly noted the concussion, shielded as they were by buildings and by indifference: if it wasn't here, it wasn't important! Winter grabbed his flight helmet, shouldered an M-14, hoisted the mission bag, and followed Captain Pyburn out to the flight line. He was flying with the boss today, both of them pushing administrative duties into smaller and smaller corners, while daylight hours were mostly given over to flying. Since visual orientation for the fixes required daylight, Third Air still was essentially a daylight job, though sometimes it strained the boundaries on either end.

After four-and-a-quarter hours fright time, when they landed and were walking back to Flight Ops, they passed SP5 Nick Selman, a fat analyst from WHITE BIRCH who liked to hang around the Air people. Selman saluted the captain, and asked Winter, "Hear about your buddies?"

Winter, who had heard nothing but static and erratic communications for the past four-plus hours, responded curtly, "Now what? What buddies?"

"Your lunch crowd. They all got blowed up, over at the terminal."

"What the hell are you talking about, Selman?" Winter demanded, he and the captain stopping on the ramp.

"What's happened, soldier?" Captain Pyburn intruded, seeing Selman's game for what it was.

"Uh, yes, sir. Sergeant Winter's friends, Sergeant Lessor, Sergeant Monaghan, Sergeant Brenner, and Lieutenant Chaldano... they were havin' lunch in the terminal. Straight up noon, a bomb went off. Planted in the ceiling. Killed some people, but nobody seems to have the straight of it yet."

"What about our guys . . . any of them hurt?" Winter had to know.

"I heard they're all in hospital. None of them killed, I don't think. But busted up pretty bad. Some Air Force light colonel was killed, and an M.P. A couple of Zip waiters, I think." He seemed uncomfortable now with his knowledge.

The captain and sergeant broke into a trot for the headquarters.

* * *

I could see from one eye, my right; the other, the bandaged one, still felt as if someone had stuck hot steel needles into it, then poured in salt. But I could make out Winter's astonished face. "Hey, hoss," I said, "to use the vernacular you're so fond of. How'd you find me here? By the way, where the hell is here? No one's said." Nobody talks to you in these places.

"The Thirty-second. Under the gentle ministrations of our comrades in harms, the Air Farce. And up your vernacular, too. How they hanging, Luther?" Expression on Winter's face was an ephemeral thing, shifting, changing with every blink of my good eye, bouncing between anxiety and worry, a narrow choice.

"Thank Christ they're still hanging." It was not one of my shining moments, erudition-wise, you might say. Couldn't seem to get the old spleen up and running, or whatever in Oz it is that keeps you humming along. Captain Pyburn came in behind Winter, leaned over and spoke to me. I don't remember now, and couldn't understand then, what he said. Something solicitous and meaningless. He must have known by then I wasn't going to die and mess up his flight skeds or personnel roster.

"Do you know what happened?" Winter asked.

"We got our shit blown away. What else?"

"Can you remember any details, dip shit?" I had a quick hint of something I wanted to say, something I thought was funny, something brilliant, but I lost it before it got to the lips.

"We'd just walked in. Sat down. The four of us, sitting there, bullshitting. Had a beer. All of us," and as I said it, I checked the captain's response. I didn't know if he still kept watch on Chaldano's drinking habits. Maybe not; he didn't appear to notice.

"You had skipped out, you fink," I made the point to Dave. "Bomb must have been set for straight up twelve. There was no warning. I don't remember hearing the blast, and now I'm not hearing anything all that great. I guess it was directly over our table. I heard some airdale colonel bought it. And some indigenous people."

"Yeah, and an A.P. from Air Force headquarters, I think." Winter offered. "Was it a bomb or what? A grenade?"

"No, they think bigger. An ordnance guy in here earlier said it was an anti-tank mine. Probably one of our own. Or maybe French, left over from ten, twelve years ago. The fact the building was built by the French, and had steel rebar in the concrete, is probably what kept us from checking out." I wondered if that was true. Was any of it true? Was I really injured? How bad? The medics never told me anything.

I asked, "What do you know about the other guys? I can't remember anything until I woke up in here, but one of the medics said they thought El Tee was brought here, too. How about the rest?" Where else could they be . . . if they were alive?

"Yeah," the captain said, "Chaldano's here, but he's unconscious still. They're prepping him for head surgery. He got a piece of shrapnel in the wrong place. He and Lessor. Monaghan's in Cho Lon with the squids. But you guys were all lucky; most of the damage seems to be the tops of your heads, and forearms — sitting with your arms on the table, I guess. And you were lucky to be directly under the blast. Most of the shrapnel blew out in a cone shape. That's what got the airdale colonel and A.P."

"Yeah," I thought, and realized I was speaking, "aren't we lucky!"

Chaldano, I later learned, had emergency surgery that night; and was shipped back to Letterman General Hospital, San Francisco, for further surgery and recuperation. And he did recover, but he never returned to the Third. Lessor went to the Phillipines, was worked over, and by the time the head wound, which was slight, and the arm lacerations, relatively unimportant, were healed, his hearing had also improved so that he was returned to duty by February.

Monaghan had been taken to the Navy Hospital in Cho Lon. Both eardrums were ruptured, and he had an ugly but not so severe head wound, as well as the arm lacerations common among us all. Winter went to visit him that evening, but he was sedated.

He learned from a nurse that Judge was scheduled to be shipped to Japan for surgery in a day or so, probably on to Letterman also, since he had homesteaded at Two Rock Ranch near Petaluma for years and had family there.

I was the least seriously wounded of the quartet. I partially recovered my hearing within three days and was back in Ops in a week, but not back flying. Not for a few weeks. And even then—I don't think anyone ever knew, except maybe Winter—but I couldn't hear half my skeds.

And it was still a short roster.

* * *

Everything local myth said about him was a lie. Well, not everything, but most.

Some.

A bit.

Oink was never an Asian Hound of the Baskervilles. He hadn't that presence. What he did have, and what primarily endeared him to his new friends in the 3rd RRU, was a deep and abiding antipathy toward Vietnamese. All Vietnamese. Such that when he took up residence at Davis Station, he automatically assumed a position of trust that was mutually manifest.

A serious problem at Davis Station—tucked away in the far, back corner of Tan Son Nhut Airbase a thirty-minute cyclo ride northwest of Saigon—was theft by indigenous personnel. Local nationals. Zips.

The war was incidental: the pillaging of GIs' belongings, cash, and club chits was food for disgruntlement. Housegirls stole from the troops; cooks and mess workers stole from food service on a commercial scale; vehicle and aircraft mechanics stole parts, tools, gasoline, and anything they found left aboard the aircraft after a flight. Theft was endemic. And the rules of engagement, regarding confrontation with a local national caught in the act, were heavily slanted in the Vietnamese's favor.

Into this stressed kingdom rode a knight, not so white.

Winter was leaving the mail room one day when he heard a loud commotion just beyond the fence in the Vietnamese Army dependents' quarters. Within seconds, two Viet adults and a clutch of urchins bounded around one of the cast-iron and sheet-steel buildings pursuing a brown flash. The flash took the shape of a shaggy pup as he flashed across a cleared space of hot, white dust. The dog was so emaciated and filthy he was hard to identify as a dog. But there was no mistaking his terrified canine yelps.

The pup hit a gap in the fence and ran by Winter, desperately seeking shelter. The Viets pulled up at the fence — they all heard the loud snick of the guard's rifle operating rod pulled back and released — and there was no further pursuit. The guards would shoot local, generic Vietnamese as soon as they would Charlie. As Putain said, "Bodycount's bodycount."

The little pup circled back, sensing he was in the clear, and swarmed the feet of Winter, who happened to be there. Immediate imprinting.

Ratty Mac put the name to him. When he barked, Mac thought he made a sound like a pig; thus he became Oink, Wonder Dog. The qualifying appellation came only after he had demonstrated his usefulness.

At first the pup was listless. Almost starved, his ribs were definitive beneath the scruffy coat. Both eyes were glued almost shut with dried discharge, mucus, dirt, and crumbling flies. His hair fell out when he was petted, which was seldom.

But he wouldn't leave Winter's side. And so Winter, and others from the flight crews, began bringing mess hall leavings to him, and he ate everything, from braised mystery meat to lime Jello. Mac and Schuyler found a vet in the AID compound downtown and had Oink treated: all his shots, ointment for the eyes, vitamins . . . some cuts and abrasions were salved over, and he was transformed into a semblance of the species. Consequently, following this unaccustomed benevolent treatment, he loved GIs, and they came to accept him. It didn't take long for him to disdain messhall leavings in favor of cheeseburgers with fried onions from the club. Even the dog recognized the threat from messhall chow, now while Benny Biggs was gone on emergency leave.

Winter noticed as he grew and filled out and his general health improved, Oink spent a lot of his spare time manning a watching post near the gate, time when Winter or another favorite human was shut away in the closed Ops building or off on a mission flight. The gate was the portal through which Vietnamese and GIs transited the 3rd RRU area en route to the aircraft parking apron, or back the other way. The first time he took a chunk out of a Vietnamese's body parts, it turned out to be one of the Viet NCOs who lived in the adjacent quarters and was likely one of those chasing the pup the day he found a new home. The ARVN sergeant made a complaint through his command, and when the complaint was extended to the 3rd RRU, Captain Crunch — an obvious cognomen for an officer named Crouch wearing railroad tracks — it was dismissed out of hand. The company commander had all his interest tied up in the new, persistently malfunctioning hot water boiler for the company area. After Davis Station's three years in the same relative location, no one in the Third had yet enjoyed a hot shower. Captain Crunch saw the dysfunctional appliance as a personal challenge, and had no time for minor concerns, like Zip complaints, a war, or such.

When Oink sensed approval for his voracious defense of the realm, he expanded his enmity to include all Vietnamese. So enthusiastic was he after his re-birth that he began costing the unit the services of local national employees. He chased and bit cooks coming to work in the dark, early morning hours; he tore strips of rayon from the cheap *ao dais* of housegirls; and he sent more than one mechanic on sick call to get stitches in his legs and buttocks, obvious bait to Oink when he found such a target bent over, working on an engine. Some wag from the Orderly Room put up an Oink Hit List, posted in the supply room, where a record of his attacks in all their variety was kept. He received snacks and handouts commensurate with the level and ferociity of attacks.

He overstepped the bounds of his contract, though, when he later took after The Token Spook, shortly after that individual's arrival. It took some convincing to make Oink understand that just because this new GI was dark complexioned did not mean he was Vietnamese. Winter enjoyed a lot of support from Ratty Mac in training Oink away from his policy of indiscriminate strangers attack, focusing him on real culprits. A hint, dropped by one of the linguists to the head Mama-san, instilled the notion that Oink could recognize a thief. Mysterious disappearances fell off. And Oink was credited.

Winter was the first to take Oink on a mission flight. In an inspired conspiracy with Mr. Stoetzel as pilot, sneaking Oink on the RU-6, the operator NCOIC initiated a legend. Later, when the 3rd RRU gained more pilots so that missions could more safely be flown with pilot and co-pilot, it was sometimes difficult to find two officers on a single manifest willing to violate standing orders. But for a while, Oink chalked up an impressive record of flight hours. His first Air Medal was a hoax: Colfax contributed the medal and a ribbon for the ceremony, and the Orderly Room clerk typed up a bogus citation.

It was some time before Oink was actually submitted, through channels, with a recommendation. The award went blindly through the system, recommended for Oink D. Dawg. The award ceremony became the *cause célèbre* for a full month, and was so commonly applauded it was a miracle that exposure to the powers-that-be never occurred.

It was nine months into his Davis Station residence, following Winter's departure and transfer of allegiance to McCombs of the Air Section, that the guard dog's rewards were extended into the arena of sexual favors. He'd accompanied any number of Ops downtown Sai Gon over time, and he was known in several of the bars. As with most Air Section Ops, The Casino was his favorite. But the Big C was only for drinking and a little Sai Gon Tea. Ratty Mac, in a particularly beamish mood one evening, took him to The San Francisco Bar in Gia Dinh and paid the tab for Oink's "hound handjob" by one of the seamier bargirls.

In the days following, everyone noticed a licentious glimmer in Oink's eyes. Mac swore that Oink began to lobby for cyclo trips to Gia Dinh.

chapter fourteen

Token Spook

Viet Nam: December 1964

Whitfield Blanchard came in on the repo-depot truck from Bien Hoa the same afternoon Crazy Bruce and I returned from TDY in Thailand. Just another replacement, he would have been shuffled off north to Phu Bai, probably, and nobody would've noticed. Except for one thing —contrast!

Soldier-san, we had Vietnamese coming out our ears, and Koreans and Thais and Filipinos and I don't know what-all, and the whole roster of them the same yellowish-brown. Most of the rest were your so-called whites, being a misnomer, a euphemism of some sort, I suppose, since I'd always pictured whites as albinos, and me and my kind as something else— pinks, maybe.

But Whitfield Blanchard was coal tar black. Sort of shiny. And in a sea of pink and lemon and umber he stood out, a raisin in the flan. Sure, I know. There were lots of blacks in The 'Nam. But Blanchard was the first ever in the 3rd Radio Research Unit— another euphemism of sorts. The Third, like the rest of the Army Security Agency, had always been a bit on the elite side. Or they aspired to that . . . which meant the color bar stayed up.

Jews, A-rabs, New York Sicilians, California Zionists, New England Methodists, and Tennessee Fundamentalist rattlesnake kissers, truck drivers, college professors, crop dust pilots, and even a thin scattering of career Army— ASA took them all. But they didn't favor anybody with a criminal record—not one that was known about or admitted to, anyhow—and no fags. No fags, period! And I have to tell you, James Meredith had a four-year lawn party at Ole Miss compared to the first black who tried to cross over into ASA, tried to pass in that cloistered service.

When Blanchard showed up in the Third, I think we all knew right off he was some kind of crazy. Some terminally stubborn bastard, considering what all he must have gone through to get there. Into ASA, to The 'Nam, to the Third. But, then, there were many who came to 'Nam, lots of volunteers even, and they all came for different reasons.

I remember Ratty Mac at the time, smiling that be-evil, do-evil smile of his as we watched the new kid offload the six-by. I was thinking what a tough time he was going to have, and wondering how they'd manage billeting without some Christian lad burning a cross on his footlocker. Mannie Barr twirled his finger in a circle alongside his head indicating that, in his opinion, the new black PFC was batshit. Mannie would know; his whole family was congenital silly putty.

"Spook don't know what he's got a-hold of," Mannie said. "I don't think. Look at him, starin' around, hopin' he'll find some more of the same persuasion." Mannie spit in the white dust and nine eyes watched the ball of saliva bounce off the hot soil and roll like a tiny crystal sphere, clear and untouched by Asia. Cockeyed Clyde kept one eye on the ground on the spit ball and one on Whit Blanchard, the new black dude, though of course we didn't know his name at that red-hot moment.

"Yep, guess he's goin' to be our token spook, I guess," said Barr, turning to me. "You know what I mean, Brenner? That's if he stays. I guess." Mannie, always cautious about committing himself to anything he couldn't back out of, was willing to give the black PFC the option of going or staying. As if he, as if any of us, could exercise any option.

"See to that, will you, Mannie," I told him, and went on to the hooch to crash in flames, forgetting the new arrival and Barr's specious concerns. I'd worry about the new man stayin, or going when it happened or didn't happen, or I wouldn't worry, or who gave a shit? The goddamned Air Force flight had beat the ass off me and Bruce, and I had more things to concern me than the well-being and happiness of one more straggler in our little world of grief.

Like the flight out! Man, I tell you, if that flight had been going anywhere else but Bangkok, I would have refused passage. Same on the return. It was that bad. May-y-y-be to Sydney, down under. But that's all. Just there . . . or Hong Kong. Or Manila. Or anywhere outside The 'Nam, come to think of it. Crazy Bruce swore he wouldn't take another R and R, even if he never saw another round-eyed female again. But Bruce lies like a rug; he took the resident Red Cross bimbo to Kuala Lumpur some months later on a contrived R and R and never complained once about the flight. It was only our return flight that was bad, anyhow.

* * *

Token Spook is how Blanchard was labeled, and when days passed and he didn't get on a plane going north to Det J, we accepted the fact that he'd be with us permanently. Nobody really gave a rat's ass. I mean, it wasn't as if we were looking for trouble, or for understanding. I guess we were all racists of one kind or another, considering what we felt about the locals, but we didn't work hard at it. Charlie country sort of took that out of you.

When our token spook's security clearance came through and he showed up for work at WHITE BIRCH, there were a lot of jokes— you could tell those boys had been anticipating— about property values dropping and the neighborhood going downhill. But you could have bought the whole goddamned country for a sixpack of Lucky Lager, and the bitching was written off to pure soldierly prerogative. If it hadn't been the Spook, then lousy chow and miserable weather, no air conditioning, or the bargirls' escalating prices would've been the excuse.

The war was accepted: mortar attacks and occasional sappers, the heat itself, bar bombings, Primaquine tablets with the resultant drizzling shits, incidental malaria, and the long days you hated that slipped by so slowly and left you frustrated to the point of tears, because the only alternative seemed to be no more long days. No more days!

And that was no choice. New aluminum boxes stacked in a hangar at Tan Son Nhut were issued on single-copy requisition forms. Prices were rising downtown, and a blow bath and steam job was up to a carton of Salems, a dollar at the Post Exchange. Indian booksellers on Tu Do Street were getting rich on the black market, and the PXs stocked the sidewalk stalls like chain store outlets, merchandise moving directly from supply ships and planes and AFES trucks, still on pallets, to storage compounds where rip-off artists scurried like ants on a burning stump, and from there down the main streets into Sai Gon and Cho Lon and appeared, as if by magic, on street corners, where it was sold back to us cheap. Low overhead makes for volume sales.

That could all be assimilated, though. Accepted. Even understood.

But American boys like to go to war in style. We'd all heard Daddy talk about the cheap price of cognac, and Uncle Ed reminiscing over the two-legged cuisine in Paris and Rome of the forties, sorta' wistful like, and as the new generation we never realized we were hearing only the tinsel coating, the thin good side of a so-called good war, sometimes so good it never happened, but was maybe a generation's dreams of what it should have been like and could have been when going to war was the right thing, the only thing, for a man to do. We American boys expected the same creature comforts, and better, in today's computer-assisted crises.

So if the food was bad — which it invariably was and no amount of practice wars were ever likely to change that — or if the water in the latrines and showers wasn't hot — which it never was — or even if some over-vigilant VC terror squad put a hit on the perimeter that wiped out a green guard or two, but worse, caused personnel restriction to base — there was instant outrage. It may be that a purpose was becoming obscured; that was not quite clear to me at the time.

But, the Spook. Well, that young troop turned out to be a ditty-bop extraordinaire, an oh-five-eight, a manual Morse operator of rare talent. A black echo of the white Wilmouth. Beyond that distinct categorization, nobody ever asked. Nobody needed to. We lost Louie; we got The Spook, both aberrations of the genre and the system.

It was not until months later, after the legend began, when the Admin Clerk informed us that the black operator had neglected to reveal to us a Master's Degree in Medieval Languages. Why it was privileged information, nobody ever knew. Like I said, lots of reasons.

But Spook could snatch some dits and dahs, right up there with the best. Almost as good as Laughin' Louie. He took to the airways like it didn't matter if he blew his ears and made grits of his brains. He moved within the mild hysteria of the 3rd RRU like it was another southern bus station lunch counter. And none of it touched him.

Whit Blanchard became the Token Spook to everyone but his white bunkmate from Alabama. Briscoe, a living, breathing redneck throwback who never called the new operator anything but Mister Blanchard. Always with emphasis. But beyond a sort of implicit denigration, Briscoe never got on the Spook's case. On some levels, they were the closest two troops in the Third, held together, if in no other way, by an adversarial, co-existent history and a cautious, wary respect for each other's absolute space.

It was Briscoe, a few months later, first told us Blanchard was seeking transfer out of the Third. When he said it, there was a touch of regret in his voice, a hint of loneliness.

But when Blanchard's little bomb hit the Orderly Room— *Shazam!* Specters of suddenly bleeding hearts! Liberal rules-change time.

Off-duty tricks were mustered in the company street for ass-chewings. Affirmative action became the order of the day. It was assumed by the staff coolies that we'd somehow conspired to ". . . get rid of the nigger." Spook had to know what was going on, what the command was accusing us of, but he never took a hand, one way or the other. He never made the lectures or the formations, and he never volunteered anything to anybody. He just lowered his head and kept on snatching dits while waiting for his transfer to go through. Didn't take long.

As much as the Old Man wanted to keep the unit's record clean, up to snuff on the civil rights mandate, he was like USARV staff: he mistakenly assumed that the Third had in fact wanted to get rid of Blanchard, and he was more afraid of the crazies in-house than he was of the longer range threat of the NAACP or the ACLU or even the Army. Fragging was a future phenomenon, but a fledgling concept coming into favor. Captain Janes declined to be the first victim in ASA. He was just a good ole boy.

So, orders arrived, Blanchard moved out. Transferred down the road to the 68th Armed Helicopter Company, an assault outfit with new Hueys. Neat choice. Made us look racist and coward-chic in a single, two-hundred yard bug-out.

But then, in short order, all the louts who'd never given him the time of day when he was in the unit, suddenly began watching for the Token Spook every day as he walked through the company area on his way to or from the chopper pad on the other side of the corrugated metal fence. They'd invite him to the club, inveigle him to play tennis on the tricky court by the motor pool—a challenging enterprise, made so by the potholes from incoming rocket detonation—even offered him social enticements of a higher order: "Hey, Spook. Wanna go get laid? I got my back hostile fire pay today and I think I'll get me to town to blow the whole thing. Can't have dying money lying fallow. Wanna go watch how it's done? Or let me watch?"

It was a little obvious at first, now that the choice was ours; but then I guess the guys were sincere. I can't say with any assurance that any of us ever knew absolutely why that sudden benevolent shift, but eventually Blanchard did begin to stop by the club after the day's flights. To take the odd trip downtown with the old hands. To drink the freebie beers and eat the conscience burgers. I don't know if he was as aware of it as some of us, but we became closer than when he was in the unit.

Dragged on like that through late summer, into the fall and then it was winter, though who could tell in this tropical petrie dish. I wasn't short but I'd grown nervous, cautious with superstition I maybe inherited from Winter. I hardly ever left the base anymore. I still had months to go.

* * *

Must have been late winter. The monsoons were dumping recycled Mekong sewage on the land like water buffalo making wee-wee on a Bailey bridge. Two recidivists—Ratty Mac's term for re-enlistees—in the Air Section, half of a four-man comedy team who'd upset a delicately balanced international understanding, were celebrating their return. Trangressing into Cambodian airspace on a lark, they had been promptly blown out of the sky for their trouble, and their return from truncated captivity was an event. They'd been held, rather indelicately to hear them tell it, for two weeks by another funny, mixed group of Viet Cong and indecisionist Cambodge reactionaries. When we first heard they'd gone down but were thought to be alive, there began a grass roots effort to convince the Cambodians to keep Trotman, but it didn't catch on with the seersucker crowd from State. They could deal only in whole packages, it seemed.

About the same time the government negotiated with the polyglot committee of Asian subcultures and subinterests comprising the government in Cambodia to gain the release of Trotman and Fort and the two pilots—the same day, in fact—Viletsky was released from the Cho Lon Navy hospital. His lungs were healed, they said, chancre sores gone, and his vision restored. To reaffirm the "keep your ass intact" motive, an emergency party alert was issued throughout the Third and peripheral units. What greater cause?

Mids Trick was tagged for the PX run, and every swinging Richard on Mids contributed a carton of Salems off his own ration card. Day Trick used their collective heads, upping the ante with a case of hair spray for the whores and ten pounds of salted peanuts for petty tipping. When the Third partied, nobody was left adrift. Except Swings, of course, but they'd be working through party time, so they were out of it anyhow. Sorry 'bout that!

Since Mids Trick sprang for the exchange, they got to pick the site. The vote was unanimous for The Fuji in Cholon, a Japanese shtick eatery, sly cover for a Chinese restaurant of which there couldn't have been more than nineteen hundred in the Sai Gon-Cho Lon area. Pure genius!

The garden at the Fuji was the big attraction. Once the owner was slipped a couple of extra cartons, he forgot he'd banned the Third forever from his restaurant after the last party when Crazy Bruce ate the banyan tree, and Ratty Mac threw up on the Swedish Ambassador's secretary's boyfriend's dog, and Archie Krebs burned the Navy Jeep in the latrine. But the Salem speaks, and by the time the party rolled around, festival was in the air, inflation imminent in Cho Lon.

Parties in the Third, particularly those initiated by Air Section, were artfully conceived rites. Finely crafted affairs of the heart, put together like a delicate work of Oriental tapestry. The menu in this instance was exotic. It was always exotic: it was whatever The Fuji offered, exotic for being printed in a subtle amalgam of Japanese and Chinese and it didn't matter whether there was any difference in the ideographic languages or not, since nobody in the Third could read either. But it was a matter of no concern, since parties never depended for their success-failure criteria upon whatever mystery food was offered, only the booze and females — not to say femininity. Air Section parties were never failures; this one would be no different. Members of the unit made their plans, gathered their supplies; guests were invited and many came from foreign lands. Chaos and mayhem promised lusty events in Cho Lon.

Came the night of the party, Minkus was on duty. Shields had been on break and drinking for two days, and was in extremis. Simonetti, who boasted some sort of religiously oriented abstinence, though it was common knowledge he kept a bottle of Old Grandad in his foot locker, volunteered to take the duty for Minkus. Simonetti, in his pious devotions, was a solitary drinker and never cared for parties.

Minkus said, "Hell yes!" and poured a gallon of hot coffee down Shields and brought him along, a wide-awake drunk. It reminded me of some nervous family sending a reprobate uncle along with a wallflower debutante.

Simonetti sat in the Orderly Room and got drunk.

All it takes, I always said, is a bit of clear thinking to make any system work.

Blanchard was invited. Expressly, specifically invited. Ratty Mac sidetracked him on his way through the company area from the chopper ramp and told him if he didn't show up at the party, Crazy Bruce would come and sit on him where he found him. Spook asked if Briscoe was coming, and when Mac told him probably, Spook accepted.

And he was there. Showed up on the leading edge of the party, and was going strong when it ended in disarray.

* * *

"Spook, you black muthafuckah! Whups! That's Mistah Mutha Spook, you black mistahfuckah!"

"Briscoe, Briscoe. You wretched, southern, po'-white trash, you're dog-ass drunk already." Whit Blanchard was an observent black muthahfuckah, if nothing else, I commented.

He Roger-ed that.

"Well . . . no shit, Mistah Blanchard. *No shit!*" Briscoe nodded in time with emphasis and the movement carried him, flailing, off the table, though he had his feet braced in the punch bowl at the time. The Alabama soldier crashed head first into the goldfish pond, which was not a pond but a bathtub-sized sunken spot in the tile of the courtyard. There were no goldfish in there, either, only the piranha that Bruce brought back from South America, where he went on a faked emergency leave for the faux burial of his non-existent Indian mother. And everyone knew the tiny eating machines would've been dead by now, anyhow, from Ratty Mac's habit of making water in the pool on every occasion, though I will give him this much—he had the graciousness not to do it while the pond was occupied.

"Hey, Briscoe. Don't pull a 'Ratty Mac' while you're in there."

"How's the water, Briscoe? Wet, you say. You simple asshole."

"Get outta there, shit-for-brains. We gotta use that for the punch bowl, since you washed your Ho Chi Minh sandals in the other one."

"Everybody outta the pool."

Had Briscoe been capable of response, he probably still would not have exited the pond, just for the oneryness of it. He was that way, southern and stubborn. But he sure had a sweet backstroke.

"Hey, Spook. What you been up to?" Minkus demanded. "Man, you're making me crazy. Everyday you come back from a mission and walk through that fence, the odds go up. I'm gonna lose my ass on you." When he blurted out his un-swave teaser, there was a sudden stillness in the courtyard.

"Sshh-h-h, Minkus, you motor-mouth turd," Crazy Bruce shushed him like he would've a country cousin who'd cut one in the front pew: uneasy, too late. Ratty Mac cursed under his breath, almost silently. Then there was only the sound of the tiny wavelets rippling in the pond, the insipid slurp against the sides where Briscoe was trying to dog paddle.

"Odds?" Blanchard said, and you just knew, watching his big old yellow eyes roll, he knew exactly what the hell Minkus had meant with his blunder.

"Uh, well . . . uh, I mean, you know . . . that's shaky duty. And I—"

"You mean you fuckin' Chucks are running book on my charcoal ass."

"Aw, Spook, what the hell! It don't mean nothing. It'd be the same if Westmoreland made those flights ev'ry day; he'd get the same treatment," Mannie Barr said, looking like he wished he was somewhere else at the time. "I reckon."

"Yeah, Mannie. I reckon. But he sure as hell don't," Spook said with a leer. "Do he?" "Reckon not," Ratty Mac answered for Mannie.

"Bet on that, Mac. Bet your cool, white ass on that."

Somebody snickered nervously; Bruce laughed. A murmur of small talk grew, became louder, and the tension bled away. A steady clinking of crumpling beer cans drowned out the mumbling, and Briscoe climbed out of the pond. A constant parade of Chinese waiters and Vietnamese bargirls bringing drinks, food, and comfort moved the party back mainstream, and the star shells burst over Sai Gon to the total disregard of the capitalist running dog puppets in The Fuji.

"Hey, listen up, you clowns," Blanchard said. "You almost had me going there. Forget that shit."

"Sure, Spook. You're a real great guy."

"Yeah, tell us why you're so tight, Spook. I can just see you straining to talk."

"Oh, yeah. I got nothing I want to hear more than your feeble, racist bullshit. Whip it on us."

"You had a bleak childhood, right, Spook? Freud got you by the ass, I bet. Right?"

"Let's hear it, Spook. I mean, who gives a shit, but let's hear it."

Laughter rippled along the table. In our mutual misery, any story worth the telling was worth the listening.

Token Spook waited until he had everyone's attention, which he was able to command by the simple act of silence. He called for a fresh drink. There was a decided lack of scramble to oblige, but a guest is a guest, and finally a new glass was had from one of the bargirls. He sipped at it and was silent a moment longer, letting anticipation build. Doing it well. Spook had more than a touch of the con in him. He leaned back, put his feet up on the edge of the table, and laid a tale on us.

If we were a misbegotten band of outlaws, a thing asserted by the command, then The Spook could well have been our minstrel, so classic was his re-telling of adventure.

* * *

"I'm beginning to wonder about this whole foreign legion bit. Man, I been on missions everyday this week. Eagle Flights, recon, every hostile mission they got. Then yesterday they posted a new manifest. I'm on for today and tomorrow for maintenance check flights. Now y'all know, check flight is cushy duty. Sweet air time, counts for the log, for flight pay, Air Medals, hostile fire pay, and all. So, you might say I was not totally displeased."

Nobody could tell that was true from his face.

"This morning, I got out on the line, flying with Mister Michenor and Captain Rice. Michenor's the maintenance officer in the Sixty-Eighth; I've flown with him before. Captain Rice is too good a man to be an officer, and he don't count; he's so young, for one thing. He's like an automatic pilot, too: everything by the book. Clean, safe, comfortable. So, I thought, all right! Let's wind her up and go." He took a long pull on the drink.

"Well, we rolled seven-seven-four out of the maintenance hangar and pre-flighted her. Skids were banged up; they'd been repaired but hadn't been painted. The Captain wanted to wait until everything was completed, but the engine work was done — she took a point fifty-one round through the engine housing three days ago — and we loaded up for a check ride. Got cleared west of the field and took off."

Briscoe leaned on the table and dripped water over what was left of the food in front of Blanchard. "Hey, Spook. Why'd you try'n drown me? 'Scyush me . . . Mistah Spook."

"Go way, Briscoe. You're diluting the sweet 'n sour."

"Yeah, ain't that the shits?"

"Might be. Only the taste will tell." Spook ignored Briscoe's fallout and continued his story. "Anyhow, didn't take us long. After we'd checked out everything and she was running smooth, we made a pass down along the Song Vam Co Dong and were swinging back east, up a small canal, headed for the field. 'bout that time, *Pow!* One round, right through the Perspex. Missed Mister Michenor by inches. Scared the shit out of the captain, 'cause, you know, we weren't out looking for trouble." I would have thought Spook would have lost some of his naivete by now.

"Michenor was plane commander, and he had to fight Rice for control of the ship, screaming at the kid, trying to get him to release the stick, and when he did, Michenor pulled the nose down and whipped that mutha below some tree cover. Right then, I spotted the sampan edged up to the bank of the river, a puff of smoke hanging over it. I jacked a round into the chamber and told Michenor to haul us around so I could bring the gun to bear."

Every head in the courtyard was turned toward us now. Flying stories were our favorites. Flying stories with hostile fire, even better. And shooting, flying stories that ended well, as this one obviously had, were best of all. I think by then we'd begun to believe the WW One jive talk, the myth — Winter called it, in his inimitable way, a synthetic milieu — the myth we'd crafted in our minds and our PR releases to explain our enthusiasm. Or lack of it.

Blanchard looked at me and said, "Brenner, remember when you rode with me on the Eagle Flight last month? We took some fire up near Tay Ninh? Well, this was a repeat of that trash. This time, we had only one gun manned, since we were only on a check ride, and we had to keep maneuvering the ship on every pass to get an angle of fire. Ship was a slick, so we had no good shit."

I nodded. I'd manned the starboard gun that time after Spook's partner-gunner was hit, only because I was so goddamned scared I had to hold onto something; just holding my ass wasn't enough. I was distracted; I sniffed. The smell of rancid cooking oil and nuoc mam spread like a curse through the garden.

Blanchard said, "You should have seen Brenner, qualifying on that M-sixty like a pro. O.J.-fucking-T. We burned some ass that day, good buddy. *Burned some ass.*" He was grinning and nodding. His shiny face held a grimace like someone who'd died with a bad taste in his mouth. His eyes were focused on something beyond the limits of the courtyard.

"Come on, Spook. Never mind that. What happened today?"

"Yeah, forget that other shit. Brenner's told that story. That's history."

"Hell, comrades. What else? I raked that bloody little scow, back and forth, fore and aft, front, back, top to bottom, from the scuppers to the crapper. It was one of those reed jobs—you know, bundles of reeds all bound together into something like little logs. Chewed me some of that reed off, and I just knew there couldn't be anybody left alive on that sampan. We pulled into a hover and watched . . . nothing. So, Mister Michenor dropped her down a few meters. Don't you just know . . . *Pow!* Another round."

We'd all known what was coming, I think, listening to Spook's story build up and up, but everybody in the Fuji's garden jumped when he mimicked the shot.

"He missed us that time. Guess he did; I didn't hear the round strike, and we were okay. So the boss pulled some Gs and got us a little working room, and I went to work on the sampan again. Shit, man! There's no way in hell I could have missed a single square inch of that boat. Pieces of bamboo, junk from on board, baskets, everything . . . floating around in that brown, streaming shit they call a river." He took another long pull on his drink.

"Well?" There was a long silence. "Did you get him?" Bruce was fidgeting.

"Him? I did say 'him,' didn't I. Well, I don't know if it was a him or not. Never saw who was doing the firing. But the asshole fired again, right there while we're hovering over the boat. I saw the muzzle flash. So I cut loose again. Fired and fired and fired until I'd burned up both belts of ammo, then opened another box, reloaded and put some more into it. Bastard fired again. Every time we'd come in close, we'd draw fire. I don't know if the fucker thought we were going to board him or what." It was plain that Spook was exorcising an abnormal demon.

"I burned up the rest of the second can of ammo. I was unduly disturbed." He said it without a trace of irony. "Man, if he'd just quit that nonsense—just kept a low profile after we made the first pass, he'd have been all right, because I was sure I'd got him." Blanchard's face exhibited the look that used to come on grunts sometimes when they'd been in one too many firefights. He was seeing something on the horizon that the rest of us didn't see. Didn't want to see. He took another drink.

"By then, I'd burned up every round in the gun. I told the pilot to do it again and see, and sure enough, we drew fire again. I grabbed my M-16 and fired four magazines into that goddamned boat. Fucking thing couldn't have been twenty feet long. The captain was leaning over, firing back out the side with his .38; even Michenor emptied his sidearm into the thing, or in that general direction. Then we hovered again, and Pow! One round.

"We were completely out of ammo and that little mother down there was still kicking us in the balls. He wasn't hitting us anymore, not after the first shot, I don't think, but he was some kinda' pissing me off. And we were hitting him. We hit him with every goddamned thing but the rotor blades. Michenor dropped down right over the sampan, and I could see it was listing. Barely floating, crooked in the water, it looked like a friggin' set of Tinker Toys, all spidery and fragile. I don't know how the thing stayed afloat." He shook his head.

"I was truly pissed. Don't you know I was some kinda pissed. While Michenor was trying to use the rotor wash to sink the damned thing, I was looking for a flare to ignite it. Or something to throw. The only thing I could find was a toolbox. We were on a maintenance flight, so naturally we had a toolbox, and that mother must have weighed a good ninety pounds. I dragged it over to the door and while Michenor and the captain were busy, I just nudged it out.

"Like a frigging A-bomb. Cut that boat—what was left of it—in half. Some of it sank. The rest just drifted away from the bank and started spinning real slow in the current. We were getting low on fuel and we hauled ass out of there. The last thing I saw was just some chaff, headed downstream toward the South China Sea."

"But you got a confirmed kill?"

"We got zip-shit! Hell, we can't even tell the man about it. How we going to explain that toolbox?"

It wasn't the toolbox on his mind, though, as his voice went soft. "You know, I got a funny feeling. About that dude on the boat. It was scary. I was, like . . . somewhere through the looking glass. Didn't feel real. Sort of . . . well, I guess it was more like a religious experience. Sort of." He looked up quickly, and his eyes darted about, sensing a slide into something out of bounds.

All of a sudden, everybody was talking at once, the courtyard of the Fuji buzzing.

"Oh, shit! Here we go. Black Jesus gonna give us a coupla' groups on religiosity," MacGantree said.

"Shut up, Mac. I know what he means. I felt like that the first time I saw a hooch torched," Bruce said.

"Oh, sure, it's the same thing. Blow up a boatload of fishermen, burn some babies. What's the difference?" Minkus's voice was tight with righteousness and White Label.

"Back off, mouth. You're out of line," I said before I realized it. According to the story—and that's all any of us had—even in an otherwise clearly authorized case of response to hostile fire, playing by the rules of engagement, the shooter had fired first and repeatedly.

"Up yours, Brenner. I'm talking to the warrior here." Minkus's sentiments, in the public view, were commonly as interesting as a rock-polishing race, and he could have been saying Mass with the Pope and it still would have gotten a rise.

"Hey, Minkus. How's your ass?" Briscoe had his head down on the table, his left cheek in a rice bowl full of cigarette butts.

"My ass is A-Okay, Briscoe. How could you tell? You're in your usual falling-down-drunken state. And you don't need to take up for nobody. Spook's a big boy. Keep out of it."

"I may be drunk, but I ain't no goddamned bleedin'-heart left-wing, pinko fag commie asshole who's primin' for a stomping, making something outta nothing." Briscoe pulled himself up from the table.

"Come on, Tommy, stay out of it," Blanchard said.

"Yeah, stay out of it, Tommy boy. You might get some kinda hurt besides hangover," Minkus chided, and it was the wrong move. The wrong words.

That was the last coherent statement Minkus made until they took the wires out of his jaw two months later, so I'm told. Briscoe, on the cue of "hangover," hung one on Minkus that must have come all the way from Mobile. Sure made for an interesting evening, all that talk about action, topped off with some real, down-home gettin' it on.

But when the MPs and the QCs and some mister cool in civilian clothes whom I used to see coming and going from the Air America hangar, who was sitting in the back corner of the courtyard, got through sorting it out, and the MPs hauled Minkus back to Tan Son Nhut to the dispensary, the party was on its last legs. There was nothing could top a left hook.

I saw Briscoe leaving with Blanchard, holding his knuckles and laughing, and the rest of the trick just vanished. Tail-end Charlie in the courtyard was Ratty Mac, pissing in the pond. And it was probably the last time I ever saw the Token Spook.

* * *

I've thought back on that night many times, remembering what Spook said about a religious experience, and I think I know now what he meant. I don't know if I would call it religious, being unfamiliar with the genre, but coming so close to a first hand view of immortality's bound to be unsettling. And I guess that's how Spook felt about the sampan sniper.

Maybe the others did come to understand— some of them, some of the mystery—but nobody ever talked about that party much. Maybe because that's when the legend started.

* * *

The day after the party, which was a Saturday, Spook flew again we learned later. They'd yanked him off the maintenance manifest because of the toolbox, and he went out as a mission gunner. It was his final flight.

I saw a transcript of the investigation later; it was incomplete and didn't help much. We'd already heard all there was to hear from the pilot, who used to drink occasionally in our club. Thing was, nobody in the damned helicopter ever really saw what happened to Spook.

The gunship he was on, and three others, had been flying cover for some ARVNs on the Vung Tau Peninsula, and sometime during the action Spook . . . well, just left, I guess. Forgive me if I take a Mannie Barr position—i. e., taking no position—but on the basis of what I knew then, and what happened later, I'm not making any commitment. I don't think!

On that mission the ARVNs got into some shit and the gunships went hot. The other gunner was busy keeping his ass in one piece and the pilots had their collective minds on maintaining some space between them and a whole world of hostility below. After the insertion, and when the choppers broke off, beating feet out to sea, and then back inland up the coast, the other gunner realized Blanchard wasn't in the chopper. They backtracked over the ops area, but could find no trace of Spook. There was no blood in the chopper, no evidence he'd been hit; his safety belt was intact, didn't appear to have malfunctioned. His M-60 had not been fired. So nobody knew if he'd been hit and somehow knocked out of the Huey, just fell out in a turn, which could have happened if he had for some reason unhooked his belt, or . . . if he had jumped.

In his unit, the 68th, opinion opted for the fall, since that was how they were reporting the loss of the toolbox the day before, on up the channel to USARV — a combat loss; write it off; write him off. Fell out taking violent evasive action in a hostile encounter.

In the Third, opinions were less consistent. The only thing we knew for sure was Token Spook was gone.

The first hint of strange came with a report from a Green Beanie sergeant, said he saw a colored fella running with the Cong in the mountains of Two Corps. I asked him what he meant by colored, since I knew of damned few creatures had no color at all of one shade or another. He called me a wiseass and said the man he'd seen was not Cambodian, either — I guess somebody'd already suggested that to him, because of the dark coloring — swore he was a real, live, African-American, black, colored Negro.

Nobody paid much attention to the report. It was just a story, a tale for telling in the club. There was always some ding-dong grunt who'd been in the bush a couple of weekends too long who thought he'd seen some guy who'd definitely been killed months before. And there were the rumors about the turncoat GI who was leading VC sappers into our lines. Always some kind of shit like that, though even then, believing it or not, I never associated the rumors with Spook. I was always convinced those sightings were semi-legitimate, not just wild stories, but that the so-called "disaffected" GIs were in fact holdover French, either settlers or maybe abandoned or deserting legionnaires.

The second notion—and when the legend really began—came when Crazy Bruce said he saw Token Spook in Gia Dinh, on the edge of Bamboo Junction. Bruce, out for a night on the town, was coming out of Melba Co's whorehouse when he saw somebody he thought was The Spook. Said he couldn't believe his eyes, but he ran after the guy, yelling for him to wait up. Before he could get near, there was a hell of an explosion in the White Mice police station across from Melba's. Knocked Bruce off his feet, killed a whole bevy of little indigenous persons. Bruce was sure he saw The Spook running off into the paddies with the sappers. Listening to Bruce's improbable bullshit, that's when I thought of the Special Forces sergeant and put the two tales together.

Later, we got a call from the seersucker crowd downtown. Had a second-hand report from one of our counterparts who heard it from a snake eater who worked with the Nungs near Dalat, who said he heard it from a French priest. Story was, there was a black American running with the VC, wearing Cong garb and all. The priest said he heard the man singing once, when he came on him and some Zips wiring an ARVN artillery command post with charges after they'd killed or run off the ARVNs, and the Cong wanted to blow the priest away and this black dude stopped them.

The priest clearly remembered the man singing in English. Third hand, through the priest, the snake eater, and the government civilian, the reported lyrics sounded to me like Brook Benton's hit from a few years before, "It's Just a Matter of Time." The Spook used to say that was his song, a special sort of tribute having to do with getting even. He'd had a gal back home —Vonelle, I think was her name—who'd married his best friend after Blanchard left for the Army. Blanchard had managed one last fling with her the day after she came back off her honeymoon, just before he shipped out to The 'Nam. Guess she felt she owed him something.

Well, he must have felt he owed her something, too, so he left her with a case of clap, San Francisco's finest, VD extraordinaire! Some kinda debilitating. Didn't tell her, either, so I guess she and her new husband had something in common to remember Blanchard by

Anyhow, even after what the priest had reported to the Special Forces sergeant who passed it on to the other guys, and the song and all, and thinking back on all the other rumors, I still had doubts about something as far out as what I was thinking. For a while.

I couldn't figure how he could have gotten out of that chopper on his last flight, and that bothered me some, but I finally figured it was all coincidence and didn't have anything to do with a man who was reportedly, and presumed to be, obviously dead.

And then, just two days before I rotated back to the world on my extension leave, I was downtown Sai Gon, buying some souvenir trash to bring home. I was in a shop on Tu Do next door to Broddard's and there was this humongous explosion nearby. I ran out into the street thinking it was a rocket and I'd better find a bunker, when here comes this apparition down the street, hell-bent for perdition. Runs my ass over, knocks me down. The guy who hit me stopped, waited while I was getting up to whip some ass. When I looked up, I was staring into the eyes of the biggest, darkest VC I ever saw. I could see him plain as day—hell, he wasn't more than three feet from me—but my brain didn't seem to function, to accept what I was seeing. The Spook looked slightly ridiculous in black pajamas—not silly or anything approaching comic, but strange.

He backed up against the wall with an AK-47 trained right on my gut. I didn't even have a weapon, for all the good it would have done me, and I just kissed my ass goodbye right then. We stared at each other for a moment—only an eternity, you understand—and he smiled that big old Pepsodent smile and loped on off up the street and disappeared down the alley by the Brinks BOQ.

When the MPs asked me what happened, asked me to describe the terrorist, I told them it was just some guy. How the hell am I to tell one Zip from another; they all look alike. Just some Vietnamese farmer, bigger than most. Maybe Cambodge. They were dutifully persistent but, No! I didn't know why I thought that, unless it had to do with his size. He was one great-goddamned-big Cong. I never mentioned he was dark. Very dark. A matter of perception.

I really was aced out after that, and I was ultra-short, too . . . and then I was gone . . . for a whole thirty days. Orders, queues, Goodbye Viet Nam! protests and bus rides: all that shit.

But after a while back in the world, I began to have doubts. It was as if it all happened in a story, or to someone else — not like it happened to me at all. But then, most of 'Nam seemed like that. I'm not sure now I ever really saw the Token Spook that final time. It could have been short-timer jitters, and the three Ba-mui-ba I had at The Casino. 'course, there was Bruce and his story. And the sergeant . . . and the green beanie. . . .

In any case, I never told anyone. I never put much stock in ghosts. I quit believing the newspapers and the bulletin board, the PR lies and whitewashing, the bullshit and ballyhoo. Why should I expect anyone would want to believe something as illogical and far-out as the tale of The Spook. And when I came back to 'Nam after leave, it was to that whole episode with Winter, and there was no more room for fantasy.

chapter fifteen

Into the Void, Junior Birdmen

Viet Nam: January 1965

Curtailing the quiet, cool, early morning bliss of a Dawn Patrol, reluctantly disembarking to the inhospitable earth, Winter returned to Operations and read the message stuffed in his distribution box.

The clerk had written: "Monaghan left word (URGENT!): 'Please visit me Cholon Hosp. today. Will ship Japan/CONUS tomorrow. Jerry.' (Repeat URGENT!)"

Jerry? Who the hell was Jerry?

He frowned into the void, trying to match the name with someone he knew. First to mind was Jerry Baines back home, reputed to be a cousin of some derivation, though relationship was denied by family members. But that was ridiculous; Baines had evaded the pitiless grasp of the draft, fleeing at oh-dark-thirty on a north-bound train, and the last Winter had heard, his erstwhile kin was living in a commune of Lithuanian lesbians in Calgary. And the clown only had three toes on each foot — the military wouldn't have taken him on a bet.

His eyes roamed over the chalkboard above the clerk's desk where was printed THOU SHALT MAINTAIN THY AIRSPEED, LEST THE GROUND RISE UP AND SMITE THEE MIGHTILY. Aviator humor. Losing its appeal with each succeeding flight into the beyond.

Jerry. Who the hell — he looked at the clerk's note again: "Monaghan left word . . ." Jesus, Winter, he thought, shaking his head to clear it of fuzzy, high altitude clutter. Get one's head out of one's ass.

Monaghan! Winter stared at the yellow sheet, gears grinding exceedingly slowly. Blind spot! Of course, the message was from Monaghan. He'd known the staff sergeant only by his self-imposed *nom de guerre,* Judge; had he ever known his name was Jerry? But, had to be; he was the only one in Cho Lon hospital. Winter had visited him the day of the bombing, two days before, but Monaghan was sedated at the time, more out of it even than usual. And flying back-to-back missions, trapped in yeoman paperwork, Winter had not gotten back to Cho Lon.

At his hooch Winter peeled himself out of the sodden flight suit, missed chow while showering, donned civvies, and caught a cart for the front gate. He was slurping down a bowl of U/I meat and noodles by 100-P Alley when he talked an MP into a ride to Cholon Navy Hospital.

Monaghan was propped up in bed, sheets thrown off his immense, hairy body, naked but for skivvie shorts. He was reading a paperback copy of Irving's *Sketch Book* — Brenner obviously having an impact. Winter, standing in the door of the two-bed room, blandly surveyed the wounded sergeant, the most un-military NCO he could name. He could but smile at Monaghan's insistence on wearing white military boxer shorts, trashed as decadent by even the most fervent militarist. He was an unlovely sight as he swiveled his head toward Winter, looking startled. Well he might, thought Winter, considering his encasement in swathes of white.

"Yo, Judge. Or is it now to be Jerry?"

"*What?*" The patient leaned forward, cupping hands behind both ears. His forearms were bandaged and, where visible above and below the gauze, the skin was pitted, hundreds of small wounds scabbing over. The bridge of his nose looked to have been chewed by a bad-tempered dog, and now glistened with salve. Both eyes were bloodshot.

Winter placed a small, brown paper bag on the bedside table and closed the door to the hall. The other bed in the room was empty. Before speaking, he picked up a bottle of rubbing alcohol from the second shelf of a metal nightstand, poured the contents down the tiny sink drain on the wall, rinsed the bottle, then took a pint of vodka from the brown bag and poured it into the alcohol bottle. He placed it back on the stand and threw the bag in the trash, stuffing the empty Stolichnya bottle in his pocket. All while Monaghan watched silently, smiling.

It was difficult making conversation: the wounded sergeant could hear only snippets of any string of syllables, his eardrums gone in the blast. Winter felt awkward, trying to make himself understood without shouting. He had opened the door again and there were Navy medical personnel, military visitors and, likely, enemy infiltrators up and down the hall in a steady stream. He forgot any notion of trying to find out—if the man even knew— why Judge had been brought to the Navy hospital in Cholon, rather than the Air Force facility on Tan Son Nhut, nearer the scene of the bombing. It was probably considered information he did not need.

"*Dave*," Monaghan grated loudly, with an air of conspiracy. Winter nodded.

"Dave, you gotta help me. My lockers are full—"

It suddenly occurred to Winter what the urgent call was about. He leaned forward, his finger to his lips, and dramatically, with eyes wide, shushed Monaghan. At the bedridden man's startled look, Winter mouthed, "Not . . . so . . . loud!" The patient nodded.

"I got weapons in my foot locker," he said more softly but, unknown to him, still loud enough to be heard in the street. "Handguns. Ammo. And four, five long guns in the wall locker." He reached into a small top drawer of the stand and took out a ring of keys. "Here. Keys to everything. Do something with the guns. Sell 'em, trade 'em, give 'em away. Don't care. Keep the money. Just get them out of there before my gear's inventoried."

Army policy dictated that any person, dead or alive, not present for reveille in his unit, was treated as a loss on the morning report, whether a casualty, on R&R, leave, AWOL or a deserter. All personal property of said "loss," if not otherwise accountable, was inventoried and stored, or shipped forward, depending upon circumstances. Any officer delving into Monaghan's lockers would be initiating courts-martial charges against the NCO. Being in a place where war was happening did not convey the right for an individual to maintain a weapon. Most officers retained their issue sidearms at all times, but enlisted men—even senior NCOs—were not accorded that privilege.

But it wasn't in this case just a weapon, even a personal weapon. That might have been overlooked, even if not condoned, the weapon deposited in its proper armory location, the matter forgotten. Monaghan, however, was dealing weapons like some middle eastern, back-*souk* entrepreneur. He kept, for his own use, a Swedish-K; he had one more K for sale; he also had an M-2,

.30-caliber carbine, full auto; two Uzis; and an M-14 with scope, ordnance-precisioned for sniping. In his footlocker, the handguns: two .45 caliber Colt 1911A1s, a .357 Magnum Combat model, a German Luger missing a firing pin, and assorted others Winter couldn't specifically remember. But he understood the urgency.

After agreeing to take care of the "little problem," as Monaghan referred to it, and about to leave, not anxious to extend the one-way conversation, Winter pulled the Rolex from his left wrist. Weeks before, his old Bulova had conked out on him. Bought with his first Marine re-enlistment bonus at the PX on the Marine depot, San Diego, nine years before, it was not waterproof and the festering climate had invested it with moisture, dust, dirt, fungus, sweat, and various microbial invaders until it ground to a halt. He'd mentioned his dilemma at the table in the messhall one morning, and recalling his grandfather's bequeathed old railroad pocket watch, said he was going to write Nicky to pack it up and ship it to him. Even then, he squirmed when he thought of the harassment he would endure from everyone: a pocket watch!

Winter required a watch for missions and could not afford to buy a new one. Monaghan offered him the use of the Rolex there in the messhall as casually as he would have loaned him a shoe brush. The Judge's military pay was supplemented with family money, and to him, the watch—one of several he owned, of which he currently favored another with a display of ganged dials and gears, time zones and bezels, buttons, and buzzers—meant nothing more than a favor he could do a friend.

Now, when Winter tried to return the watch, Monaghan's eyes opened wide and, waving his hands, he yelled, "*No! You keep it! You still gotta fly.* Give it back when you see me again." The not-so-subtle trade-off, a gift accompanying disposition of the illicit weaponry, was blatantly obvious.

Monaghan had dealt in weapons only to offer other GIs an opportunity to safeguard themselves in the quirky but accelerating hostilities. He never would have sold a weapon on the black market downtown. To be sure, however, though never to be acknowledged, he *was* operating a black market operation of a sort, all his own.

In the next few days, with the delighted conspiracy of a Green Beret from the 400th SOD, every weapon in Judge's lockers was moved from Davis Station compound, disappearing into the shadowy world of indigenous support — all except the .357. Winter found a niche for that in his own locker, looking over his shoulder as he stowed it away. The Green Beanie paid Winter a pile of local currency, which he didn't bother counting; but later, through various enterprising exchanges, and at a loss but not to a usurious degree, converted back into American currency. He used the laundered funds to buy money orders, which he sent on to Monaghan's home address in Petaluma. It was some weeks by the time Winter dropped the last envelope through the mail slot, sighing with relief at the end of the threat to Monaghan, and himself.

* * *

Laughin' Louie Wilmouth, the Third's best intercept operator-turned-Air Section's best op, had already been in country for more than two years. He'd deployed with the original levy of personnel TDY from the field station in the Phillipines, and when he was to be replaced through established personnel turnover a year later, had opted to remain. He became the first operator for the Air Section when it was formed. He trained other airborne ops until his hardly-unique affectation became officially known and it was deemed unwise to use Laughin' Louie anywhere except actual operations in the plane.

Louie was a drunk.

He wasn't a problem drinker. He wasn't threatened by alcoholism; it wasn't a sickness. He liked to drink. He insisted, "I don't have a drinking problem. I drink. I get drunk. End of story." Louie was perhaps the epitome of the enlisted drunk in the Warp Zone. Finesse did not enter into it; it was a gift at birth. Being from Arkansas had nothing to do with his affliction, as some suggested.

But he could copy code with the best, pull a signal out of a maze of electrical and meteorological garbage, read it, understand it, copy it, recognize it — he knew the "fist," the characteristics of each enemy manual Morse operator's style and sound and technique — and could identify enemy targets by the fist of the radio operator. All Laughin' Louie wanted to do was fly, snatch dits, and come back to earth to debrief with a bottle.

But the Army, in its lock-step mentality, couldn't let that alone. Laughin' Louie's *condition* became a command issue when he stepped off the bottom rung of the ladder of a Beaver at the end of a mission, passed out, and sustained a concussion on the tarmac. He might have squeaked by with the injury, but some well-intentioned ground clerk, thinking to reward Wilmot's twenty-seven months of dedicated service, wrote up a citation for award of the Purple Heart for his ladder-launched injuries. The circumstances of his injury did not merit such award. Since the Third had sustained so few bona fide instances of proper award of The Heart, a close review by the Group Adjutant led to a query, to an investigation, to a board hearing, and orders for Wilmouth to be mailed to the Phillipines for drying out.

It was not just another hit on the manpower pool of Third Air; it was a *major* blast.

* * *

When Brenner reported back to the section, initially he was not cleared to fly, due to hearing loss. Though they'd talked a few times since the bombing, he and Winter had spent little time together, due simply to the extraordinary demands for time on the few remaining flying ops, including Winter. Brenner was pleased to be back on duty, even on the ground.

"Welcome back, Luther." Winter said. "Ready to work?"

Brenner seemed to have to digest Winter's query, then said, "Feel good. Still got ringing in my ears, but it comes and goes. No worse than working a full shift in an electrical storm. Arms are O.K." He flexed his scab-covered hands and arms before Winter. "Need to get out there and get some."

"Can't be too soon to suit me. You heard they grounded Wilmouth, sent him to the P.I."

"Fucking straphangers. I heard Zwick's been on a roll, too. Border incursion and all. Man lives a charmed life."

"Hmunh!" Winter snorted. "Man at least still *has* a life. You know Dann? Herb Dann? A-Slash at Whitebirch—"

"Yeah, worked my trick for a while."

"He's on board now, flying. Probably due to him Zwick's still alive, insisting they get the hell out of Dodge when that yo-yo was playing games over some Cambodge triple-A site. But he's also responsible for Zwick's weenie being in a wringer. Dann reported it to me; I had no choice but to take it to Pyburn. *Đai-úy* came down hard on him." Winter looked grim.

"Well, fuck me, Dave. You'd rather everybody looked the other way until Zwick drives one into the ground playing Combat Kelly? Be thankful those Cambodians didn't blow his shit away." He wrinkled his brow, "Wonder why not."

"Dann said they were doing tight, spiral turns, directly over the gun pits. Maybe they don't have a protocol for direct overhead fire." He laughed as Brenner nodded distractedly.

"Uhh, listen, Dave —" Brenner changed the subject, " — do we have any new guys in the unit? Latinos? Spanish-speakers?"

"You mean Puerto Ricans, Mexicans, like that?"

"Don't think so. Sounded like pure Castilian. Or Manchegan." He spoke with an air of evasive dread.

"Don't know Manchegan. What's that?"

"You know, as spoken in La Mancha. Province in Spain, south of Castile. South of Madrid. Weird. "

"Then that would be Castilian. I don't think the citizens of Don Quixote country speak a separate language."

"So you say. Well, whatever . . . I was in the messhall and there were these two. . . ."

"What about 'em?" Winter effected disinterest, as if only half listening, and continued marking a map sheet with hi-lited coordinates and sked times. But something raised a flag in his memory, something . . . *Familiar* was too strong a word.

Brenner realized it was too weird to try to describe.

"I don't know. I was in line behind them in the mess hall, and they didn't seem like anyone from . . . today's army. You know what I mean?"

"No. No, I don't. Hey, give me a hand with this map board will you."

"Sorry, Dave." Brenner held up his scabbed arms. "Got these bad paws, you know."

* * *

The day after New Year's, the First Sergeant of 3rd RRU called Sergeant Winter and Specialists Portugal, Malthus, and Horgan to the Orderly Room. He handed each of them a list from MACV, an alert order on which the four were named as candidates for a newly enacted Rest and Recuperation program.

"Portugal, you and Sergeant Winter are next up, so you choose first. The dates of the flights are fixed for the destination: ninth through the fourteenth for Hong Kong; sixteenth through the twenty-first for Bangkok. Six days total, counting coming and going. Free flights aboard Air Force birds. First two guys from the Third R.R.U. on the list in this new program left for Bangkok this morning. You have 'til roll call tomorrow to choose. But you have to tell me now, this red-hot instant, if you don't want to take any R-and-R. That's all."

After refusing to commit such an act of heresy as turning down time out of country, and finding themselves back out on the company street without further explanation, the four stood and looked about in confusion. "Do we all have to choose the same place? Do two of us have to go to Hong Kong and the others to Bangkok? What the fuck, over?" Portugal made sounds, but the other three knew it meant nothing; he would go anywhere he was offered, just to get away from Sergeant Timmons, his Trick Chief.

Winter and Portugal walked away from the other two, Winter saying, "They been telling us R.-and-R. was coming. But how'd we manage to wind up near the head of the list, Leon?"

"As if I would know, Sarge. Maybe in your case, for being Straight Arrow; mine, I haven't a clue. Can't be the same."

"Well, I already know I'll take Hong Kong. I just got back from T.D.Y. in Bangkok."

"Yeah, that can't be all bad. The British Crown Colony has much to recommend it. I guess if we choose Hong Kong, being first up, Horgan and what's-his-name get Bangkok."

"Yeah, right," Winter replied, cutting his eyes toward his fellow worker. They were not particularly good friends, but got along. "I can guess what you have in mind . . . what you'll base your choice on. But, hell, the girls in Bangkok come in gaggles, too." He stepped around a soldier he didn't know, who was on his knees in the dirt, vomiting up today's culinary deliberation from the chow hall or street corner cart. "Gaggles of giggles," he smiled.

"Just point me to the plane."

* * *

Above the engine noise on the C-54, Winter said to Portugal, "What's in that brown paper package I saw you stuffing in your overnight bag this morning?" He hoped his R-and-R partner wasn't entering the international marketplace of illicit substances. But he knew, too, that could not be the case; Portugal likely disdained drugs as much as he. But it was a known fact, however unfortunate, that Viet Nam was an up-and-coming player in that market.

"Just a little something from my friend Singh I'm taking to his brother."

Winter knew Singh; he owned a tailor shop just off Tu-Do, downtown Saigon. The Indian expatriate and Portugal had become friends through an unlikely progression of events that Winter did not choose to delve into. He had not known the Indian was internationally incorporated.

"I don't know what it is," Portugal admitted blandly. "He just learned last evening, when I ran into him at dinner in The Taj, I was going to Hong Kong. He asked me if I'd take a 'little something' to his brother who lives there. How could I refuse? He paid for dinner and the Johnnie Walker."

Feeling it unwise to pursue the subject, Winter said no more.

* * *

When they'd landed at Kai Tak Airport, they were bused to the Park Hotel in Kowloon and given the new, still-developing R-and-R briefing: "You can stay here at the Park, an old Brit favorite — great breakfasts: kippers and scrambled eggs — or you can fan out, find a place of your choosing. If you go somewhere else, check back and let us know. Keep your whereabouts current on the roster here so we'll know where to find you." Standard VD warnings with a wink. Instructions on currency exchange; warnings about unlicensed taxis; information about visiting the New Territories and the risks of inadvertently crossing the ill-defined border and becoming a guest of China.

Both men chose to stay at the Park. They knew of nothing better, and it would save time and trouble. As soon as the rambling briefing was concluded and they had signed in, they bolted for their rooms.

"Let's change," Portugal urged. "Don't forget, we only have six days, minus flying time here and back. Time's-a-wasting." Winter didn't feel on the same anxious schedule, but he caught the infectious sense of adventure from his traveling companion.

Agreeing, first things first, out of uniform they took a taxi to an address on Cameron Road. The security steel flex was closed over the door, but following Singh's instructions, Portugal pounded on the door. A thirties-something, well-dressed Chinese gentleman opened the inner glass door of the clock shop, and when they'd identified themselves, he smiled and unlocked the security door. Pulling them in with firm handshakes, he led them into a back room, invisible from the street. When Portugal handed over the innocuous brown parcel, Marcus Singh immediately ripped through several layers of brown wrapping paper, exposing a stack of American currency, fifteen-to-twenty thousand dollars worth, Winter judged. Hundreds, fifties, nothing smaller than a twenty, and not many of them. The two soldiers stood witness to the ambitions of displaced merchants in the war-besieged country.

Singh smiled openly, friendly, but blocked the view of the combination as he opened the safe, deposited the cash, and twirled the knob. He stood. "How's for some grub?" he asked in colloquial English he was obviously proud of. The soldiers found the Indian food at Singh's private club to be a good choice. Both often ate at Indian restaurants in Saigon. The Taj, where brother Singh had passed on the currency to Portugal, was their favorite. Marcus's club could hold its own.

The one thing they found odd was that no drink was offered — no water, no tea, no coffee, no wine — nothing, except the bottle of Johnnie Walker black that Singh picked out of a desk drawer and brought with them from the clock shop. He and his Sai Gon brother shared at least that affinity. JW black made for a gracious dinner.

Following the long, slightly festive dinner, celebrating the Singhs' upper-hand maneuver over the Sai Gon government, which forbade transfer of funds out-of-country, the group split up. Marcus Singh went home with reiterated expressions of great thanks; Winter returned to The Park Hotel, too drunk to read, but unable to sleep. Winter sat down and labored over a letter to Nickie. Portugal went back out to a bar across the street from the hotel, seeking company. Drunk or sober, if the two soldiers considered that Marcus Singh was a little light in the thanks department, they didn't worry. Both knew future curries at The Taj were going to be well within their budget.

* * *

Portugal found her in the parochially named Kowloon Bar, across the street from the Park Hotel: "Won't have to crawl far if I fall off a stool," he promised Winter before they split up.

Introducing himself to Linh Heung, sitting alone at the bar in the Kowloon was, when he walked in, like coming home. He never considered looking further. Portugal could never remember whether one considered Chinese names, as given, to be the reverse of English names, or the other way round, but she would be Linh. No one except Linh and the mama-san paid any attention to him. Accustomed as he was to bar habits of the world, Portugal took this as a positive sign. No one asked him for a drink. No "Sai Gon tea," which would have been the invitation *de jure* back in 'Nam. He had to make all the moves.

And when he'd asked, been accepted—after close scrutiny worthy of a Southern Baptist teenage queen's mom, and then had to go through the ritual with the bar mama-san: set the terms and prices—only then was the deal concluded. One major attraction to Portugal, beyond her beauty, was her facility with English. Linh carefully gathered her things, led him onto the street where they stepped into a waiting taxi, and took a lengthy drive to Repulse Bay. Portugal afterward could never have found his way back to Linh's on his own, but the following morning, after she had fed and cared for her mixed-blood infant—Linh, herself, was of mixed blood: a gorgeous blending of east and west—she made breakfast for the two of them.

Afterward, she shyly accepted the "tip" he offered. He had already paid her fee up front to Mama-san back at the bar. Before he left her apartment, she wrote out her name and address on a scrap of paper for him. She was obliged to work today, but they agreed he would come back that night at eight. The following four days she would spend entirely with him. All the time he had.

Portugal felt good. He'd passed muster. She had withheld commitment until after their first night. He would be back.

* * *

Winter saw him once more, during that second day, when Portugal appeared at the Park and checked out of the hotel. He told Winter just enough to off-set concerns for his continued absence.

Winter was on his own, making the solitary rounds of tourist sites: Aberdeen Bay, the Hong Kong Island tour, Wangchai, the New Territories' long frontier, Tiger Balm Gardens. He allowed himself to be talked into R-and-R-sponsored bus tours, a mode of exploration he deplored. Dinner two nights in a row at the Crown Palace Restaurant and Club.

Linh did not reappear in the Kowloon Bar, and Portugal was on the missing list. Winter's gain, he considered, was the uninterrupted hours in a comfortable, even sumptuous bed, sleeping without a mosquito bar, and the oft-repeated long, lazy, hot showers without water rationing.

Winter and Portugal met back at the Park Hotel on the day they flew back to Viet Nam. Portugal, quiet, subdued on the flight to Sai Gon, was back in harness the following day, none the worse for wear.

A mortar attack the night they returned helped in their re-acclimation.

chapter sixteen

Black Virgin

III Corps, Viet Nam: March 1965

McBride lectured to a captive audience. Two Morse operators and an analyst were clustered by his desk listening to his take on things: the war, the world—petty matters. Private McBride, a well-read man, was another college breakaway whose fall from classroom grace had invested him with an involuntary cruise to Southeast Asia, a popular event on which the Army was having a run. But even there he would prosper, for he was adept at seeding his conversation with plagiarized material, exhibiting only a fine residue of bitterness: someone else's thoughts, filtered through his own quirky vision.

Zoltan McBride, offspring of a Chilean mother and Icelandic father, boasting family ties no stronger than his institutional devotions. The McBride travail had begun with the Irish diaspora in famine when his great-great-grand*da* sought a life in Canada. A century later, his father, proudly illiterate, succumbing to homesickness for the land of his forbears, had mistaken for his homeland the destination of Iceland on a freight line's shipping schedule, thinking Rekjavic must be down near Cork. That Celtic connection held firm in the cold clime, and the latest generation had all the attributes of the most dogged, peat-loving *shanachie* from the ould sod.

"It was well put by Robert Leckie, in a *wa-a-arr* book," McBride said in his soft burr, "non-fiction, as unlikely as you might think that—can't remember the title—in which the speaker, in a similar situation, said, 'He had no authority; he needed none. He had a theory.' Spot-on!" McBride had the good taste, always, not to overreach when mesmerizing bystanders.

He had even been known to advise listeners, caught up in the fascination of his monologue, to "Close your mouth, man; you're attracting flies."

Now he continued, in parallel, some menial task which occupied much of his time at the desk, and added, "Well, I, too, have a theory.

Wanta hear it?" He looked up, as if surprised to find an audience, and grinned fatuously.

Winter and Brenner pushed through the obstruction of bodies in the narrow hallway, too soon after lunch for the benevolent rectitude of McBride and a gaggle of sycophants. McBride had that Irish gift of gab. And it did not harm his credibility that he was authoritatively correct in most matters.

"Sergeant Winter." The call echoed up the hallway from Operations area. Winter saw Captain Pyburn motioning to him and followed his lead into the plotting room; Brenner hung around, indulging curiosity. Now that he was a hard-stripe NCO, fewer people pinged on him.

The captain, seated now, swept his hand over a map on the desk. "We're going to do something about our comms breakdowns, from the planes to base. We've been *instructed*," he said grandly, connoting authority to those descended from the gods, "to check out places of possible location for a relay site. Somewhere, preferably high elevation, where we can put a low-profile repeater and set of antennas to re-transmit our signals when we're far afield. Make sense?" Pyburn spoke through a cloud of noxious smoke, indulging in the Vietnamese home-grown variety of cigarette. Mekong Queens smelled like perfumed excreta. *Heavily* perfumed. Ordinary, old, run-of-the mill, plain excreta would have less seriously offended the olfactory sense.

"Well, sure. I guess, sir. Any place particular in mind?" Winter signed up.

"As you know, one of the areas we have most trouble with is working up along the Fish Hook, the Parrot's Beak — that area. Engineers think a site on top of the Virgin would work. Got plenty of elevation, for sure. And it is in our hands . . . so to speak." He grimaced.

"Whadda you mean? Don't we hold the top? Sure we do; we have Green Beanies up there." Winter had cultivated a modicum of intelligence about the mountain.

"Well, yes. Point taken. But an ARVN major runs the show. C.O. of that Viet signal operation on top. They have maybe twenty-five, thirty troops up there to our ten or twelve. And the Viets have their dependents and property there." From his expression, such was not the ideal scenario for troop deployment.

"All right, Captain. And you're telling me this because? . . . I mean, it's interesting, of course, but I still have tasking skeds to get out this pee em." Winter did not want to know where this might be going.

Necessarily.

On the other hand. . . .

"Got you a ride to the top of Nui Ba Dinh. You 'n' Lieutenant Biddle—you know the Commo Officer, don't you? Well, you will—I want you to take a look at that site, decide if we can isolate a piece of ground there for the antennas and a few boxes of relay equipment. See if there's a power source, either from the Viets or the Special Forces people. Talk to the Beanies; try to talk to the ARVN major, if he speaks English. Make nice with both. I think a master sergeant is the senior man on the Special Forces team. Anyhow, do what you hafta do to make it work. 'kay?"

The captain really expected only a "Yessir."

Winter gave it to him.

* * *

It was past 1600 hours when the Huey settled through a thick fanning of dust and grit, thumping awkwardly onto the volcanic residue atop Nui Ba Dinh, "Black Virgin Mountain." Lieutenant Biddle, sightseeing, stepped blindly off the landing skid onto the back of a young, muddy pig that had sidled up when blade rotation ceased . The porker squealed, fled, and spilled the officer onto the ground, making the day for the half dozen GIs and ARVN troops who had gathered to see what all the fuss was about, this unscheduled helicopter arrival. Winter gave Biddle a hand up. The young officer laughed it off and Winter thought the better of him; having just met, he'd so far been unable to get any impression of the lieutenant's personality. On the chopper, the noise had kept them both speechless. It wasn't much better here: a diesel generator cast a cacophony of mean proportions over the mountain top.

Master Sergeant Billups was offensive guard material, running somewhere near 275 pounds, standing six-and-a-half-feet tall, his skin the shade of well-smoked venison. And he might have been a civilian, ballplayer or not, for he was missing any semblance of rank or allegiance to any military cause. His dress was barely a pair of shorts, ripped from tiger-stripe fatigues, the legs torn off at the crotch, and Ho Chi Minh sandals, made from some expatriate's Peugeot truck tire. Nothing else adorned his body: no shirt, no hat, no belt, no weapon, no watch–not even a tattoo that Winter could discern. No smile. Handshake like a truck driver's arm-wrestling grip.

He was not happy to see the duo, and was disposed to let them know it. "You people," he launched into his un-welcome, no vestige of a Sir or other obsequiousness for the lieutenant, "are bringing attention down on my house." He offered nothing to relieve the implicit dissatisfaction evident in his growl.

A second soldier, only slightly less *déshabillé*, but sporting a set of faded SFC stripes, stuck his hand around Mount Billups and said, "Don't let this ugly asshole scare you off. He worries Charlie will mortar us tonight for landing a chopper up here in daylight . . . but then, he mortars us every night anyhow. What the hey?" Sergeant First Class Condace did not seem to hold the threat in high regard. The big master sergeant continued to grumble, but it was only background noise. Billups was, no doubt about it, the top NCO, evidenced by the deference of everyone on the mountain top. But Condace made things work.

After Biddle explained their mission on the mount, Billups disappeared, scowling, and Condace squired the two of them about the surprisingly small, cluttered space. It was a mountain top: site of an ARVN signal operation, and a Special Forces — what? Winter posed the question in his mind. There was not even a full A Team here. And it was not truly a compound, not a camp. Certainly not a fort or a firebase. But it *was* a mountain top.

Go with that!

Winter saw only one effective structure, a building of sorts the size of a two-car garage. The core of it built from stone, it had been added to with timbers, loose stones, sandbags, empty ammo boxes, full ammo boxes, one small and one large Conex, and other emptied cartons, bales, crates, and a host of unidentifiable leftovers. Condace proudly spoke of this architectural anomaly as the dispensary, the kitchen/dining hall, storage shed for night-vision scopes and other, unnamed "sensitive gear," and quarters for the ARVN major. The major was not in evidence; he would not appear during the time the two visitors were on his mountain.

Their guide did not specify how many ARVN troops called the mountain top home, but Winter observed somewhere between 20 and 25. "Maybe ten of them have wives with them, and a few have children; you'll see them walking naked about the site," Condace said. Hard core, Winter thought—the Vietnamese military policy which placed soldiers' families with them on outpost duty. Draconian. It was deemed insurance against soldiers abandoning their posts under enemy attack. It didn't mean they didn't run; it just upped the ante when they did. *But, Đai Úi, what happens to the wife and kids when the troops are overrun, or just run away? Con biêt?*

Hard core.

Pigs and chickens, a couple of goats, and a few ducks rounded out the menagerie on this fixed ark. Winter and Condace stepped around them as they pecked and groused, shit, nibbled, flittered, flapped, and squawked about the dirt enclosure without regard to people. One small rooster, a flurry of feathers about his feet like busy socks, made mock attacks on Condace's bare feet. The sergeant, finally tiring of the game, booted the cackling upstart some twenty feet toward a sandbagged machine gun emplacement.

As they walked about, hustling against the loss of daylight, examining the ground for a likely site for the proposed relay system, the failing light was further debilitated by an advancing bank of black and puce-colored clouds blowing in from the northwest. Winter recognized a Cambodian moment as imminent. Just when he began to feel concerned they were cutting it pretty close for getting their ride off the peak, an unfamiliar Spec-5 caught up with them and told Biddle the chopper pilot had called, advising he would be unable to get back in on the mountain to pick the two tourists off tonight. Weather had closed in, and the would-be passengers would have to "overnight on the hill," as he put it. Like a pair of banjo pickers when the gig ran out, the Biddle & Winter duo found themselves dumped on the mercies of the community.

They chowed with Special Forces. Condace found them space under a shelter half lean-to against a dry stone wall along the edge of a precipice, a drop of several hundred feet. A rectangle of sandbags formed a sort of room against the stone; a shelter half had been pegged from the tops of the bags to the wall. The threadbare roof and threatening sky offered little hope of a dry night. The sergeant found them a couple of blankets, surprisingly clean, but smelling strongly of burnt oil and something less pleasant. Winter chose not to identify the odor.

Biddle chose to find other accommodations.

Later, sitting around a small fire built in a shallow pit near the stone wall, Billups offered as much as they could have hoped for. "If you can get Major Thuy to go along, and that's not a given . . . but if you can, as far as Special Forces is concerned you can put a relay anyplace it won't interfere . . ." Winter and the lieutenant waited for the second shoe to drop.

". . . anywhere it won't interfere with our passes in review on the parade ground," Billups added with a straight face.

Which pretty well limited the location, Winter thought wryly. You couldn't march a two-man band ten paces in one direction anywhere on the mountain top.

The rain held off, though the clouds initially brought fog, but by 2300 hours it had lifted and it was breezy with a slight chill. It was nearing midnight when Condace came by and invited the two stranded travelers to ". . . come watch the games," and they accompanied him to one of the machine gun emplacements. From the wall there they had an unobstructed view out across flat ground and rice paddy heaven more than three thousand feet below. In the distance the meager lights of Tay Ninh City glowed. In other directions, the ground was covered with rubber trees as far as sight allowed in the on-again/off-again moonlight flickering between clouds.

Occasionally, a light would appear following a straight line across the ground far below them, and Condace explained the road. He pointed to where another road intersected with the one showing traffic, and directed them to keep their eyes on the intersection. "Sometimes the local Teamsters gather at that crossroad to party. They're constantly moving shit on both those roads. And they know we're watching. They gather at the intersection sometimes, put on a show. Morale builder for the dudes humpin' the trail, Major Thuy says. I think their main purpose is to yank our chain.

I've seen people playing musical instruments and dancing in front of a crowd. They're so goddamned cocky, they build fires there sometime. Don't know if this's one-a those nights or not." He leaned his chin on his crossed hands atop the sandbags and stared across the land.

"Don't you ever call in fire on them? Try to get some ARVN to hit 'em?" Winter asked.

"Hmmph!. We've only had any fire support within range for about a month or so, now. Pre-registered a few points for fire, but haven't had occasion to experiment. Mostly be wasting shells, likely." He sounded as if calling down fire on the bold enemy, even given an opportunity, wasn't high on his wish list. "Marvin the ARVN don't wanta screw with 'em."

The three soldiers talked about where the war was going, acknowledged they had no idea, and drifted to reminiscences of home, girlfriends, places served, places visited, homes away from home, girlfriends, hunting dogs, girlfriends . . . The lieutenant seemed content as one of the boys.

Condace was from Georgia—though Winter could find no trace of it in his speech— and thought the epitome of gracious living was sharing a trailer with a pack of Morgans. Winter, bread-and-buttered in a similar environment, remembered the bear dogs his grandfather in Mississippi had kept. He soon tired of that subject and had decided to test the queen bed comfort of his blanket on sandbags when he saw a small flare of light at the place Condace had labeled a crossroads. He pointed.

"Yep. By damn, we got lucky. The Ho Chi Minh traveling circus looks like they're going to perform," the Green Beret sergeant said. As they watched, the fire grew and the observers could see movement of ant-sized players about a cleared area. It would be the crossroads, but the glow from the fire was not enough to define the area as such. Condace chuckled. "Let me get a radio. If we're *really* lucky, the one-oh-fives might have a couple of rounds they can spare us. We'd never hit the Gooks, but if we even came close, it'd send a hell of a notice." He hurried away from the gun emplacement.

"Wouldn't that be something," Winter said. "I wouldn't mind calling one in on the bastards." He smiled grimly.

"You know anything about directing fire?" Biddle asked, shuffling himself into a position with a better view. He had a small pair of binoculars which he peered through in the direction of the fire, but did not offer to share them.

"Used to. Transferred from infantry to arty in Korea. Eleventh Marines, artillery regiment. Forward Observer team." There was nothing of fondness in his memory . . . but there *were* memories. And serving the guns, tasking Fire Direction Center, bringing down hurt on night stalkers, was like swimming or riding a bike: you don't forget the good stuff!

* * *

Condace came sprinting back to the parapet, a packboard with radio in one hand, a large pair of binoculars in the other. He grinned at the lieutenant, "Time to pay for the tickets."

"You get many opportunities up here to call fire?" Biddle asked.

"Not much. We have one man, S.P. Five Jones, who trained as F.O.. But he's in Thailand on T.D.Y."

Winter thought, Hell! Everybody's doing it.

Condace commenced checking the battery on the radio, switched on the power. "Everyone else's just had minimal instruction. But maybe I can drop one into the same county, with a little help from my friends," he nodded toward the distant Fire Direction Center.

"Sergeant Winter here has some background," Biddle offered. "You might consider giving him the chance. See if he can do any good. Unless there's some prohibition —"

"Nahh, no problem. I don't mind. I'd likely just be wasting shells," the SFC said. "How about it, Sarge? Wanna give it a shot? Hah!" he said, startled at his own joke.

"I don't mind. Been a while . . ." he reached for the handset. "What's the call sign for the F.D.C.?"

"Wombat. And we're . . . let's see, this is Tuesday . . . we're Mongoose. No, my wrong; we're Meercat today. Meercat niner niner. Freq's set." Condace passed the backpack to Winter, who placed it on the parapet.

Looking below again, across the plain, he saw the blaze had grown to practically a bonfire. "Cheeky bastards, aren't they," he said, breaking squelch a couple of times. He depressed the switch on the handset and called, "Wombat. Wombat. This is Meercat niner niner. Fire mission. Over."

Southeast Asia's ether was devoid of response.

"Wombat, Meercat niner niner. Over."

There was a spasm of white noise, followed by a series of clicks, merging into a tone of rising pitch and intensity. Then a disembodied voice rent the air. "Meercat. Roger your fire mission. Wait one." Winter turned the volume down, not wanting every enemy soldier on the mountainside chuckling over his outdated procedure.

In the waiting seconds, the three men watched a colony of ants flicker about the fire far below them, the firelight dancing red and gold on drab black garb.

"Meercat. Meercat. This is Wombat. Ready your fire mission. Over." Winter imagined the flurry of activity, finding plotters, waking gunners, un-boxing shells, cutting powder bags, and all done with counterpart ARVN cannoneers.

"Uhh, roger, Wombat. Fire mission." Winter had a quick thought: he didn't know if the firing protocol was different for Army arty or not. Must be enough commonality to make it happen. Well, at least the FDC comms was manned by a GI. He focused on the map that Condace held before him, a hooded flashlight directed onto it, one grubby finger stabbing at a pre-registered firing point.

"Fire mission," Winter repeated, slightly nervous as he thought of the years since he'd done this for a living. "Base tango Blue One One," and he looked through the powerful glasses the Special Forces sergeant had furnished him, squinting at the familiar mil scale imposed on the lens, "left . . . uhh, eight zero. Add . . . six hundred. One marking round Willie Peter. On your command. Over." He turned to Condace, "We still using mils?"

"Yeah, using mils, but Willie Peter might be out of time. Maybe not, but it's been a while since I heard that term."

Winter, stuck in Korea-speak, chuckled, embarrassed. Willie Peter was old phonetic alphabet for WP, an abbreviation for White Phosphorous, a devilishly horrendous affliction to render unto anyone, but because of its high visibility—exploding in a coruscating eruption of white smoke trailing streamers of highly visible burning phosphorous—it was used as marking rounds for artillery fire. When it burst on the landscape, it was hard to miss, and from its placement, a forward observer then visually adjusted fire, calling back changes to the FDC, thus to the guns.

"Meercat, Wombat. Base TANGO Blue One One, left eight zero, add six zero zero; one round, Willie Peter. On the way. Adjust on my shot."

Right in stride.

There was a brief eternity of silence. No one spoke. The radio remained quiet. Then they heard from a great distance a muted *Boo-om!* They never heard the round in flight; the guns were on the far side of the target from them. But before them, on the flats below the looming peak, as if the central focus in a diorama, the bonfire exploded suddenly into a massive eruption of fire and flying, burning debris, a momentary impression of ants blown away by wind, followed belatedly by a dull cracking sound. The nimbus of light from the fire-explosion quickly faded. Only a grotesque, night-blooming flower of pristine white phosphorous tendrils remained, splayed in broad circumference, hanging in the breezeless air halfway up to where he stood. The lingering P-trails were clearly visible, glowing in the patchy moonlight through the glasses. All sound died away across the rice paddies below, diminishing into the stands of rubber trees beyond.

No one moved. No one spoke. Lieutenant Biddle continued to gaze through his glasses at the world below, focusing on a few tiny sparks that glowed, flickered, and went out, one by one, until there was near dark. He nodded once in affirmation, said nothing.

Winter keyed the handset, "Wombat. This is Meercat. Cease fire. Cease fire. End of fire mission. Out." He handed the pack to Condace.

The sergeant stared wide-eyed at Winter, a gaze of admiration—or disbelief—fixed on his face. He, too, said nothing, but looked back at the plain below. He sought out the meager fireflies on the dark land, all that remained of the Viet Cong Ideological and Morale Cooperative at the crossroads. He made a soft, almost soundless whistle. "No one will ever believe this. *No* one. Not since Basilone's mortar shot on The Canal has anyone pulled off a single-shot scene-stealer like that—"

"What?" Winter asked distractedly. "Who'd you say?"

"Basilone. Sergeant John Basilone. Marine in World—"

"I know who Basilone is. What's the connection . . . to this?" Winter turned toward the sergeant first class, away from the astounding darkness below.

"Well, if you know who he is . . . was . . . then you know the story."

"*What* story, for Christ's sake?"

"Jeez . . . John Basilone was a sergeant in the Marines." Condace's voice took on a begrudging aspect in reaction to the testiness in Winter's demand. "In the battle for Guadalcanal—he was a mortarman—they were being shelled by a Jap destroyer, coming down The Slot. He—"

"He was a machine gunner."

"Well, he fucking well fired a mortar at this destroyer. He musta known what he was doing; the fucking round dropped down the Jap ship's stack, straight into the engine room. Blew the fucking thing completely out of the water." The Special Forces sergeant's animation seemed overdone, Winter thought.

"Bullshit!"

"*Bullshit?* What the hell you mean, bullshit? Man, he won the Medal of Honor for his action." There. Proof positive.

"Where'd you get that tale, Condace?"

"Before I joined the Army and made Georgia my home . . . I'm originally from Flemington. New Jersey. Next town over from Raritan, Basilone's hometown. I been there a million times. Played ball there. Got drunk. Got laid, got indoctrinated there. I *know* about John Basilone."

"Bullshit! Sergeant John Basilone won the The Medal for action on the Tenaru River, holding a thin line of Marine defenders about Henderson Airfield against Japanese infantry. October, nineteen forty-two. He was a machine gun section leader with two gun sections. He lost one gun—hold on, let me finish—one gun out of action in sustained *banzai* attacks; he picked up the other gun and tripod, ninety pounds of steel, and ran several hundred yards to reposition the gun for a better field of fire, got the gun back in action, and continued to fire until the barrel almost burned out." Winter seemed intent on the telling; he wouldn't look over the parapet, but stared into Condace's eyes. His narrative had a rote sound.

Condace stood frozen, his mouth slack, half open. "But—" he began.

"He had to repair the gun, jammed with mud and sand. He had just one assistant gunner alive, and he was wounded. Lost a hand. But for hours he held off repeated attacks. This was at night, in heavy rain. When the Jap bodies piled up so high—so close—around him that he couldn't bring the gun to bear, he repositioned it again and continued to fire.

"At times, when the charging Japs got around behind him, Basilone used his forty-five and dropped a number with that. When he was out of ammo, he ran two hundred yards, across open ground, under fire, grabbed all the ammo he could carry, and ran back and got the gun back in action. 'Manila John'—that's what he was called, you know, from his Army service in the Phillipines in the 'thirties—was a one-man killing machine."

Neither other man offered speech.

"By daylight, the Japs were *banzai*-ed out, their will broken. Basilone, personally, was credited with effectively destroying a regiment's combat capability. After-action confirmed thirty-eight dead bodies piled about his position. No telling how many others crawled off and died. Or were dragged away. That . . . *that*, my good sergeant, is how Manila John won the C.M.H. The first Marine to win the 'big one' in the Pacific war."

"But the ship . . . the mortar round—" Condace tried to insert.

"Only mortar shell I associate with him is the one that killed Gunnery Sergeant John Basilone in 1945, two-and-a-half years after The Canal, while directing his machine gun crews off the beach on Iwo Jima in the face of heavy fire. He'd only been ashore two hours, and had already, single-handedly taken out a bunker, an action for which he was awarded—posthumously—the Navy Cross."

There was a long, grudging silence. But no argument; Winter's soliloquy was profound in the extreme.

"How d'you know all that stuff about Basilone? A Marine," Condace asked suspiciously.

"Marine boot A.B.C.s at Parris Island. Corps history. Mother's milk."

Lieutenant Biddle, who had been staring through his binoculars silently throughout, his eyes and his mind focused on the now dark plain, pulled the glasses down and produced a minuscule smile as he watched Winter turn and walk away.

The handset squawked. "Meercat. Is that it? Will you need us again? Over." Improper comms protocol.

Condace picked up the handset, keyed the mike, and said, "Wombat, Meercat. Cease fire. That's a wrap. Thanks for your help. Out." He stared after Winter's fading form.

"Uhh, Meercat. Wombat here. Okey dokey. How'd we do? Was it a clean shot? Over." The query could be heard in the voice for all the other things the cannon cocker wanted to know.

"Wombat, you . . . you wouldn't believe. Out." Condace flipped the power switch off. No encore was possible.

* * *

Walking back across the dimly lighted compound, Winter struggled to keep the quaking in his legs from betraying him. If he could only make it to his lean-to, he'd sit a spell. Think about resting.

His hands trembled uncontrollably; he felt a strong urge to urinate. But he had gone to the latrine less than a hour ago. He knew the symptoms: nerves. Hell, *scared!* The sequence of events, culminating in the . . . *miracle* – dare he use the term in an event of death and destruction? – was frightening.

A matter of pure luck. Obviously. No one, to his knowledge, had ever placed a hit so accurately on target, so deadly. Even Manila John, he thought, close to smirking. He shook his head in amazement at Condace's worshipful tale. But, maybe . . . *had someone, sometime* dropped a mortar round down the stack of a Jap destroyer? Maybe Lou Diamond? The Mortar Maven. Covering the beach at Guadalcanal? Elsewhere? Blown it out of the water?

Apocryphal? Assuredly . . . though not necessarily untrue. Not all war stories were without substance. But if the tale had a basis in fact, Winter had copied the unidentified gunner's act – on his *registering* round, no less. Jeez-us, it *was* unreal.

Bizarre, but he wouldn't be the one to tell them, his Black Virgin companions, that. He put his hands under opposite armpits and squeezed himself. He felt cold. No, he wouldn't volunteer what must already be obvious: he'd just witnessed divine intervention. Was God on our side in this fracas, after all?

A giggle shook him. Or was it the mountain-top cold?

He wasn't laughing. He imagined, wildly, what version all this weirdness would take in the re-telling. He knew he would never tell anyone anything about it, thus avoiding being branded the most flagrant kind of liar. He heard behind him shouts and laughter as Viet soldiers ran to the parapet hoping to take in some part of this phenomenal gunnery. Someone else had seen and passed the word.

Master Sergeant Billups appeared at Winter's bedding-down spot later, stared at him without speaking in the dim light of nearby Vietnamese guard-post cooking fires. The massive sergeant hunkered down and sat on air for a while, like a Vietnamese coolie, morbidly as silent. Winter gazed back at him, letting no expression corrupt his face, equally silent. After a few minutes, Billups rose, shaking his head, and vanished into the gloom.

chapter seventeen

Never Get Out of the Plane

Viet Nam: March 1965

A young soldier, feeling harried and put-upon by circumstances, sits at the console, staring blindly into the black box before him, turning a dial. In the headphones an irregular rush of static and aural confusion assails his eardrums, occasionally coalescing into the sharp, chattering dot-dash of manual Morse code as he tunes through a CW signal. The operator is unidentifiable, wearing no jacket, therefore no nametag, no indication of rank. He has memorized his nametag, thus no longer requires it; and when anyone addresses him as Mickey, PFC Michael Seiders lets it pass. Close enough. His once-white T-shirt is stuck with sweat to his wiry body.

Next to him, Specialist-4 Planert might be equally anonymous, without even the false modesty of a T-shirt covering his hairy, tanned, sweating torso, but this operator, in action like Seiders, advertises himself with a tattoo of Planet Earth high on his right shoulder, superscripted with the name Dale. They are two in a line of similar figures, slumped in the oppressive heat and humidity of WHITE BIRCH Operations Center, Tan Son Nhut, Saigon, Republic of (South) Viet Nam.

"I hear a guy from the thirty-ninth lost his arm riding in a cyclo last night. In Cho Lon. Booby trap," Seiders mumbles between bursts of code.

"Heard that, too. Thank Odin . . . that shit mostly happens up country . . . or down." Working his fingers quickly, heavily pounding the keyboard of a solid-looking typewriter, Planert cranks the carriage return lever, lifts up the chatter roll of six-ply paper and carbons, and scans what he has just typed. "You here last year . . . when they set off the bomb in the American theater . . . downtown?"

"That time last year I was still a civilian puke. You?"

"Never got to the theater. Knew the two guys killed, though. Bunch more wounded." He again pounds out a quick flurry of keystrokes, double-shifts the lever, types some more, reaches forward, grabs a large hand dial, and begins rotating it quickly, clockwise. "Fucker's movin' on me again. Q.S.W. thirty-seven. *Aaarrrrgh!*"

"Sic 'im, Dale," from the next row over.

Their speech is clipped, succinct snatches of pseudo-conversation wedged between bursts of coded communications. The subjects of their abbreviated discourse are eclectic and erratic, the pace dictated by their targets. Loud, piercing signals squeal across the sweltering bay where ineffective air conditioners swirl the dense atmosphere lethargically, ensuring distribution of misery. A high-toned rip of printer chatter dominates for a moment, then is gone. A rank fug of humid, charged air hangs like a damp towel over the bay which smells of feral animals.

"Got him." The op leans back, complacently pecking away in reponse to the slow-speed signal, now that he has reacquired his target. The ubiquitous cigarette is clamped in the corner of his mouth, the rising smoke in the stagnant atmosphere keeping his left eye scrunched shut. His booted foot never leaves the table that supports his mill, a military commo version of a typewriter with no lower case letters, and beefed-up construction to accommodate around-the-clock pounding by insensitive GI hands. Another cigarette smolders in the slide-out ashtray of the metal table.

"'nother coup attempt last night. They're—" The anticipated pronouncement is interrupted as the operator pursues his target up the band.

" —silly assholes," he finishes as he zeros in. "Khanh's in it for the long haul."

"Yeah, 'til the next Zip general's proles pull a one-up on Khanh's proles."

The third console in line is manned by a tall, slim, elegant soldier from Panama City who seems to thrive in the invidious atmosphere. He is in complete summer fatigue uniform, only nominally acknowledging the ambient atmosphere by rolling his sleeves up on white, hairless arms. He is known as The GQ Clone. He is between skeds now and engaged in broadening his horizons. "Hah!" he shouts. "Talking oxymoronica—*military intelligence*," he offers, shaking his copy of the *Stars and Stripes* GI newspaper.

"I have to read this yellow-sheet rag to find out what's going on outside yonder door."

As other ops, splitting their attention between two radio dials and a promising diatribe, home in on the bitching, The Clone shifts into high dudgeon: "We gather all this useless crap, feed it upstairs, but the bastards never come back and tell us anything. Whether we're doing any good or not."

"Uncle Sammy don't write," comes from an unidentified source.

"Roger that. Listen to this . . . uhhh, it's talking about increased fighting in the countryside—what else? Says . . . President Johnson, 'still refusing to authorize bombing strikes on North Vietnam, has taken the—'*Machiavellian*, my word '—step of authorizing—' get this '—*retaliatory bombing raids in the future event of continued escalation.*' Now ain't that some shit?"

"Means we don't do it right now, but *Watch out! you silly fuckers. Next time . . .*" another chides.

"Wait 'til he gets back. Catch him in the club sometime. You gotta hear Sergeant Winter on this cluster fuck," Planert urges.

Aping the BBC, with grave inflection The GQ Clone ponderously intones, ". . . and as the Tet Truce winds down, a fog of substantial weirdness securely envelops Washington."

* * *

Damson, newly arrived in Vietnam, ignored all caution regarding off-duty activities. His second day in country, as soon as his briefers released him from the headquarters drill, he changed into civvies and, relying on solicited directions, caught a cart to the front gate and a cab into Sai Gon. He ate at Cheap Charlie's and made his way down Hai Ba Trung to the Kit Kat Klub, an unprepossessing drinkery that harbored only soldiers, mostly troops of the 39th Signal Battalion.

With some five years in Army Security Agency when he reached Viet Nam, Damson preferred the company of other than his on-duty colleagues. This was acceptable to them, as he did not fare well in their appraisal. Comrades-in-arms considered him somewhat sub-par: neither good soldier nor qualified malcontent; not STRAC, but not quite a dirtbag either. One factor to his discredit: Damson never repaid money he borrowed. But since that was quickly well known in any new assignment, no one would loan him money, so that was a wash. But the cruncher, in the cloistered world of security clearances, background checks, and admonitions toward straight-arrow behavior, was that no one had ever seen him chatting up the hooch maids, spending money on bargirls, or visiting any of the popular whorehouses, anywhere he'd served. He wasn't thought to be, necessarily, light in the loafers; he just didn't fit well with the common run of ASA wastrels.

His first night on the town, finding no evidence of 3rd RRU in the Kit Kat, Damson relaxed and drank an indecorous number of the unfamiliar *Ba-mui-ba* beers; and whether the nine percent alcohol or the fifteen percent formaldehyde put him under, he was shortly beyond any ability to stand, see, or talk. A perfect customer for Suzi Kew, the Kit Kat Kween.

After a couple of hours double-billing his drinks, purloining his bar change, and a little sticky-finger wallet work, at closing time Suzie, assisted by the barman and mama-san, got Damson into a taxi at the street edge. Giving her regular driver the usual instructions, Suzi directed the erratic journey from Hai Ba Trung to some back-street palace of delights far off the beaten path, a scaled-down Xanadu. From her small but well-appointed pad, even Ratty Mac, the most accomplished white hunter in Southeast Asia, would have been at pains to follow a trail of breadcrumbs home.

What degradations the Kit Kat Kween engaged in with the hapless soldier were to remain forever a mystery. Suzi may or may not have worked her wiles on the unawares Damson, but there came a time, far into the early morning hours, when even the dark sciences paled and their minions slept.

With the streets emptied of all but the hardest-core, dedicated little purveyors of dialectical materialism, there was no one or nothing to offer succor to the beast. With a scream portending horrendous intentions, the dragon swooped down upon Suzi's shack, it's monstrous snout breathing fire, its talons clutching the torn, macerated bodies of earlier victims, even as it sought further prey. The piercing wail woke Damson, brought him upright from a supine position on Suzi's bed to vertical on his feet on the filthy floor in one seamless move, undecided which way to flee. He could not see through the walls of the room, though immediately from its flare he was aware of the dragon's glowing eye already sweeping the outside of the house, seeking entry. He was almost unaware of the smell of incense.

As the mythical beast roared nearer, its scream grew, became angrier. It threatened to break through the back side of the house, through the solid wall opposite the dimly outlined door Damson could barely make out in his transfixed state of terror.

Awakening at Damson's screams, not the rage of the beast, the whore, Suzi, contributed to the din, wailing, out of bed and running in place while praying to her ancestors for protection from these thousand devils. Though she might have accommodated the dragon, Suzi Kew was unaccustomed to screaming customers, and in her newfound confusion, took a natural course.

Taking the route of least resistance himself, screaming in bursts, Damson fled out the door, splintering it back against the wall and off its hinges. He ran without breaking stride off the low porch, hitting the ground while maintaining his balance. He would have shot forward directly into the maw of the monster, but he stumbled over the rusting handle of a switching control and fell onto the cinders on the verge of the tracks.

The Vung Tau-Saigon local, a Toonerville Trolley-like train comprising an old steam engine of French Indochine origins trailing a string of motley cars bearing a variety of products of minimal value, chuffed angrily past where he lay, ignoring Damson's naked efforts to flee. It disregarded, equally, the naked and screaming whore who danced in a circle on her low porch, still without opening her eyes.

Her myth-induced panic, however, would not affect her fiscal well-being. Suzi had already collected her fee, and every other dollar and piastre Damson had in his wallet, along with several documents that might be of some value to her brother who was leaving soon, newly recruited in the local Viet Cong popularity contest.

Damson, lying stunned in the filth of backstreet Saigon, dimly recalled through his current haze and stunned senses a scene of similar proportions that reeked of salt sea air, camel shit, and cobblestones.

* * *

The GQ Clone is bitching because someone has lifted the sports section from his four-day-old *Stars and Stripes* when he left his pos to take a leak. The only sport he cares for is pro football, and the championship has been played and reported on more than a month ago — he's even read the copy — but if you let someone get away with that crap, skiffing your paper without notice, it'll just get worse, he knew.

"Read something else, G.Q. I'll post the N.B.A. scores for you later," Planert offers.

"That's not the point, goddamn it . . ."

"For Christ's sake, give it a rest. What's happening in the rest of the world?" SP4 Vern Garvin asks. He's read the duty *S&S* from cover to cover, but if he can get the Clone diverted, maybe he'll stop yapping.

Clone shakes out the creased front page once more and, still grumbling, peruses the large type for worthy subject matter. He reads, mumbles, shakes the paper again.

After several minutes of relative quiet, the Clone announces, "Well, no shit. About fucking time."

No one takes the bait.

Clone waits, and finding no encouragement, tries again. "It had to come to this. Maybe things will change around here now."

"Nothing's gonna change. Tomorrow'll be just like today. Same-old, same-old," Garvin laments.

"No. Did you read this timetable in here? Remember, about a month ago, I read you how Johnson signed off on us kicking the shit out of Charlie if he kept on with the attacks? Says here — must have been the day after that — on the seventh of February, the V.C. upped the ante. Charlie must have read about Johnson's threat, wanted to test us. On the seventh was when they hit the advisers' compound and airfield at Camp Holloway, up near Pleiku? You must remember! Killed nine Americans and wounded more than a hundred."

"That's old news, G.Q. We been on alert ever since. How'd you miss that?" an op down the line smirked.

"I'm not reading it as news, asshole; it's part of this timeline of events. Just hold your water." There are no rebuttals; Clone explores the timeline. "Well, when that happened, Bundy convinced the president to finally authorize retaliatory strikes. And we did, and we were surprised — *I* was, anyhow — when the Navy immediately launched sorties off carriers and hit those barracks in the north. Tit for tat."

"I'm all for a tit," floats above the noise.

Ignoring the plaintive interruption, Clone labors on: "That attack was above the D.M.Z., but far enough from Hanoi that Kosygin didn't jump in with Soviet troops, as I thought he might. I lost five bucks to Jensen, betting Kosygin had the balls."

"I'm guessing it's not over yet, G.Q."

"You are not wrong," he laughs. "Because of bad weather, V-NAF couldn't follow up the swabbies' strike that day, so they came back and hit another target the following day. We'll call that part of the same tit for tat. Anyhoo, after Johnson's lead, the House . . ." his eyes roll, ". . . *discussed* raising the stakes. So much for the threat. On the tenth, Charlie *did raise the stakes.* That's when they blew up the billet hotel in Qui Nhon, got some G.I.s again."

"Still old news. What happened last night?"

"Hell, Seiders, how do I know. This goddamned rag's four days old." There is a burst of harsh laughter across the bay. GQ is such a bite.

"Let me get to the point, damn it. This whole pick-up game has become one of showdown. So where was I? Yeah-h-h, the president. Well, to take the metaphor a step further, Johnson had reserved the right to check and raise. After Qui Nhon, immediate retaliation was not forthcoming — his check; but two days later Johnson finally got his game face on and raised, authorizing, I'm quoting here, '. . . a program of measured and limited air action in areas south of the nineteenth parallel.' Gentlemen," he says with serious mien, "the cheap bidders folded." But even GQ realized he had pushed the metaphor to its limits.

"Then, two weeks ago, we acknowledge for the first time that we're flying combat missions into North Vietnam. On the twenty-fourth. Then — here's the good shit" he reads verbatim again, "' — on March nine, five days ago, a combined U.S.-South Vietnamese air strike hit an ammunition dump and a naval base in the north.' Qui Nhon must have been the final straw, buckled the hoary camel's back. That's what all the activity's been about this week." The GQ Clone is in his element now; he has the attention of enough ops he could charge admission.

"Fellow running dog capitalist swine, we are now pursuing a policy of kick-ass. This particular phase of confusion and angst shall, heretofore, be known as Operation rolling thunder. We've been ramping up to this state forever, now. First queried, then teased, I guess Charlie finally embarrassed the Washington weenies to take the Operation out of the planning/saving-for-a-rainy-day bin and nudge it into the action category, thereby raising the game to the house limit." He's back into Vegas.

* * *

Winter jerked awake. The dreams were still with him, but he couldn't make them out. Muddled. Nickie. Fireworks. Someone crying, as if down a long corridor.

Where was he? The mountain! The goddamned black bitch. What woke him? A sharp rattle of—Was it shots?—No shit!— more shots, followed by the detonation of a grenade. Sounded like serious shit.

Under attack.

And it was raining.

He was wet, soaked through. Clouds hung a few feet above the mountaintop, wringing out a deluge onto the ground and the men and women and kids and dogs and ducks . . . and sandbags and supplies scattered across the compound. The shelter half that had been stretched above him was gone, a tribute to the winds conspiring now to further his destruction. He was open to the elements.

He had no helmet. His fatigue cap was soaked through, but he jammed it down on his head, trusting the bill would divert the rain enough to sight the rifle. He grabbed his M-14 and sprinted through the downpour to the nearest machine gun emplacement. Two Special Forces men were mounting a Browning light machine gun on an elevated tripod. Beyond, another trooper dropped 60-mm rounds into a mortar tube in quick succession, the rounds exploding with hollow pops high in the sky. The detonating rounds freed flares on small parachutes to float back to earth, illuminating the mountain and countryside with a surreal, unworldly wash in silver, blue, and green. Wind and rain blew the chutes out away from the parapet where the light continued far down the mountainside, the brilliant little torches drifting to the valley floor.

Winter heard machine gun and rifle fire and the crump of grenades from the far side of the compound where ARVN guards were alert. He looked cautiously over the edge of the sandbags, and in the uneasy light cast from swinging airborne flares, he thought he could make out movement. He spotted dark blobs that appeared part of the mountainside, but he knew they were the still forms of Viet Cong, caught in the flare light while climbing toward the compound through the wire. There was only an occasional shot fired from below — the VC had admirable fire discipline — and nothing seemed to be threatening this position. Winter leaned over the parapet and began firing at suspicious, lumpy shadows.

Another M-14 opened up near him. As he changed magazines he saw Lieutenant Biddle, off to his right, pouring a stream of fire down at unseen attackers. Winter had the good sense to feel frightened, thankful for the fear.

There was a space of some thirty yards to the left of him where no one manned the stone-and-sandbag wall. Winter checked repeatedly down the slope below and to his left, looking for any activity in that quadrant.

Inserting another magazine, Winter found himself in one of those unaccountable lulls in combat that occurs at some time in every firefight when, for whatever reason— changing magazines, out of ammo, the rifleman hit, wounded, position abandoned— every soul engaged in the fight stops shooting at the same moment. In the shrieking silence Winter heard a tenuous scraping sound. Looking left, he made out movement just a few feet below the crest of sandbags. One of *them* had managed to reach the top!

Winter swung the M-14 left and loosed off half a magazine, the recoil jerking the sight picture around until he couldn't be sure he was anywhere near target. As the flutter of firing about him grew loud and sustained, he heard a sharp, high-pitched scream, and could no longer make out the form of the nearby VC. He felt a funny quiver in his stomach; at the same time, relief. As he turned back to his front, the sandbag wall blew into shreds all about him.

The sharp burst of AK-47 fire missed him by millimeters, though he could not understand how; it fairly encompassed his position.

Condace, crouching and barking an alert to his presence, ran up behind Winter and thrust a pair of hand grenades at him. Winter pulled the pin on one immediately, reached over the sandbags, and let it roll out of his hand. He heard the *clink-pop* as the spoon flew and hoped it didn't get hung up on the wire. But when it blew, he knew by the diminished blast it had fallen straight. When Condace disappeared to bring more grenades, Winter was reluctant to use the only one he had left. He was low on ammo, and being unarmed was not a desired scenario.

"El Tee, how much ammo you got?" Winter called to Biddle during a lull in firing.

"What? Who said that?" The lieutenant sounded as if he were on the phone from Anaheim.

"It's me, Winter. You okay?"

"Yeah. Oh yeah, Winter. *Sergeant* Winter. Yeah. I'm all right. You got any ammo? I'm out." Winter had a quirky flash: Teacher, I don't have any paper for the test.

"You sure you okay, El Tee?" Winter crawled over to him.

"Yeah, all right. I just—" he giggled. "I think I wet my trousers." More giggles.

"Hey, no sweat. Be grateful that's all." Winter was not trying to offer solace; he meant it. He'd been there.

Condace and a staff sergeant whose name Winter couldn't recall ran up, a wooden box slung by rope handles between them. The box of grenades was opened but full. Condace set it on the ground, started pulling grenades from the packing. As he did, Winter decided he could afford the gesture, pulled the pin on the one he still held, let the spoon fly, counted to two, and lofted it gently over the wall. When this one blew, it was accompanied by a scream nearer, downslope, chopped off short. The sergeant first class grinned nastily and commenced passing out magazines of 7.62mm ammunition.

By the time he and Biddle reloaded and the two ammo humpers had disappeared, it had grown quieter. A few shots sounded from the far side of the compound, but soon even that ragged firing ceased. Billups walked across the compound, urging quietly but insistently, "Conserve ammo, troops. We're running low."

"You've used up your ammo stocks?" Winter asked incredulously, stopping Billups in his crouching stroll. Hell, they'd only been under fire a few minutes—forever. How could they be short of ammo? Biddle beside him looked at the looming master sergeant as if he were speaking Swahili.

"Just about used up *ours*," Billups said.

"What's that mean?"

"What I said. We have our ammo; Marvin the ARVN has his. Ne'er the twain shall be shared."

"You're shitting me," Winter offered. Could this get sillier?

"Never you, G.I. I shit thee not." Billups crouched suddenly as a poorly aimed round cracked through the air above him. "Our supply chopper didn't come in. For three days, now. Weather. Yet, they managed to get you in here." He did not seem particularly put out by the obvious truth of his comment. "We're just about out. And, no! We cannot draw on *these* ARVN supplies. The Major," he said with curious emphasis, indicating the mystery Vietnamese Army major who commanded the mountaintop, "says we don't overlap. *Insists!* Rations, ammo, medical supplies. Nothing." He looked somewhere between Winter and Biddle.

"Who supplies this mountaintop?" Winter asked.

"Uncle Sugar, of course. Don't matter. Once Major Thuy gets supplies, they become the personal property of Major Thuy. And Major Thuy is scrupulously private, jealous, and stinnn-gee." Billups didn't expand on his low-voiced comments. Winter, looking about in the uneasy after-shock of the firefight, understood that Billups knew there were ears everywhere.

"Well, fuck me," Winter said with feeling. Lieutenant Biddle shuffled nervously about, as if forced to share the propensities of the foreign national officer corps.

"A word to caution you, young Sergeant: don't stand still . . . or someone will." Billups moved off, avoiding response.

Condace stayed with Winter, waiting for the light. Biddle went off, probably, Winter thought laughing to himself, to share the benefits of command with the major. But it was quiet now, on and below the mountain. And the rain had stopped. To the east, gray . . .

The first hint of dawn came with cold, shrouding effect. Both sergeants were shivering. Winter was still wet through, Condace in similar condition.

Adding to Winter's still-heightened mood was the presence of an enemy soldier's body, caught in the lower strands of barbed wire strung atop, and hanging out beyond, the sandbags along the parapet. The wire maze continued down some twenty feet below the crest, and in the lower edge of it, Winter saw the tangled body of one of the attacking VC. He felt sure it was the one he had shot when he'd heard movement during the lull and opened fire.

As the light grew stronger and he could see more clearly, he couldn't take his eyes off the small, dark bundle of one-time humanity that hung there as if chiding him for ignoring the commandment. He stared at it, bothered by the lack of bulk, remembering the high, shrill cry in the dark, wondering, aching to determine if this was a female or just a young man. Small, for sure. He tried not to be particularly bothered by either possibility; he wasn't silly enough to take it personally. But he was curious.

It was completely quiet on the mountaintop now. Condace went away and came back with two canteen cups of coffee. Or so it was rumored. It tasted like nothing Winter had ever labeled coffee, but it was hot and formidable, smelling strongly of iodine. As they stood, looking out over Three Corps, both unavoidably aware of the bundle in the wire just below them, Condace said, "Only one casualty last night for the good guys. Marvin caught his weapon on the wire, shot himself in the foot. Don't have a count on the bad guys."

It was rapidly growing lighter now. Winter asked, "How do we go about getting him—" he thrust his chin toward the offending, dark presence "—out of the wire down there?"

Condace looked over the edge. "Or her," he said, sniffling with the early chill.

Despite his convictions, his training, and his last-war experiences, Winter felt a slight tug at his guts. "Yeah, or her. Well? . . ."

"We'll get one of the ARVN to go over, get a line around it, pull it up. They have some little guys who clamber up and down these slopes like monkeys. No slur intended, you know."

"Course not. So we just wait."

The Special Forces sergeant did not reply; they waited in silence.

* * *

Before dawn transitioned fully into tourist brilliance, Winter had moved to his left, peering moodily down at the dark mass. He grunted, said to Condace, "Get your man. Let's get that thing out of the wire. I don't think it's a body."

"Yeah, I been thinking that for about ten minutes now. Didn't want to make any wild guesses, though. Looks like a bundle of unfilled sandbags, blown over the edge during the fight. You disappointed?" he grinned at Winter, "Dead Eye."

"Oh, sure. Thought we definitely had a kill," Winter said, a measurable relinquishing of tension rippling through his belly muscles.

"Stick around. We'll give you another chance tonight. Don't worry, though; we likely accounted for more'n a couple of the bastards. Up here, no way to check for blood trails, we never get confirmeds." This lack of accountability seemed acceptable. Condace didn't bring up the miracle of the single 105 round.

Lieutenant Biddle walked over from wherever he had been and said, "The chopper will be here for us about six." He looked up at the mostly clear sky, the few gold-tipped cumulus along the eastern rim of the world drifting without menace. "Weather's not a factor now." He sniffed and chewed on some of the coffee he carried in a ceramic cup.

* * *

Except for Condace, no one saw them off. Billups, true to form, left them to think what they would about his absence. No one else seemed to be awake on Nui Ba Dinh.

* * *

The UH-1B Huey, which had returned to the mountain for the two stranded 3rd RRU men, struggled across the early sky, its cargo bay empty but for Winter, the lieutenant, and one gunner cradling a machine gun on a strap, leaning into it and out the open door. The soldier wore only a T-shirt despite the cool air at altitude. There were no flight helmets with courtesy headsets on the chopper. The co-pilot, a second lieutenant, had told Biddle the ship was returning to Tan Son Nhut following a pre-dawn Eagle Flight, inserting ARVN troops into the bush along the Cambodian border. They had been advised to pick up the two hitch-hikers at their convenience.

Cool wind blew in the open doors and the bay experienced a cross-current that could sweep a man out. Both 3rd RRU men sat against the right wall of the ship propped against metal frame members that cut into their backs. Winter had caught himself referring to it in ingrained Marine jargon when he said to the officer, "We'd better sit against the bulkhead."

The lieutenant looked at him strangely and shouted, "What?"

They were at about four thousand feet, and the smudge of the Sai Gon metro area had begun to define itself to their twelve o'clock when, without warning, the helicopter swung violently to port in a steep banking turn, leaving both men looking straight out the port door at the green and brown swirl of the land below. The door gunner disconnected his helmet commo cord from the line feed and flailed over to shout in Winter's ear over the rotor noise. "Gotta make a detour . . . into a hot area . . . El Zee taking fire . . . keep your weapon handy." He skittered back across the decking without waiting for a reply, re-hooked his belt, reconnected his headset, grabbed the handle on the gun, and jacked in a fresh round.

The Huey swung in a wide circle and Winter, who had crawled nearer the open port side, visualized them anchored to a radial, centered on a cleared space in heavy brush and trees below. It was not quite jungle down there, but would have offered impediment to a casual stroll. He could see troops, some glancing up with a sudden light flash of face, most concentrating on matters at hand. A light haze partially obscured the landing zone. Winter could tell from the untidy litter the LZ had been blown recently: scattered logs and branches and shredded bamboo, still green, and the detritus of combat — ammo crates, empty; ammo bandoliers, empty; and shipping tube cartons for mortar rounds — made a questionable environmental statement across the LZ. Now he saw strawberry smoke spewing from the edge of the clearing.

Completing his second orbit of the LZ, the chopper pilot suddenly dropped his ship into the center of the tiny clearing, sinking toward waving grass. A Vietnamese rifleman wearing a red beret, secreted in the rippling green ground cover, leapt to his feet and dodged away from the helicopter's set-down. He held his rifle with one hand, and with the other, projected a universal single middle finger skyward toward the Huey driver.

Biddle and Winter jumped from the idling chopper. Biddle sought someone of authority to check in with. The gunner shouted to Winter, "Don't go far, Sarge. We're gonna pick up wounded. Don't know how many. Maybe you can give 'em a hand loading. I gotta stay on the gun," he yelled, looking rapidly about the perimeter.

Winter, bent over and, looking in every direction, made his way toward a small knot of child-soldiers on the edge of the LZ, hunkered down by what looked like a giant ant hill. One over-sized soldier, dressed as the ARVN were, was not a surprise: the American had to be an adviser. All of the troops wore red berets and Winter knew them for airborne or Rangers.

The sergeant first class looked him over with curiosity as Winter sprinted into their area. "Whatcha need, Sarge?" he shouted over the chopping of the Huey blades. Winter saw the sergeant was flanked closely by two ARVN exhibiting the body language of guards.

"Casualties. I was on the chopper. We were diverted here to pick up wounded. You got casualties, right?" he yelled.

"More every minute. This was supposed to be a cold zone. Somebody fucked up. Big time." He glanced around, raised up a few inches and swept his arm over his head and pointed, directing some infantryman to a new position without words. "Any more choppers coming?" he asked, swinging back to Winter.

"Don't know. I'm just a passenger. How many casualties you got?" He couldn't see anyone who appeared to be wounded among those about the clearing.

"Three serious, four or five more that ought to be outta here. But we're down to about two squads out of a short-handed platoon. The platoon leader's off there with the wounded now," he motioned with his head toward the densest patch of brush and trees. Slithering to one side, he grabbed the handset of a radio phone and began talking. Winter couldn't see his nametag.

Winter started crawling toward where he thought the ARVN officer might be, and saw Biddle scurrying in the same direction. Gunfire was desultory about the clearing, but he could hear well-disciplined bursts of three or four rounds being ripped off by an AK-47 from a longer distance. An occasional muffled *Crump!* of a grenade. Nowhere did he hear the comfort of outgoing mortar or artillery.

An ARVN first lieutenant, whose nametag in red embroidery read Kien, about twelve years old Winter judged, was holding nervous court beyond a screen of brush, just in the edge of a tree line. The officer was talking to another American NCO and an ARVN second lieutenant. Round about lay a disorderly lot, young Vietnamese soldiers in various stages of undress and differing stages of activity, most of it subdued. All of them bore bandages, bloody and dirty, hastily applied to heads, shoulders, a stomach-abdominal application, the inevitable common hand, arm, foot, and leg wounds. Winter counted six men on the ground and two sitting up, propped against trees. A couple lay ominously silent on the ground.

The ARVN lieutenant crawled over to where Biddle and Winter shared questionable sanctuary behind a scruffy bush that smelled like licorice. "Are you he'p get wound from here?" he asked in better-than-average English. He looked uneasy, but not scared. If he was frightened — and he should have been, Winter thought — he was controlling it well. His concern seemed mostly for the wounded. They agreed that was their intention, and he waved them on.

The two tourists moved to lend a hand and, dragging their rifles, they scurried bent over to the first of the wounded men. He was an ARVN sergeant; he waved them off, pointing to another soldier, motioning them to take him first. They complied, grabbed the silent form by the feet and under the arms — they had no litter — and crashed through the brush with him. He was not heavy.

The two pilots, a young lieutenant and a young warrant officer, were out of the helicopter, helping a walking wounded into the ship's bay. When he was secure, they ran toward Winter and Biddle.

"There're more in there," Biddle yelled, inclining his head toward the brush, waving the pilots past. He and Winter lifted the bloody, unconscious soldier into the bay, where the gunner grabbed him by the belt and pulled him to a far corner. They ran back.

No one was attempting a triage process; the unit's medic was one of the silent ones who waited. They grabbed the nearest man each time they returned to the gathering point. Between the two 3rd RRU men and the two pilots, within a few minutes they had five wounded on board the ship. But there were more casualties still, some appearing while loading was being accomplished. There wasn't room for all of them plus the two passengers, late of Nui Ba Dinh.

Winter caught his breath and said to Biddle, "El Tee, I'm going to wait here for the next chopper. Give my space to a casualty." He was breathing hard, the humidity and heat continuing to build. It was still early morning, but a full-bore Vietnam scorcher was working up.

"Wish I could do the same," the lieutenant said, "but I *have* to get back; I have a meet at J.G.S. at ten o'clock. Ten hundred hours, I mean." He looked about anxiously. "Are you sure you want to do this? We can just get on board; we're here by accident —"

"Yeah, I'm sure. With them in the shit, there must be other choppers on the way. You can make sure when you get to Tan Son Nhut. But I can't justify leaving wounded here while I *di-di* out. Besides, somebody's covering my job." He thought quickly, "Can you get word to my boss, Captain Pyburn? At the aviation shack? Tell him I'll be there A-SAP."

"No sweat." The lieutenant looked around. The two pilots were loading the last casualty for which there was space; one of them sprinted for the left seat; the other waved at Biddle and Winter, signaling them toward the helicopter. "O.K. Be careful," Biddle said softly, reached out and shook Winter's hand, then grasped a walking wounded about the waist and said, "Let's go, *quân nhân*. You get the last seat on the bus." They hobbled away together as the blades on the chopper began whipping faster. The second pilot stared at them as they approached, then turned and jumped into his seat. When Biddle had cajoled, pushed, and thrust the last wounded man aboard the heavily laden helicopter, he jumped in after him, stepping on one of the casualties on the floor. He winced and looked down. Blood ran in rivulets across the aluminum floor panels, channeling in the slots between. The man he stood on was unconscious.

The helicopter leapt toward the sky.

* * *

Winter made his way back to the advisor, the SFC whose nametag he now read as Velakian. Before he could speak, a nearby explosion shook the group of them, declaring the newly added factor of mortars. Not their own.

"*In-comm-innnnng!*" the sergeant yelled. Similar exhortations in Vietnamese filled the air. Succeeding bursts of fire bracketed the clearing. Over the noise and pulsing pain of concussion, the *Whop! Whop! Whop!* of another helicopter could be heard, as if it were on top of them. Rolling onto his back, Winter sought but could find no sign of the bird. He did hear a long, sustained burst of machine gun fire seemingly coming from the sky. As fallout from some inexplicable connective, he flashed on the lines from Yeats's "Host of the Air" —

> *But above him he heard*
> *High up in the air*
> *A piper piping away . . .*

He was making good time across the open clearing, heading for the promise of cover along the edge of the treeline, when he felt himself suddenly flung toward that same encroaching sky, disoriented and, in that shocked instant, felt he'd been struck below the waist by a bus. Then burning, suddenly wreathed with fire, he fell back toward the ground, pain erupting . . . And the sky faded to black emptiness.

chapter eighteen

LIMA ZULU

III Corps, Viet Nam: March 1965

Deep cool oases, shadows of towering trees fell long across the battlefield. Sunlight flickered through leaves, dappling a soldier who ran over the hill and down along the edge of a field past rippling grass. He abandoned the open space and dove headlong into a ravine, heedless of branches whipping his face, vines clawing at the rifle in his hands. He crashed to the bottom of the depression and found a path, worn with use. Experience in this kind of combat had taught him a path was a mistake, but it was easier going and he followed along it, gasping for breath.

The enemy were close behind.

The hysteria he felt from being hunted, counterpart to the excitement of the chase, allowed the soldier no glance backward. No chance to reconnoiter, to cover his tracks. His only hope lay in pushing on, reach a position he could defend.

Where the trail bent to parallel a brackish stream, tumbled branches and logs formed a horseshoe-shaped windfall, enclosed on three sides. The open side backed onto the bank of the ravine and was hidden in dense brush. A natural fortress camouflaged by nature, now mostly dried and twisted bramble. He knew he must make his stand here. He would not find better.

He paused at the edge of the tangle, listening. Above his own labored breathing he heard their careless, sure pursuit far back up the ravine. Rabbit-like, he crouched and wriggled through the brittle branches until he was safely behind the largest trunk. The stream was motionless, tepid swamp water dark with the sap of ferns and cypress. The rifle was heavy and slippery in his hands.

He sighted along the barrel, found the black fin of the front sight blade, and let his vision focus beyond to where the trail he had followed opened out onto the stream. He would not have long to wait, he knew. A sense of calm overtook him as he crouched and forced himself quiet, burrowing deeper into the tangle. His breathing slowed.

He became silent.

Readying himself, he accepted his tenuous position, obvious as it was.

With a trembling hand he wiped salty sweat from his eyes, off his forehead, painting it onto the dead white branch before his face. In the humidity the smudge dried slowly, imperceptibly. He stared, entranced: perspiration was a new-found phenomenon.

When the first one came into sight—slowly now, picking his way along the trail, his head swinging side to side as his eyes swept the trail, the submachine gun raised before him—the front sight of the soldier's rifle was centered as a dark blur on the enemy's chest. The ambusher waited . . . tense, motionless, his breath a painful ball at the back of his throat. A second, then a third one of the enemy patrol crept forward into the clearing. Cautious. Nervous in exposure.

The leader of the tracking party stopped, searching the ground. The soldiers bunched closer to the leader, shuffling their feet in the dry crackling leaves. They were otherwise deathly silent, skilled in their craft. No one spoke.

With the first one only yards away the hidden rifleman's finger tightened on the trigger . . . slowly took up the slack . . . adjusted his sight picture . . . then jerked.

The sharp report shattered the stillness of the forest and echoed away through the trees. The three enemy soldiers were caught, marked for death in the deadly open. Shocked by the single shot, they hesitated too long, then broke for cover in the trees as the sniper slammed the bolt back, then forward, firing twice more in rapid succession.

"*I got you! I got you all!* You first, Sonny . . . and John. You too, Tim. You're all dead!" he shouted exultantly, savoring his triumph. If he could have expressed it he would have said his smugness was well-earned.

"Boy, are you dumb suckers." The voice of the still hidden rifleman crackled across the clearing, laughing from tree to tree, shaming their vulnerability.

"You missed me!" bounced back from behind a large oak. "I was behind the tree. *Pow! Pow!* I got you! I can see you now."

"Dead soldiers can't shoot, Tim. You're dead. I killed you all," the sniper gloated, "and you didn't either see me. Ever." Davey Winter, age ten, veteran of countless battles, would brook no argument. "All you Japs is dead," he stated firmly, twisting his way free of the brush pile.

"We wasn't Japs nohow, stupid. We was the 'mericans and we was trackin' you down, you dirty yeller ambusher." Tim's voice wavered with uncertainty. The sun crept down the western sky.

"Durn you, Tim. I was *too* the American, 'cause I was the German this morning with John, and we all said I'd be the American this eve'nin and y'all'd be the Japs." He stalked up to his last score, glaring belligerently in the boy's face. As the others emerged scowling from their ineffectual sanctuary, Davey's tanned, dirty young face cracked across in a victorious grin.

There were no further protests. Only muttered threats for next time and nostalgia for what almost was.

The last dead soldier turned quickly onto the path leading up into the autumn woods. He yelled back at the group over his shoulder, "I'm a new man. Let's go!" He crashed away through the low-hanging branches firing a series of staccato bursts on the roll-fed cap gun . . .

* * *

A sudden hammering brought his eyes open. Another burst of machine gun chatter from farther out echoed. The constant feathery swish and whine in the background increased in tempo and intensity, becoming a frenzy, a hard choppy flutter as a helicopter lifted off, sending sand, leaves, and dirt over the clearing in a stinging spray. The soldier closed his eyes against the aggravation and fantasized on a cigarette he did not have.

Winter, David D., Staff Sergeant, US Army, lay in a muddle of casualties. Standing he would have been considered moderately tall; lying, his booted feet hung off the end of the litter, one of them oozing a rusty liquid from below a heavy pressure bandage that bore the same rusty stain. He was slimmed down from meager rations, little sleep, and too much time on the job, his hair spattered, matted with mud and bits of leaf and grass and clots of unidentifiable matter. His usual close-trimmed crewcut had been ignored into a scraggly whorl resembling a chicken's rear end.

He reached one hand up and again patted his pockets. Empty! He knew that, though. Habit, like the smokes themselves. Hell, he hadn't even smoked cigarettes for a couple of years now. He cursed himself again for leaving his pipe behind, back at his hooch. He raised himself to locate someone with a butt; then saw there were only the small, silent ones close enough. He slumped back onto the litter, realizing he was the only one in the clearing on canvas. The other wounded lay on blankets, at best; most on bare ground. He accepted the pain in silence.

When the last helicopter had come in, it settled as near the casualties as possible , blowing LZ chaff—bits of cane and brush and dirt, empty ammo bandoliers, ration boxes, soda cans—over wounded and sound alike, into open gun ports, open wounds, open mess kits, mantling everything with a gritty residue, like ash from a demonstrative volcano. The ARVN medic and a child-like rifleman attempted to lift Winter's litter to give him priority on the bird, but he had waved them off, pointing to an ARVN sergeant with severe head trauma. The bearers set Winter back on the ground and loaded the head casualty onto the chopper before the dust of the landing settled.

There was no prioritizing scheme for evacuation, beyond the necessity for the ARVN to get the Americans out first; it was their helicopters, after all. Two casualties, wounded in a sudden flare-up of firing, were hustled from the brush and tagged for immediate evacuation. Then two others from the general patient roster. Sergeant Winter, straining to see just how bad were the wounds, was content to consider himself fourth or fifth. If not on this one, he would be on the next ship out. Maybe. If he didn't bump himself again. He tried rationalization: it was only a leg wound. Unavoidably, he thought of bullfighters, dead from a *cornada.*

The dead waited farther back, a dark green bag marking maybe an American; the rest—little people—Zips, he thought—Marvin the ARVN—were stacked like hideous firewood. For them there was no rush for liftoff. He felt a flash of guilt for the disdainful characterization. The dead American must be the SFC he spoke with early on the LZ. He was the only GI Winter had seen.

Winter wondered, almost idly as if it didn't really matter, if he would *ever* get through that gaping square in the side of the helicopter, or would the line go on, extending in front of him, stretching back out each time it appeared to be dwindling, forever accordioning in and out like a Slinky Toy, until it was too late. He had no one to blame if that happened; he'd insisted he take a back seat in the evacuation. Wound severity dictated. He tried to care, but the morphine lessened any anxiety he might have felt.

No sweat!

He heard that chopper lifting off through an echo chamber, understood he hadn't made it. He tried to remember where he was in the process. Did he have a number? Was he in a queue? Must be his number, right there, written on the side of the *DUSTOFF – Big number; could he be that far down in priority?* – then lost it in the fury above. He could only wait anyhow, and the battle sounds were dying away.

The firing faded to sporadic shots and the occasional muffled crump of a grenade beyond the LZ. He was aware that his loss of interest was due more to failing acuity than to a change in status, but Sergeant Winter couldn't seem to care. The sounds, the smells, the tastes, even the pain melted away into the green, wet world of the jungle. He was beyond even the relentless heat.

Above the tiny man-made clearing the sky was faultless. Winter remembered yesterday, just yesterday, how he had played war games with his younger brother and friends. But the old oaks—burdened with the magic mistletoe visible in the fall after the leaves had gone, bark scarred with heel marks of correctional shoes, scuffed by ball-ankled sneakers, branches splintered by Batman Club daredevil tests—were replaced by these palms and mangroves. Whispering harshly on the air, elephant grass grew twelve feet high and threatening where boxwoods had been carefully nurtured.

A flight of three A-1Es in echelon, mimicking a banshee's homecoming, screamed over at treetop level. Their barking cannon caused a warm and fuzzy in Winter's mind, comforting above the incredible roar of the engines. The aircraft snapped him out of his reverie. He jerked his head up, but they were gone while still their spent brass rained down over the LZ like good luck charms.

Winter knew the VNAF would sweep wide and make another firing pass. The Viet Cong still probed, menacing the encircled ground. He watched carefully to try to catch the shrinking of the clearing even as it happened, but he could see only the jungle wall pulsing. Raising himself on his elbows, he gasped at the sudden dizziness and nausea which arose, counterpoint to the now-constant pain. Morphine didn't touch it. He looked down for the first time and noted the poncho covering him below the waist soaked a dark, splotchy magenta, mottled throughout with camouflage print, and beyond the canvas the olive green straps of the bandage fluttered. He didn't lift the cover, but looked away at the scattered wounded, counting.

He saw that he was almost alone now in the tiny clearing. He envisioned the next helicopter as it might appear when it came, finally, for him. All that power and noise and monster blades and . . . and pilot training and hardware dollars and bullshit headlines about the Hueys, you'd think they'd carry more than six litters at a time. Or was it six? He had a flash of awareness: Didn't matter; they weren't on litters, anyhow. It was bodies . . .

He could see one other casualty near him with a bandaged shoulder; the Vietnamese private looked like a grade school child. And beyond that one, another, though Winter had no idea of that man's wounds. He thought of them as Numbers 1 and 2. He wondered about number 2 lying beyond the near private whom he'd labeled number 1, whose face he now saw was concealed in a mask of gauze as well as the shoulder binding. Number 2 mumbled incoherently, struggling to regain consciousness. Or to lose it, Winter thought. He turned his head to stare in the other direction, regretfully.

In a moment of new awareness, there was a Number 3 on the other side of him, unrecognizable. His mind was thrashing; of course he was unfamiliar–he didn't know these troops. The man's face was exposed and entirely unmarked. Odd, Winter mused, how immaterial such an oddity could be. For a moment he wished that number 3 was the next in line for evac; then that would make Winter number 1 instead of . . . what? He thought 2, enviously. For number 3 was dead. He felt a twinge of guilt, but the logic of it seemed so . . . logical. Inescapable. That is, given that the man was already dead . . .

The jungle pressed in on the litter, the blankets and ponchos and poncho liners and their gory burdens, and the dark, splotched ground. The somber, shrouded tangle beyond the edge of the clearing was the enemy: mysterious, evil by definition. The VC who used the jungle for cover — a sniper in every tree, a booby trap on every limb, beneath every bush — were only transient interlopers. The jungle was the real enemy. He saw that clearly now.

The Skyraiders made their second pass at low level, banking up and away into the sun, waggling their wings in playful farewell as their exuberant pilots must have learned from some late-night war movie where things like that were done. He looked, seeking some sign . . . Then they were gone and the farewell flourish was little comfort. Even ominous. Except for the spaced-out stuttering of a machine gun in the distance, it was silent on the LZ.

Winter tried to lose the consciousness that was only pain piercing the numbing sheath of morphine. "I guess it was better back then," he whispered to a still pair of boots now just visible beyond a bush behind him. "Playing at war. Just playing. Nobody ever really died. Choose sides and start over." For a moment — or an hour — he lay and reviewed this observation, and in his morphia-induced somnolence was wistfully satisfied with the calm manner of his appraisal. His remarkably profound perception. "Dying was so easy then," he murmured. And he waited. For unworldliness . . . for the chopper. For something.

Suddenly from behind his head, where he could not see without rising and twisting about, two moves he was unlikely to accomplish at the moment, a voice spoke weakly. "Hey, Sarge. You got a smoke?"

"Sorry 'bout that. I quit." The answer was mechanical, unthought. "Who's that?"

"Yeah, guess you can't see me." He said a name Winter couldn't hear. "Adviser. Talked to you before." His voice trailed off, grown weaker.

The speaker hacked and strangled. Winter said, "You really should do something about that cough." The adviser was quiet. Winter lay back and asked the sky, "You hit in the throat?"

"Huh-uh. Chest. Hurts like a bitch, off"'n' on. But I'd risk the pain for a Camel. If I could walk, I'd walk a fucking mile for one." He made a sound grimly akin to a chuckle. "Even if it leaked."

How utterly predictable they should both be out of cigarettes, Winter thought. Man, I've seen this dog of a movie. He flailed about and turned his head on the litter to take in the wet, glossy swathe of bandage around the speaker's chest; still, he couldn't see the man's face. The macabre vision of tiny wisps of Camel smoke streaming from perforations in his flesh was startlingly comical, and Winter was vaguely aware what his own condition must be to react so to silliness. "You okay, Sarge?" he asked.

"Fuck do I know? I look like Ben Casey?" His voice sounded like Taps. "I know I'm hot, though. Numbah ten-thou' hot." His hoarse speech was accompanied by a thin, whistling after-note. After an anxious pause, "I saw you get hit."

"Why haven't they taken you, with that chest wound?"

"Un-n-nh. Advisers stay with their advisees. Good days and bad." An ominous silence ensued. "No, I got wounded just after that last chopper went." Winter was startled; had he been unconscious? Then, the adviser said wistfully, "Wish that Dust-Off'd get back here. I hear they got wards with air conditioning in the Thirty-Second." He was seized suddenly with a spasm of coughing, and he hacked twice and spat several mouthfuls of bloody phlegm into the grass, over his chest and shoulder, and onto the unconscious form of number 1 below his feet.

Winter tried rolling onto his side, arching his head back to better see the neighboring casualty. The pain, down through his thigh and leg, was incredible as he moved, but he could see the sergeant propped against a soldier's pack on the ground. Velakian! That was the name, Winter remembered, gratified he could keep the memory in what was a cycling flutter of consciousness-near consciousness. He looked to confirm it but the casualty's nametag was part of the jungle fatigue jacket that was shredded and blackened with powder burns and clots of drying blood. A gory sheen glazed the sergeant's chest and shoulder, like the picadors' work on the flank of a fighting bull he'd seen in the *corrida* in Tijuana.

Jeez-us! Flake time. A second bull fighting metaphor. What would be the do-gooders' take on that?

Velakian, who looked to be about Winter's age, muttered between coughs in a hoarse, rasping croak. As the coughing subsided, Winter saw a bright new stain spreading through the crusty chest bandage.

"Lay quiet, Sarge. You're going to be all right," Winter lied. "Don't move around. You open the wound." They lay silent for several long minutes. A mortar shell burst close beyond the clearing and Winter instinctively burrowed under the tarp of poncho, seeking even that deceptive protection.

The single explosion was all, but it was several long minutes before Winter's grip relaxed on the camouflaged cover.

Finally the adviser rasped aloud: "I heard what you was sayin' . . . 'bout the games and all. Did you . . . when you was a kid, did you play war games too?"

"Oh, hell yes . . . combat legend. I played every kind of game. Long before this." Winter winced and dragged in a painful fragment of breath. "I've been German, Japanese, British, Italian — that one was easy; you just wave your hands a lot and talk gibberish — Greek guerillas, Yugoslavian partisans, Americans of every service." He caught his breath. "You name it, I've been it. Never got wounded before, though, not that I can remember. All new to me. Got dead many times. Always dead — never just hurt." He seemed surprised at such unforgivable complacency.

"Me, too. One shot — *Bang!* One grenade — *Boom!* Never thought — *Whoo-o-o-ee* — about this." The SFC's gray face reflected astonishment. Betrayal. Pink foam bubbled along the bandage edge.

"Yeah" Winter agreed. "Clean, neat. You got shot, you were dead. Never messy. Never painful. Very glorious. Very . . . *Whoa!*" he whispered as a sharp tug of pain rippled up his leg. "We always . . . we always knew who the enemy was, too. Easy to become a new man in a new game. Start over."

"Should-a stuck to games, I guess," Velakian said. "These little bastards don't know from games." He broke into another spasm of uncontrollable, strangled hacking. Tiny bubbles rose through the gauze and burst in the dusty air. *"Saau-u-u,"* he murmured. "Numbah ten-thou'."

* * *

The taller of the two boys, carrying a fielder's glove, looked down at his brother and said patiently, "I told you a hundred times, Larry. I don't play war anymore."

"But Davey —"

"No! The real war's over. Long time now. And I quit playing that a long time ago." A silent half-block later he said, "Larry, . . . I'm seven years older'n you. I played war games when I was your age." He smacked a hard, knobby brown fist into the pocket of the Eddie Stankey glove, continuing, "I'm sixteen now. I wanna play baseball. Not war. I had my war, and it's over. There's another one for you. You go on, play with Arnold and the boys. Get some of the younger guys to play with you; we used to let you play with us. You've got enough for sides. I'm gonna play ball."

He hesitated, conscious of the disappointment on his brother's face, then spoke softly, "Besides, not long ago I was still having bad dreams about dying in the war like . . . well, in the jungle . . . like Dad."

He reached out and tousled Larry's hair. "But your war's got mountains and towns and stuff. It's better. In Korea. Anyhow," he added, "I'm gonna play ball."

* * *

Jerked back from semi-consciousness, Winter was faced with the specters of that war. Korea! A long time ago, it seemed. As if blessed for something he'd not earned, he'd walked away from the contact sports on that peninsula without a scratch. In payment thereof, he allowed himself to ease back into a don't-care mode.

In hazy deliberation he dreamed of baseball and children's games. He remembered crisp, magic autumn days, full of pecan picking and blue, smoky mornings, and the first frost. Then on some other plane he was a part of spring and picnics and not-so-childish games, the world resplendent with the wonder of barefoot, long-legged girls chasing through meadows of cool clover. He adhered to those visions as long as he could. Then, slipping reluctantly back into the conscious world, his eyes focused and he watched a squad of flies lifting sticky feet as they scurried back and forth across the crusting poncho that covered his lower body.

How they could smell it, he never understood. He couldn't smell anything. Like all of them here in the jungle, the smell of cordite and blood, the sour reek of mud and cankered vegetation, the rotting dead, sweet with the gasses of decay, human waste, and the incomparable sharp familiarity of burned flesh, all meant nothing to him. Though pervasive and dominant in some realm of higher faculties, such landmarks of the subconscious no longer registered on his jaded senses. He didn't smell a thing in the fetid world he now felt he'd been born to, so long had he been a part of it. He exaggerated. He lived in a sterile, steambath microcosm of all the hated places on the earth, places which simply did not emit odors, existing only as abstracts.

But they felt. Oh, yes, they felt. They felt . . . green, and they tasted. Of fear. Of fear for which there was not even the hope of an ending or getting better, but was a solid fear until it was less than fear, an end to fear. And the fear of ending.

Someone farther down the line of casualties, speaking English, broke into his thoughts, voicing Winter's own unspoken question in a scream, "W'ere is go'dam' Huey? Have only one?"

"Shut up, Linh," Velakian growled. And then as if addressing competence in language, "The whole brigade's in the shit. They're getting us out faster'n they would if this wasn't Big Minh's favorite division. Be thankful for small favors."

Someone — it did not sound like the same Linh — responded in Vietnamese, angrily.

"Now remember," Velakian mock-ordered, "rape, pillage, *then* burn, you stupid assholes. Get it right for the media."

"Velakian? . . ."

"Yeah?"

"How many G.I.s out here?"

There was a long pause. "Just two." Another pause. "No, I count one dead — Garmble. Monk's nearby . . . but he ain't down. They'll have to kill him."

Shit, Winter thought. He didn't know the TO&E for advisers and the commands they advised. He thought two sounded chicken-shit skimpy.

A fit of strangling seized one of the men on the ground, whether from laughter or a punctured lung, Winter couldn't tell, but laughter seemed unlikely. All the other Vietnamese were silent, except for one he couldn't see, somewhere very close to him, who was crying steadily.

Winter heard, "I don't hurt. I ain't hot or cold. I ain't even uncomfortable. But I'm afraid to move. Friggin' Charlie almost blew my crotch away. Christ, I hope they don't breach the perimeter and get in here. The ARVN Ranger company's shot to shit . . . I don't know if I could make the choice to get up and try to run and lose my goodies, or just lay here and go all at once." The speaker's words came between deep shuddering breaths.

Winter looked about as he could but saw no other American.

"Velakian. You said two. There's a third. And he said a company. I thought you said a platoon." Winter questioned.

There was no answer for several moments. Finally, in a spectral voice: "My platoon here, three more . . . scattered. 'nother company." Winter, not looking at him, sensed movement as if he'd swept his arm in an indistinct motion. "More . . . Jesus!" The advisor went silent.

A weak ripple of grunts and sighs, groans, and cries marked the conscious ones. A Vietnamese corporal near the far end of the line, back where chances looked slimmer—he was midway between the wounded and the un-bagged dead; nobody knew which he was marked for—screamed and moaned alternately, rising up and falling back with metronomic regularity. No one on the ground paid him any attention.

Winter would join Velakian in wisecracking, but like the old saw, it hurt when he laughed. It hurt whether he laughed or not. It hurt so he couldn't laugh.

He felt an irresistible need to contribute some witticism, though it would be phony. All the macabre, desperate jokes were phony. This was not grace under pressure. All of them here, with no exceptions but for the dead, were intimidated, terrified at the possibility of not making the next chopper flight out . . . or the next one . . . or the one after. He lay flat, too weak to comment; too scared to try, scared not to. Silence was a statement, perhaps, but not one he was comfortable with.

Velakian broke into his musing again. "Sergeant—"

"Winter."

"Yeah . . . Winter. When they comin' back, you reckon? They been gone a long time. You reckon it's too hot on this LZ for them?"

Well, hell, thought Winter. He was wondering the same thing, but no sense spreading the grief. "Be here soon," he said with barely concealed disbelief. "Smilin' Jack and the boys aren't going to let a bunch of ragtag Vee Cee keep them from earning their flight pay. They're probably refueling. They been on the go since early morning." He paused to listen to the empty air, then tried to cover the obvious silence: "How do you feel now? Still feverish?"

The adviser's voice was slow in coming. Weaker. "No, I guess I feel okay now. Doc did me good," he crooned, recalling with a dreamy smile the lightning stab of the needle. "My chest still hurts, but I guess I gotta expect . . . something. Purple Hearts ain't free." There was another long silence before he continued. "I think they got me with one of our own grenades. Old frag. There's a piece stickin' up by my collarbone, just under the skin. It feels like that same steel Ex-Lax. Don't hurt too bad. I guess I feel a lot better," he concluded, his voice unsure.

Winter wondered how many Evac-Expedite cases might be brought out of the bush, stretching the line out, before a chopper returned. Would he make the next load out? More important from the sound of him, would Velakian make the next one? It had better be soon. The adviser recognized he'd been the victim of a grenade, but from the spacing of bandages and the front-back wounds, he'd also apparently been shot.

The sky was still silent, the ephemeral queue static.

* * *

The ARVN second lieutenant, whose name Winter didn't know, was acting platoon commander now, since Lieutenant Kien, the officer he'd encountered when he and . . . what was his name? His own lieutenant who was on the chopper with him? Couldn't remember his name. But the ARVN officer they'd met was one of the anonymous dead farther back. The young officer crouched over the side of Winter's stretcher. "Ser-junt. You, too? Where you get it?" he asked inanely. If he'd been American, standard banter likely would have been, "How're they hanging?" but he was staring at Winter's lower body hidden under the stained tarp. In any language, it would not be a politic question.

While Winter considered a response, the lieutenant, requiring no answer, asked, "You ver-y strong man, you ser-junt. Why was stay here? Let Vietnamese so-jer fly safe."

"I wasn't in a hurry, *Trung uy*," Winter answered. Jeez-us! Could it be yesterday he'd left Tan Son Nhut? Just yesterday? A million years ago! That was obscene. Yesterday!

"Tough shit, G.I.," the lieutenant's enunciation was scatalogically clear. "See wings," he pointed at the flight wings on Winter's fatigue jacket. "What you do here with grunt?" The lieutenant's eyes continued scanning the edges of the LZ. He peered hard at the jungle that encroached with a menacing presence on the tiny clearing, wanting to make the right moves. Winter didn't know how to answer him, that he was just an accident, but he could read the hierarchy of problems sweeping predictably through the lieutenant's mind. Almost inevitable in his newness, Winter could read across his face a flood of concerns: command presence, ego, confidence, seeking a chance to prove, to handle . . . frightened, angry, determined, anxious about the men whose names he didn't know, but willing to spend any one or more of them to do what he'd been taught . . . anything, everything! Just as in his own army, Second Lieutenants needed opportunities to become First Lieutenants. First Lieutenants needed breaks to make Captain. Disasters created career patterns. Open a slot above; everybody move up one.

"Luck of the draw, I guess," said Winter meaninglessly

The young lieutenant seemed to be handling himself okay for the mess he was in, and Winter thought he might make a pretty cool platoon leader after all. If he didn't become a part of the statistics on second lieutenants in combat. If he got off this LZ alive. If the world didn't end in the next ten seconds.

The lieutenant added, in a meaningless attempt at comfort, "You go soon, Sarge. Hang there." His truncated Americanism offered like absolution, he moved away in a crouch, his eyes wary, scanning the jungle wall.

* * *

It was utterly quiet now, except for a solitary bird Winter heard high up in the screen of trees. Stupid bird! He felt strongly the malevolent presence of the wounded and dead all around him, the picture nudging an elusive memory. He was vaguely reminded of something, a similar scene, but in his semi-detached world of morphine, he'd been living re-runs ever since he was hit. He knew he'd not experienced this before, but there was the sense of familiarity. Not quite déjà vu. The key to the memory was the bird, he was sure.

* * *

"Hey, it's my turn to be the good guy, Jimmy. I been the Kraut all morning. Besides . . ."

* * *

It wasn't a bird. A butterfly! On the western front, for Christ's sake. As far from here as possible to get. Of course, the bird. The bird, like the butterfly, he realized with startling clarity, was symbolic. Was the bird really here? It didn't matter. As he lay, his mind filled with confusion, the line between reality and illusion ill-defined, the burst of a single mortar round sent the bird on its way. If it was ever there. That's okay, he thought; it's a symbolic war. There was irony in the thought. At least, he identified it as irony, relying on Brenner's mantra: "There is no God but Irony!"

Ain't that some shit.

* * *

The specters came closer together, the many visions blurring into one. The humid air in the hacked-out clearing swirled suddenly and was blown away by a cool March breeze. An Illinois *cold* March breeze. Through the oak leaves overhead he saw a red-white-and-blue kite, pulling from side to side. In cycles of reality and release, alternately with the sticky closeness of the jungle, Winter felt tingling blasts of icy wind driving powdered snow back into his eyes and nose as the sled plummeted down the hill back of the school near Aunt Thelma's. Man, that was the year he'd spent at his great aunt's house in Northbrook when his mother was sick, the only white Christmas he'd known as a child.

He shook with the cold. Or was it the cold? Was he imagining that too? No! The cold was real enough.

"But I don't think *this* is real," he said aloud. He tried to blink the frosty haze from his eyes, but they wouldn't clear. "The snow." It's not real, he thought, or thought he said. Or said. Or is it the jungle that's not real? The border between reality and memory was blurring, the demarcation fainter. He considered this a moment, then spoke aloud: "The hell with it. I like snow." And he ignored the jungle.

"I like . . . snow, too . . . Winter," he heard Velakian murmur. It was meaningless, another complementary hallucination, but it gave Winter focus, a bearing. Something to hold onto. The adviser sergeant needed help. The attraction, the force of that need was even greater than Winter's own frightened lapse of control. He edged reluctantly back toward the real world in the clearing. Velakian's throaty rasp was almost inaudible now.

"You married . . . Winter?" The question out of nowhere startled Winter.

Without thinking, he responded: "Sure. Wife and a son. Jeremy." He was suddenly swept up in a fury of anxiety. What would this do to them? Hell, he hadn't even thought of his wife and child since . . . when? What if he didn't—

"Me, too. Was, anyhow. Not . . . anymore." Velakian went silent. Then, "Glad, now."

Winter thought his own voice sounded perfectly normal when he said, "Lay back, Sarge. Keep still, will you. Every time you raise up, you open that wound." Where had he heard that recently? Had he urged him before? "What're you looking for?"

"That goddamned bird. That stupid . . . ignorant bas . . . tard of a goddamned bird. He can . . . shit, he can fly anywhere . . . Vung Tau, Soc Trang, Dalat, out to sea . . . to Hong Kong, if he likes. Wish I could fly . . . to Hong Kong. Why the hell does he stay here? Why don't he get . . . his feathered ass clear of this . . . this mess?"

This mess, thought Winter. This colloquial charnel house of confusion and pain and mistakes, and an end of dreams. An end of games. The bird had been gone—how long now?— at least since the stray round. The teasing in Velakian's head was self-induced. And in Winter's own.

The adviser screamed out something unintelligible. As if parodying Winter's private wanderings across the western front of a war long gone, Velakian raised suddenly to a sitting position and yelled in a surprisingly firm voice, ". . . and I'm not reaching up for some goddamned molting loudmouth who shits from a limb and don't have no brains nohow and get my head ventilated."

Velakian was dying, Winter realized with a sense of distant compassion. Velakian was already a dead man; it showed in his eyes, and if not there, then in the statistics. He had managed one good look at the wounded advisor and knew. The fragment of steel — the shard or the bullet that caused the tiny hole in his chest from which the frothy pink bubbles and the bright red stain issued — was not contaminating his body further; it had exited through his back, and what was left back there was beyond repair. Disposable. Totaled. Winter knew without seeing it. Planned obsolescence.

There has to be more than this, Winter thought, though he'd watched it before and knew there was little more. I'm wrong, he thought, begging. About the dying. I'm no damned doctor. I don't know he's going to die. That's too predictable, like the cigarettes. Like the bird. They're telegraphing the scenes. This whole scenario is too . . . too cliché.

Velakian's right here beside me. They'll patch him up with plasma and plastic fibers and nylon staples and all that new shit. Glue him together. Take a slab of meat off his ass to fill in the hole where the exit . . .

"Velakian," Winter began, as the adviser coughed, jerked once in spasm, and fell back heavily onto the blotched poncho. His collapse was flat, the message inevitable. Unforgivable. Winter fought against hearing the words even in his mind, and was conscious of a wry, caustic denunciation building behind his eyes, about to erupt from his mouth.

Alone now in his vigil, he sought refuge in the comfortable anonymity of unconsciousness once more. It would not come.

Through the sparse, almost negligible firing that had started up again, Winter
strained for the *Whop! Whop! Whop!* of a Dustoff that might never return.

He acknowledged part of the misty haze was pain, but the fog did not diminish with the realization that he now could choose his own number.

epilogue

Bad Aibling, Germany; Spring 1968

Rome, in all its eternal grandeur, was a fading pastoral interlude; Kufstein and Austria a jaundiced more recent memory.

The Bavarian *Autobahn* was busy, despite the early hour. Off the *A-bahn*, passing through Bad Aibling village, winding carefully among the morning cyclists, farm tractors to-ing and fro-ing between barn and town and field, edging the VW around cattle herded down cobblestone streets en route to lush fields of spring grass, Winter sought comfort from the recent, pre-revelatory times, and put that earlier tour behind him.

More emphatically, he thought of that landing zone as one might of any catastrophe that left one with the breath of life. A startling wonder: had it really happened? He leaned toward disbelief, but an insistent throbbing in his leg put the lie to that.

There was no talk in the car. It had all been said. He had no idea what their future held. He looked forward only into a chasm of shadows, unsure if Nicole's words of the bleak night past were truly her last on the subject. He couldn't reconcile the term "irrevocable" with their situation, but neither could he discount the threat. He listened futilely for the soft hush of boyish sleep in the seat behind him, but because the boys were still ahead — albeit close — he was deprived of even that comfort.

Approaching the front gate, Winter slowed for the MP's hand signal to proceed. He had committed to keeping the promise to himself, with the knowledge that choices were exhausted.

He could only go forward, following orders.

See where it took them.

Made in the USA
Middletown, DE
02 November 2017